Praise for
the novels of
Maxine O'Callaghan:

''Solid pacing and detection.''
—*The Washington Post Book World*

''A tidy, tight plot . . . The characters are
sharp and definite.''
—*Ft. Lauderdale Sun-Sentinel*

''O'Callaghan's polish and her eye for detail
amply entertain.''
—*Publishers Weekly*

''Fast-paced, well-plotted . . . a must-read.''
—*Booklist*

SHADOW OF THE CHILD

Maxine O'Callaghan

J

JOVE BOOKS, NEW YORK

SHADOW OF THE CHILD

A Jove Book / published by arrangement with
the author

PRINTING HISTORY
Jove edition / March 1996

The Putnam Berkley World Wide Web site address is
http://www.berkley.com

ISBN: 0-515-11822-2

A JOVE BOOK®
Jove Books are published by The Berkley Publishing Group,
200 Madison Avenue, New York, New York 10016.
JOVE and the "J" design are trademarks
belonging to Jove Publications, Inc.

PRINTED IN THE UNITED STATES OF AMERICA

10 9 8 7 6 5 4 3 2 1

For Brandon

Sincere thanks to:

Laura Apperson, my daughter and local-color expert, who provides love, support, and a home base in Phoenix;

Gary Bale, talented writer, friend, and Orange County Sheriff–Coroner's Department Investigator, for his invaluable and generous help;

Maureen Albrecht, Deputy Coroner, Orange County Sheriff–Coroner's Department, for willingly and patiently answering questions;

Dr. Mary von Aspe and Brenda Simmons for sharing insights into child psychology;

and the Fictionaires, especially Noreen Ayres and Patricia McFall.

The shadow of the balusters, the shadow of the keep
    The shadow of the child that goes to bed—
All the wicked shadows coming, tramp, tramp, tramp
    With the black night overhead.

—Robert Louis Stevenson
"North-west Passage"
A Child's Garden of Verses

1

Phoenix, Arizona

In Anne Menlo's experience, a carefree idyllic childhood was mostly an adult's myth. Forced from the haven of the womb and greeted with a slap on the bottom, children have good reason to suspect the world is a cruel place. Soon—often much too soon—they discover their suspicions are justified.

Five-year-old Jason Sills, Anne's four o'clock appointment, was not handling this discovery very well, his reaction serious enough for Deena Sills to seek professional help. As far as Anne could tell from their first visit, however, Jason was luckier than lots of other kids. At least Jason had a fairly secure home and loving—if imperfect—parents.

He and his frazzled mother arrived five minutes late. Deena had her hand clamped firmly to his small wrist and was saying, "You know the rule about parking lots, young man," as Anne came out to meet them.

Jason resisted, a mutinous look in his eyes, but he brightened at Anne's smile and warm greeting.

Recently she had heard a patronizing colleague say, "It's no wonder kids like Menlo; she's not much bigger than they are and she looks about their age." Maybe there was something to the exaggerated remark. Anne wasn't sure. To a small child, thirty-four was old. And she was still a grown-up—large, imposing, and magical—even at a height of five feet. If a child responded to her size, the kind hazel eyes, and the soft brown hair curling around what one little girl described as a smiley face, fine, but Anne didn't count on it. Instead she relied on a low-key, nonthreatening approach and her natural rapport with children.

The tactic seemed to be working on Jason. When his mother released him, he spontaneously reached for Anne's hand. The three of them started into Anne's office, but the receptionist sang out, "Doctor? This man on the phone? He says he really has to talk to you?"

Anne and two other psychologists shared the common reception area where Peggy Rettig normally sat. Peggy would never disturb a doctor who was with a patient, but Peggy, also shared by the three but who made each feel as though she worked for them alone, was on vacation. An agency had sent two different temps this week, this one a ditzy young woman named Candi with frizzy red hair, a short attention span, and an annoying habit of putting a question mark at the end of every sentence.

"Just take a message, please," Anne said.

"But he says it's urgent—to tell you it's Bern? He said you knew who he was?"

Bernard Pagett. A detective with the Phoenix Police Department. The man Anne had almost married.

"Oh, I know him all right," Anne said under her breath. To Deena she said, "Go on in, I'll just be a minute," and went to take the call on Candi's desk.

"Bern, I really can't talk right now. I have a patient waiting."

"Is it something you can reschedule?" he asked. "I'm on my way to a homicide, and there's a child on the scene."

"No, I can't reschedule."

"Anne—"

"No. I can't do it. Get somebody else."

There were plenty of other psychologists on the police department's list. She'd had misgivings about being placed on that list, and had been right. Crisis situations don't fit neatly into time slots, and her involvement created havoc with her schedule. That was the official excuse she was using for backing away. The real reason went much deeper, of course. Why on earth had she let Bern talk her into offering her services in the first place?

"Why don't you think about it," Bern said. "I'll call you back."

"*No*, don't do that. Bern—"

He had hung up. She resisted the urge to slam down the receiver. "Candi, please, if anybody else calls, just take a message. I'm not to be interrupted when I'm with patients."

Candi nodded, adding sagely, "Boy, sometimes men can be such pigs, can't they?"

Heading into her office, Anne wished she had told Bern to call Karen Doheny. Karen would be the best person to deal with a traumatized child—boy or girl? Bern hadn't said. Never mind. Not Anne's problem.

Deena Sills was waiting, seated in one of the winged-back chairs. Jason was over in the far corner venting some hyperactivity on an inflatable Puncho. One end of the rectangular room held a small sofa, two chairs—bought for comfort rather than style—and Anne's desk; the other had a low table made from a sturdy old wooden workbench with the legs sawn off, salvaged from a garage sale and used for painting and play therapy, and open wood shelving loaded with hand puppets and a brightly colored plastic basket filled with toys. A closet held more toys and art supplies.

The slate-blue commercial-grade carpet could stand up to regular cleaning. Some large floor pillows were piled beside the worktable. Posters of animals, birds, blooming saguaro, and brilliant orange Mexican bird of paradise filled the walls. Closed miniblinds covered a window with a view of the parking lot.

While Jason attacked the Puncho, Anne sat in the other chair and asked quietly, "How did things go for him this week?"

"Awful," Deena said.

Ever since starting a full-day kindergarten at a private school, Jason's teacher had been sending home daily complaints about his behavior. At home Jason had turned whiny and clingy, biting his nails to the quick and throwing constant temper tantrums.

Anne glanced over at the little boy who punched the inflatable clown so savagely it hit the floor before springing up; a cold finger of foreboding touched her spine. Her heart began that old drumming as she thought, *What am I missing here?*

Deena was watching her with a worried look. Anne carefully kept her voice even as she said, "Tell me what happened."

"I got a call at work," Deena said. "The school insisted I come right over and pick Jason up. They wouldn't tell me what he'd done—God, I was scared to death. You know what happened? He was in the bathroom with this other little boy, and the boy dared Jason to pee in the sink."

"And did he?"

Deena nodded anxiously.

Anne smiled, relief like a warm flood soothing away her uneasiness. Jason was a typical little boy coping with inflexible teachers, a situation that caused stress, a natural reaction considering the circumstances. It was Bern's phone call that had stirred up old memories and made her doubt her judgment.

"Well, good for Jason," Anne said.

Deena grinned back. "I thought it was funny, too, but this teacher—well, of course she walked in and saw him doing it. The way she acted, you'd think Jason had murdered somebody—"

The phone rang on Anne's desk. Trying to hide her annoyance, Anne went to answer it.

"I asked you to hold my calls," Anne said.

"I know, Doctor, but it's that guy again, and he said he was from the *homicide* department? And, like, it was a real *police* emergency?"

Anne's fingers clenched so tightly it was a wonder she didn't crack the plastic receiver. She ordered herself to take a couple of steadying breaths. She would have to talk to Bern. Otherwise he would just keep on bugging the receptionist, and Candi was no match for him.

"All right. I'll take it out there."

Anne apologized to Deena and Jason, excused herself, and went to the outer office to pick up the phone, turning her back on Candi who listened with shameless excitement.

"Bern, I told you you'd have to get somebody else. I'm with a patient."

"Sorry, but I've got a little kid here who needs you, too. He's been keeping a corpse company."

The wrenching scene flashed into Anne's mind as though she was there, seeing it herself.

"Bad?" she asked.

"She's been dead about twenty-four hours, give or take a few. Gas-meter reader saw the body through a window."

"And the child?"

"Paramedics are checking him out. I don't think he's hurt—not physically."

"Bern, get him out of there."

"Child Protective Services is backed up. They'll send somebody, but it'll be a while."

"Then call Karen Doheny."

"I'm calling you," Bern said. "He's been in this house with a dead body. He's sitting here, staring, won't say a word. For God's sake, Annie, he's not more than four years old."

She felt a giant hand squeeze her heart. Dammit, the man had done it again.

"All right," she said. "Give me the address."

It was cool in the Camaro—the Arizona heat no match for GM air-conditioning—but sunlight glared in through the windshield, harsh and unrelenting, as Anne drove west out on Baseline Road to the edge of town. Eighty-nine days so far this year with the temperature at one hundred plus. It was a point of pride with the locals to keep the tally. Anne thought the practice smacked of masochism and sincerely hoped she would never feel that way.

Much as she loved Phoenix, there came a point every summer when she wondered why she didn't move back to San Diego where she grew up. Well, she knew why. Even in rocky, inhospitable soil, once you put down roots, it's hard to yank them out. And she was tied to this stark, lovely, contradictory place in more ways than she wanted to admit.

When she explained there was an emergency, Deena Sills had agreed to reschedule for Saturday. Now, following Bern's directions, Anne turned off Baseline toward South Mountain. The peak loomed, steep and remote, thickly covered with creosote bush, cactus, and stunted brown grass.

The houses out here were small, sorry affairs with warped wood siding and scabrous paint. Chain-link fences guarded yards full of discards: old cars, rusty appliances, a stained mattress leaking stuffing, a roll of glittering razor wire. Beaten and dry, the ground was too hostile an environment for all except the toughest weeds, the kind furred with sharp prickles and sprouting leathery, veiny leaves. At the corner Anne caught sight of a house a block away that had tried for a touch of whimsy with a yard full of toy windmills about three feet high that spun in the hot breeze.

Anne found the address easily enough. Surprisingly the media had yet to gather. Two patrol cars and a crime-lab van were parked out front in addition to Bern's white Cherokee. The department had no better luck arguing with Bern than she did. He hated the car-pool vehicles and drove his own in spite of the memos regularly issued ordering him to cease and desist. Working in homicide required a cooperative spirit, but when it came to his wheels, Bern stopped being a team player.

She left her Camaro on the street, bracing herself but still surprised by the brutal assault of the heat as she opened the door. The air smelled of dust and sun-burned brush with just a hint of something malodorous and dark.

She got out and slung her roomy canvas bag over her shoulder, grateful she was wearing a light cotton dress.

The house was as desolate as its neighbors, the yard more barren. Next door, a skinny black dog with mean yellow eyes left the dark cavern of a hole it had dug beneath the porch to lope over, flatten its ears, and growl, the sound a low, menacing vibration as it paced Anne along the fence.

Bern must have been keeping watch. He met her at the door, wearing that impassive aura of authority that went beyond the gold shield and the holstered gun clipped to his belt. At just under six feet, he towered over Anne. But then, most everybody did. The lean face with its thinning dark hair was ordinary-looking except for eyes the blue-green of glacial ice.

"Anne. I'm glad you came."

"Where is he?"

"Kitchen. Paramedics had to leave on another call."

She went inside, and Bern closed the door. Entry was directly into a small living room, crowded with furniture that looked ready to be abandoned out in the yard. The room was only marginally cooler than outside. An old swamp cooler wheezed, fighting the heat, stirring up odors of mildew, mold, and things infinitely worse.

Nothing looked out of place except for a lamp that sat on an end table, the shade askew. A crime-lab tech was lifting prints from the brass base. On a coffee table a fly buzzed around a Coke can that stood in a litter of corn chips and plastic Twinkie wrappers. The empty family-pack carton for the creme-filled snack lay on the floor. A camera flash strobed from a narrow hallway.

Anne's instinct was to rush to the child, but she said, "I think I ought to see what he's been dealing with."

"You're sure?"

She nodded.

A hug would have been nice, or just his hand on her elbow. She expected neither gesture. She and Bern had been engaged and living together for a year before their breakup. In the five years since, they had gradually drifted back into each other's lives and beds. Anne had loved him all that time and longer, knew him better than any other person. He was a tender lover, a loyal friend. He was allergic to pistachio nuts, was deathly afraid of snakes, worried about losing his hair, and fought a tendency to go soft around the middle with punishing handball matches. The first time she saw him handling a crime scene, she wondered if she knew him at all. There was a stillness about him, a cold distance that jolted her even though she understood this aloofness was necessary for him to do his job.

She tried for some of that detachment now, willing herself to be calm and objective, and followed him as he started toward the hallway.

"Will Hanson is assisting," Bern said. "He finished out here, and now he's in the bedroom with the victim."

A patrolman and another tech crowded the hall. They moved back into the living area to let Anne and Bern through. Straight ahead was the bathroom, the door ajar. Two bedrooms, a tiny one on the left that was dark and gave a gloomy impression of disorder. Slick yellow tape barred entry to it and to the one on the right. Slightly larger, it had only a single bed and a dresser for furnishings. A rolled-up shade drooped at the window, the bracket loose on one side, providing an opening for the meter reader to look in. An overhead fixture added bluish fluorescent light.

Will Hanson was down on his haunches, methodically searching the worn green shag carpet. He wore plastic booties on his shoes and disposable latex gloves. He looked up and said a distracted hello. As case agent, Bern was the lead investigator, responsible for witness interviews and follow-ups. Hanson was in charge of the physical evidence and was following standard department procedure, which was to mark out the scene and then work in toward the victim. He was still two feet away from the corpse.

The woman lay facedown beside the bed, short and stout when she was alive, her bulk diminished in death. The stench was bad but not unbearable. Anne forced herself to look as the boy must have, to see what he saw. Decomposition in warm climates quickly bloats and mottles the skin. Mercifully, most of the woman's was covered by light blue stretch pants and an oversized T-shirt with a stenciled design of pink flowers. Brassy blond hair spilled across her face, but one eye was visible, open wide in a fixed stare. Blood matted the hair above the ear, no longer red, oxidized to a purple-black. She was about Anne's age, or maybe a little older.

Anne shuddered and turned away.

"Her name was Dorie Wineski," Bern said.

"The boy's mother?"

"I don't know. This is not what you would call a close-knit neighborhood. I haven't had time to do a complete canvass, but I turned up one person who said she was pretty sure Ms. Wineski didn't have any kids."

Anne went back into the living room. The fingerprint tech looked up from his work to tell Bern that the medical examiner's ETA was half an hour.

Anne pictured the violence that must have gone on here, seeing it from the child's viewpoint, imagining his terror. He was hiding when it happened, she decided. He had to be. Otherwise, why had the person who killed Dorie Wineski left the boy—the witness—alive?

"Okay?" Bern asked.

She nodded.

He led the way into the kitchen.

The two patrolmen kept the boy company. One hovered near the formica-topped table where the child sat on a chrome chair. The other leaned against the wall.

The boy pressed his sturdy little body as tightly as possible against the plasticized back cushion and hugged his knees against his chest. He wore navy shorts and a matching knit shirt, white with thin navy and green stripes. Straw-blond hair skimmed his eyebrows, topping a face dirty enough to show the tracks tears had made on his cheeks. Sweat beaded his upper lip. Behind a blank, blue-eyed stare lurked the knowledge that the world was not just cruel but peopled by monsters.

Bern gestured to the patrolmen and left with them as they filed out. Anne pulled a chair over and sat next to the boy, resisting an instinctive urge to gather him up in her arms.

"Hi," she said. She took a soft brown teddy bear from her canvas bag. "My name is Anne, and this is Edgar. We'd like to sit here with you if that's okay."

Nothing. Anne perched the little bear between them and stroked its head.

"It was pretty scary around here, huh? Well, you don't have to be scared anymore. All of us are going to take care of you. You know that policeman who isn't wearing a uniform? The one who was just in here?"

He turned his head slightly, in the direction of the door to the living room.

"His name is Bern," Anne said, "and I know him really well. He's the best person you could have around to protect you. And me and Edgar'll be right here, too."

She waited, letting a few unhurried seconds drift by. "You know, what happened here—it wasn't your fault. Bad things happen sometimes, and we just can't stop them."

He moved suddenly, in one motion swarming up, coming into her lap, and bringing the teddy bear with him. Straddling her, he clung tightly with his arms and legs, both his head and Edgar's pressed against her breasts. With her face against his sweaty hair and his trembling body telegraphing his need for her, she felt the connection made, like an umbilical cord attaching her to this child.

This powerful emotion also brought with it an overpowering sense of dread. This little boy's well-being lay in her hands. So easy to make a mistake. A thousand ways to go wrong. She had learned that bitter lesson very early.

Anne had always wanted to work with kids. In her teens, she had even enjoyed baby-sitting the ones in the neighborhood that everybody else avoided, labeling them brats. She had fixed her goal early on: a degree in psychology, a career that focused on helping children.

During undergraduate school at Arizona State University she worked part-time in an afternoon program set up by the Phoenix school system that offered an alternative to latchkey kids: after-school activities like computer workshops, field trips, arts and crafts, a safe place to be until their working parents came home.

Ten-year-old Nicki Craig was in Anne's group, a shy girl, beautiful with a fine mass of blond curls, rain-gray eyes, an angelic face. Anne worked hard to get Nicki to participate, actually thinking what a good job she had done getting to know the child. Six months later, after Anne had quit her part-time job and was well into her first semester of graduate courses, one of her coworkers from the after-school program called with the shocking news: Nicki Craig, just turned eleven, had gone quietly into the bathroom one night after her parents were in bed and slashed her wrists with her father's straight-edged razor.

The police quickly learned the reason for the suicide. Nicki's father had not only been abusing his daughter for years, but also he had started passing her around to his friends. All that time Anne had spent with Nicki, and she had never guessed, had not a glimmer that anything was wrong.

The experience shook her so badly her grades plummeted. She probably would have dropped out of school if it hadn't been for Rosemary Beiderman. Anne's adviser, then her therapist, now her friend, Rosemary had encouraged her to use the incident to gain insight, and helped her to deal with the pain. Anne had thought their efforts were successful—until Bern talked her into working for the department.

Holding this traumatized little boy, she knew that the terrible sense of inadequacy and fear of failure had not been banished at all. The twin demons had only retreated to a dark corner of her mind and now they were loose once again.

2

Bern gave Anne fifteen minutes, then went back to the kitchen. The sight of the little boy in her lap brought him up short, remembering how much he had wanted a child of their own, a child with Anne. They had never really discussed it. Whenever he brought up the subject, she steered the conversation away. She was trained for that, good at it, too. He knew about the experience she'd had in college, figured that incident had something to do with her reluctance to think about a family of her own, but had every confidence that they could work it out. He still thought they would have, if they had stayed together, still hoped they might be given a second chance.

Now she looked up at him, her eyes full of unreadable shadows, just an instant of anguish that made his heart turn over.

She's really upset by this, he thought. "Anne—"

"I'm sure he's going to be fine," she said quickly, her look warning Bern off. "He just doesn't feel like talking right now."

Optimistic words, more for the boy than for him. Well, now wasn't the time for personal discussion anyway.

Delores Hetch from CPS bustled in just then, saying hello. The boy tightened his grip on Anne even though

Delores was about as nonthreatening as they come, a short, plump woman with a pleasant face framed by black hair that was liberally salted with gray.

Sizing up the situation, Delores said, "Looks like this little tyke wants you to come along with us to St. Joe's, Anne. Okay with you?"

Bern took the keys to Anne's Camaro, promising to have it brought to the hospital. He offered to take the child, who was much too heavy for Anne, but the boy clung to her like a limpet, so Anne carried him as they walked out to Delores's dusty gray sedan.

They were safely away before the advance press car rolled in with a News at Ten van close behind. Putting his thoughts of Anne on hold, Bern went inside, sent the patrolmen out to secure the scene, and told them to call for backup and a department media rep.

In the Wineski bedroom, Will had finished his painstaking search through the dirty shag carpet. The simple theory of forensics is that anybody at the scene of a crime leaves something behind and takes something away: fibers, soil, fingerprints, fluids, *something*. Therefore, every inch of the scene was searched and sampled. Now Will would do the same for the body.

He squatted beside the still form. Bern joined him for a close look while the photographer snapped pictures. The woman had suffered an injury above the right temple severe enough to cave in the bone. Blood and hair on the edge of the heavy oak lamp table in the living room indicated Dorie Wineski had fallen there with sufficient force to cause the wound. The fall might have been accidental, but Bern didn't think so.

When he carefully lifted the woman's head for a look at the other side of her face, however, he knew it would take an expert to tell whether the deep purplish-red color was a result of lividity, that pooling of the blood in the lowermost parts of the body, or was caused by somebody clubbing the victim with either his fist or a blunt weapon.

Will gave his opinion: "Somebody aced her."

"Yeah," Bern said. "I think so, too."

If they were right, the boy looked to be a potential eye-witness to murder. Bern told Will he was heading to St. Joe's.

Either the press had found the crime scene uninteresting, or it was too hot outside to linger. He only hoped they hadn't found out about the boy. Press coverage might be needed to help identify the child, but Bern didn't want re-porters tracking him down like a pack of hungry wolves.

On the way out he made arrangements for one of the patrolmen to bring Anne's car to the hospital. His Jeep was parked close enough to the yard next door so that the black dog charged over, baring its teeth and barking. A chain-link fence ran around the perimeter of the neighboring yard; a gate provided access to the driveway and a ramshackle carport that sheltered an old Chevy Monte Carlo.

The presence of the dirty white car indicated somebody might be home, but Bern couldn't get to the front door of the house without going into the yard with a dog that looked like a cross between a Doberman and a black Lab. Nobody had answered his shouts. He might have to return with an animal control officer. For now, he left his card in the mailbox along with a note saying he needed to talk to the resident immediately.

In the Jeep driving away, he thought about the look in Anne's eyes as she sat cuddling the little boy.

He'd been pursuing his own selfish agenda, simply want-ing to be close to her, hoping her involvement would help overcome her dislike of his work. Should he have been listening a little closer when she complained about disruptions to her schedule? Realizing there was more there than she was letting on? Recognizing nuances was part of his job, for Christ's sake.

His cell phone rang then, and what he heard put his concerns for Anne on hold. As she had once told him, he had the human equivalent of bloodhound genes. Once he was nose down and tracking, Bern the cop rarely looked up.

In the emergency room at St. Joseph's Children's Hospital, the staff was busy with victims from an auto accident. Anne waited with Delores and the boy in a curtained-off treatment area. Harsh light gleamed off chrome and shiny white surfaces. The chill air smelled of alcohol and Betadyne. Somebody over in a corner was saying, "Ohjesus ohjesus" over and over.

The little boy clung to Anne as she quietly told him about all the ominous-looking equipment, explaining to him and Edgar how all the people who worked here loved children and how she would be right there to make sure he was okay. He still wouldn't talk to her, but he raised three fingers when she asked how old he was.

A harried nurse supplied apple juice. The boy drank thirstily. Anne coaxed him into sharing some animal crackers from the zip-locked bag in her purse with her and Delores, probably the only supper Anne would get.

Then, after much reassurance, he allowed Anne to put him on the examination table and undress him. There was a good brand name on the label of his striped knit shirt, a fading bruise on his upper left arm covered by the sleeve. About the width of a cruel hand, Anne noted. Delores saw it, too.

When the young ER doctor hurried in, the child allowed an examination as long as Anne stood right beside him, holding Edgar. Besides the bruise, there were no other visible marks on his body and, according to the doctor, no indication of sexual abuse. That was good news, but Anne couldn't help thinking that signs of trauma are not always easily read.

"A nice warm bath and maybe some scrambled eggs," Delores said as she watched Anne dress the child. "A good night's sleep wouldn't hurt either, huh, little guy?"

The boy had no idea what was about to happen to him. He didn't know Delores would now take him off to stay at a CPS home or else be placed with foster parents until the police found out who he was and where he belonged. But he sensed change, and change meant new things he didn't understand, things that might be scary, maybe even terrifying. His eyes, fastened on Anne, were huge with dread.

"I've handled a lot of traumatized children," Delores said quietly. "I'm pretty good at it."

"I know you are," Anne said, knowing her overprotective reaction bordered on becoming neurotic, but unwilling to let the boy out of her sight until she absolutely had to. "I just think I ought to go with you and help get him settled for the night."

Before Delores could answer, Bern stuck his head around the curtain that hung on rails and enclosed the cubicle. The boy stiffened, then relaxed, recognizing Bern.

"How's it going in here?" Bern asked.

"We're doing okay," Delores said.

Anne read fatigue in the line of Bern's shoulders and in his face where the skin seemed to stretch tautly over his cheekbones the way it always did when he was tired. She'd bet he hadn't eaten. At least she'd had the juice and animal crackers.

"Did you speak to the doctor?" Anne asked.

"Just now."

"Well, we're all finished up in here and about to head out," Delores said.

"Not just yet," Bern said. "I got a call on the way over. A couple phoned headquarters to report their little boy was missing. They're meeting us here. With any luck—"

He broke off at the sound of voices: a male baritone rumble, a woman saying sharply, "I'm sorry, but you'll have to wait," and another feminine voice edged with hysteria, "I have to see him; I have to see him *right now*—"

Beside Anne, still seated on the table, the boy went rigid and stared at the closed curtain with intense concentration as Bern ducked out. Anne could hear Bern speaking softly: "Mr. and Mrs. Lewis? He's in here."

The metal rings rattled back on the metal rail, revealing the man and woman with Bern. There was a stopped, timeless instant while they stood there: a slender woman with her long, dark hair escaping the elasticized fabric circlet that pulled it into a sloppy ponytail, her face scoured by sleeplessness, worry, and fear; a man who was hiding his feelings with squared-jaw determination but with worry showing in eyes remarkably like the little boy's. Anne would bet his thick brown hair had once been bleached to straw in the summer sun.

Then joy lit Mrs. Lewis's face, and she rushed to scoop the child into her arms. "Danny—Danny, oh, thank God."

Anne stepped aside to let the father move in to hug Danny, his arms around both his son and his wife, because it was going to be a while, Anne suspected, before the woman and her child would be separated.

"Looks like a match to me," Delores murmured.

And little Danny Lewis spoke his first words. He said, "Daddy? Mommy? I wanna go home."

•　　•　　•

After brief introductions and assurances to the Lewises that the doctors had found nothing wrong with Danny, Delores left, declaring she had a husband and two kids who'd be happy to see her in the evening for a change.

Mrs. Lewis looked to Anne. "You're sure Danny's all right?"

"Natalie, honey, look at him," her husband said. "He's fine."

"How could he be fine? He was in a house with a— where somebody was murdered. Glen, they brought in a *psychologist*."

Holding Danny, Natalie Lewis sat down abruptly in a chair next to the examination table as though her knees had given way. She looked thin and breakable in a dress with an empire bodice and a pleated gauze skirt. Anne suspected she was near her limits, functioning on sheer nervous energy.

"Of course this was a traumatic experience for Danny," Anne said. "But I'm sure we can help him through it. I was called because the police were concerned. They wanted a professional there to take care of him."

"We appreciate that, Dr. Menlo," Glen Lewis began, but his wife interrupted, fixing her gaze on Bern. "Did you get him? Did you arrest the man who took Danny?"

"No arrests were made," Bern said. "All you told the duty officer was that your son was missing. Are you saying he was kidnapped?"

"Can't we talk about this later?" Glen took a protective stance beside the chair, ready to do battle. The blue polo shirt tucked into tan slacks displayed a hard-muscled body and the kind of well-defined biceps that only came from lifting weights. "My family's been through hell. I want to take them home now."

"I understand that," Bern said, "but I'm afraid I need

to ask you some questions right away. I'm sure there's a lounge here we can use.''

Anger darkened Glen Lewis's face. "For God's sake, man—'' He broke off, reading Bern's unyielding expression, and turned to Anne. "Dr. Menlo, you say you were called in to take care of Danny. Don't you think my boy's had enough to deal with? I know my wife's exhausted.''

Danny had lapsed back into silence, and his eyes had a dulled, switched-off sheen, but Anne could tell the heated exchange was raising his anxiety level. He seemed to burrow against his mother, and his thumb had crept into his mouth.

Anne knew Bern wouldn't like it. He needed to know the details of the kidnapping, to find out what had happened to put Danny in that house with a corpse. She wanted to know, too, but she said, "Yes, Mr. Lewis, I certainly agree.'' She added formally to Bern, "I'm the child's doctor, Detective Pagett, and I want him in his own home, in his own bed as soon as possible.''

Well, dammit, Bern dragged her into the case; now he could bloody well abide by her advice.

Bern usually kept a lid on his temper, and he did now. Just a jaw twitch and an icy coldness in his eyes belied his anger. As a substitute for a physical display, however, he could use words the way some men use their fists. Anne steeled herself, but the assault didn't come.

Instead he nodded curtly and said, "All right, Mr. Lewis. We'll talk at your house after the boy's in bed. I'll be there in an hour. Now, I'd better walk out with you. I don't think the press knows about Danny yet, but let's not take any chances.''

From the look on their faces, the Lewises had just realized their nightmare wasn't over yet.

•   •   •

Leaving the refrigerated air of the hospital, Anne caught her breath as she walked out into the full force of summer heat. The sun had set, but the western sky glowed with a bright, hot twilight. If anything, the temperature was higher than it had been all day. Contrary to popular belief, in the Arizona desert the thermometer did not fall rapidly at night. By dawn, the temperature would be much cooler—relatively speaking—maybe even down to eighty degrees. Evenings, however, were usually hotter than the daytime hours, especially in the city, where concrete and brick and stucco radiated back heat accumulated after long hours of baking in the fierce sun.

No reporters were lying in wait, so she and Bern had parted company with the Lewises at the ER entrance, then walked out to the parking lot without speaking, the tension between them like a wall. She was almost glad for it. She was sure he'd noticed something earlier back there in the Wineski kitchen. She just hoped he wouldn't ask any questions. The last thing she needed right now was to deal with his police-honed probing.

Maybe this flashback to little Nicki's death was just a result of the larger stresses in her life. If asked, back when she was a naive twenty, she would have predicted that by this age she would be married with a child of her own—along with a thriving practice, of course. At twenty she had believed not only that she could be superwoman, but also in happy endings.

Well, she had her practice. But her expectation of a happy personal life was another matter. She loved Bern, and he loved her. It should be simple. She had been trained to understand human interactions, so why hadn't she seen what was happening and fixed it before it was too late?

All this time she'd blamed their problems on his job. The Bern she loved was funny and kind, his only flaw a streak of pessimism instilled by his father. Bern the cop was distant and relentless, his natural cynicism deepened by his daily exposure to the worst of situations and people. The disparity in their outlook, a small rift in the beginning, had quickly turned into a chasm. Or at least that's what she had told herself.

Good Lord, listen to me.

Of course, it was Bern's job that had split them up, that still kept them in a go-nowhere relationship. And since he liked his work and was very good at it, a career change was not a viable possibility. Anne knew that his pressuring her into working for the department had been an attempt to bridge their differences. She let him talk her into it for the same reason.

Now she was afraid they'd both made a big mistake.

The Camaro sat next to Bern's Cherokee. Bern stopped beside the Jeep, dug out his keys, and said, "Sorry. I'm sure you think I acted like a real asshole in there."

"Now that you mention it, I guess I do," Anne said.

"Can't help it, babe." He gave her a wry grin. "It's part of the job description." He reached out to lay his fingers lightly against her cheek. "Don't be mad?"

She went into his arms and let him hold her. Mutt and Jeff, her father said the first time he saw them together. The top of her head barely touched the bottom of his chin. Pressed against his chest, she could hear the faint, steady beating of his heart.

"Want to talk about it?" he asked softly.

She shook her head.

"Okay, we don't have to talk. How about something to eat?"

At home there was half a roast chicken in the refrigerator, fresh salad greens washed and ready for the dressing, some chilled white Grenache. In the hour or less before

Bern was to meet with the Lewises, about all they could
do was hit a fast-food joint and eat burgers and fries.

"Please?" Bern said.

At the nearest McDonald's Anne virtuously ordered a
salad, but when Bern asked for a Big Mac, she said, "On
second thought, make that two. And a chocolate shake."

"Good idea," Bern said. "Two shakes. And a large coffee."

"You're a bad influence," Anne told him as they tore
into their meals.

"Always have been."

Anne felt herself relaxing. Nothing like fat and choles-
terol to calm anxiety. While they ate in companionable silence, she vowed to eat only water-packed tuna the rest of
the week. Extra pounds showed quickly on her small frame.
Fortunately she had a good metabolism. Watching her diet
was still a cautionary habit, but she liked to eat and occasionally had to call to mind her mother's short, barrel-
shaped body to keep her appetite in check.

They had the place to themselves except for one other
couple who sat at a table out in the playground area, drinking from large cups and watching their two kids jump in a
bin filled with brightly colored plastic balls. The girl was
about five, the boy three—Danny's age. Their crows of
laughter were audible even through the glass window sep-
arating the playground from the restaurant.

Following her gaze, Bern ate the last bite of his burger,
pushed aside his unfinished shake, and opened the container
of coffee.

"Anne, you realize the boy may be our only witness to
what happened to Dorie Wineski," he said quietly.

"Maybe it was an accident. Maybe she was drinking and
fell."

"It's possible. I still have to talk to Danny about it."

"Yes, but not tonight."

"Things get lost—forgotten—"

"No."

"Especially with a child."

"No," she said. "And I'm to be there when you do talk to him, understand?"

"You're a hard woman, Annie Menlo."

"I have to be, dealing with you," Anne said.

Feeling suddenly stuffed, she put the remains of the burger back in the cardboard container, wiped her hands, and began cleaning up the table, putting things on the tray. Bern's beeper went off. He excused himself and went to make a call. She picked up his coffee and sipped.

In the play area the children jumped and shrieked. Their parents didn't notice. They sat hunched over their soft drinks, and Anne didn't have to hear them to know they were arguing. Body language spoke volumes. In-law problems, money problems, sex problems—whatever the reason for the fight, it would be the overstimulated kids who would suffer the fallout. Anger, demeaning words, slaps—and sometimes things infinitely worse.

Cut it out, she told herself.

Not all parents were like Nicki's father; they were merely careless and self-absorbed, things most kids survived very well.

She took another sip of coffee and looked at Bern questioningly as he slid into the seat.

"That was Will," Bern said. "The M.E.'s report's preliminary, but I'd give odds it won't change. Dorie Wineski's death was no accident."

Despite the hot coffee in her hands and the hundred-degree heat waiting outside, Anne felt suddenly chilled. Danny may have been sleeping; he may not have witnessed the murder at all or, if he had, remember it with a three-year-old's distorted view. Until he talked about the experience, they wouldn't know for sure.

"Why don't you come with me to the Lewises'?" Bern asked. "I ccould call Will, but you already have a connection, at least with Natalie. That's always a help when you question people."

"*Question*—you mean interrogate, don't you?"

"Yes," he said flatly, "I do."

It was one of the things she disliked about his job—he always had to assume the worst. But then that was part of her job, too, wasn't it?

It occurred to her then that she could tell Bern what she was feeling and withdraw from the case. That maybe, given her anxiety, she wasn't fit to be entrusted with Danny's care.

But she remembered Danny's small body pressing against her, the trust in his eyes. He might not forge that bond so easily with another therapist.

"All right," she said. "I'll go with you."

3

The Lewises lived in a new two-story house tucked into a neighborhood of older homes on the edge of the Encanto area of Phoenix. Except for palms, some orange trees, and an occasional splash of brilliant bougainvillea, the street, with its well-tended lawns and hedges, looked as though it belonged in a Midwestern town rather than the arid Southwest. The Lewises' house with its raw, oversize look didn't quite fit in.

Only a few lights shone dimly behind drawn curtains and closed blinds. When Bern turned into the driveway, however, security lamps blazed on. Bern parked beside a white Lexus; he and Anne got out and went up to ring the bell.

Glen Lewis let them into a tiled entry with a vaulted ceiling. Stairs were on the left, the flight topped by a railed landing. Glen gestured them into a living room off to the right, and asked if they'd like something to drink. In a land where dry heat sucks moisture out of the human body, offering beverages is a standard gesture not to be necessarily interpreted as hospitality.

Anne shook her head, and Bern said, "No, thanks."

Glen sank down in one of two big overstuffed chairs upholstered in navy corduroy and left them the sofa that was covered in a cotton fabric, a stripe of light blue and cream. If Anne sat all the way back on the firm, deep cushions, her feet wouldn't touch the floor, so she perched near the edge.

Her first impression was that the room was distinctly masculine. The floors were covered in plush camel-colored carpet; walls were painted a light cream. Drapes in a cream open-weave fabric hung over white miniblinds. Glass-doored bookcases flanked the fireplace, a dark, reddish wood, cherry—like the coffee table. Matching cherry-wood end tables held brass lamps. Three huge pink roses drooped in a crystal vase, shedding petals on the glossy wood. Anne could smell the flowers, the scent mixed with furniture polish and a faint odor of cigarette smoke.

Decorations included a few Remington prints and a large painting of a cattle drive that hung over the fireplace. Except for the dying roses, a few needlepoint pillows in shades of rose and mauve supplied the only feminine touch.

"Natalie's asleep." Glen offered the information with a trace of defiance. "Danny wouldn't go to bed alone, so she laid down with him. She was out of it right away. It's the first time she's slept in three days, and I won't wake her up."

"That's all right, Glen," Bern said. "She must be exhausted. Okay if I call you Glen?"

"Sure." Anne thought Glen had picked up on the steel beneath Bern's soothing, sympathetic tone, but he made an effort to sound cooperative. "Tell me about your finding Danny, Detective Pagett. I didn't want Natalie upset any more that she had to be, but I need to know how bad it was."

"All right, but first let's hear your story." Bern took out a notebook and uncapped a pen. "Your boy was missing— you said three days?"

Glen nodded.

"But you didn't call the police."

"Damned right I didn't, not after what happened to that little Carter girl out in L.A."

Anne remembered the case. Anybody who watched TV or read a newspaper had suffered along with the parents of five-year-old Sarah Carter. Two months ago the child had disappeared from her backyard in Riverside, California. A note was found demanding a large ransom and warning the parents not to call the cops. But the father called the FBI immediately. Nothing else was heard from the kidnappers, and the little girl's body had been found a few days later in a gully out in the Mojave by some weekend dirt bikers.

"The Carters did the right thing," Bern said. "It was unfortunate—"

"*Unfortunate?* Jesus Christ, somebody killed their baby because they brought the police in. Do you have any kids, Detective Pagett?"

"No, I don't."

Anne caught an underlying note of hurt in Bern's voice. He'd had dreams of happy endings, too.

"Well, then, you can't understand what I was going through," Glen said. "I wasn't, by God, going to let anything like that happen to my boy."

"Glen, let's get something straight," Bern said. "I can't fault you for doing what you thought was necessary to protect your son, but I've got some big problems to solve here. I started off with a murder, and now I find out there was a kidnapping, too. I'm sure you want to find the person who took your son, and if you paid a ransom, maybe recover your money. So you need to help me out."

Glen stared at him. "The money—to tell you the truth I figured it was gone. Do you think there's really a chance to get it back?"

"Maybe. With your cooperation."

"Glen?" None of them had heard Natalie come in. She stood at the edge of the tiled entryway, looking like a sleep-walker.

Glen jumped up and rushed to her. "Natalie, you ought to be in bed."

"I heard voices. I told you to wake me up when they came."

"I didn't have the heart. Honey, I don't think you're ready for this. Why don't you go back upstairs?"

"Glen, I'm not an invalid." Irritation blazed in her eyes, then quickly died. "I'm all right, really."

The popular myth is that trouble brings families together. Anne knew that quite often the opposite was true, so the strain between the Lewises was not surprising. Or was it more than simple strain? She vowed she wouldn't be blinded to any secrets hidden in this pleasant, well-kept house. But she had to be careful, too, not to see things that weren't there.

Natalie went to sit in one of the chairs and said to Bern, "I heard what you were saying—about the money. It would be nice to have it back, but the important thing is, I want you to catch this—this animal. I want him to go to jail. I want him to suffer the way he made us suffer, the way he made Danny suffer the past three days."

"Believe me," Bern said, "that's what we all want."

"What about the FBI?" Natalie asked. "Glen doesn't think they'll be involved. Will they?"

Bern explained that since Danny was missing longer than forty-eight hours, the FBI could be brought in, but under the circumstances, their participation wasn't automatic. Because of the murder, the Phoenix police would probably want to take responsibility for both cases. A decision would be made tomorrow.

"Right now," Bern said, "I need to interview the two of you separately."

"Oh, come on," Glen said. "We agreed to talk to you. Can't we get this over with?"

"It's routine procedure." The steel was back in Bern's voice.

"Routine . . . what is this? You *suspect* us of something? If you do, I want to know right now." Natalie put a hand on her husband's arm, but he shook it off. "I'll call our attorney, and we won't say another word."

Anne thought he meant it. She could see Bern weighing the situation and knew that the last thing he would want was to have an attorney monitoring the conversation.

He didn't like it, but he said, "That's your privilege, of course, but it's not necessary, not now. Let's just talk. Start at the beginning and tell me what happened. Take your time."

"All right." Glen took a pack of Marlboros from his pocket, shook one out, then hesitated. "Do you mind?"

Both Anne and Bern disliked smoke, although he tolerated it better than she did. Natalie didn't object. Well, it was their house, and this was no time to keep Glen from his calming hit of nicotine.

Bern said politely, "No, go ahead," and waited while Glen lit up.

"I gave these up three years ago because of Danny, and now—" He took a deep drag, then went on, "It was Monday afternoon. I came home from work a couple of hours early."

"And you work where?"

"Fitness Unlimited. That's my company. I mean, I own it. We make exercise equipment." He glanced down at his cigarette with a wry grin. "Anyway, I was going to run some errands, so I took Danny along to get him out of Natalie's hair and to spend some time with him.''

"He's giving up his nap,'' Natalie said. "He gets so crabby in the afternoon."

"We were only out about ten minutes when he fell asleep,'' Glen went on, tapping ashes into a large, crystal ashtray. "My first stop was the bank. I used the drive-through, then I had to pick up some dry cleaning. I knew I shouldn't leave Danny in the car. But he's really cranky when you wake him up."

"He was out there in the heat?" Anne asked, appalled, thinking about how quickly temperatures rise in a closed vehicle.

"No, I wouldn't do that. I left the engine running and the air on. It was just for a couple of *seconds*. I know it was a stupid, *stupid* thing to do.''

More than stupid, Anne thought grimly, mentally cataloguing the other dangers—but then, of course, Glen Lewis had learned about them the hard way.

"When I came back, Danny was gone." He took another drag of the cigarette. "There was a note. It said to go straight home and wait, that if we called the police, Danny would be killed.''

He ground out the cigarette, plowed his fingers through his hair. Bern just sat, saying nothing.

"All I could think of was the little Carter girl. I did exactly what the note said. I went home, and we waited.''

"That night—it was the hardest thing I ever had to go through.'' Natalie's voice trembled. "I kept thinking we were making an awful mistake not bringing in the police. But Glen insisted we couldn't take the risk.''

"And I was right, wasn't I?''

Natalie nodded with that attitude of long-standing ac-quiescence that told Anne that Glen usually called the shots.

A dangerous position to be in, because the person who insists on making the decisions takes on a terrible responsibility. If Glen had been wrong, the consequences could have been even more shattering for him than for Natalie, Anne thought.

The kidnappers finally called at ten o'clock the following morning. A male voice on the phone, demanding one million dollars.

Glen shook out another cigarette, stared at it, put it back in the pack. "He said if we called the cops or did something dumb like marking the money, we'd get Danny back in—in pieces."

Natalie made an anguished little sound that would have softened stone. In spite of her suspicions and her intention to remain objective, Anne's heart went out to both the Lewises.

"You paid the ransom?" Bern prompted.

"Of course. I couldn't get the whole million—not a chance. And I was really scared when the guy called back because what I had was a little over eight hundred thousand. Wiped out our savings and my business capital." Glen's face was grim. "He didn't like it, but I guess I convinced him that's all I could lay my hands on."

At seven o'clock the night before, Glen left the ransom in a Dillard's shopping bag in a rest room at a Mobil minimart on Camelback. Miles from Dorie Wineski's house, Anne realized, which might or might not mean anything.

"Okay. You dropped off the ransom—then what?"

"I came home."

"What time was that?"

"I don't remember. Eight, eight-thirty."

"Maybe you remember, Natalie," Bern said.

"I wasn't here," Natalie said. "I went out, driving

around, looking for Danny—it was crazy, but I just couldn't sit and wait.''

"She didn't leave a note," Glen said. "My first thought was that the son of a bitch came and took her, too.''

"I'm sorry," Natalie said. "I told you I was sorry.''

"I know, Nat. It's okay.''

"What was supposed to happen after the ransom was paid?" Bern asked.

"He said they'd leave Danny in a shopping mall today, but he wouldn't say which one.''

"And we didn't hear anything," Natalie said. "We waited and waited. I knew Danny was dead. I just knew it. We argued—''

"It wasn't an argument," Glen said. "We were just upset.''

Natalie didn't contradict him. She stared off toward the corner of the room, as if the ugly scene still played there. Glen looked at Anne, an appeal for understanding. People expect a psychologist to understand, to verbalize their feelings.

"Anybody would be upset," Anne said. "It was a stressful situation.''

"It about drove me crazy just sitting here, hoping mall security, *somebody*, would call," Glen said. "So I went looking for Danny. Another stupid move. It was rush hour. I only got to two malls.''

Meanwhile Natalie was home, slowly losing her mind. "I couldn't go on just doing nothing. I told Glen we had to bring in the police.''

"So I came home, and we called and found out about the little boy in the hospital . . .'' He trailed off. "That's it. That's what happened.''

"Okay. First of all I need the ransom note.''

Glen nodded and pulled open the drawer of a lamp table.

"I'll get it," Bern said.

He took a sheet of white paper from the drawer, picking it up carefully by an edge and laying in on the coffee table. "Both of you touch this?"

They said they had.

The note had been typed using a manual typewriter with a dim ribbon on what looked to Anne like plain white copier paper. It read: WE HAVE DANNY. WE'LL KNOW IF YOU CALL THE COPS. IF YOU DO, WE KILL YOUR SON. GO HOME & WAIT. WE'LL BE IN TOUCH.

Upstairs, Danny began to scream for his mother. Both Natalie and Anne jumped up.

"I'll come with you," Anne said as Natalie headed for the stairs, calling, "I'm coming, Danny. Mommy's coming."

In the glow of a night-light, Anne had the impression of a spacious room done in cheerful primary colors, furnished with child-size furniture. Danny sat bolt upright in a small bed, his body rigid, his eyes wide with fear.

"Bunny," he wailed.

"It's okay," Natalie said, rushing over to pick him up. "Mommy's here."

"Bun-nee."

"You want your bunny rabbit? Anne—" She looked up at a netting hammock slung across the corner of the room, loaded with dozens of stuffed animals.

Anne took down a soft gray toy with long floppy ears and offered it. Danny recoiled, screaming "No!" and knocking it from her hands.

"Don't wanna—" His back arched. He almost bucked out of Natalie's arms. "No, no—no bunny face."

At least that's what Anne thought he said. His words were practically incoherent. Natalie looked up at her, pleading for advice.

"Just hold him," Anne said. "Let him know he's safe."

It sounded so inadequate, but it was about all that could be done just then, and Danny's mother was the best person to do it. As Natalie sat with Danny in a rocker, Anne went out, closed the door, and leaned against it. She could hear Danny's cries and his mother's soothing monotone as she comforted him. The child had had a bad dream, a normal reaction to the kind of trauma he'd suffered. Still, Anne had the feeling that he'd tried to tell her something important. She only wished she had some idea of what it was.

Glen paced around and lit another cigarette, listening to Danny's wails, looking as though he wanted to rush up the stairs and tend to the boy himself.

"I'm sure Dr. Menlo and your wife can take care of him," Bern said, and sure enough the boy's screams modulated to a desolate sobbing.

"Can we please wrap this up?" Glen said. "You can't have any more questions."

"A few," Bern said. "Back to Monday—what time did you leave the house to run your errands?"

"I don't know. Three-fifteen, about then."

"You notice anything different? A strange car parked on the street? Somebody following you?"

"What?" Glen's attention was on Anne, coming downstairs. "What is it? What's wrong with him?" he asked as Anne walked into the living room.

"Just a nightmare," Anne said.

Bern thought she looked unsettled and distracted, but she quickly composed herself and added, "It's a natural reaction, Glen. It's to be expected."

Glen nodded but didn't look relieved.

Bern was still sitting. Anne gave him a questioning look. He said, "We have a few more things to discuss with

Glen.'' After Anne joined Glen on the sofa, he went on, ''I was asking him if he noticed anybody following him on Monday.''

Glen glared at him, sat down, and stubbed his cigarette out in the ashtray. He might have to answer Bern's questions, but he didn't have to like it.

''No,'' Glen said. ''I didn't notice anything like that.''

''Do you pick up cleaning at that same shop every Monday afternoon?''

''No.''

''Good timing on the part of the kidnappers, wasn't it?''

''I don't know what you mean.''

''They just *happen* to show up, and there Danny is, alone.''

''I didn't say they weren't following me. I said I didn't *notice*. My God, who would be expecting something like that?''

''Do you always leave your son in the car while you run errands?''

''No, I never do.''

''Never?''

''Never,'' Glen declared.

But he had on Monday. He locked the doors. The car had a keyless pad. A combination could be punched in. You could use a key, but you didn't need one.

''And when you came back with the cleaning,'' Bern said, ''was the door locked?''

''I don't know. I looked in and I didn't see Danny. That's what I was thinking about. I don't remember anything about the door. But I'm sure I locked it. I know I did.''

From the stricken look on Glen Lewis's face, Bern knew he wasn't sure at all.

''You were gone—how long? A few *seconds*—''

''A minute,'' Glen snapped. ''Maybe two.''

"And it wasn't a random snatch, was it?"

"I don't know."

"Couldn't have been. Danny's name was in the note." Bern doodled something on his pad and asked in the same level tone of voice, "Do you know Dorie Wineski?"

Glen sat bolt upright. "What?"

"You know her?"

"Dorie? Well, sure, she—Jesus, *Dorie's* mixed up in this?" he asked, stunned.

"How do you know Ms. Wineski?"

"She was our nanny for a while."

"When was this?"

"Back in February. February to June, four months. Natalie decided she wanted to get a job."

"Why did Ms. Wineski leave?"

"I fired her. I never really trusted the woman. And I was right. She was an alcoholic. One day I came home and found her passed out on the couch."

"She very angry over being fired?"

"No, not really."

"No threats or—"

"No."

"—strange phone calls? Hang-ups, breathers—"

"No."

"Was she married?" Bern asked.

"I don't think so."

"She have a boyfriend?"

"I've no idea. Why are you asking about—oh, Christ, Dorie's dead, isn't she? She's the woman who was with Danny. How did she—? What happened?"

"We don't have the results of the autopsy yet, but it looks like somebody smacked her around. When's the last time you saw Dorie Wineski?"

"In June. The day I fired her. You know—we keep spare

keys in a drawer in the kitchen. She could've taken one to the car. Or Danny could've woke up and opened the door. He knew her.'' Either of these possibilities let him off the hook, but neither cheered him up. ''She must've been hanging around—she and this guy, the one who called me— waiting for a chance to get to Danny. And I gave it to them.''

''Sounds like a good possibility,'' Bern said.

''When did she die?''

''Preliminary estimate is eleven o'clock last night.''

''She was dead all that time, and Danny was there—my God, I never thought—'' He looked sick.

''There was no way you could've known,'' Anne said. ''You can't blame yourself.''

She glanced at Bern, sending a silent message: *Enough*.

He said, relenting, ''She made it into the bedroom after the fall. It looked like Danny was sleeping in the other room. At this point we're not sure how much he saw.''

''Didn't he tell you? Didn't he say anything? I'm sorry, but he hasn't talked about it, and I guess I just need to know what we're facing here, how to handle things.''

''Danny didn't say a word,'' Anne said, ''not until he spoke to his mother in the hospital. That's understandable, under the circumstances, but he is going to need help dealing with the trauma.''

''Well, of course, we'll help him.''

''Professional help,'' Anne said.

Danny had stopped crying, but the memory of his screams lingered in the room.

''Listen to her, Mr. Lewis. She's very good at what she does.'' Bern capped his pen and put away the notepad. ''We'll go over this again tomorrow.''

''Again? Why? We've told you everything.''

''Well, sleep on it. Maybe you'll remember something

else. Ten o'clock in the morning? I'll come here if that's easier for you. Oh, and we'll need to print both you and your wife.''

"Fingerprint us?"

"To eliminate your prints on the note."

"Oh, right. Okay."

Bern hadn't mentioned talking to Danny. No point in pushing it with Anne right now. He took a large evidence bag from his inside jacket pocket and carefully put the ransom note inside.

"Say good night to your wife for us," Bern said.

Glen said he would, got up, and followed them out. Anne told him to call her office to set up an appointment for Danny, which got her a distracted nod.

Bern paused at the front door. "If I were you, I'd think about calling a locksmith. If somebody's walking around with your car keys, maybe they have a house key, too."

"God, you're right. I'll do it right now."

It looked as though the Lewises would be spending another night without much sleep.

4

In the Jeep driving away from the Lewises' house, Anne thought about Danny's cries when he'd awakened. She'd been so sure that his words had meant something, but how likely was it that they did? Nightmares have their own distorted images and landscapes. Even if significant, children Danny's age have a hard time translating those dream scenes.

More likely she was letting her professional guard down, giving importance to something totally meaningless.

"Penny," Bern said.

"Not worth it."

He gave her a sidelong glance that said he really didn't believe that. "Danny's going to be okay, isn't he?"

"I hope so, in time. What did you think of Glen and Natalie?"

"You first, Doc."

"They come across as two ordinary people who have been through a horrible ordeal." She paused.

"But," he prompted.

Unable to confide how unsure she was of her own impressions right now, Anne found herself saying with more conviction than she felt, "They really love that little boy. I can't imagine either of them being so desperate to siphon off money by doing something to hurt him, especially Natalie.''

"No? You noticed neither of them had an alibi for the entire evening when Dorie Wineski was killed. As for Natalie, try this. It's obvious Glen's running her life. She tried a job. That didn't work. Maybe she's getting desperate. What she really wants is to divorce him, but she figures if she does he'll hide the money and she'll get little or nothing. She liked the nanny. She feels okay about leaving the boy with Dorie for a few days in spite of Dorie's history of drinking. It's for his own good—their own good—in the long run. But Dorie is more abusive than Natalie knew. They have a fight, maybe over Danny, maybe over money, and—'' Bern shrugged.

It depressed Anne to realize she could easily believe Bern's speculation, but she had to point out, "It was a man who called about the ransom. Where does he come in?''

"Don't know. Hey, it's not a complete scenario, but it's plausible.'' Bern turned into the hospital lot and parked beside her car. "I can see something's bothering you about this one, Anne. If you'd just tell me—''

"It's nothing,'' she said. "Long day. Too many long days lately.''

Talking about the feelings stirred up by Danny could easily open a big can of worms that she wasn't prepared to deal with. Not tonight.

"Okay, babe,'' he said. "I'm not going to push it. What about tomorrow?''

"If you plan to talk to Danny, I want to be there.''

"Would you like me to pick you up at your office in the morning?''

Anne had one early session scheduled, then she was free until two-thirty. She had planned to use the time to catch up on reports, pay some bills, and talk to her accountant. She sighed. "I'd better meet you."

"Okay." He leaned over and brushed her lips with his. "Drive safe."

She took off the seat belt and reached for the door handle, hesitating a second, wanting to ask Bern to come home with her.

She was an independent spirit. She liked living by herself in her own house, way out in the foothills, miles from town, liked the isolation. On the average, Bern stayed with her two nights a week—her limit, not his. If she said the word, he'd move in. Probably better to leave things the way they were. Better not to have to sidestep his questions, even if she suddenly and desperately didn't want to be alone.

"I was going to get a jump on the paperwork," Bern said, "but on second thought, to hell with it. I'll drop off the ransom note, and then—okay if I spend the night at your place?"

Anne slipped out of bed just before dawn. Bern lay snoring softly, an arm over his eyes, as she pulled on shorts and a T-shirt and stuck sockless feet into an old pair of Keds. No need to tiptoe. Nothing short of dynamite would wake Bern up.

After a brief trip to the bathroom, she went out through the shadowy house to the kitchen. Facing east, the room was full of pearly light that muted the bold sunflower print border and rendered the whitewashed cabinets in shades of pinky-gray. She poured some orange juice, took the glass out on the back deck, and leaned against the wooden railing. Above, the hills loomed, still dark and secretive against a luminous eastern sky.

A faint breeze, dry and warm, caressed her bare arms and legs. She wondered how Danny had spent the night, then resolutely pushed the thought away. She had made a pact with herself. Problems and work were to be postponed, at least until after breakfast. She took a deep breath, clearing her mind, enjoying air cleansed by blowing over a hundred miles of wild desert mountains, air that smelled of sunburnt mesquite, creosote bush, and purple sage.

As the sky brightened, she scanned the brushy slope—and froze. Something sat, still as stone, atop an outcropping of boulders about a hundred feet up. Just a dark shape at first, but coming rapidly clearer as the sun rose. Compact body, square head, pointed tufted ears. The bobcat sat for another full minute, staring back at her, before he moved off, wary but unhurried, up the hillside.

Anne let out a pent-up breath in an exultant sigh.

The rock behind the boulders was hollowed out to form a natural basin. The previous owner had run a water line up there and had made Anne promise to keep the basin filled. Jackrabbits, coyotes, and javelina regularly came to drink. This was the first time she had seen the more elusive bobcat, however.

Finishing the juice, she went back inside, put house keys and a small cellular phone into a fanny pack, and belted the pack around her waist. *O modern pioneer,* she thought as she went to take her bicycle from the storage area in the carport, a sturdy mountain bike with special tires made to resist penetration by cactus barbs.

She pedaled down the patchy asphalt drive, staying alert because the most plentiful wildlife out here was rattlesnakes and lizards, including nasty-tempered Gila monsters that grew to be eighteen inches long. This morning, except for two startled jackrabbits, she had the narrow street to herself. Remoteness was the appeal in Cave Creek, certainly to Anne. Houses sat on one- and two-acre lots, well back from the road that followed the contour of the land, dipping down into arroyos that became flash-flood channels when it rained. The half-hour ride provided a good workout. Her skin was sheened with sweat and her calves had started to feel the strain when she arrived back at home.

Riding up the drive, she was struck anew by how much she loved it here. The house was sand-colored adobe and weathered wood, the carport tacked on as an afterthought. Only the two big paloverdes that shaded the house from the worst of the afternoon heat had been planted there; the rest of the landscape had been designed by nature, an acre and a half of sandy soil, rocks, and cactus.

On the edge of the wild foothills north of Phoenix, her house was old, inconvenient, and in constant need of repairs. Bern seriously thought she'd lost her mind when she bought the place. A man who dealt regularly with the dregs of society, he was uneasy with the wild expanse of mountains outside the back door—and he was terrified of snakes. For Anne the house was love at first sight, worth the expense, hazards, and the long commute.

Inside, Bern was sound asleep atop the covers, sprawled on his stomach. He slept in loose pajama bottoms, short ones, and always kicked off the sheet, complaining the house was too warm. He was still in the same position when she emerged from her shower. She slipped into a cotton robe, then went to sit beside him on the bed and put her hand lightly on his bare shoulder.

Both his work and disposition kept him out of the sun, so he had a farmer's tan. She liked the warmth of his skin, white beyond the demarcation of collar and short sleeve, liked the feel of it, supple and smooth over the power of muscle and bone. The touch evoked the memory of their lovemaking, the joining that always made her think that if she let it, the sweet force could sweep all obstacles aside.

She knew better, of course. Things between them were much too complicated.

She leaned down to kiss the back of his neck, then gave him a shake. "Bern, time to get up." A little louder: "Bern, up."

He finally stirred, groaned, opened one eye, and closed it again. The problem with mornings out here, he always said, was that they came too damned early.

"I guess it's shock therapy for you." Anne flipped on the radio next to the bed.

A bolt of loud rock music drove him up and sent him stumbling off to the bathroom, swearing and muttering about sadistic women.

After making sure he was actually in the shower, she went out to the sunny kitchen to start the coffee and scramble a couple of eggs for herself, reflecting how quickly all personal problems give way to practical concerns.

She was eating the eggs and spreading guava jelly on her second piece of toast when Bern came in, dressed in tan slacks and a white shirt with the sleeves rolled up to the elbow, carrying a jacket and tie and his holstered gun. The inventory of clothing he left here kept accumulating, bit by bit, like the accretion of liquefied minerals dripping slowly to build a stalagmite. He dumped his stuff on a chair, poured himself some coffee, and slouched down across the table, eyeing her morosely.

Conversation was painful for Bern until he had an infusion of caffeine, so she read the paper and finished her meal. He finally said, "Don't you know those things are bad for you?"

"I like them."

She ate the last forkful of eggs, remembering the Big Mac and shake she'd eaten the night before and feeling less guilt than she should have. So much for the water-packed tuna.

He drained his coffee, looked at his watch, and said, "I have to get going."

She lifted her face for a kiss as he picked up his jacket and gear. "See you at the Lewises'."

She was heading toward the sink with her dishes as the front door closed behind him. A moment later he yelled from the carport, "Anne! ANNE!"

She dropped the dishes with a crash and raced out in her slippers to find him standing by the back bumper of his Jeep, ashen-faced, staring at the snake that was coiled up by the front tire and rattling its tail in a furious warning.

Anne grabbed his elbow. "Back up. Come on. Give it some room."

It was a mark of his fear that he had a loaded .9mm Glock semiautomatic pistol in his hand but hadn't used it. He let her walk him backward, his gaze still fastened on the poor reptile that was even more frightened than Bern was. The snake slithered off the back of the cement carport pad and headed for the brush.

"Just stay here," Anne said. She did a visual check around and under the cars. "Okay. All clear."

"This goddamn place," Bern said, still pale and shaken as he climbed into the Cherokee.

"Look at it this way," she said. "After this, the rest of the day should be easy."

To outsiders Phoenix might conjure up visions of the Old West, but it was really a city with over two million people in the growing metropolitan area, and Bern was a city man. His only concession to the frontier culture was the occasional wearing of jeans, boots, and a bolo tie. Wild desert mountains were fine as a backdrop, but he liked the security of cement and other people.

That damn house of Anne's switched on some primitive alarm center in his brain. During most of the long black night, he remained on guard, waiting to repel wild animals or raids by outlaws and Apaches, rarely sleeping soundly before dawn, prepared long ago by his father's warning: *Consider the worst thing that can happen, because it will.* Getting up earlier than usual didn't help either; it was sheer torture for somebody who was not a morning person to begin with.

He was certainly not up to talking to Anne about her unsettled reaction to little Danny Lewis. And last night— well, if she'd meant to distract him, she'd succeeded, all right. Maybe it was just what she had said: She was tired. And she may have been reacting to the murder scene itself. He tended to forget that most people weren't used to seeing corpses.

There was no freeway going through town in the direction of Cave Creek. After his confrontation with the rattler and then an hour spent fighting rush-hour traffic on surface streets, Bern arrived at the Police and Public Safety Building on Washington and Sixth Avenue with his nerves frayed and his stomach unsettled the way it always was when he lost sleep.

Frank Trusey was on his way out of the homicide detail as Bern was coming in, an alert bird dog of a man who, Bern would bet, never missed hitting the sack early.

"Uh-ho," Frank said. "Another night in the country, huh? Looks like you need a cup of that Jamaica Blue I just made."

"Straight in the vein," Bern said, although the aroma wafting through the door was almost enough to do the job.

Frank had come down from Seattle three years before,

bringing with him a connoisseur's love of freshly ground beans. The division's urn filled with metallic-flavored Maxwell House had soon given way to a Braun twelve-cup dripping French roast and Colombia Supremo.

At this time of day, most of the detectives were in the squad room, hunched over computer keyboards or huddled in small groups for case discussion. Such a group was collected around Will Hanson's desk, but Bern headed with single-minded purpose to the coffee machine.

He barely had time to fill a mug before Will hurried over to say, "Jane wants to see us." With no respite at all, Bern followed him into Lieutenant Jane Clawson's office.

Five years ago Jane Clawson had earned her position as head of the homicide detail with intelligence and such unstinting hard work that not a single detective here—man or woman—had been surprised or resentful.

At forty-nine Jane fought the effects of desk work and gravity by spending her lunch hour on the treadmill in the gym downstairs. She was sturdily trim in a blue skirt and plain white blouse worn with costume jewelry—a necklace of gold beads and seed pearls, and small gold hoop earrings. A blue jacket waited on a plastic hanger on a hook behind the door, ready to be donned for the endless upper-echelon meetings that made up a good portion of her day. Jane *O'Reilly* Clawson's Irish father, a Boston cop, had passed along the dark hair and fair skin as well as his love for his profession.

"Morning," she said, and then, not one for chitchat, added, "fill me in on Wineski."

She listened without interruption to their briefing. Will reported gloomily that the killer had left damn little physical evidence behind. Scrapings from under the victim's fingernails revealed no foreign skin or hair; the victim had not had recent sexual intercourse. The few fingerprints lifted in the house were being run, including one from the typewriter used to write the ransom note.

Will had gone over early and found the machine, an old Smith-Corona manual portable. Following the theory that the killer would have taken something from the crime scene with him, Will had collected plenty of house dirt and fiber samples ready for matching.

"The victim's family was notified?" Jane asked.

"Yeah," Will said. "I talked to her father up in Salt Lake. Said as far as they were concerned their daughter died years ago. Guess the county will be burying her when the time comes."

Bern's turn. He told Jane about the interviews he had done in the neighborhood and what he knew so far about the kidnapping.

Jane said, "Tell me about the parents."

Bern gave her his impressions: a fairly well-off couple with rumblings of marital discord. Dominant husband, submissive wife. No suggestion that he was abusive, but something to keep in mind. Hard facts about their background and Glen Lewis's business remained to be uncovered.

"You think they're hiding something?" Will asked.

Bern shrugged. "Can't tell at this point. Lewis could be a pedophile who gets his kicks beating up his wife every night after he finishes with the kid. Hell, Mrs. Lewis could have planned the whole thing to siphon off some money and get out of an unhappy marriage."

"Or they could be two normal people driven to the breaking point, which is just what the creep who took their baby wanted. This isn't the first time parents have paid a ransom without calling us in," Jane observed. "I say we leave the Feds out of this one. What do you think?"

"Fine with me," Bern said, and Will nodded agreement.

Given a preference, any detective on the squad would opt not to waste the time and energy required to work with the FBI.

"Too bad there was no spontaneous statement from the little boy," Jane said.

When children are witnesses, something said immediately, without prompting, to identify the killer would carry the most weight in court.

"He was in bad shape, damn near catatonic when we arrived," Will said.

"Yes—well, I guess we all agree he may be useful," Jane said. "The question is: Is he in any danger?"

Will said, "Seems to me if the killer knew Danny saw him hit Dorie Wineski, he'd've taken the boy out, too."

"Yeah," Bern said, "but he may not have realized how hard he hit her, so Danny didn't seem like a problem at the time."

"Well, I can't justify a twenty-four-hour on the boy," Jane told them. "I'll order more frequent patrols in the neighborhood, and of course this is the one thing we have to keep out of the media if possible. Okay. Paperwork yesterday." She rose from her desk, and the men stood up, too. "I don't have to tell you we need this one, guys."

They knew what she meant. It wasn't just high-profile cases the media fixed on these days. A few years ago the focus was on bad economic news, and God knows there was plenty of it. Phoenix had plunged into the recession early and suffered badly before things turned around. But the government poured money into massive freeway projects; fleeing riots, earthquakes, and high taxes, businesses had been relocating from California in droves. TV ratings weren't built on good tidings, however, so the press had moved on to that hot-button topic: crime.

Phoenix had always boasted of its safe, small-town atmosphere; in particular, homicides were far less frequent than in comparably sized cities, and the clearance rate much higher. Unfortunately the new prosperity had a down side: more people, more crime, more murder. The homicide detail had been stretched thinner and pushed harder. Not surprisingly, the clearance rate was dropping. This guaranteed a media bonanza, but was not something that made Jane Clawson happy—not to mention the chief of police and the mayor.

"We're on it," Will promised.

"Good." At the door, Jane reached for her jacket, said, "Bern," and he waited while Will went out.

"Might have been a good idea if you'd gone back last night to talk to the rest of the neighbors," Jane said. Coming from her, the low-key rebuke was the equivalent of a tongue-lashing.

"It was a little late," Bern said, trying not to sound defensive. "For them, not for me."

When a person signed on to be a homicide detective, he committed to working long days without complaint. But Jane was right. The first forty-eight hours after a homicide were the most critical, half that already gone when Dorie Wineski's body was found.

Jane just looked at him.

"I'll get on it right away," Bern said.

"Take some men if you need them. And, Bern, I know you trust Anne's judgment, but you have to talk to the boy."

"I'll do it this morning."

"Good." She slipped on her jacket, ready for battle. "Keep me posted. And I meant what I said. This one's got to be quick."

Don't they all, Bern thought as he went back to his desk and checked for messages. Dorie Wineski's neighbor, the one who owned the dog, hadn't called. No big surprise. Will would do the check on the Lewises, including a verification of Glen's route with Danny the day of the kidnapping. Bern would complete the rest of the canvassing after his stop to talk to Danny and the Lewises. They would meet back at the morgue for the autopsy that was scheduled for four-thirty.

By then he was running late so he made a quick call to Anne before going out into the fierce midmorning heat. He said nothing about Danny. He hoped the boy would be recovered enough to talk. Bern sighed as he got into the blast furnace of his car where the steering wheel and shift lever were hot enough to burn his fingers.

In retrospect, talking Anne into consulting for the department was probably not a good idea. Jane was not going to let up. He couldn't blame her; she had people to answer to higher up. But it sure as hell wasn't going to help his situation with Anne.

God knows he didn't want to fight with her. Their relationship had settled into a routine, but he never for a minute fooled himself into believing it was stable. The last thing he wanted was to go head to head with her over the boy.

A fine old mess, his father used to say, and nobody to blame but yourself.

His father had said a lot of other things, too, all of them negative, until he choked to death on a hunk of rare sirloin in a restaurant where Bern's mother had insisted they go to celebrate his fiftieth birthday, an event he would have pointed to as fate offering confirmation of his pessimism.

It pained Bern considerably at how often his father's cynical observations came to mind, and how often they were right.

5

With Bern running late, Anne made it to the Lewises'
house before he did. There was a truck parked out in front
bearing the logo for Az-Tec Security. A dark-haired work-
man was planting a sign near the entry announcing that the
house was now guarded, warning of armed response to in-
truders.

Anne rang the bell. Glen answered, surprised to see her.
He stood in the doorway as though blocking her entry.

"Dr. Menlo, I didn't know you'd be coming back."

"Make it Anne, please," she said. "Detective Pagett will
want to talk to Danny. I told him I had to be present when
he did."

"And not a damn thing I can do about it, I guess."

He moved aside to let her in, closed the door, and engaged a heavy-duty dead bolt. Sunlight angled in through
a window set in the high wall above the door and reflected
off the polished tile.

He looked like a man who had spent few sleepless nights
in his life and wasn't handling them well. His tanned skin
showed a hint of gray pallor; tired lines radiated from his
eyes. He wore white cotton slacks and a chambray shirt, so
either he dressed casually for the office or he wasn't planning to go in.

"I really don't mean to be uncooperative," Glen went on. "I just hate the thought of Danny being grilled by the police. I don't know; maybe I'm being overprotective."

"I'd say you're having a normal reaction." For either a concerned parent or for somebody who was afraid of what the child might reveal. "I think you'll find Bern to be very careful with Danny, and I'll make sure he is. Has Danny talked about what happened to him?"

"Not a word." Glen held out his hands, palms up. The whorls and ridges of his fingers were still stained with ink. "Somebody from the police came by earlier to take our fingerprints. Can't get the damn stuff off. Sorry, I don't mean to leave you standing in the hall. Natalie's up with Danny."

"Were there any more problems last night?"

"No. We were so tired, and we just couldn't stand the idea of being away from him, so we brought him in bed with us. I know that's not a good idea, and we don't want to make a habit of it—" He broke off and smiled ruefully. "Do people always feel like they have to explain themselves to you?"

"All the time," Anne said. "Look, this has been a terrible ordeal, so you wanted to be close. My advice is to be sure Danny knows it was a special occasion. It's easy to fall into a pattern with a child and hard to change it."

From upstairs came the sound of Danny giggling and shouting, "No, no! I'm a monster, I'm a soap monster!" Then he pounded down the stairs, dressed only in red shorts, traces of toothpaste foam around his mouth, obviously an escapee from the morning routine of teeth brushing and getting dressed. Natalie was right behind him with a towel in her hands.

Glen scooped him up at the bottom of the stairs, saying, "Whoa, there, partner."

"Make me fly, Daddy, make me fly," Danny cried, the wild glee on his face replaced by fleeting expressions of apprehension and terror as he saw Anne. Suddenly he lunged away from his father, seized Natalie, and buried his face in her neck.

Anne felt a stab of dismay. Had he blocked out everything from the day before? It wouldn't be uncommon if he had. Remembering the depth of Danny's terror last night when he awakened from his nightmare, she reminded herself that the mind has a way of locking things away until they can be safely processed. To tell the truth, after her instant bonding to Danny, she felt a stab of rejection, too. The reaction was totally unprofessional but just as real as the feeling of relief a second later as she realized how brightly the sun dazzled off the tiles and that she must have been a shadowy figure to the boy.

"Honey, don't be scared," Natalie said. "It's Dr. Menlo."

"You had a hard time seeing me just now," Anne said, hoping it was true, stepping into the light. "It's Anne, remember?"

Still clinging to his mother, Danny turned his head slowly, regarding her for a long moment before he said, "Edgar snores."

Glen laughed. "I have a feeling that was me, Dan."

"We all slept in the big bed," Danny said.

"You must have had a lot of fun doing that," Anne said.

"We ate breakfast there, too. Daddy made it."

"Yeah, Dad's a real chef." Glen ruffled his hair. "Frozen waffles and bottled apple juice."

Shirtless, the bruise on Danny's arm was still faintly visible. The mark was too wide to have been made by Natalie's small hand, Anne decided. If one of his parents did that, Glen was the better candidate. She had her doubts,

though; not just from observing the loving way Glen held
his son, but from the fact that it was much more likely that
Dorie Wineski had made the bruise, or that it was the im-
print of the man who helped Dorie kidnap Danny, the man
who killed her.

The doorbell rang. Natalie went to let Bern in. In the
time since he left her house, he'd retreated to that other
persona, Bern the cop. She could measure the distance by
the cool remoteness in his eyes even as he said hello, his
only smile for Danny.

Anne thought the boy recognized Bern, but the context
of the memory was too much for him to handle. He lapsed
back into an anxious, watchful silence.

Natalie said, "I'd better take him up and finish getting
him dressed."

Her loose sage-green dress was smeared with toothpaste,
her hair hastily combed, her face bare of makeup. Relief
had smoothed out some of the distress of the past few days,
but there were still plenty of worry lines visible. She reminded Anne of a newly hatched bird, so nakedly vulnerable, especially because her every emotion was easily read.

"Anne, why don't you give Natalie a hand?" Bern suggested. "Glen and I will talk."

She could take a hint. Obviously Glen was in for a second round of questioning. Danny was her primary concern,
so she said, "Fine with me—if it's okay with you, Natalie."

"Yes, of course. Let's take Dr. Menlo up to your room,
Danny. I'll bet she'd like to see all your toys."

Natalie tried to put him down, but Danny whimpered and
clung, locking his legs around her waist. Anne remembered
the weight of that chunky little body. He was a load for his
slender mother, but she carried him up the stairs while Glen
went into the living room with Bern.

Today, blinds tilted open at two windows to flood Danny's large room with light. The walls were painted a bright blue, the furniture and storage cubicles in white; reds and yellows were added in the bedspread and drapes. The bed had not been made, and Anne saw the gray, lop-eared bunny on the floor where it had fallen when Danny knocked it from her hands.

Natalie took a knit shirt from a drawer, then sank down on the floor with Danny. He straddled her lap, his head against her breast.

She said, "Let go just for a second so Mommy can put on your shirt, okay?"

He shook his head and stuck his thumb in his mouth.

"You can't show Dr. Menlo your toys until you get dressed."

Anne sat beside them. "It's Anne, Natalie. We're old friends, aren't we, Danny?"

No response.

"This isn't like Danny at all," Natalie said helplessly. "Being there in that house—it must have been so horrible for him. He will get over it, won't he? Glen says it's just going to take time."

As questions go, Natalie's didn't peg the insensitivity meter; Anne had heard worse. But it reflected the tendency parents had to talk about their children as though they weren't there, as though they were on a communications link that could be switched off and on at will. Anne never said anything in front of a child she didn't want that child to hear because it was amazing how much a three-year-old could understand, even one who was deliberately tuning out the world.

She said, "What happened to Danny was very frightening. You can't just ignore scary feelings like that and hope they'll go away, but with all of us helping, I'm sure he's going to be just fine."

She gave Danny a reassuring smile, then got up and began a circuit of the room, commenting casually on the animal posters on the wall—giraffes and zebras and monkeys from the Phoenix Zoo—and on the wallpaper border, drapes, and bedspread of nonthreatening dinosaurs done in crayon colors. More realistic-looking dinosaurs sat on a child's table next to an overflowing toy box. Anne picked up a tyrannosaurus rex, the teeth bared in a ferocious grin.

Taking his thumb from his mouth, Danny said soberly, "That's T-Rex. He bites people."

"He's very scary-looking," Anne agreed. "What's this one?"

"Brontosaurus. He just eats vegetables."

He left Natalie to come over and identify the others: stegosaurus, diplodocus—"he spits"—pronouncing the long names carefully. Then he moved on to the toy chest, pulling out cars, airplanes, and Ninja Turtles at random, demonstrating the things they could do.

"Who's this?" Anne picked up the rabbit.

"Easter Eggs," he said, then returned to excavating the treasure trove of the chest with none of the fear he had exhibited when Anne handed him the stuffed toy the night before.

Children have to take you where they want to go; you cannot lead them. Anne could hear Rosemary Beiderman's voice giving that favorite piece of advice. And Rosemary's second favorite: *Remember when you interpret, you do it with an adult's mind, an adult's experience.*

Knowing Rosemary was right, Anne limited herself to physical observations, judging that there was no problem with his motor skills, not after the way he had bounded down the stairs and handled the toys. He had a good vocabulary and could relate things in a logical sequence. There was a frenetic edge to his actions, and it was hard for him to maintain control, but children don't have grown-up methods of coping.

Suddenly her skin prickled with the feeling of being watched. Perhaps because she spent so much of her time observing other people, she was always acutely aware of finding herself observed. Glen stood in the doorway, his face expressionless. She wondered what she might have read there a second earlier. Freud would assume something sexual, no doubt. Anne thought resentment more likely— she was part and parcel of this painful intrusion into their lives.

Whatever the emotion was, irritation replaced it, and Glen said, "Jesus, Natalie, isn't he dressed yet?"

Stresses like the ones the Lewises had undergone these past few days quickly strip away the niceties of civil behavior. Natalie reacted instantly, ugly red color rising in her cheeks.

"I'm doing the best I can. If you think you can do better, help yourself." She wadded the shirt and hurled it at Glen.

Danny dropped the toy he was holding, his glance darting fearfully from Glen to Natalie, then turned and threw his arms around Anne, clinging tightly, burying his head against her stomach. A surge of protectiveness welled up; Anne hugged the child close, murmuring comfort as Natalie rushed over to kneel beside her son.

"It's okay, baby," Natalie said. "We're sorry. Mommy and Daddy aren't mad. We're just a little upset, that's all. Come on to Mommy."

Slowly Danny let go of Anne and climbed into his mother's arms, leaving Anne shaken by the reminder of her attachment to the little boy.

"Pagett's hell-bound to talk to Danny about what happened," Glen said. "I guess we'd better get down there."

Anne understood the frustration in his voice, having dealt with Bern's implacable will more than once.

"Don't worry," she said. "I'll make sure Danny's all right."

6

Anne led the way downstairs. Danny had allowed Glen to put on his shirt but insisted on being carried by Natalie, refusing even Glen's offer of a piggyback ride.

In the living room, Bern sat on the blue-and-cream-striped sofa. He smiled at the little boy and said, "Hi, Danny. We met yesterday, remember? Why don't you and your mom sit right here beside me so we can talk."

Natalie sank down next to him with Danny on her lap. Glen stood beside the lamp table as though he were preparing to snatch them up and take them away on the slightest provocation.

"Dad, why don't you sit down, too," Bern suggested pleasantly, but the way he looked at Glen brooked no argument.

After Glen took one of the chairs, Danny eyed Bern apprehensively, then shifted his gaze to Anne who perched on the coffee table. She reached to pat his shoulder and said reassuringly, "It's okay, Danny."

"I'm a policeman," Bern said. "Did you know that?"

After a second, Danny nodded.

"Do you know what a policeman does?"

"Kills the bad guys," Danny whispered.

"Only if we have to," Bern said. "Most of the time we

just try to find them and put them in jail so they can't hurt people. Sometimes we need help to do our job. You could help me, Danny. Would you like to do that?''

A cautious nod.

"Good. All you have to do is tell me about being at Dorie's house. Can you do that?''

Danny shook his head and hunched close to Natalie.

"I know it was scary for you," Bern said. "But you're safe now."

Danny's thumb crept into his mouth. Natalie gave Anne a look of mute appeal. Anne could hear Glen make a noise in his throat.

"Bern," Anne said.

"Can you try, Danny? Come on, son. Anything you can remember—"

"That's enough," Anne said sharply.

Questioning Danny had been against her better judgment, and now she knew she was right. Danny's knees were drawn up, and his blue eyes had taken on a dull sheen.

Bern sighed, nodded.

Glen sprang up and took Danny from Natalie. He'd put a tight lid on his emotions, so he didn't say anything. His body language expressed his anger as he strode toward the stairs with his son. A shaken Natalie stood up, clearly torn between the urge to run after Glen and a need for official permission to leave the room.

"Go ahead," Anne said. "Take care of Danny. I'll come up in a minute."

Anne studied Bern as Natalie left and went upstairs. He looked withdrawn and utterly weary, reminding Anne he'd cut his sleep time short by several hours, making the long drive out and back to her house because he'd sensed she needed him last night.

She said, "Now you see why I didn't want you to question Danny."

He nodded. "I don't like this any better than you do, but that little boy may know something. If he does, you can be damned sure the person who kidnapped him and killed Dorie isn't going to want him to talk. The sooner we wind this up, the better for Danny."

"I know that," she said, "but, my God, Bern, he knew that woman. She took care of him. And he was in that house with her—saw her, smelled her, probably touched her. I'm not going to ask him to relive that experience, not until I'm sure he can handle it. And right now he's either withdrawing or using hyperactivity to handle the stress."

"Okay, I won't push it again. But I have to tell you Jane wants this one cleared as soon as possible."

"For Danny's sake?" Anne asked tartly. "Or to keep the press off her back?"

Bern gave her a wry smile. "Partly that, but Jane really is concerned about the boy. And it's not just bad publicity we're fighting these days, it's the caseload. The next homicide I catch goes on top of the stack; Dorie Wineski's murder gets moved down in priority. That's the way it works, Anne. Nothing any of us can do about it."

The ramifications of what he was saying made Anne's blood run cold. As long as Dorie's killer was free, Danny might be in danger.

Bern stood, reached for Anne's hand, and pulled her up.

"Annie," he said, "keep in mind we're on the same side here. You need to start working with Danny as soon as possible so we can find out what he knows."

"You're right," she said. "I will."

Glen came down then, his anger and resentment tightly controlled. Bern lingered only long enough to remind Glen that there might be more questions and that the Lewises should keep themselves available—the polite equivalent of don't leave town.

All that pent-up rage visible in Glen's face—Anne wondered what he did to work through it. Judging from his muscular upper arms, she assumed he used the equipment his company made. At least she hoped that was the way he let off steam.

"How's Danny?" Anne asked.

"Better."

"Where is he?" She took a step toward the stairs. He moved in front of her, blocking the way.

"That's okay," Glen said. "We can take care of Danny."

"I know you love him," Anne said. "But sometimes love isn't enough. He needs professional care, Glen. Are you uncomfortable with me treating him? Do you want me to recommend somebody else?"

The easy way out. But maybe the best thing for Danny.

"No," he said. "No, no, nothing like that. Listen, Anne, I can't tell you how much it means to us to know you were there for him yesterday. And today, in there with Pagett— we can't even begin to thank you. But right now, we need to be by ourselves—just the three of us. Please."

"Natalie agrees with you?"

"Yes," he answered, although Anne wondered if he had really consulted his wife.

"All right," she said reluctantly. "But call me later."

He promised he would, mostly to get rid of her, she suspected. There were all sorts of reasons why Glen might be resisting therapy for Danny. He was in denial, that much was clear. He blamed himself for the kidnapping, so Danny's psychological trauma was Glen's fault, too. The only way to alleviate the guilt was to deny the severity of the problem. Another thing: People like to think of themselves as thoroughly modern and accepting in their thinking; still, the old notion lurks in the subconscious that only crazy people need therapy.

Or—as she knew Bern would remind her—Glen Lewis could just be protecting himself.

Driving away, Anne told herself she should have been more blunt with Glen, stressed the danger Danny might be in if he had seen Dorie's killing. And while she was second-guessing herself, maybe she should have mentioned that episode to Bern, the thing with Danny and the toy rabbit— Easter Eggs, as Danny called him. No, there was nothing to tell—was there?

Better to wait . . . and pray that she could recognize the important detail, and distinguish substance from shadow.

The old Chevy Monte Carlo was gone from the driveway next door to Dorie Wineski's house. Bern had run the plates and come up with the owner's name: Florence Louella Mosk.

The Mosk house squatted without benefit of shade under a blistering sun. Instead of a stoop, somebody had used planks to make a porch across the front, put the thing up on cement blocks, and topped it with a wooden overhang set on spindly supports. Maybe the person had fond memories of red Alabama dirt and cotton fields.

Sometime recently a coat of white paint had been applied to the siding. This was probably done without a primer, however, because the white coat was peeling off to reveal the original bile-green color underneath.

Ms. Mosk might not be home, but the dog was there. Bern could see him, way back in the hole he'd dug under the porch, his yellow eyes glinting in the deep shadow. Conserving energy, Bern guessed, because the animal didn't bark or venture out. Bern thought he could probably cite Ms. Mosk on an animal cruelty charge, something to keep in mind, if he ever got a chance to talk to her.

By two-thirty Bern had loosened his tie and discarded his jacket—which meant the gun clipped to his hip was in plain sight, not a bad thing in this seedy neighborhood.

He had caught three more people home. A couple two doors down were in the middle of an argument and not happy to be interrupted, the quarrel sounding sullen and long-standing, something to do while they finished a couple of six-packs. No, they didn't know Dorie Wineski, didn't know anybody around here, and didn't want to.

Across the street from these friendly folks was a skinny man with pop-bottle glasses who said he was a Seventh-Day Adventist. Although he had a passing acquaintance with Dorie and would really like to help, he was walking in a neighborhood down in Chandler the night Dorie died, passing out pamphlets. He pressed a handful on Bern when Bern left.

In addition to these three, Bern reinterviewed two others, learning nothing new. Between each interview, he came back to the Cherokee parked down on the corner in the only shady spot, started the engine, and turned on the air conditioner. While he rehydrated himself with bottled water, he stared at a house a block away where a yard full of miniature windmills turned lazily.

None of the houses had inside temperatures below eighty, a combination of poor insulation, inferior coolers, and astronomical electric bills. The last house had no cooling at all; closed doors and windows kept the temperature to about a hundred degrees, turning the place into a stifling oven that seemed hotter than the 115 degrees that it was outside.

Should've taken Jane's offer of help with the interviews, he told himself as he swigged water and let the full force of the cold air from the vents dry his shirt. Even his scalp was sticky with sweat, and he wanted nothing so much as to stand under the shower for about an hour.

What the hell was he doing? Making up for his failure to get something from Danny, maybe. Playing Mr. One-Man Macho Cop—not the kind of behavior encouraged by the department.

His second interview with Glen Lewis had yielded nothing new. Maybe Will had dug up some background information. If not, Bern could always do paperwork back at the station until it was time for him and Will to attend the autopsy. Or he could wait around out here for Florence Mosk, wasting gasoline and polluting the air.

Just then the old Monte Carlo cruised down the street, making the decision for him. He left his Jeep and went to intercept the car as it turned into the driveway. A woman got out, a very large woman. Bern's father would have described her as being three ax handles wide, not exactly politically correct but accurate.

She was almost as tall as Bern; he put her weight at 275 pounds of dense, solid flesh. She wore stretchy knit pants and a knit polo shirt that Bern guessed came from the Big Man's department. Her short red hair had a metallic sheen and showed dark brown at the roots.

The dog came out from under the porch, legs stiff and black fur bristling, and barked with his lips curled over his teeth.

"Shut up, Duke," the woman ordered, and the dog stopped barking but began a menacing rumble deep in its throat.

"Ms. Mosk?" Bern told her his name and presented his identification, which she ignored.

Her "Yeah?" was husky and masculine.

"I'm investigating the murder of your neighbor, Dorie Wineski."

"I figured."

She settled the handles of a large vinyl handbag over her left arm, slammed the car door, and headed for the trunk. Bern could feel the sun burning his skin right through his shirt, and he briefly considered going out first thing in the morning to buy himself a ten-gallon hat.

"I'd like to come in and ask you some questions," he said. "Just routine. I'm questioning all the neighbors."

She grunted, opened the trunk, and took out two full paper grocery bags.

"Help you with those?" Bern offered, but she grunted again, stuck one under her left arm, let the handbag slide down, and grabbed the handles along with the top of the other grocery bag with her ham-sized left hand. This freed her right hand to deal with the trunk lid and, after striding over without a word, the gate.

Bern followed cautiously, resting a hand on the butt of his gun. The dog was about ten feet away, the rumble changing to a snarl.

Florence gave Bern a contemptuous look and stabbed a finger toward the porch. "Duke, go lay down."

The dog retreated, still growling. Bern was no expert on animal behavior, but he'd bet the growling was directed more toward Florence than at him. Still, he didn't take his hand off his weapon until he was inside the house with the door shut.

Room-darkening shades covered the windows. Coming in from the bright sunlight, he had a moment of blindness while his eyes adjusted, standing just inside the door while Florence clomped out to the kitchen. The place was warm, of course, but pleasantly clean, he noted after he could see again, and it smelled of lemon Pledge. Not much furniture, but what was there was oversize and sturdily built.

Florence came back from the kitchen, opening a can of Miller without offering him any, and detoured over to adjust a shade for light and flip on a window air conditioner. Then she sank down in a chair and took a big gulp of beer. Bern wondered if she treated all her guests like this or just cops. He sat across from her and began trying to extract answers of more than four words to his questions.

He discovered she worked varying shifts in the laundry room at Good Samaritan Hospital, graveyard the night Dorie died. She had lived at her present address for three years, known Dorie for two.

When he got down to the nitty-gritty, shrugs and shakes of her massive head outnumbered the actual spoken words.

"When did you last see Ms. Wineski?"

Shrug.

"The day she died?"

A head shake.

"Did you see her the day before?"

Another shake.

"I need a time frame here, Ms. Mosk."

"Week, maybe."

The condensed version was that she had seen nothing, heard nothing, and had no opinion whatsoever about her neighbor's death. She watched him with a cunning intelligence that convinced him she was lying through her large square teeth, but it would take a hell of a lot more time than the hour and fifteen minutes he'd spent here to uncover the truth.

Exhausted, feeling as if he'd been banging his head against a wall, he said it was very likely he'd have to talk to her downtown. He took her silence for consent. She stayed in the chair as he walked to the door, and he was outside before he remembered the dog. He drew his gun, fully prepared to shoot the damn beast, but it stayed under the porch, emitting the ominous rumble.

In the Jeep he switched from water to Coke, washed down Excedrin, and chugged the rest of the can. Then he drove directly to the morgue. What had Anne said about the rest of the day being easy?

As autopsies went, Dorie Wineski's was routine. That is, bearable through stoic disassociation. And it yielded no surprises. Dorie had been struck on the left side of the head, probably with a fist, then she had hit the right side against the table hard enough to cause a subdural hemorrhage. She died approximately one hour later, sometime between nine and eleven P.M., plenty of time to get from the living room to the bedroom.

At home Bern stood in the shower with water streaming over his body, trying to wash away the sights and odors of the day, trying to shake a feeling of impending loss. Delayed reaction after a session in the morgue, he guessed, understandable but overwhelming, especially because his father's favorite axiom crept back into Bern's head.

Better consider the worst thing that can happen because it will.

His thoughts went immediately to Anne, of course. Except for their disagreement over the boy, things were going along as usual—which meant they were stuck at this nice, pleasant plateau. They ate together a couple of times a week, had sex with the same frequency. Better than those years apart. God, yes. Still . . .

One afternoon, pre-reunion with Anne, he had been spending a weekday at home, off from work, bored, doing a little TV channel surfing when he flipped into a talk show with some feel-good guest psychologist. She was saying,

"Love's like a *plant*; it must grow or die—" before he gave up and hit the off switch.

He'd dismissed the remark as psychobabble at the time. Anyway, just then love wasn't something he wanted to *grow*, thanks very much. Given a choice, he'd yank the emotion out of his heart, roots and all.

The little sound bite of advice must have stuck, though, because it popped up now, and sappy or not, he sensed the truth of it. Things couldn't stay where they were between him and Anne. Change must be coming, some kind of change.

Was that what caused the foreboding—the fear of another breakup?

The worst thing that can happen . . .

Jesus. Enough.

Lately he'd begun to think this streak of pessimism was not just a matter of conditioning by his old man, that it had been passed along in the genes. After all, his mother had thrown the dismal outlook aside like shedding an old dress. She was up in Prescott, happily married to a retired stockbroker, not a gloomy day in sight.

He told himself it had just been a hell of a day, that's all. He was working on making himself believe it when he got a piece of good news: The computer had found a match for two sets of the unidentified prints in the Wineski house.

7

After her last appointment, Anne jotted down some case notes and went through the mail. Cynthia Lynde, one of the psychologists who shared the suite, had left her an envelope with a scribbled note on a Post-it: *Anne, how about it?* Inside was an invitation to the opening of a new gallery in Scottsdale called Kristobel's. Anne wished she could look forward to something as pleasant as going with Cynthia to a gallery opening, but she had been distracted and unsettled all day, replaying the scenes with the Lewises and Bern.

She knew Bern was right; he urgently needed to question Danny. Had she stopped Bern too soon? Maybe if he had probed a little harder—no, Danny had been withdrawing. More questioning would have been useless.

So far neither of the Lewises had called to make an appointment. Therapy was not an instant process; it took time, and in Danny's case time was precious.

Maybe she should call them.

She picked up the phone, hesitated, then dialed Rosemary Beiderman's number instead.

They talked for a moment before Rosemary, observant as ever, said, "I always love to hear from you, Anne, but I get the feeling you called for more than just a chat."

"I really need to see you," Anne confessed. "Do you have some free time this evening? Say around eight o'clock? I promise not to stay too long."

"You're not home already?"

"No, I'm still at the office."

"Surely you're not driving all the way to Cave Creek and back to see me."

"Oh, I'll have dinner here in town first, maybe do some shopping."

"You'll do no such thing," Rosemary said firmly. "You'll have dinner with us. We eat at seven, but come as soon as you like."

The Beidermans lived in Paradise Valley, about thirty minutes from Anne's office. Their unassuming house sat in the middle of a cul-de-sac, one story with white stucco walls and a flat roof, much larger and more expensive than it looked from the street. The front yard was done in what was popularly called desert landscaping, although compared to Anne's place, there was no mistaking the professional design of river rock and plantings of sweet acacia, fairy duster, and sand verbena, along with one huge multi-armed saguaro.

When Norman and Rosemary had built the place twenty years ago, Rosemary had already been diagnosed with multiple sclerosis, so the house was designed with ramps and doorways wide enough to accommodate the wheelchair Rosemary would eventually need.

Norman answered the bell, a bearish man with a grizzled beard, wearing a white polo shirt and olive-green shorts that revealed his knobby knees. A healthy sixty-three, he watched his diet and exercised, conscientiously taking care of himself as much for Rosemary's sake as his own, Anne suspected.

He gave Anne a hug and said, "We're having drinks on the patio. Rosemary's looking forward to seeing you."

"How is she?"

"Today was a good day."

This was as much as Norman ever said about his wife's illness, although Anne knew the ratio of good days to bad was now appallingly slim. The medical journals often carried reports of new treatments for multiple sclerosis. So far, none of them had helped Rosemary. She had been managing fairly well when Anne studied with her nine years before in the doctoral program at ASU. Then, within two years the disease had progressed so rapidly that Rosemary retired from teaching. Since then she had produced one scholarly book and was at work on another.

"Never think it's easy," Rosemary had told Anne once. "There are times when I just want to give up. But then I think that if Norman can put up with me, surely I can stand myself in this condition."

Norman Beiderman had resigned a federal judgeship to stay home with Rosemary. He loved his work, but if asked, he would simply say he loved Rosemary more. He had not martyred himself. On the contrary, he golfed and gardened and did some writing of his own, although none of these activities ever took precedence over his primary concern, which was taking care of his wife.

The Beidermans had surmounted enormous problems to fashion a steady, supportive marriage. Why couldn't she and Bern, with far less to overcome, do the same? In this house the lesson seemed clear: commitment and acceptance. Anne had never thought of herself as having trouble with either one. But here she was in the midst of a relationship she had ended once because she thought it was a mistake, still unable to commit herself fully. Well, what was wrong with wanting to go slowly, to keep things as they were at least for now?

Norman led the way through the house where a collection of Navajo rugs decorated the walls rather than the polished oak floors, and the low tables and sofas were grouped to leave lots of empty space to maneuver a wheelchair.

Sliding glass doors opened onto a covered patio as big as a room, cooled by water vapor sprayed from misting devices installed around the edge of the patio cover. Old wine barrels held ferns and trailing ivy. Hanging baskets dripped fuchsias in shades ranging from palest pink to deep magenta. Pots contained Rosemary's favorite butterfly orchids, Phalaenopsis, with their fleshy leaves and fragile sprays of white blossoms on curved twiggy stems. Strangely, it was the dun-colored hills behind the house that looked unreal.

Rosemary sat on an upholstered lounge chair, a long loose cotton dress in a dark antique print covering a body grown painfully thin. Her silky black hair, cut short for comfort and manageability, was winged with white at the temples. Illness may have ravaged her body, but the smile was as warm as ever, the brown eyes luminous and lively.

"Anne, dear, hello." Rosemary held out her hands, and Anne took them, careful not to squeeze.

"I've been neglecting you," Anne said, remembering with a pang that it had been almost six weeks since she had come here.

"It's called living a normal life. Never mind that. Norman will get you some wine. Unless you'd rather have raspberry tea?" She indicated the beverage in her own glass.

"No, wine will be great."

"Good choice. Here, sit."

Norman provided a wrought-iron chair cushioned in a

SHADOW OF THE CHILD 77

floral print, the chair taken from a round table already set for dinner.

"I always forget how beautiful it is here," Anne said.

Because the brutal summer heat was so hard on Rosemary, she became a virtual prisoner for six months of the year, rarely venturing out. To compensate, Norman had created this retreat for her.

"Sometimes I feel a little guilty about using all this water." A mischievous grin. "But not for long."

Norman brought the wine, then excused himself to go finish dinner. While they ate salad and angel hair pasta with homegrown tomatoes and basil, Norman asked about Bern. Anne said Bern was fine and changed the subject to Norman's golf game and Anne's family; Rosemary told how Norman had brought the Amabile string quartet here to play Mozart in her garden patio for their anniversary. Pleasant conversation during which Rosemary studied Anne's face and, Anne was sure, missed little.

After coffee, Norman let Anne help him clear the table, then sent her back outside, saying, "I'll finish up in here. She won't say anything, Anne, but another hour is about her limit."

Anne assured him she wouldn't stay too long and went back out to sit next to Rosemary. Beyond the light fog created by the misters, above the low hills, the hot twilight purple of the sky was muted to soft indigo. Orchids hovered on invisible stems like white moths in the growing dimness.

"All right," Rosemary said. "Tell me."

"I've had—well—a flashback, I guess. That little girl— Nicki Craig—remember?"

"Yes, of course I do."

"After all this time, all the work we did, there was a moment yesterday, a memory so intense—as if I were back there just hearing the news. I'm sure it happened because of my work with the police . . ."

It was almost dark when Anne finished telling Rosemary about the cases she'd become involved with through Bern. The first had involved two young children held hostage by their father who barricaded himself and the little boys inside his apartment and fired on the social worker who came to take them away. The mother had won sole custody and was taking them to New Mexico. The second had been a six-year-old girl kept virtual prisoner in a run-down trailer by her guardian, an aunt who was sinking deeper and deeper into paranoid schizophrenia. In both instances Anne had been there only for the crises; the children had gone off to live elsewhere.

"It's easy to see why you'd be reminded of Nicki," Rosemary said.

"I never expected to forget her," Anne said. "And it's understandable that I'd think of her more. But it—it shakes me. I feel such panic. Not for long. An instant. Long enough to make me doubt my judgment."

"So this has been building up. Tell me what happened yesterday."

Anne described the murder, her first contact with Danny. She didn't elaborate because the details really had no bearing on what she was trying to resolve.

"What do you think you should do?" Rosemary asked.

"The obvious thing? Withdraw. Insist that another psychologist be brought in."

Rosemary waited.

Several lights came on, low wattage lamps in square frosted glass shades spaced around the patio. Either operated by timers or else Norman was keeping vigil.

"Solutions aren't always obvious," Anne said. "A very good therapist told me that once. Danny must feel he's already been abandoned twice, once by his father in the car, again by Ms. Wineski dying and leaving him alone in that house. If I bow out, he'll see it as another abandonment. But if I stay and make a mistake . . .''

Rosemary said, ''Do you remember what else that therapist told you? Solutions are usually not easy either.''

''Oh, yes. I remember that part.''

Beyond the softly lit patio, the night seemed impenetrably black.

''Did I really deal with Nicki's death?'' Anne asked. ''Or did I simply bury it? Oh, maybe I'm just overreacting. Could that be it?''

''What do you think?''

Anne smiled. ''How did I know you'd say that?''

''Whatever's going on, we'll find out,'' Rosemary promised. ''We'll work on it.''

She shifted her position on the lounge and pain flashed, minnow-bright in the dark depths of her eyes. The hour wasn't up, but Anne could see that Norman had miscalculated Rosemary's stamina, that her energy was flagging.

''Yes,'' Anne said. ''But not tonight. You're tired. You need to rest.''

''I guess I do.'' Rosemary leaned back and closed her eyes, adding with rare, dark bitterness, ''God, I hate being like this. Well, that's old news, isn't it?'' She managed a wry smile. ''Your decision about treating Danny can't wait, Anne. What are you going to do?''

''I don't know.'' Anne leaned over to kiss Rosemary's cheek, then stood up. ''Sometimes I feel like such a fraud, telling other people how to manage their lives when mine is so screwed up.''

''So you speak with a human voice—what's wrong with that?''

Anne allowed herself to be comforted by this as she said good night, promising to call soon and arrange a session.

After a stop to say good night to Norman, she let herself out the front door. Stepping back into the reality of the Arizona night heat, Anne knew Danny's treatment couldn't wait while she sorted out her feelings.

It would take time for him to adjust to another therapist. If Bern caught Dorie's killer quickly, that time lapse might not be so important. If he didn't, the delay would increase the risk that the killer might find out Danny could be a witness.

Anne really had no choice. All she could do was try to help the little boy—and pray she was up to the job.

It was a slow drive home up Tatum Road. The traffic moved sedately, the motoring public having gotten lots of tickets in the mail courtesy of the photo radar in Paradise Valley. Anne didn't see any of the small Suburbans the police favored and wasn't sure they would be snapping pictures of license plates in the dark, but she went along with the other cautious drivers, turning on the radio to a talk show to keep her mind off Danny.

She'd made her decision. So, enough already.

At home there was a message on her answering machine from Bern. Something had come up on the Dorie Wineski case, he said with a note of worried urgency in his voice. The urgency must have nothing to do with Danny; if it had, surely Bern would have paged her.

Still feeling particularly vulnerable, she debated about waiting until morning to call him back. He might pick up on something in her voice, and she certainly didn't feel like trying to explain what was going on with her.

Or them, if the subject should come up.

If she was committed to helping Danny, and she was,

she had to put her problems with Bern on hold. She washed her face, brushed her teeth, and put on her oldest, softest short pajamas. Bern's shaving gear was in the bathroom, his clothes hung in the closet. In bed, the smell of his body lingered on the pillows and sheets. She sat up, turned on the light, and picked up the phone.

"Sorry to call so late," she said.

"No, that's all right. I'm glad you did. We found a match for two sets of the fingerprints in the Wineski house," Bern said. "One was for Florence Mosk. The other's a man: Anthony Edward Sales. He's got a rap sheet a mile long. Mostly DUIs and narcotics-related. But he spent a stretch in Perryville for armed robbery and assault. We've put out an APB."

Anne felt a rush of excitement and relief. "He sounds as if he could be the one."

"A prime candidate, anyway." He hesitated. "Anne? Everything all right out there?"

"Yes," she said, thinking, *Oh, Lord, here it comes.* "Why?"

"Oh, nothing. It's just—when you didn't call me back, I got worried."

"I went to see Rosemary."

"Oh. I see."

The words were carefully neutral, but she heard the unspoken resentment. It was an old sore spot between them. He had liked the Beidermans but came to avoid them, jealous of the fact that Rosemary was privy to whole chunks of Anne's life before he knew her, hating the thought that Anne confided in Rosemary about their problems, and demanding, "How can we work things out between ourselves when you talk more to your damn shrink than you do to me?"

"We didn't discuss you," Anne said. "Jesus, Bern, I had dinner with an old friend."

"If you say so." He paused, then blurted out, "Babe, let's stop this fooling around. Move in together—hell, let's drive up to Vegas, now, tonight, and get married."

"What?"

"I'll turn the Wineski case over to somebody else. Jane won't like it, but fuck her. You call Karen Doheny—"

"Bern, we can't do that."

"We could," he said, but his voice had lost its urgency and conviction.

"No, Bern. What is it? What's the matter with you?"

"Oh, overworked. Not enough sleep. I need you around in case there's an invasion of rattlesnakes."

Anne thought she had heard fear in his voice, but he seemed determined to make light of it, so she played along. "Yes, third-floor apartments have a real problem with snakes."

"Damn straight," he said. "They can crawl up drain-pipes, trees—come up through the toilet."

"I think that's alligators," Anne said, "and you're not afraid of them."

"That's right. I'm not, am I? Annie? I love you."

He hung up before Anne could reply.

Feeling more unsettled by the conversation than ever, she went around checking the doors and windows, aware of just how isolated the house truly was. And for the first time since she moved to Cave Creek, she spent the night filled with an uneasiness that disturbed her sleep and snapped her awake at the sound of coyotes out in the hills, howling at the moon.

8

Already tense and edgy after a restless night, Anne dreaded going into the office. Both Cynthia and Andrew Braemer, the third psychologist who shared the suite, had ducked out early the day before, leaving Anne to deal with the temp service after Candi announced that no way was she coming in on a Saturday. The service promised only that they would try to find a replacement, but it was the weekend after all. Anne decided unemployment must not be as big a problem as the newspapers made it out to be.

When she walked in and saw Peggy Rettig sitting behind the desk, Anne's spirits soared.

"Peggy? What are you doing here? I thought you wouldn't be back until Tuesday."

Every summer Peggy would announce that the relentless sunshine was driving her crazy, and she'd head for her mother's place in Astoria, Oregon, on the mouth of the Columbia River. Anne understood the urge. Sometimes she was overcome by a longing to stand beside the Pacific and feel the cool, salty breeze against her skin.

"All it did was rain," Peggy said. "I forget about that. Not like the storms we get here, just this steady, gray downpour all day long. I paid the money to change my ticket and flew home. And from the looks of things, not a minute too soon.''

She had three stacks of files in front of her, one for each doctor. This included everything the temps had touched, Anne guessed, which would now be redone to suit Peggy's exacting standards. The Lewis file was on top of Anne's stack, but Peggy would pointedly never mention it since Bern was involved. Fifteen years ago her own husband had walked out and left her with a four-year-old daughter. ''Good riddance,'' Peggy always said. Otherwise she kept her opinions about long-term relationships to herself.

A solid, buxom woman, Peggy was square-jawed with short brown hair and bangs cut just above her eyebrows. She always wore sling-back low-heeled pumps, straight skirts, and frilly white blouses. No jewelry. Reading glasses hung on a chain around her neck. Her calm, no-nonsense voice worked wonders with rambunctious kids and nervous adults; her organizational skills freed Anne to think about her small patients; and Peggy's ability to get the parents to pay for these sessions in a timely manner made the difference between a profitable business and one that barely stayed ahead of the malpractice insurance payments.

On Saturday mornings Anne scheduled back-to-back appointments with patients whose parents worked and couldn't bring them in during the week. The Lewises didn't call, and she had no chance to phone Natalie about Danny's therapy. There was also little time to puzzle over Bern's strange behavior the night before, but both situations stuck in her mind like a couple of sandburs that couldn't be dislodged.

At eleven she took a few minutes between patients to call Bern. He wasn't at his apartment. When she tried the office, he answered on the first ring.

''Why aren't you at home?'' Anne asked.

"Paperwork, what else?"

Anne knew the typical case could generate a hundred-page report with every aspect of the investigation carefully detailed.

"Did you find Anthony Sales?"

"Not yet. What's up, Doc?"

"My last patient is due at one. Would you be interested in a late lunch?"

"It's a poor substitute for eloping, but I guess it'll have to do." At least he was joking about it although the humor sounded strained. "Can you come pick me up? I dropped off the Jeep for an oil change."

She agreed she would, hung up, and went out in the reception area to greet her next patient.

Jason Sills was her last appointment at one o'clock, the little boy she had to reschedule when Bern called about Danny Lewis. Both Jason's parents had come along. Anne heard Travis Sills's voice through the closed door, commanding the boy to sit down and stop fooling around. If Travis was annoyed, it wasn't because Anne was running late. Peggy had kept the schedule running smoothly.

Anne went out in time to hear Deena tell her husband if the damned basketball game was that important, he should've stayed at home. Jason rocked back and forth on the edge of a chair next to Travis, his head hunched into his shoulders, actually sitting on his hands to keep himself under control.

Anne looked directly at the little boy and said a warm hello. Jason brightened. The grown-ups might assume the greeting was for all of them, but he knew it was directed to him. He sat there and said nothing, however, until Anne came and held out her hand.

He took it, his moist little fingers clinging tightly, and went willingly with her toward the office.

"This sure does cut up the weekend, Dr. Menlo," Travis was saying as he and Deena followed. "I guess emergencies come up, but seems to me this could've waited."

Anne glanced back at Peggy before she closed the door. Peggy would never do anything as blatant as rolling her eyes or making faces. But Anne had learned to read her expression and knew Peggy had Travis Sills pegged: an ex-jock chained to a desk, discovering it took more and more time and effort to keep in shape and growing daily more dissatisfied with life.

Mothers didn't have a corner on concern about their children; fathers cared, too. Even Travis did, Anne was sure; he just didn't want to have to devote any energy to it. He'd made his position clear the first time they came: This was a waste of time and money; kids needed to learn to do what they were told and get along. So he lounged on the small sofa and looked bored while Deena told Anne about talking to the principal at Jason's school, asking again to have Jason transferred to another class, and getting a polite but firm refusal. And Travis was more than happy to escape back into the waiting room with Deena while Anne worked with his son.

During play therapy Jason set up a dark cave of blocks. A big mean-looking plastic rat herded a handful of little mice into the cave, then crouched outside, refusing requests to go to the bathroom and denying pitiful cries for food and drinks of water. When one brave little mouse made a break for it, he was grabbed and thrown back inside where all the mice were ordered to lie down and stay perfectly still. If they didn't, the rat threatened to get some rope and tie them up. Busy watching the mice, the rat didn't see the big cat puppet Jason brought over to gobble it up.

Anne made a few notes after the session and then mulled over her observations during the drive down to Bern's office. Even allowing for a child's egocentric perspective, it was becoming clear to Anne that the problem was not simply a matter of Jason's adjustment to a strict teacher. Instead, Anne was beginning to think this teacher had either little experience or no talent at handling five-year-olds. One of the realities of life, however, was that school was not always wonderful. The thing that Anne had to determine was whether to help Jason accept the situation and learn to cope, or if the issue was serious enough to suggest something as drastic as removing him from the school.

Or was there something here—even more serious—she wasn't seeing? Something dark and evil.

No, she told herself firmly. Not every case was a horrendous repetition of the things that happened to Nicki Craig.

Anne found street parking on Sixth across from the Police and Public Safety Building, locked her car, and walked back half a block to the intersection of Sixth and Washington.

For several years the city of Phoenix had gone to great lengths to banish the homeless from the area. The effort had not been entirely successful. Two men sat in the shade on the low wall of the cement planter that attempted to soften the square structure with some generic cactus and scrubby olive trees. Both were imbued with that peculiar grayness of clothes, skin, and spirit that came from living on the street and looked too stunned with the heat to get up and approach her.

Inside the front entrance an older man and woman waited on turquoise plastic chairs in a small walk-in area. Their eyes were fastened on the activity at the front desk that lay beyond a wide glass partition and big glass doors, their faces full of the dread that comes from knowing that terrible things are about to happen. Anne left them to their vigil, checked in at the front desk, and went up to the homicide department.

The squad room was a big area with islands of desks, low ceilings covered in acoustical tile, and gray linoleum on the floor. Today the place looked deserted. Most of the detectives must be in the field, Anne decided. One man she didn't recognize sat over in the corner pecking at a computer keyboard. Bern talked on the phone behind a desk covered with stacks of reports. He often said he was waiting for the day when TV live-action shows demonstrated the real side of police work, which was dealing with the snowstorm of paper.

Since it was his day off, he had compromised on the white shirt and tie that was the department's standard dress, wearing instead a print sports shirt and a silver bolo. He waved Anne over, said a few more words into the phone, then hung up.

"That was the desk sergeant. A patrol unit just brought in Anthony Sales. Sorry, Anne, but I'll have to skip lunch."

"That's all right. I'm just glad they caught him. Listen, if I bring you back a sandwich, will you take time to eat it?"

"Pastrami?" he asked hopefully.

"If that's what you want."

"It's a deal."

As Anne turned to leave, the door to the squad room burst open. Two muscular patrolmen strong-armed a handcuffed man inside, the man writhing and fighting against them, ignoring their commands to "Settle down, Tony. Knock it off."

Tony Sales was skinny, but a tank-style undershirt revealed ropy muscles bulging in hard knots as he struggled. Jailhouse tattoos decorated his biceps. His snug-fitting, dirty jeans were tucked into scuffed boots. Long black hair, held in a ponytail by a leather thong at the back of his neck, was coming loose to fall in his face, and there was a mad gleam in his black eyes.

"This is fuckin' bullshit," he screamed. "Draggin' me in here. This ain't right—this ain't fuckin' *happenin'*. Let go, you assholes. Fuckin' turn me *loose*."

Obscenities keep pouring out as he fought to get away. His wrists were cuffed in front. The officers had a good hold, their arms clamped around his at the elbow, but his legs were free, and he knew how to use the high-heeled boots.

"Stay here," Bern said to Anne.

He moved fast around the desk and hurried to help with Sales.

Things happened so quickly then that it was only afterward that Anne's memory began to replay the sequence in a slow-motion action that would haunt her dreams for a long time: Sales's legs scissoring high off the floor, the heel of his boot coming down hard enough on one patrolman's foot to crack bone while Sales sank his teeth into the other patrolman's shoulder; both men bellowing in pain and Sales pushing free and moving snake-quick to grab a gun from the second officer's belt; Bern rushing forward as the gun went off, the blast of sound loud enough to shatter the world.

9

Anne rushed across the room, crying Bern's name just as he threw himself to one side. Her throat ached with the shout, but she heard nothing. The smell of cordite burned her nose and eyes, and her head was full of an eerie, ringing silence. Bern turned toward her, his mouth stretched wide and moving. She understood he was yelling a warning, even though she could barely hear the sounds he made.

Tony Sales was yelling, too—the words indistinct and garbled but the meaning clear enough. He held the gun in both cuffed hands, holding it straight out and whipping it back and forth at the patrolmen; at the detective over in the corner, just getting up from his chair, hand on his gun; at the door where more officers were pouring in; at Bern jumping up to grab Anne and pull her to the floor beside him.

"Stay *down*," Bern said and thrust his body between Anne and Sales.

She heard that all right. She pressed tightly against Bern, feeling the broad planes of his back against her breasts, his body whole, unhurt, no blood that she could see. Relief loosened her terror. She began to shake violently.

"Stay away," Sales screamed. "I'll fuckin' *kill* you. I ain't goin' to jail, so back off, back the fuck *off*."

"Okay, Tony," Bern said. "Take it easy."

"I didn't *do* nothin'. I didn't kill *no*body. *Get back*." His voice rose as the officers in the doorway edged forward. The gun zeroed in on Bern and Anne. "Tell 'em to get out or I'll shoot, I fuckin' swear I will."

"You heard the man," Bern said. "Go outside. You, too, Frank." This was for the other detective in the squad room. "Follow procedure."

"And shut the fuckin' door!"

When the door swung closed, there were just the four of them in the room besides Tony Sales. One patrolman was on the floor near Bern and Anne, clutching his ankle, obviously in pain. The officer Tony had bitten leaned against a desk, eyeing Tony and sweating profusely.

Tony Sales said bitterly, "*Procedure*. Waitin' to blow my fuckin' head off, that's what they're doin'. Well, let 'em try, I'm gonna take some people with me. You." He gestured to the patrolman by the desk. "Get over here with the others."

"Do what he says," Bern ordered sharply when the man hesitated.

"And you—get away from the woman," Tony said to Bern. "I wanna see what she's doin'."

"Listen, Tony—"

"I mean it. *Move*. I'll fuckin' blow a hole clear through you right into the bitch."

"It's all right," Anne said, leaving the shelter of Bern's body, feeling suddenly terribly vulnerable.

"Hands, let me see your hands," Tony barked.

She slid over a foot or two, keeping her hands out and flat on the floor so she could scoot along on her bottom.

"Okay, Tony," Bern said. "We're all cool here. Come on, let's talk about this—what do you say?"

"I ain't talkin'. You wouldn't listen anyway."

"Sure I would. We can work this out—"

"No, we can't, so shut up. *Just shut the fuck up.*"

Spittle flecked the sides of his mouth, and the black eyes shone with reckless fury. The pupils were dilated—some kind of drug in his system cranking up his reactions. Besides this, Anne could almost smell the overabundance of testosterone from the four men mixed with the rank odor of the sweat that soaked their shirts. She clamped down on her own fear, forcing herself to speak calmly.

"Tony, I can see you're frightened."

"Anne," Bern began, but she ignored him.

"I'm scared, too, Tony," she said.

"You better be scared. You better be good and fuckin' scared, lady."

"I'm Anne. Anne Menlo. And I'm shaking. My heart's pounding like crazy. I'll bet yours is, too."

"Yeah. Oh, yeah. I'm strung out," he admitted. "I got a right to be."

"You certainly do," Anne agreed.

Bern was studying her, staying silent, letting her handle it. Probably hoping to God she knew what she was doing. She hoped so, too.

"Maybe we can make things easier for you," Anne said. "Maybe if you sat down. Would you like to do that? How about a cigarette? Or something to drink—"

He shook his head. "Nothin's gonna help, don't you understand? They're gettin' the fuckin' SWAT team ready. They're gonna kill my ass. Help me? *Shit.*"

"There must be something." She racked her brain for an idea. "I know. We'll get you some protection—a bullet-proof vest."

He looked at her like she was the one who was crazy. Bern and the other two men stared at her with the same expression.

"Wouldn't that make you feel safer?" Anne persisted.

Tony blinked. "A flak jacket?"

"Yes. One of those Kevlar things. We could do that, couldn't we?" she said to Bern.

"Sure," Bern said, agreeing much more readily than she thought he would. "I'll have somebody bring one up."

"Yeah," Tony said, warming to the idea. "A vest. Okay."

Bern yelled the request to the men outside the squad-room door.

"Nobody comes in," Tony warned. "I ain't takin' no chances."

"Of course not," Anne said soothingly. "You sure you wouldn't like a chair, Tony?"

"No," he said, but the idea of resting had been planted. He backed up against the desk and eased down on it, relaxing for just a moment only to spring up again when somebody tapped on the door.

"Stay there," he yelled, making stabbing motions with the gun at Bern. "Tell 'em. Tell 'em I'll blow their fuckin' heads off."

"Don't come in," Bern called out. "Open the door and put the vest inside."

The officer complied, dropping the vest and closing the door again. Tony's eyes darted from it back to Bern and the two patrolmen.

"It won't do you any good over there," Bern said. "Go ahead, Tony. Go get it."

Fresh fury ignited in Tony's eyes. "Yeah, you'd like that—set me up, didn't you set me up? I go get the jacket, and they start shootin'—fuckin' *shit.*"

"Nobody's going to hurt you, Tony," Anne said. "I'll get the vest, okay?"

He gave her an assessing look. Half Pint, her brother

Kevin used to tease. He still called her that. She hated it as a kid, still hated it, but God she wanted to see Kevin's devilish grin and hear him use the nickname again.

She waited, willing herself to look small and nonthreatening. After a moment Tony Sales said, "Yeah, okay."

Bern called sharply to the men outside, telling them she was coming to the door. She got up, went over, and picked up the vest. It must have weighed five pounds—my God, how could anybody wear one of the things all day in the summer heat? Some people did—routinely, she knew.

She brought the vest back, stopping a few feet from Tony, put the vest on the floor, and slid it the rest of the way to him, suddenly sure she was making a terrible mistake.

Tony stared at it for a second and swore. "How'm I supposed to put the fuckin' thing on? Gimme the keys," he said to the patrolman on the floor. "No, give 'em to her. Slow. You reach for anything else, and I mess up your other ankle."

"Go on," Bern told the man.

He carefully extracted the keys and handed them to Anne.

"Okay, Anne," Tony said, extending his hands while gripping the gun. "You ain't gonna try nothin', are you?"

"No, I just want to help you, Tony."

"Okay. I got nothin' against you, but I'll fuckin' shoot you anyway if I have to. You keep that in mind, hero," he said to Bern.

Close enough to insert the key in the cuffs, Anne could see that Tony fairly thrummed with excitement. There was a kind of strange intimacy between them as her fingers brushed his skin. When the lock clicked open, she stepped back, more than happy to put some distance between them.

He dropped down on his heels, put the cuffs on the floor,

and picked up the vest, managing to shrug it on with the gun still pointed in their direction. The reassuring weight of the body armor calmed him enough so he eased back against the desk without any urging.

"Better?" Anne asked.

"I guess so. You sit down, though."

"All right." She sat on the floor near Bern.

"It don't change nothin'," Tony said. "They're still gonna try to kill me, Anne."

"No, I really don't think so, Tony. They won't start shooting with me in here."

"Like hell they won't."

"Trust me, Tony. I'm a civilian. Think about the bad press if something happened to me. Besides, everybody understands you're scared. And when you're scared you get desperate. We all know that. The police just want to work it out so nobody gets hurt."

"Yeah, well, then they shouldn't come and drag people outta their place. Shouldn't hassle 'em and threaten to put 'em back in jail for something they didn't do."

"No, they shouldn't," Anne said firmly. "But acting this way—it doesn't help you, Tony. It just makes things worse. I don't think you really want to hurt me, Tony. I don't think you want to hurt anybody here."

"Well, I don't mean *you* no harm," he said.

"I'm sure you don't, Tony."

"You act like I do."

"It's just the gun. It makes me nervous."

"Oh—"

And he lowered the gun. Not all the way, but enough.

Bern was on her left, the patrolman who was nursing his foot was next to him, the other patrolman on her right. Maybe there had been some signal among the men. She had been too engrossed with Tony to notice, but they must have communicated because suddenly she was aware that the two patrolmen had quietly inched away from her and Bern.

The realization hit Tony at almost the same time.

"Go," Bern ordered, shoving Anne out of the line of fire.

Before Tony could bring the gun up, the three cops swarmed over him, quickly and efficiently. He was disarmed and facedown on the floor while Anne stood there, trying to adjust to the fact that the danger was over.

Bern shouted an all-clear. Every cop in the whole building seemed to have been outside in the hall, and they all poured into the room. Tony was hauled up and taken away, his nose pouring blood, a stunned look in his eyes.

Bern helped Anne to her feet, saying, "Oh, Christ, Annie," as he held her tightly. She could hear his heart pounding in his chest.

"I'm okay," she said.

He held her away from him, checking her over as though he needed visual confirmation.

"I'm all right, Bern, really."

She wasn't, though. She had a hollow, shaky feeling compounded of shock, fear, and too much adrenaline. While she was in it, she had done what she thought best to defuse a dangerous situation, but what if she had guessed wrong? Added to that nagging doubt was an unsettling feeling that she had betrayed Tony Sales's trust.

The watch commander came over and said to Bern, "She seemed to be doing just fine, so we figured we'd go with it." He grinned at Anne. "You ever want a job as a hostage negotiator, Dr. Menlo, I'll put in a good word. And the thing with the vest—outstanding."

She said a shaky thanks and hung on to Bern's arm because she was afraid her knees would buckle if she let go.

He took her over to a chair by his desk and yelled, "Frank, get Anne some coffee." To her, he said, "Back in the good old days I could offer you a slug of whiskey."

"That's okay. I hate whiskey," she said. "What the sergeant said about the vest—I thought everybody would be upset about my giving a criminal something to keep him safe."

"Anne, you only gave him the illusion of being safe," Bern explained gently. "There were two SWAT team members here today. They didn't have time to get into their gear, but they did have their Heckler and Koch submachine guns. Believe me, those bullets can cut through Kevlar like butter."

"Oh," Anne said, not only feeling foolish but sickened by how little true protection there is for any of us.

10

The coffee that Frank brought was wonderful, aromatic, hot, and reviving. Frank hovered while Anne sipped, adding his own congratulations on her brilliant maneuver. Bern kept his hand on her shoulder. She knew he could feel that she was still trembling.

"I have to question Sales right away," he said. "How about I have somebody take you over to my place? I'm not sure you ought to be driving."

She nodded. She would have preferred to go home, but she couldn't ask to be driven all the way to Cave Creek. And Bern's observation was right: She didn't trust herself behind the wheel.

"I'll take her," Frank volunteered.

The two men dealt with the logistics. Bern would drive Anne's Camaro; he'd call the shop and have his Jeep delivered to his apartment building. Anne really didn't care what they arranged. All she wanted was to be someplace away from here, in a bed, preferably with Bern's arms around her.

"I'll come home as soon as I can," he promised.

"Hurry," she said.

•   •   •

Bern had Tony Sales placed in an interrogation room immediately. Sales's hands and feet were manacled to a good strong chair, and two of the biggest, brawniest uniformed officers on duty stood guard. Whatever fight Sales had left was pretty much gone by the time Bern walked in.

There was dried blood under his nose and on his chin, a splash on the white undershirt. The leather strip that had tied his ponytail was gone, so the oily, dark hair straggled across his shoulders. Sweat stuck a couple of strands to his face. The mean, sullen gleam in his black eyes reminded Bern of Florence Mosk's dog, watching and growling from under the shadowy porch.

With the vision of Anne flying across the squad room and the sound of the gunshot echoing in his head, Bern would have liked to grab the man's hair and hammer his head against the table in pure primal rage. The worst thing that could happen almost had, all because of this slimebag.

With monumental restraint, Bern sat down in a chair across the narrow table. "Okay, Tony, you ready to talk to me now?"

"Yeah, just let me loose, willya?"

"You're ready to behave yourself?"

"Yeah, I'm cool. I really am."

Bern turned to one of the officers. "Kellum, take the cuffs off his hands, but leave the feet."

Kellum shot him a skeptical look. "You really trust this guy?"

"No, but if he tries anything else, just shoot the son of a bitch."

When his hands were free, Tony rubbed his wrists and then dabbed at his nose with the tail of his undershirt. "Thanks, man. Listen, where's the doctor?"

"What doctor? You need a doctor?"

"Yeah, I need one. I'm bleedin'. Dr. Menlo. The broad who was in there."

"Forget it," Bern said harshly. "You haven't lost more than a couple of pints. Anyway, you've got a hell of a lot more to worry about than a bloody nose."

"I didn't mean none of this to happen," Tony whined. "Them two assholes? They busted in when I was sound asleep. I didn't know what was goin' on. I was scared. I just flipped out for a few minutes. I wasn't gonna hurt nobody."

"You could've fooled me," Bern said. "You have any idea how much trouble you're in, Tony? Assaulting a police officer in the line of duty, assault with a deadly weapon, attempted murder—"

"I wasn't gonna *kill* nobody," Tony said with a touch of indignation. "If I was gonna do that, you'd be fuckin' dead by now."

"You held us against our will, Tony. We can probably add kidnapping, too."

"Kidnapping?" He paled a little, fear swimming just below the scum of meanness in his eyes.

"You had some experience along those lines, Tony?"

"Hey, no, this is bullshit." But Bern thought the mention of kidnapping had scared him badly, and knew he'd probably pushed a little too hard. A good guess because Tony's next words were: "I get a phone call. I know my rights. I want to call a lawyer."

"Sure you do, after I've arrested you. But I didn't do that yet. We're talking about possibilities here."

"I still think I'd better call one."

"Okay, Tony, but you know what that means—we stop talking. And once that happens, I'm going to hit you with everything I can think of."

"Oh, man, you're gonna do it anyway."

"Maybe. Maybe not. Why don't we just discuss things for a while, see what happens."

"I don't see what we got to talk about."

"How about your friend Dorie?"

"I don't know nothin' about Dorie," Tony said, and Bern could see the freeze setting in for sure.

He was losing the guy. Tony Sales was a pro with too many busts, too many times around the criminal justice system's revolving door. Bern said quickly, "You know she's dead, don't you?"

"Yeah, I saw it on TV."

"Was she alive when you left her, Tony?"

"I ain't sayin' another word."

"Because she didn't die right away. I'll bet you didn't know you hit her hard enough to kill her. What did you fight about? The money?"

"I want a lawyer."

"We can probably come down from murder one, Tony, if you help us out. Tell me what happened, give up the ransom, things could go a lot easier for you. Talk to me, Tony."

"Listen up, dickhead. I'm only sayin' it one more time, and these guys are witnesses." He gestured to the two uniformed cops and bellowed, "I WANT A FUCKIN' LAWYER AND I WANT ONE RIGHT NOW!"

After Tony was taken away to a holding cell, Bern wrote up his notes and reviewed all the ways he'd gone wrong: too antagonistic, too aggressive. And don't forget too personally involved. He also had to consider that part of his anger was directed toward himself because somewhere inside, right about gut level, he knew he was responsible for Anne being in the line of fire.

To hell with second-guessing.

He went home.

• • •

Anne prescribed warmth, caffeine, and sugar for herself to combat what she recognized as the aftereffects of shock. So, huddled on the sofa in Bern's flannel winter robe, she drank tea and ate pecan sandies from the supply of cookies Bern always kept stocked.

The couch was old and comfortable, covered in a brown plaid fabric—Herculon, she thought it was called—that never seemed to wear out. Bern had bought it used through the *PennySaver* along with the rest of the furniture. He had brought little when he moved in with her and had taken little with him after they broke up.

Bern was not a man who wasted money on expensive grown-up toys, but he liked nice furnishings and could afford them. Looking around the orderly room, she saw clues into Bern's current mind-set. The place reflected Bern's need for comfort and order, but it showed no investment of either money or personal energy. Anne had a feeling this was a way station because he still expected they would get back together.

Remembering that scene in the squad room, she was torn by conflicting emotions. She wanted to grab Bern and never let go, and she wanted to run like hell away from a man whose work exposed her to so much potential loss.

The job—always the damn cop shop, but she had to ask herself: Would Bern be Bern if he'd been a construction worker or a CPA? The job had shaped the man as surely as his early home life.

The sound of his key in the dead bolt stopped her existential questioning. She rushed to him, and they quickly reduced the broader quandary of their relationship to the immediate sensation of mouth against mouth, skin against skin.

After they made love, she nestled, spoon fashion, in his

arms, drifting and content, and thought how simple their life was as long as it was enclosed by parameters the size of a bed.

Hunger drove them from the safe haven of the bedroom soon enough. The incident with Tony Sales had short-circuited their plans for lunch, so they were starving. Since neither wanted to face the hordes of people out on a Saturday night, Bern cooked pasta and heated jarred spaghetti sauce while Anne managed to salvage enough lettuce and green peppers from the refrigerator's crisper for a salad.

They sat at a small kitchen table, Bern dressed in shorts and a tank top since he had let the temperature in the apartment drift up for her benefit; Anne wore one of his T-shirts that hung down to her knees.

Anne occasionally came to Bern's apartment, of course, but she kept none of her things there and rarely spent the night. She preferred that Bern come to her place. A matter of control, she supposed. No, admit it. Of course she felt more in control of the relationship on her own ground. She needed the feeling, because so often she felt at the mercy of her emotions when it came to him.

While they ate, Bern told her that Tony Sales had clammed up, admitting nothing about a connection to Danny's kidnapping and Dorie Wineski's murder.

"Basically, I blew it," Bern said gloomily. "You've got to work these guys. I came on too strong and scared him."

"I think you're entitled to a few hostile feelings," Anne said. "The man might have killed you."

"He might have killed *you*—that's what I couldn't get out of my mind. I should never have questioned him by myself. Maybe I shouldn't have questioned him at all."

He took their empty plates to rinse them in the sink while Anne put on water to boil for coffee.

"Do you think he's the one?" Anne asked.

"Well, he's got the temperament for the killing, we know that, don't we? I can't see him as being smart enough to pull off the kidnapping, but maybe Dorie was the brains."

They both stopped what they were doing as a pager began beeping in the living area. "Mine," Anne said.

She dialed her service to find that Glen Lewis wanted her to call him right away. Glen answered on the first ring. Anne could hear Danny's frantic crying in the background.

"I'm sorry we had to bother you at home, but we didn't know what to do." There was desperation in Glen's voice.

"That's all right," Anne said. "What happened?"

"I have no idea. He was just fine—had his bath, then Natalie brought him down here to say good night. When she said it was time to go to bed, he started screaming, and nothing we did seemed to help."

"You did the right thing to call," Anne said. "I'll come right over."

"You don't have to do that. If you could just tell us how to calm him down."

"It may not be as simple as that. Keep holding him and reassuring him everything is all right until I get there."

"Danny?" Bern asked when she hung up.

Anne nodded distractedly. She headed for the bedroom, pulling off the oversize T-shirt as she went.

"I'll come with you," Bern said from the doorway as she dressed quickly.

"No, Bern, I really think it's better if I go alone."

It wasn't easy for him to defer to her judgment, but he said, "Okay."

"Can I tell the Lewises about Sales?"

"No. I want to tell them myself—assuming we can keep it out of the papers and off TV for a while."

Her clothes were rumpled and her panty hose ruined by crawling on the squad-room floor. Never mind. She stuck bare feet into her sandals, swiped a comb through her hair, and picked up her purse on the way through the living room toward the front door.

Bern followed her and gave her a quick good-bye kiss. "Come back when you finish?"

"I don't know how long I'll be," she said. "Don't wait up for me. Go to bed. I'll call if it's not too late."

"Call anyway," he said. "Whatever time it is, especially if you get anything from Danny. And—Anne?—remember that at this point Tony Sales is a *suspect*. We don't know for sure if he killed Dorie."

In other words, Danny might still be in danger. Danny needed to remember what he saw—if he saw anything. It was up to Anne to get him to face the trauma and talk about what he knew.

11

Glen met Anne at the door, looking relieved, saying, "We finally got him calmed down. Sorry we dragged you all the way over here."

Anne assured him she was glad to come and followed him into the living room. The fact that Danny's screams had stopped might have been good for Glen's jangled nerves, but Anne was more alarmed at the sight of the little boy than she would have been by some good healthy crying.

Danny lay on the sofa with his head in Natalie's lap, his knees drawn up. He was clutching Edgar and sucking his thumb, with that glazed, fevered look in his eyes, looking not much better than he had when she left him the day before. Anne went to kneel beside him and stroked his hair.

"Hi, Danny." She kept her voice steady and apprehension-free. "I heard you and Edgar had a really bad time of it to-night, so I wanted to come and check on you. Would you like to tell me what happened? No? Okay, maybe a little later. I'll talk to your mom and dad first."

Anne looked up at Natalie who shook her head, bewildered, and said, "I have no idea what set him off. After he had his bath, I brought him down to say good night to Glen. Then he began stalling. He wanted a snack; he wanted to snuggle for a while. He was falling asleep, but as soon as Glen picked him up and said it was bedtime, he made a fuss.''

''Did Danny say anything specific?''

''Just no, no, and that he didn't want to go upstairs. He hung on to me, begging me not to go up, not to leave him. We tried to talk to him, but he got worse. Glen was going to just take him to his room anyway.'' She shot Glen an accusing look.

''I thought he was overtired,'' Glen said defensively. ''And maybe all the attention is spoiling him.''

''Well, you should've listened to me,'' Natalie said. ''Danny began screaming and kicking—it was awful. I started yelling at Glen—which made it worse, I guess, but I wasn't going to force Danny to do something that was upsetting him so much.''

''Understand I'm not taking sides here,'' Anne said. ''But Natalie was right. Children have their own logic that's sometimes difficult to follow, so I think Danny had a reason for not wanting to go upstairs that made sense to him.''

''If you say so.'' Glen sounded a little testy and not quite convinced.

''Anne, were there stairs at—where Danny was found?'' Natalie asked.

''No, it was a one-story house.''

''Then is this connected to what happened to him?''

''I think so, in some way,'' Anne said. ''We ought to start his therapy immediately. I'm willing to go into my office tomorrow if you'll bring him in. Say, ten o'clock?''

''We'll be there.'' Natalie looked at Glen as though daring him to disagree.

''Sure,'' he said with only the slightest reluctance, ''ten o'clock. I called Danny's doctor after I spoke to you,'' he told Anne. ''His pediatrician. He suggested a mild sedative to get us through the night. I'm going to pick it up at the all-night pharmacy.''

"I don't like the idea of giving Danny drugs," Natalie said.

"Oh, for Christ's sake, Natalie, it's *medicine*, not crack cocaine.''

"Well, I still don't like it. Anne, what do you think?''

"You might want to have a sedative handy," Anne said, "but I wish you wouldn't use it unless you really have to.'' Anne studied Danny as she smoothed his hair back from his face. His skin wasn't quite so clammy, and his gaze seemed focused on her as she said, "How about it, Danny? Are you ready to go upstairs if we all go with you? You could sleep in Mommy and Daddy's bed again.''

He shook his head, and she could feel him tensing up. She said quickly, "That's okay. You don't have to. He can sleep down here, can't he?'' Anne asked Natalie. "You need to stay with him so he won't be scared if wakes up.''

"Of course he can," Natalie said. "Maybe we ought to bring down the mattress from the guest room. It would be a lot more comfortable.''

"Where would we put it?'' Glen demanded, clearly unhappy with the suggestion. "It's going to be a real mess in here.''

"Oh, for God's sake, Glen. Danny's more important than the damned living room," Natalie said with what Anne was sure was uncharacteristic spirit.

Glen closed his mouth on another protest and smiled ruefully. "Yeah, sorry, hon. Now's not the time to worry about how the house looks.''

After moving the coffee table aside, he went up for the mattress. Anne studied Natalie's exhausted face.

"Don't you have family here who could help out?''

Natalie shook her head. "My folks live in Buffalo. Glen's are in Dallas."

"A friend, then—someone who could come and stay for a while."

"My sister and I were always close. Kelly lived here in Mesa for a while. After she moved, well, I guess I don't make friends easily. Kelly would drop everything and jump on a plane, but she's got two little kids of her own and another on the way. My mom offered, and it would be wonderful for about half a day. She has this way of making me feel so inadequate and like everything that happens is my fault."

"What about Glen's family?"

"I suppose they'd come if we asked. But they'd insist on staying at some cheap motel, and then they'd come and sit on the living-room sofa and say nothing. I'm sorry. I don't want to sound mean. I just know how they are."

Glen came back, lugging a double-bed-sized mattress, and put it in the empty space between the chairs and couch. Danny held his teddy bear and watched, wide-eyed and wordless, but he did remove his thumb from his mouth, and he sat in Natalie's lap while Anne helped his father tuck in sheets and a blanket. He only got upset when Natalie tried to leave long enough to go up and change for bed. After Glen went for her nightgown and robe, Danny let his mother out of his sight long enough so she could use the downstairs powder room.

"Well, in you go, partner," Glen said. "You, too, Mommy."

"And Edgar?" Danny asked.

"Of course, sweetie," Natalie said. "Now, come on. Let's crawl under the covers."

Glen tucked them in. After Anne kissed Danny and Edgar good night, Glen gave his son and the teddy bear a big kiss, too. Then he turned toward Natalie, but she moved away.

When Glen reached for the lamp switch, Danny said anxiously, "Don't turn off the light."

"Okay. I'll just turn it down a little." He added, a little too heartily to Anne, "We'd better let these two get some shut-eye."

Anne squeezed Natalie's hand and mouthed: *Don't worry.*

In the hallway, Glen said, "Anne, if you have time, come on out to the kitchen and have something to drink. Maybe some iced tea? I don't have to go to the drugstore right away."

Anne felt thoroughly drained and needed to go home, but if Glen wanted to talk, she knew she should listen. "All right, sure. That sounds good."

The kitchen must have looked wonderful in a designer's drawing. All Anne could think about was how hard it must be to keep an active little boy from scratching the pegged oak floor, getting fingerprints on the glossy white cabinets, and smearing the black glass fronts of the appliances. A granite slab formed counters that were meant to be uncluttered, Anne was sure; however, dishes spilled over into the sink, and the surfaces needed wiping.

"We just can't seem to get on top of things," Glen said, more uncomfortable with the mess than Anne was. "Please—" He gestured to an oak table placed in a small bay window area where pleated fabric shades had been lowered to shut out the night. "How about something stronger than iced tea? Wine? A beer?"

"No, tea's fine."

He went to take a pitcher from the refrigerator. "We haven't heard from the police. Do you know if they've found out anything?"

Anne repressed a shudder as she thought about Tony Sales and that scene in the squad room. She wished she could reassure Glen that some progress had been made; instead, she gave him a vague, "I really couldn't say."

He brought the drinks—tea for her, a glass and a bottle of Heineken for himself—and sat on the other side of the table. "I wanted to explain something, so you wouldn't get the wrong idea. About Danny's therapy—it's not that I don't want Danny to get whatever help he needs. It's just—this is hard." He poured beer, tipping the glass to keep down the foam.

Anne waited, saying nothing.

He put down the bottle and took a breath. "My sister had—well—mental problems. I know she went to a psychiatrist after she tried to kill herself the first time. Therapy didn't help. My folks finally committed her to a state institution, but she managed to finish the job."

"I'm sorry," Anne said. "How old were you when this happened?"

"Eleven, almost twelve when it started."

"And your sister?"

"Seventeen." He stared down at the beer in his glass. "I came home from school one day, dying to use the toilet. The bathroom door was locked. I figured Angie was in there—you know how girls are at that age; they live in the bathroom. My mom was at work. I pounded on the door, but Angie didn't answer. So I kept pounding and then suddenly I got scared—I mean, really scared. I was a big kid. I ran at the door and smashed it open. She was in the tub and the water was—it was so red . . ."

Nicki's mother found her, Anne. I went over there, to see if I could do anything. They'd taken the—the body away the day before, but nobody had done any cleaning. Just let

the water out. The bathtub was still—it was still—stained,
like rust . . .

"Are you all right?" Glen asked.

"What? Yes, I'm fine." She took a sip of her iced tea,
wishing she'd asked for wine or maybe vodka, clenching
the glass tightly so her hand wouldn't shake.

"I'm sorry," Glen said. "I didn't think telling you about
Angie would upset you."

"It doesn't. I was just—I can imagine how you must
have felt finding her there. How you might have blamed
yourself somehow."

"Yeah, well—" He picked up his beer and drank several
long swallows. "I guess I did, a little."

It's not your fault, Anne. My God, none of us ever sus-
pected a thing.

"It's a natural reaction," she said, feeling as though she
was merely repeating the reassurance, parrotlike.

"I know you're right, but I'm not sure I could've handled it if she died. Well, thank God she didn't, not then
anyway."

"What caused the suicide attempt? Do you know?"

He shook his head. "My folks are not exactly open people. I guess they thought if you didn't talk about bad things,
they would go away. I just keep wondering how Angie
could go over the edge like that without somebody noticing
something was wrong."

"It can happen." *God knows, it can happen.* "I have no
way of knowing what your sister was going through, Glen.
It might have been organic. Maybe she was clinically depressed. This thing with Danny is quite different. There's
no reason to think he won't recover."

"I know—my *head* knows, but—" He gave her a pleading look. "Anne, be square with me. My stalling around
has made Danny worse, hasn't it?"

"I can't answer that," Anne said. "I don't know for sure. The important thing is you're ready to have him treated now, aren't you?"

He nodded—although she still sensed reluctance.

"I know it's been rough," Anne said. "You and Natalie are both under a lot of pressure."

"Yeah, I guess that's easy to see. I've always been kind of a neatness freak." He gave Anne a crooked grin. "I'll bet you could make a lot out of *that*. Like the stuff with the mattress. It just bothers me. I know it shouldn't, but it does."

"Don't be too hard on yourself. But be prepared. The tension may get worse before it gets better. You'll be dealing with Danny as well as stress between you and Natalie, and I'm sure there'll be financial problems if the police don't find the ransom."

"Oh, Christ, yes," Glen said. "I haven't even started to think about that."

"You ought to. And talk to Natalie. You need to make sure the two of you discuss everything."

"I guess so, but she's not a strong person, and she's gone through a lot already."

"Give her a chance. You may be surprised at how strong she is." Anne took a last sip of the tea. "I have to get going. No, stay here. I can find my way out."

Back in her car, she found herself heading for Cave Creek, still shaky from that flashback to Nicki's death. If she went to Bern's apartment, he was bound to sense something was wrong. She didn't want to talk about it tonight. She was just too tired.

She called him on her cell phone to tell him she had learned nothing from Danny and to say good night.

"I was really hoping—" He sighed. "Anne? The press know about the kidnapping. It was on the ten o'clock news.

They don't know Danny's name, and they haven't connected up Sales's arrest, but it's just a matter of time. We've got so many leaks around here, it's like a goddamn sieve.''

"Don't you think you should warn the Lewises?"

"Yeah, but it's late. Tomorrow. How about you? Are you all right?"

Afraid he was going to offer to come out to Cave Creek, she said quickly, "Don't worry about me. I'm fine."

"Well, if you're sure. Talk to you tomorrow."

At home in bed, her body longed for sleep, but her brain kept doing a replay of the scene at the police station. She hoped Bern could connect Tony to the kidnapping and murder and quickly close the case. Then she could let Danny set the pace for his therapy. And she could work with him without constantly wondering if deeper, darker motives had put him in that house.

But what if Tony hadn't killed Dorie? That meant the killer was out there right now, wondering—as they were—exactly what Danny saw.

12

Bern was at his desk by nine o'clock the following morning even though it was Sunday and he was not scheduled to work. Long hours went with the territory because time and caseload were the homicide detective's worst enemies. Bern was due to testify on one of his cases in a week, barring more delays; he had two cases on the back burner, refusing to call them unsolved and doggedly putting in a few hours on them when he could; and unless somebody else cleared an ongoing investigation, he was next on the roster when another body turned up.

He didn't need Jane Clawson to remind him that he had only a narrow window during which he could devote most of his attention to the Wineski murder—although he was sure she would remind him anyway at the next briefing, especially since Channel 12 had broken the news that a kidnapping had been connected with Dorie's murder. Jane would be hammering home the point right now except for the fact that she'd gone to a conference in Vegas.

The machine had picked up when he'd called the Lewis house earlier. He'd left a warning to keep a sharp eye out for the press and advised that it might be a good idea to screen all their calls.

The squad room was nearly deserted, but somebody had

started the coffee. Bern had his second cup with a Hostess fruit pie he'd picked up at a minimart on the way in—the one where Glen Lewis said he left the ransom on Wednesday at eight P.M. The manager had been there during that time period, running the register as a matter of fact.

Had he seen Glen Lewis?

"What? Are you crazy?" was the reply. "You know how many people are in and out of here?"

Bern figured he'd get the same response to Tony's description, and he did. Would it help to have the manager come in and take a look at Tony? Bern would have to run that past Jane and Will.

Jane would not be happy to hear that Danny had frozen up on him—Jane was not happy about a lot of things these days. He just hoped Danny would start talking to Anne at their session this morning. Or maybe Bern could squeeze something out of Tony Sales before the next briefing.

Yeah, sure. To quote his old man: *When pigs fly.*

Bern had already fallen asleep when Anne called from her car the night before to say she was going on home from the Lewises'. He knew he should have offered to drive out to Cave Creek and spend the night, but to tell the truth, much as he wanted to be with Anne, he'd been just as glad when she said she would be okay. He never rested well in her house, and God knows he needed to sleep and have his head clear.

He opened the Wineski file and contemplated the stack of paper the case had already generated: witness interviews, Will's meticulous report on the physical findings, and notes on the autopsy with a reminder that toxicology reports were still pending. Will must have come in the day before after Bern left because he had appended three new items. One report gave background data on Fitness Unlimited, Glen Lewis's company.

A quick scan of the information painted the picture of a small but growing company, competitive and well managed, without much debt and with plentiful cash reserves, that last bit sure to be altered now because of the ransom payment. Will also noted that Fitness Unlimited began as a partnership. Two years ago Glen had bought out the partner, a man named Joseph Ferraro. The name pinged dimly in Bern's memory. He thought a minute but couldn't make the connection.

He'd already decided he needed to question Glen and Natalie again, this time here, officially, in an interrogation room, without any distractions. Glen had spoken to the kidnapper on the phone; maybe he would recognize Tony's voice.

Bern figured an hour for Danny's therapy, half an hour for the Lewises to drive home. Hell, he was a nice guy, so he'd give them an hour for lunch before he called.

Anne's office was located on the fringe of a group of high-rises clustered near St. Joseph's Children's Hospital, an area known as uptown Phoenix. The older, two-story complex enclosed a U-shaped parking area. Plantings of feathery Mexican bird of paradise softened the plain stucco and rough wood buildings. Today Anne was grateful for her ground-floor location because of Danny's sudden fear of climbing stairs.

Anne arrived at nine-thirty to make sure she didn't miss the Lewises and to set up her office for the therapy session. Usually she liked to take a slower approach, especially during the first few sessions. She always remembered Rosemary's advice that the therapist must be where the child is, so she let the child lead the way by choosing among the toys and setting up the play. But in Danny's case the problem was specific, the trauma known. Or rather, she cautioned herself, she knew the broad parameters. Only Danny really knew the things he had seen and experienced.

Still, it was a good idea to accelerate the process, wasn't it? She stood in the middle of her office for a moment, torn by indecision. How close was Danny to the edge? What if something she did sent him back into that state of traumatic shock that bordered on catatonia, the way he was when he was found in Dorie's house?

Stop it, she told herself.

There was always a possibility of going too far with patients, but she would be careful and observant. This kind of second-guessing was destructive; if she kept it up, eventually she'd have trouble deciding about anything.

The doubts were still there, like a dark shadow in the cheerful room, as she selected specific things for the play table. From the storage closet she took out a doll house with two floors and doll house furniture, added blocks, and filled a basket with miniature cars, assorted doll figures, and small toy animals. Then, because three-year-olds can be easily distracted, she took the rest of the toy-filled baskets from the open shelving and put them in the closet out of sight.

In the remaining time before the Lewises arrived, Anne made a few brief notes, sitting at her desk with her office door open. She never used an intake form for patients. She would, however, ask Glen and Natalie to fill out an office form that provided the information that Peggy would use to start a formal file.

She thought about calling Bern, but she didn't need any pressure from him before her session with Danny. Anyway, there was no time because the Lewises walked into the outer office five minutes early. Anne left her desk and went out to meet them.

•   •   •

The other two reports from Will interested Bern more than the one on Glen Lewis's company. One said that a search of Tony's apartment had not turned up the ransom or anything else to link him to the kidnapping. The other gave background on Florence Mosk, which explained why her prints were on file. Florence had a record: one drunk-driving conviction and an arrest for aggravated assault. Seems she had gotten into an altercation with a man over the use of a dryer at a laundromat a couple of years ago and beat the man senseless with a nearly full sixty-four-ounce bottle of Tide detergent. After Florence spent a month in the Maricopa County jail awaiting trial, the victim dropped the charges.

How well did Florence know her next-door neighbor? Well enough to use those ham-sized fists on Dorie, dealing a blow that sent her crashing into the lamp table with enough force to crack her skull?

Florence's home phone number was on the report. A machine answered. Bern hung up without leaving a message and called Good Samaritan Hospital. Florence was not at work but was scheduled three to eleven P.M. today. Bern dialed her home number again, waited through the impersonal, robotlike announcement in a male voice that was warmer and chattier than Florence's was, and left word that Florence was to be in his office at nine A.M. tomorrow morning.

Come to think of it, Florence's own voice was almost as husky as the one on her machine. He'd have Glen listen to her as well as Tony.

Bern closed the file, sipped coffee that was rapidly growing cold, and thought about the night Dorie died. Since the time of death was between nine and eleven P.M. and the killing blow was struck approximately one hour earlier, her attacker had to be in the house somewhere between eight and ten, probably exiting right after the fight.

How had he—or she—arrived and left? In a car? On foot? Easy enough for Florence, living right next door. The only neighbor who had shown the slightest bit of cooperation was the Seventh-Day Adventist, Wayne Jensen, and he had been down in Chandler passing out pamphlets. Or so he said. But wasn't there some cutoff time for knocking on doors? People who go to work early also go to bed early and are not apt to be receptive after a certain hour.

Bern was fairly sure Saturdays were church day for this religion, and figured he was right when Wayne answered the phone, home on a Sunday morning.

"Oh, this is strange," Wayne said. "I was just going to call you."

And, yes, as a matter of fact, he did make it a rule not to disturb people after nine P.M., so he and Dale—that's the guy who was with him—left Chandler about that time.

"Dale's over here now," Wayne said, "and we were talking. What I told you about not getting home until ten-thirty? That's true, but, see, Dale reminded me that we were here in the neighborhood earlier.

"Neither of us had eaten dinner," Wayne went on. "At first I said I'd make something at my place. Dale was driving, using his gasoline, so that only seemed right. But Dale kept saying we really ought to go out, that we were both tired and did I really want to cook that time of night. Finally we decided to just go to Shoneys, but by the time we did, we'd already turned onto my street. And, you know, I saw somebody walking—let's see—going the same way we were, so that would have been from Ms. Wineski's house. I mean from that direction. I don't *know* that the person actually was coming from there."

"What time was this?"

"About nine-thirty."

"This person—male or female?"

"Well, I didn't get a good look, just a glance, but I'm pretty sure it was a man."

"Can you describe him?"

"Oh—boy, I don't know. It was dark. We don't have many streetlights out here. And he was walking the direction we were driving, so I only saw him from the back."

"How about your friend—Dale?—did he see the man?"

"He says he sort of vaguely remembers it."

"Tell you what," Bern said. "I'd like both of you to come down here. I'll get a sketch artist to work with you. You may remember more than you think."

He would also put Tony Sales in a lineup, which might jog some more memories.

After Bern arranged for the sketch artist, the front desk called to say that Tony's P.D. was on his way up.

Anne observed that at least Glen looked rested. Violet-tinged shadows smudged Natalie's eyes, and weariness rounded her shoulders. Holding his mother's hand, Danny walked slowly, as though he had lead weights tied to his ankles. When he saw Anne, he brightened, visibly relaxed, and came willingly into her office as the adults exchanged "good mornings."

His attention was immediately drawn to the play table, but Anne said, "Let's sit down and talk for a minute, Danny, and then we'll play."

Anne sat in one of the chairs; Natalie took the other one, leaving the sofa to Glen. Danny stood in front of his mother, up against her legs. Natalie leaned forward to keep an arm around him.

"How was it camping out in the living room, Danny?" Anne asked.

"I had a bad dream, and I wetted the bed," Danny said, shame-faced.

"I know you didn't like that," Anne said, "but sometimes when we're upset, those things can happen."

"I was all smelly," Danny said. "Mommy gave me a spunch bath in the sink."

"A sponge bath," Natalie corrected, then said to Anne, "There's just the powder room downstairs. I'm afraid I only had a sponge bath, too. He wouldn't let me leave him."

Danny's attachment to his mother might present a problem. Unless Anne wanted the parents to interact with the child, she usually found their presence distracting and inhibiting. But what if, in this case, Danny needed his mother more than Anne realized? What if—

Quit it, she told herself.

My God, this wasn't a life-or-death decision. All she could do was put the question to Danny, and if he showed any resistance, she wouldn't insist on seeing him alone.

"I'd really like for you and me to play by ourselves, Danny," Anne said, "while your mom and dad wait outside."

"I thought we would be part of this," Glen said. "I mean, especially because Danny wants to stick so close to his mother right now."

Danny pressed closer to Natalie, but Anne suspected this was more in response to Glen's words and the tone of his voice than out of separation anxiety.

"How about it, Danny?" Anne said. "Is it okay if your mom and dad sit in the other office while we play?"

After a moment of hesitation, he nodded and moved away from Natalie so she could stand up.

"We'll be right out there, pumpkin," Natalie said.

Anne handed Glen a clipboard that held the information

form and asked him to fill it out. He lingered in the doorway for a moment as though he was about to change his mind, rush back in, and scoop Danny up. Anne thought it was a real effort for him to step outside and pull the door shut.

When they were alone, Danny gave Anne a look of sheer panic that quickly changed to resigned acceptance. He knew why he was here; children always do. Sometimes they resist what lies ahead, but often they welcome it.

Anne held out her hand.

Danny took it, squared his small shoulders, and walked with determined bravery over to the play table.

The public defender, Larry Fries, was a short dumpling of a man who looked as if he could think of about a dozen places he'd rather be than here in the squad room on a Sunday. He carried his gray suit coat draped over his arm, sat down with a sigh across the desk from Bern, and dropped his heavy briefcase with a thump.

"Coffee?" Bern offered after saying hello.

"No, thanks. How can you drink that stuff in this heat?"

Without waiting for a reply, he got right down to business. Fingerprints at the scene and the mention of a possible eyewitness go a long way toward promoting reasonableness. A tiger where a client was concerned, Larry was still a reasonable man, especially when that client's butt was in a sling.

"He knows he screwed up here yesterday," Larry said, "but he swears he didn't kill Dorie Wineski."

"Guys like Tony always swear they didn't kill anybody."

A wry grin. "Well, there's that. Listen, Bern, Tony has a request, and it may go a long way toward getting him to cooperate if you help him out. He wants to see Anne Menlo."

"No way," Bern said. "Out of the question."

"He has a right to seek treatment from a psychologist."

"Anne treats children. Besides, there are plenty of other shrinks."

"Yes, but I take it he's formed some kind of attachment to Dr. Menlo. Look, tell you the truth, I advised against it, but I can't talk him out of it. I can ask her directly."

And if he did, Bern wasn't altogether sure Anne would turn down Tony's request. Knowing how stubborn she was, she just might go along with it. And there was a chance Tony might confide in her, or that she could convince him to come clean with Bern.

Bern the man loved Anne, didn't care about how much an interview might help the case, and didn't want that slimebag anywhere near her for any reason. But Bern the cop was taking a cold, objective look, figuring that safety precautions could be taken, and thinking that Anne just might provide a shortcut to Tony, and if she could, he'd be a damn fool not to take it.

"All right," Bern said. "I'll ask her."

For the first fifteen minutes Danny picked through the basket of toy figures, pushed a little truck around the perimeter of the table, stacked blocks, and ran the truck into them in experimental crashes while Anne sat on a floor pillow beside the table. Finally he began arranging furniture in the house, approximating the layout in his own home, and selected figures of a mom, dad, and little boy.

He made comments to Anne about the toys in the beginning, but grew more and more absorbed as the family did ordinary things: The dad went to work, the boy played in the yard, the mom cleaned and made dinner. Most of

Anne's little patients didn't have moms who stayed home full-time and if they created such a scenario she might suspect they were copying old reruns of *Father Knows Best* or *The Brady Bunch*. This seemed typical for Danny's family, however.

Soon, the boy in Danny's play story who had behaved so nicely turned into a brat. He threw his toys around, knocked over a lamp, refused to eat his carrots. The father yelled at him and sent him to his room, but the bad behavior persisted, so the father announced, "I don't like bad kids. I'm getting out of here."

Now Danny's story became darker. He took toy animals from the basket, the more ferocious the better—lions, tigers, alligators, and snakes. They lurked in the yard outside the house. The biggest, fiercest lion crawled up a wall and sneaked into an upstairs window.

The boy knew the lion was up there. He tried desperately to warn his mom. But she went up, and the lion attacked.

Anne steeled herself not to interfere even though there was real horror in Danny's voice as he imitated the savage growls and the terrified screams. Several times the lion chased the mother to the edge of the stairs and the little boy cried, "Look out! Look out!" Just as the lion knocked the mother to the floor, the boy found his father's gun and raced up to shoot the lion.

Danny stood very still, staring at his created scene, unable to go on.

"Isn't it safe for the mom to come down now?" Anne asked softly.

"No. She hurt her leg. She'll fall down and die."

"Maybe the boy could hold her hand and help her."

Danny thought about it, nodded, then manipulated the toys so that the boy guided his mother down the stairs. As soon as she was safely down, Danny dropped the toys and crawled into Anne's lap. Quite often children don't need to talk about their play therapy, and Anne never asked them to discuss it, especially not young children.

So it went against her rule to push things further, and she only did it out of her urgent concern for Danny's safety. Hoping to lead him into telling her more about the murder, she said, "You know, Danny, people don't always die when they fall down. Sometimes they just bump themselves and get an owie."

"Uh-uh," Danny said, his body growing tense. "Blood comes out. Bugs crawl on their face." His voice dropped to an anguished whisper. "Bugs crawl on their eyes and their eyes stay open and they don't wake up and—and—"

"I know, oh, honey, I know. Bad people do things, and people can die. But it isn't always that way, Danny. It isn't."

She held him for a few minutes, murmuring reassurances until he said, "I don't want to play anymore today."

He looked a little pale, but at least he hadn't withdrawn from reality.

"Okay. Then let's tell your folks you're ready to go home."

The Lewises jumped up anxiously as Anne and Danny came out. "We had a productive session," Anne told them. "I think Danny's worried that stairs can be dangerous places for grown-ups, and he'd really like it if he could hold his mom's hand every time she goes up and down, just to make sure she's safe for now. Is that what you'd like to do, Danny?"

He nodded soberly.

"Is that all right with you, Natalie?"

"Well, of course."

"Promise?" Danny asked.

She dropped down on her heels to hug her son. "Yes, sweetheart, I promise."

"Was that it?" Glen asked. "I mean, was there anything else?"

"Not today," Anne said. "Therapy's not a quick process, so, please, both of you, don't expect miracles."

Natalie readily agreed to another session the next day. Glen went along with her decision, but Anne thought he still was not sold on the idea. Now, knowing his background, she understood why.

After the Lewises left, Anne sat in her quiet office, making notes and marshaling her thoughts. Danny had revealed nothing at all directly related to the kidnapping during the play therapy. The little boy in the drama never left the house. Anne thought this was because he was dealing with his most immediate fear. Dorie had fallen down and died; the same thing might happen to his mother. He had seized on the stairs as a threat—not such a reach, after all. People did trip and fall down steps; clumsy three-year-olds did it all the time.

Wild animals had massed outside the home, she noted, and not a lop-eared bunny in the bunch. Although the animals seemed an obvious symbol, Anne had learned through experience that at best her interpretations were only useful as a guideline since they were based on her own experience, not the child's. And she cautioned herself about another observation: The toy parents were affectionate with the child, but they never touched each other. Still, if she had to speculate, she'd guess that Natalie and Glen Lewis's problems had started long before Danny was kidnapped.

And for all her doubt, the session had gone well enough. She'd kept the stress at acceptable levels for Danny until the end. She shuddered, remembering his description of

Dorie's corpse. She'd had no choice but to end the session there. But now she knew one thing for sure: He had seen Dorie fall. And if he'd seen that, he must have seen the person who hit her. He must have seen the killer.

13

Anne knew Bern would want to know what she had learned from Danny right away. He answered his phone at the station with a distracted hello, then asked her to wait while he put her on hold for a second. When he picked up again, he told her he was in the lieutenant's office because he had a couple of people at his desk.

"A neighbor of Dorie Wineski's and one of his friends. They saw somebody on the street the night she died."

"Was it Tony Sales?" Anne asked, hoping it was true.

"Actually, the description's pretty vague. But the artist's going to work with them. How did it go with Danny?"

"He saw the murder, Bern."

"He said that?"

"No, not exactly." She told him what had happened during the session.

"Doesn't give us anything to go on," he said. "Anne, can't you hurry this up a little? It's for Danny's own good."

"I'm trying. But it's easy to push him over the line—" Especially when you're not sure where the line should be drawn. "Today—he talked about seeing somebody dead. Not Dorie specifically. I don't think he's ready to get that close yet. But at least it's progress."

"How about bringing him in for a look at Sales? Too soon?"

"Yes, but maybe, in a day or two—"

And if Danny had seen Tony hit Dorie, if he stood and witnessed that terrible violence, heard the ugly words and the sound of fist striking flesh, the thump of Dorie's head hitting the table, would she cause irreparable harm by forcing such a horrible memory?

"Anne?" Bern said sharply. "Are you okay?"

"I'm fine, just tired, and—I'm all right."

"Then maybe you're not up to this, but I said I'd pass it along. Tony wants to talk to you."

This didn't surprise Anne. In situations like the one with Tony Sales, a bond is formed, even though the therapist might prefer it hadn't. To tell the truth, just the thought of being near the man made her flesh crawl.

Suddenly she was aware that Bern was anxious to hear her answer. "Did you say I'd do it?"

It was Bern the cop who said, "It might not be a bad idea."

Just doing his job, and what difference did it make? She would do it because of Danny.

"Okay, I'll see him."

"Today?"

"I'll come as soon as I can."

Bern took her back to a small interrogation room that held only a table and two chairs and smelled of stale cigarette smoke. Tony waited in one of the chairs, ankles shackled to the heavy legs. He had been brought over from Maricopa County's Madison Street jail and wore the jailhouse uniform: a loose blue shirt tucked into blue pants, baggy on his wiry frame. The black hair straggled, lank and oily, around his face. A tic jumped in his cheek, and his cuticles had been bitten raw. He'd come down from the drug- and emotion-induced high of the day before, but he looked even more dangerous. He reminded Anne of something in the weasel family—a mink or a ferret—never adjusting to imprisonment no matter how long the animal is caged, always looking for a way out.

Was he the thing that haunted Danny's nightmares?

"I've already explained the rules, Tony," Bern said, "but here they are again: One, either somebody's in the room with you and Dr. Menlo, or the cuffs stay on. So which will it be?"

Tony glowered, not liking either choice. "Keep me chained up like a fuckin' dog, I guess."

"Okay. Now, two: Nothing you say is privileged. She works for the department."

"Yeah, yeah, you told me."

Bern had other rules he had explained to Anne. Do not, under any circumstances, go within reach of the prisoner. Keep the table between you. Call the officer stationed right outside if you feel you need him. Call him immediately.

As soon as the door closed behind Bern, Tony said, "That ain't right, is it? You're a doctor, so you can't tell him what I say."

"This is not quite the normal doctor-patient relationship," Anne said, "so nothing is confidential. If you're uncomfortable with that, then we don't have to talk. I'm only here because you asked me to come."

He thought about it, weighing his chances, then shrugged. "Nobody else is gonna know where I'm comin' from, you know? You were there. You saw the kinda shit they pulled on me."

Anne put her arms on the table and leaned forward, making direct eye contact, thinking how much he reminded her of the rattlesnake Bern had surprised in her carport a few mornings ago. If she had to choose, however, she thought she'd rather deal with the snake.

She kept such preferences out of her voice as she asked, "Why do you think they treated you that way, Tony?"

"Because they like to hassle people. They like comin' into your place and pushin' you around."

"Why don't you tell me what happened."

She didn't have to ask him twice. One of the problems working with children was their difficulty in verbalizing situations and emotions. This was not a problem with Tony. He told her in vivid detail about the cops storming into his trailer. How they jacked him up against the wall, jammed a nightstick in his kidneys, twisted his arms.

"They kept talkin' about a murder charge, for Christ's sake. It didn't make no sense. No wonder I was freakin' out. I didn't wanta hurt nobody. You saw that."

What she saw was the cunning intelligence in his eyes, and she suspected he wanted an ally, hopefully one with a psychologist's credentials who would stand up for him in court.

"I understand that you were scared," she said. "But the police did have reason to bring you in for questioning. They found your fingerprints in Dorie Wineski's house."

"I never said I didn't know her. But I didn't kill her, Anne. And I sure as hell didn't kidnap no little kid. The cop said something about a ransom, but that went right over my head. I fuckin' couldn't believe it when my lawyer told me. I mean, Dorie's maybe murder two, but kidnapping— Jesus Christ. And they're gonna nail me for it, too."

There was true despair and desperation in his eyes, although Anne realized this was no indication of innocence.

"It's a frightening situation," Anne said. "Maybe you ought to cooperate with the police. I know Detective Pagett, Tony. He's not out to railroad anybody."

"Yeah, right," he said bitterly. "You never had to deal with the system. They need to hang somebody, and I'm the fuckin' fall guy. The thing is, I didn't even see Dorie for at least a week before she died. When the news first came on TV, I couldn't believe it. I thought somebody musta broke into her house, was maybe robbin' the place. They didn't say nothin' about the kid."

"It's always a shock hearing about the death of a friend."

"Yeah, you said it. I mean, Dorie and me weren't real close. We just got together once in a while, and it was okay, but somebody like Dorie—I mean, I'm real easy, but anything permanent I want a woman who's strictly into guys, you know?"

"And Dorie wasn't?"

"No, but, hey, live and let live, I always say."

"Did you know any of the other people in her life?"

"You mean like who else she was sleepin' with?" He leaned forward, a confidential note in his voice. Anne was sure he had wanted her to ask this question.

"Well, she always mentioned Florence," he said. "I think that's that big-assed woman next door, but I don't know for sure. Hey, that would be cozy, wouldn't it? The two of them snatchin' the kid."

And it would let Tony off the hook.

"The last time you saw Dorie—what did you talk about?"

"Oh, nothin' special. This and that."

"Did she give you any hint of her plans? Was she nervous? Preoccupied?"

And when did she stop being the observer and listener here and become the interrogator? And what made her think she knew what she was doing?

"Dorie did seem in a hurry to get rid of me." Something

shifted in the black gaze. The tic jumped in his cheek. "But—no, she didn't say nothin'."

Although Anne had no basis for the feeling except pure intuition, she was sure he was lying. And she realized she was out of her depth here. More than likely the man sitting across the table had conspired with Dorie to take Danny from his father's car and hold him for ransom, then fought with Dorie and killed her. That he had not killed Danny, too, was the only fact that made Anne hesitant to believe totally in his guilt.

"I keep thinkin' about that poor little boy," Tony said. "They said on TV last night he was there when they found Dorie. Makes you wonder—you suppose he saw her gettin' whacked? I mean like the Lewis kid's an eyewitness?"

Her heart gave a sudden, painful lurch. "How do you know the child's name?"

"Hey, this is America. If they're gonna accuse you of something, they gotta tell you what it is."

Aware of the animal brightness of Tony's eyes, she said carefully, "Well, if you're innocent, you don't have to worry about the child identifying you, do you?"

"He could make a mistake. He's a little kid. Hell, half the time people don't know what they're seein'."

"All the more reason for you to talk to Detective Pagett. Give him something to work with—like the information about Dorie's neighbor."

"I don't know, Anne. I don't trust him. Maybe if you stayed with us—then I'd be sure he couldn't pull any shit. Would you do that?"

"All right, if you want me to."

"Yeah, well, I'd better run it by my lawyer first, but I guess it couldn't hurt. There's just one thing. Anne? My stomach's in knots, and when I woke up this morning, I was shakin' all over. Maybe you could write me a prescription, nothin' too strong, just something to take the edge off, you know?''

"I'm sorry," Anne said. "I'm not an M.D. I can't prescribe medication. I'm sure they have a physician on staff. Ask to see him."

"Oh, yeah, lotta fuckin' good that would do." For an instant frustration wiped away the earnest facade and let her see the ruthless con man underneath. Then he managed to cover up with a halfhearted grin. "You see how they treat people." He jerked on his ankle chain to demonstrate. "Tell the guy out there he needs to come and walk the dog, will you?''

Anne and Bern sat in a corner of Morrie's Deli, drinking iced tea and waiting for their food. Since it would take some time to get Tony's P.D. back down to headquarters, Bern had insisted on taking Anne for the lunch they missed the day before. He listened intently as she recounted her conversation with Tony, especially interested in Tony's mention of Florence.

"Florence Louella Mosk," Bern said. "Good old Flo."

"You met her?" Anne asked.

"Oh, yeah."

He told Anne about Dorie's heavyweight, taciturn neighbor.

"Maybe she's the one," Anne said.

"A possibility anyway."

The food arrived, and they ate in silence for a minute or two before she said, "How did the sketch turn out?"

Bern chewed a bite of his pastrami sandwich and swallowed. "Pretty much a bust. My two guys came up with a tall-average, skinny-medium, Caucasian-Hispanic male. The more they talked about it, the more they thought they wouldn't know the guy if they fell over him. I went ahead and put Tony in a lineup, and guess what?''

"They didn't recognize him.''

"Well, it was a long shot.''

"I hope you get more out of him than I did,'' Anne said. "I know he was trying to manipulate me, that most of what he said was lies.''

"They always lie, Anne. They try to work you, they try to work me, they try to work the system.''

Bern's father had died before Anne and Bern met, so she never met the man. But, just then, she felt his presence as surely as though his ghost were sitting at their table. Bern's job naturally reinforced the cynicism he'd learned from his dad. Police work, by its nature, required an expectation of the worst in human behavior. After her talk with Tony Sales, she understood more than ever why this was so.

"Bern, is there any way Tony could have found out that I'm Danny's therapist?''

"I guess so. Maybe his attorney told him. It's not exactly a secret. Why?''

"I don't know. The idea just gives me the creeps.'' She put her fork on the table, feeling a little sick. "I keep wondering—if Danny saw Dorie's murder, why wasn't he killed, too?''

Bern pushed aside his plate. "Don't forget. Dorie didn't die right away. He—or she—probably had no idea Dorie was in such bad shape.''

"Or maybe the killer didn't see Danny.''

"That's another possibility.''

"Something else that bothers me,'' Anne said. "Aside from the murder, do you think this person tried to arrange it so Danny never saw him—?''

"Or her.''

"Or her—because wouldn't it be a risk that Danny could

identify his kidnapper? Of course, Danny knew Dorie. He could tell the police where he had been held. Unless . . .''

Anne was suddenly struck by the full horror of her chain of thought. ''They were going to kill him.''

Bern was already ahead of her, had thought of it before. ''Probably.''

They sat in silence. No need to put into words what they were both thinking: Danny could finger this person for murder and kidnapping. And they weren't the only ones who knew this. The killer knew it, too.

14

Anne had heard Bern talk enough about how jail seemed to have a swinging door these days. Back at Bern's desk waiting for Tony's attorney, she said, "You're going to keep Tony locked up, aren't you?"

"I'll give it my best shot," Bern promised. "We've got plenty of charges without the murder and kidnapping."

But it seemed that Tony and his attorney had their own ideas about those charges. When Larry Fries, Tony's public defender, met them preparatory to the interview with Tony, he declared his client wanted a deal before he would talk. After all, he had not been identified by Wayne Jensen in the lineup.

"Deal?" Bern said incredulously. "In the first place you know I don't have the authority. Second, I haven't even begun to put together a case. I can probably nail his ass with or without any conversation. You two better have another talk, Larry. He needs me. I don't need him."

Anne knew Bern was bluffing, but did Larry Fries know it?

"You got to give the guy something," Larry said. "He says he didn't kill the woman or take the little boy. But he did know her. If he cooperates fully, maybe he can help you close the case."

"And maybe he's blowing smoke. Look, unless he wants to confess or he can ID the killer, all he can do is save me a little time. If he does, I'll go to bat for him with the county attorney. That's all I can promise till I see what he's got."

"Okay. I'll ask Tony what he wants to do."

Tony must have decided he had no choice because Larry was back in ten minutes to say his client had agreed to cooperate. Or maybe, as Bern had said back at the restaurant, Tony thought he'd have another try at working the system.

The three of them went to the same interrogation room Tony and Anne had been in earlier. Tony was already there drinking something, dark and bubbly over ice in a big paper cup decorated with golden arches. Anne smelled the fizzy odor of cola along with a faint stench of perspiration. Tony's hair had been scraped back from his face and was held at the nape of his neck with a rubber band. His cheek still twitched, and his collar was damp with sweat.

Two more chairs had been brought in. Larry joined his client on one side of the table; Anne and Bern sat on the other. Anne noticed that Tony was no longer cuffed; however, a uniformed cop stood outside the door.

"You had lunch, Tony?" Bern asked solicitously.

"Yeah. Larry brought me a burger—some real food."

"Good. Like a cigarette?" Bern gestured to a lone ashtray on the table.

"No, man. I don't smoke. Those things'll kill you."

"Okay, then. Let's do it."

Bern turned on a tape machine and went through the legalities of identifying everybody present and having Tony acknowledge his consent to being taped.

"I just want to say," Tony added earnestly, "that I wouldn't be doin' this if it wasn't for Dr. Menlo. She made me see it was the right thing to do."

"Yeah," Bern said dryly. "I'm sure that's why you're doing it. Are you employed, Tony?"

"I was. Probably not anymore," he said bitterly. "Baby Time Warehouse. I run a forklift."

"How long did you know Dorie Wineski?"

"More than a year and a half, because I was at her house for a Christmas party. Not this past Christmas. The one before."

"She invited you?"

"No. I came with a friend."

"Who was that?"

"Some guy I met in a bar. Said there was gonna be free booze and food." He shook his head, disgusted by the memory. "Frozen pizza and no-name beer. I remember that. And eggnog. Jesus, I hate eggnog."

"But you liked Dorie."

"Yeah, sort of. We hit it off, I guess."

According to Tony they became intimate right away. Anne wondered if this was true or was simply presented to boost the man's ego. He might be in big trouble, but she was sure he enjoyed the drama, playing mostly to her, probably fantasizing about the terrible things he could do if he put his mind to it.

Tony sipped Coke and said in the beginning he saw Dorie maybe once a week, sometimes staying over. He figured she might be seeing other guys. What did he care?

"You told Dr. Menlo Dorie also had affairs with women. Did that bother you?"

"Nah. I'm a broad-minded guy. And I think it was just that one woman, Florence—the one who lives next door."

He said Dorie had a problem with booze but never got mean when she was drinking. "You know Florence's dog? Dorie was the only one could get near that mean bastard. She used to buy liver for him."

He drained the Coke, keeping a chunk of ice in his mouth, rattled it against his teeth as he said he'd never heard the two women argue, but one time Florence was leaving just as he came in, and Dorie was crying.

"She had this red mark on her face. I think Florence hit her."

"You ever hit her, Tony?"

"Me? No—"

"Never knocked her around a little?"

"That's enough," Larry said. "He told you he never assaulted Dorie Wineski."

"He hits other women, though."

"No, I don't," Tony declared, a little hurt by the accusation, looking to Anne as though she could verify this fact.

"No?" Bern took a notepad from his jacket pocket and flipped it open. "How about Crystal Stumpf? She was beaten so badly she wound up in the emergency room. Signed a complaint against you."

"Oh, yeah, Crystal. That was different. I was drunk."

"And when you beat up Maria Munoz—you drunk then?"

"No, I was smoking some bad shit that night."

Bern put away the pad. "But you never got drunk or smoked any bad dope around Dorie?"

"No."

"Come on. You said Dorie drank. You mean you never had a few beers with her?"

"Well—sure."

"How about last Wednesday night. How much drinking did you do then?"

"A lot. But not at Dorie's. I was in a bar, a couple of bars."

He gave a list of the ones he remembered but was vague

about who he'd seen or talked to, telling his attorney, "You got to make the cops check that out, Larry."

"Oh, we will," Bern promised. "Back to Dorie. Was she employed during the time you knew her?"

"Most of the time. At first she worked at this day-care place. Real little kids. She liked kids. But I guess she missed too many days, 'cause they canned her. After that she got jobs workin' in people's houses. A nanny, she called herself. The jobs didn't last too long."

Anne wondered about people like the Lewises who had hired Dorie Wineski. Didn't they check her references? Of course, her love for children would have weighed heavily, maybe even influencing parents not to look too closely at her background.

"Did Dorie talk to you about these families?" Bern asked.

"Some. Mostly what the rug rats did."

But according to Tony they never discussed how rich the families were, and he wasn't ever curious. Sure, he knew they must have had some dough. They could afford to pay Dorie five or six bucks an hour, cash most of the time and no taxes.

"What about the Lewises—did Dorie discuss them with you?"

"Lewis—that's the little kid she's supposed to've snatched, ain't it?"

"That's the one. Do you know Danny Lewis?"

"No," Tony declared.

And he never visited Dorie while she was baby-sitting, never picked her up there after work, didn't even know where they lived. Anne watched him begin to tear the top of the paper cup, making quarter-inch slits all around the rim. The cuticles on both hands were red and raw.

"But did Dorie ever talk to you about the Lewises?" Bern persisted.

"Some. She liked the little kid. And the mother—Dorie said she was nice."

"How did she feel about Mr. Lewis?"

"I don't know. She liked him okay, I guess. Of course, after the guy fired her, he wasn't her favorite person."

"Did she have a grudge against him? Talk about getting even?"

Tony finished with the rim of the cup, stared down at his handiwork for a second, then set it aside. "Nah, she wasn't mad at him. She knew she fucked up. She hit the bottle pretty hard." He looked at Anne. "Something like that can make you real depressed, can't it? That's what she mostly was: depressed."

Dorie only worked one other job after the Lewises, and that lasted a few weeks. He didn't remember where. She said she couldn't get unemployment because of the way she got paid.

"So she was having money problems?"

"Sure. Ain't we all?"

"Okay, Tony, let's talk about the day Dorie died. What time did you leave her?"

"I didn't leave her," Tony said indignantly. "I told you: I wasn't there."

"Oh, right, so you said. When did you see her the last time?"

"Had to be at least a week before she died—maybe longer."

He said he just went by to say hello. Brought a six-pack. Dorie didn't want any. She was on the wagon. She was cleaning the house up a little bit, running the vacuum and using one of those fluffy white dusters on a long stick. While he talked, Tony picked up the cup and began bending down every other torn section around the top. He had asked if she was expecting company, but she said no, she was tired of living in a pigsty. "Now, looks like she was cleanin' up for the kid."

A child she was fond of, Anne thought. At least Danny would have been well cared for while Dorie was alive. Could she really have planned to kill the boy after the ransom was paid?

Tony was getting bored. He slouched down in the chair, his mind on other things. No, Dorie hadn't mentioned the Lewises that day or Florence, didn't talk about much of anything. "I could take a hint. I picked up my beer and went home."

"And that's the last time you saw her?"

"The last time."

"Tell you what, Tony," Bern said. "How about we set you up with the polygraph tomorrow?"

"You mean a lie detector?" He sat up straight and turned to his lawyer. "Larry, what's this shit?"

"First I heard of it," Larry said.

"If your client's innocent, I don't see why he should object," Bern said.

"I know guys in Perryville who got put there by that damned machine, guys who never done half the stuff the cops said they did."

"Tony, the test is not admissible in court," Bern said. "This would just be a way to eliminate you as a suspect."

"Well, I don't care. I ain't takin' no fuckin' tests," Tony declared.

"Okay. Your choice," Bern said. "But it would go a long way toward convincing me you're telling the truth here." Bern took a pad from his jacket pocket and began writing something on it. "Right now, you can do something for me."

He finished the writing, holding the pad where Anne could see the block letters. YOU CALL THE COPS OR DO ANYTHING DUMB LIKE MARKING THE MONEY, YOU'LL GET DANNY BACK IN PIECES. Anne remembered Glen's account of the kidnapper saying this to him on the phone.

Bern handed the note to Tony. "I want you to read this into the tape recorder."

Tony scanned the page, his lips moving, forming the first few words. "What is this? What kinda shit are you tryin' to pull? Will you fuckin' *do* something here?" he demanded, glaring at his attorney.

"Stop the tape," Larry said, and Bern complied.

After Larry looked at the note, he said, "I take it this is the ransom demand made over the phone in the Lewis case?"

Bern confirmed that it was, adding, "Your client agreed to cooperate."

"I been cooperatin'," Tony said. "Ain't that what I been doin', Anne?"

"Yes, you have," Anne said soothingly. "You've answered every question. If you didn't make that call, Tony, then I don't see why you should be worried about reading this for Detective Pagett."

"They can do things with tape, make you come out soundin' different."

"I'm listening. I can tell if that tape is doctored," Anne said.

"I still don't know—"

"The sooner Detective Pagett can eliminate you as a suspect, the sooner he can concentrate on looking for somebody else. Dorie was your friend, Tony. Don't you want the person who killed her to pay for the crime?"

"Well, sure, but—" He looked at Larry.

"Keep in mind that so far your client has given me

squat," Bern said, an edge to his voice. "And remind him that just because he tells me he didn't do something, that doesn't make it true."

"Yeah, okay," Tony said without giving his attorney a chance to reply. "Okay, I'll do it."

After the recording was done, the two Sheriff's Department deputies took Tony back off to jail, and Larry Fries made a quick departure.

"What's next?" Anne asked as they walked back to Bern's desk in the squad room. "Are you interviewing the neighbor—Florence Mosk?"

"Tomorrow. I'm seeing the Lewises"—he looked at his watch—"in about forty-five minutes."

"They're not bringing Danny down here?"

"No. They'll take turns so one of them can be at home with the boy. Glen's first."

How did Bern do this day after day? Like her he was always poking and prying, digging for the truth. No, not like her at all. She used those hard-won nuggets to try to help her patient; Bern would play on a suspect's fears, use everything short of lies and coercion to find a vulnerable spot, then squeeze until the ugly truth came out, like pus from a boil.

And he did it with such confidence. Didn't he ever wonder if he'd gone too far? Overlooked some hidden truth? If he had such doubts, they never showed.

For herself, she wasn't sure if she could sort out the lies in Tony Sales's statement and didn't envy Bern the task. This suspect was a clever manipulator and a first-class liar.

Will Hanson was at his desk, telephone to his ear, signaling to Bern.

"Be right back," Bern said and walked over.

Anne sat on the edge of Bern's desk to wait, still thinking

about Tony Sales. Something had gone wrong a long time ago with Sales when he was a little boy like Danny. Nobody had seen it—or nobody cared. What went on in a child's mind was at once simplistic and terrifyingly complex. Which made it so important to watch and listen in therapy, to give the right reassurance . . .

Bad people do things, and people can die. Her words to Danny this morning rang in her head, and she realized immediately she had made a horrible mistake.

Most of the time children Danny's age accepted the blame for everything. They saw themselves as the center of the universe, controlling things around them and therefore responsible for terrible events. *Bad people do things, and people can die.* My God, what had she been thinking of? More than likely in Danny's mind he was already to blame for Dorie's death, awful enough, and now he would assign the title of Bad Person to himself as well.

Shaken to the core, she wondered how many other mistakes of omission or commission she had made. All she could do was get to Danny, try to fix this one, and worry about any more later.

15

Bern waited for Will to complete his call, observing that the stacks of paperwork on Will's desk were as high as his own, thinking how much more remained to be written after today's interviews.

Will hung up and said, "That was the guy who does the local business column for the *Republic*."

"Alan—something."

"Alan Dean. I tracked him down at home. He knew about Fitness Unlimited, about how Lewis and his partner split up. They didn't part on friendly terms. Something else. I feel like an idiot for not picking up on it. Joe Ferraro's uncle is Leo Ferraro."

"Jesus," Bern said. "No wonder the name sounded familiar."

At the present time Leo Ferraro was serving life in Leavenworth, but for years he had been the major muscle for the Vegas mafia. And, although City Hall vehemently denied it, there were those who thought the tentacles of organized crime had reached into Phoenix.

"This kidnapping—" Will shook his head. "Doesn't sound like their style to me."

"Me, either," Bern agreed. "Any reason to suspect the nephew is in the family business?"

"Lot of suspicions," Will said. "Nothing to take to court. You'll want to talk to him."

"Oh, yeah," Bern said.

"Like company?" Will asked hopefully. "My kid's swimming in a meet at four-thirty, but if we went now . . ."

Bern said he had a couple more interviews scheduled. Will looked disappointed but brightened when Bern said he would like Will to sit in on those two. While Will went off to get a cup of coffee, Bern turned to go back to his desk.

He was only a step or two away from Anne before he saw the look on her face and felt a twinge of alarm. He was used to dealing with slime like Tony, but Anne wasn't. She must be having a delayed reaction, even though he thought she'd handled the interview just fine. Now she seemed so small and fragile, her face gone pale and her eyes haunted.

"Anne?" he said, really worried.

"I have to go," she said.

"Annie, what is it?"

"I have something to do. Call you later."

She headed for the door, leaving him standing there with the premonition he had the other night returning in a cold tide, his father's dour words echoing in his head.

The worst thing that can happen . . .

Just as Anne approached the Lewis house, she saw the Lexus pull out of the driveway in a hurry with Glen at the wheel, late for his appointment with Bern. She was relieved that she'd missed him because she really didn't want to explain to Danny's father why she was here. She hadn't phoned ahead for the same reason. Glen had enough problems trusting psychologists already.

Maybe with good reason. Maybe the psychiatrist who

treated his sister had made mistakes, too. Said stupid, careless things that led to Angie being placed in an institution.

Anne parked on the driveway, walked to the door, and rang the bell. After a short wait, she heard dead bolts being turned, and Natalie opened the door, looking surprised to see her. Danny peeked around his mother, pressed right up against her legs.

"Hi," Anne said, trying to keep a casual tone in her voice, even as her heart turned over at the sight of Danny's solemn little face. "I hope you don't mind my stopping by. I was thinking about Danny and wanted to see how he was doing."

"No, of course not. Come in. We were coloring in the kitchen. Is that all right—?"

"Sure," Anne said and followed them to the room where a small boy's cheerful clutter of coloring books, crayons, and a spill of bright construction paper warmed up the designer coldness of glossy white cabinets, black appliances, and oak floor.

"Danny was really tired after we left your office," Natalie said. "He went to sleep in the car and didn't wake up when we brought him inside. Then he slept for a couple of hours."

Danny climbed up on a chair at the table, selecting a crayon and ducking his head away, although Anne was sure he heard every word.

"He hasn't talked about his therapy," Natalie went on. "Is that normal?"

"Whatever Danny decides to do is perfectly okay," Anne said. "He may feel it's a personal thing right now, just between him and me."

Danny looked up through his long eyelashes and rewarded her with a shy smile. "I'm doing Tiny Toons. Wanta see?"

Anne took the chair next to him and gave the coloring book her full attention. Vivid scrawls splashed across pages filled with kiddy-sized Looney Tunes characters. Green ducks and red pigs, colored approximately within the lines.

"Good job," Anne said. "Can I help?"

"Sure. I want red, though. And purple."

Anne took a yellow crayon and looked up at Natalie who leaned against a counter. Her skin had a transparent quality with hollowed-out shadows under the cheekbones. "If you'd like to go rest for a while, I'll spend some time with Danny."

Natalie was not slow on the uptake. She understood Anne wanted to be alone with her son. "Okay. That would be nice."

There was a delay while Danny escorted his mother upstairs, and another while Anne and Natalie convinced him it was all right to leave her there and go back to the kitchen with Anne. He agreed reluctantly only after Natalie promised to call him before she came back down.

When they were settled once more at the kitchen table, Anne let a few companionable minutes drift by before she said, "Remember earlier when I said something to you about bad people, Danny? I want to make sure you understand what I meant, okay?"

"I know," he said. "Like robbers. Gang baggers." Even if he'd pronounced that last word correctly, she doubted he knew the definition. "Killers and stabbers and shooters and guys that throw matches on you and burn you up." He finished in a rush with fear alive in his eyes.

"Yes," Anne said. "That's who I was talking about. Not you. You're a good person."

He didn't argue, but she wasn't sure he believed her. He went back to his coloring, making hard purple slashes that obliterated a tree, then shoved the book away. Construction paper scattered, revealing some drawings he had made.

"Oh, look at these," Anne said, hoping to redirect his mood.

Natalie's hand was evident in the first, a sticklike sketch of a swing set that Danny must have drawn, with more realistic flowers and trees in an adult perspective.

"Very nice." Anne selected a second that showed an irregular black oval outline overlaid with scratches of blue. "What's this one?"

"Free Willy," Danny said.

Yes, Anne could see it: a killer whale in a vast ocean, rendered in a natural Picasso style.

She picked up another drawing, but barely had time to glance at it when Danny snatched it from her hand, crying, "No, I hate it, *I hate it*," as he tore the sketch apart, quickly reducing it to shreds.

A sweep of his arm sent crayons and books flying off the table. By then he was completely out of control, stiffening his body and throwing himself around. Anne caught and held him, surprised as always by the strength in small angry bodies. Too much, too soon, coming here after a session in the morning. Kids can only process so much. She didn't dare push him anymore, so she just gave him calm reassurances until he settled back against her, sobbing.

Then she rocked him a little, her face against the top of his head. The odor of his sweaty hair mixed with the smell of crayon wax and a scent of bananas ripening on a nearby counter.

While she did all the things necessary to soothe the little boy, her mind raced frantically, replaying everything she'd said and done. Even though she was preoccupied with double-checking and second-guessing, the feeling grew:

Something important had just happened here. She only wished she knew what it was.

By the time Glen Lewis arrived, Bern had rationalized his feeling of foreboding away, or at least enough to bring it down to an acceptable level so he could go on with his job.

Glen did not like being in the police station, definitely did not like being in the interrogation room. He was edgy, ill at ease, and probably feeling outnumbered with Will there. At least Bern hoped so.

"This is damned inconvenient." Glen lit a Marlboro without asking and eyed the microphone the way Bern eyed a snake. Bern thought he might start making noises about having an attorney present, but he only muttered, "I don't see why it couldn't wait."

"I figured it would be better for you to come in on a Sunday since you have a business to run. How is your business these days, Glen?"

"Why do you want to know that?"

Bern shrugged. "Well, you've been so preoccupied with Danny."

"Nice of you to worry," Glen said. "Fitness Unlimited is solid enough, so my taking off for a week isn't going to hurt anything."

"Good. When you split up with your partner—Joe Ferraro? Did that set you back any?"

"You've been checking up on me."

"I did." Will lit a cigarette, too. "Routine."

"Then you probably know Joe and I didn't part on the best of terms."

"That's what I heard. Why was that?"

"Nothing personal. We had different ideas on how to run things."

"Did Joe feel like you cheated him out of some money?" Bern squinted through the smoke, his eyes beginning to sting.

"Is this going somewhere? I thought we were here to talk about my son's kidnapping."

"Just wondered if your ex-partner had a reason to want to even the score with you."

"What? Joe? That's crazy. Where did you come up with an idea like that?"

"You don't think there's any possibility that Joe Ferraro might have kidnapped your son?"

"No," Glen declared. "Of course not."

"You knew he was connected to the mafia," Will said, making it a statement of fact.

"His *uncle* is. I don't believe in judging people by their relatives."

"You never had occasion to observe any dealings Joe Ferraro might have had with organized crime?" Bern asked.

"No, I never did," Glen said irritably and ground out his cigarette with more force than was necessary.

"How did you happen to go into business together? Were you old friends?"

"I worked for him."

"Doing what?"

"Sorry to disappoint you, but I wasn't breaking knee-caps. I managed one of the fitness centers he owns. I heard that the company that made some of our equipment was going under. I thought they turned out a good product and that the market was going to expand, especially for home equipment. I couldn't buy the company on my own, so I went to Joe."

"Okay," Bern said. "Just for the record, we're going to

go over everything that happened when Danny was kidnapped.''

He took Glen through it—leaving Danny in the car outside the dry cleaners, the note, the phone call from the kidnapper, dropping off the ransom. Everything jibed with his earlier statement.

"The thing with the ransom," Will said. "Run that by me again."

"The money was in a shopping bag from Dillard's department store." Glen had smoked two more cigarettes, and his voice was hoarse.

Will had not lit another one. *Doesn't have to,* Bern thought. The air was so thick, Will could get a hit of nicotine just by breathing the stuff.

"I left the bag in the rest room," Glen went on, "behind the wastepaper bin."

"At eight o'clock."

"Yes."

"Funny, isn't it?" Will said to Bern.

Bern said "Yeah" with no idea where Will was going.

Glen looked from one of them to the other.

"According to what the manager told you, Bern, he didn't see Mr. Lewis," Will said.

"So what?" Glen snapped. "I wasn't waving a flag."

"Seems strange, that's all. Here you come in carrying a shopping bag. You'd think the guy might have been suspicious, a little worried about shoplifting."

"Well, I didn't give too much thought to what the guy might suspect. I had a few other things on my mind at the time."

"Still," Bern said. "We only have your word that you were there."

"My word?" Glen said, astonished. "I don't believe this."

If they needed proof, he said he had some: a credit card receipt for gasoline he bought. Bern and Will started over again, picking at any detail that seemed out of line. Glen lit another cigarette, his hands not entirely steady as he struck the match, and Bern's head began to ache.

"You didn't hang around inside the station, try to get a look at the person who picked up the ransom?"

"Of course not," Glen said. "I'm not a cop. I'm just a father who was scared to death some maniac was going to kill his son if he screwed up. I could barely put gas in my car, my hands were shaking so bad. I got out of there as quickly as I could."

Suddenly Bern was struck by the conviction that he was grilling a man whose only crime was in leaving his son unattended for a few minutes, a man who had lived through hell. *I really hate this,* he thought, even as that cooler, detached side of his brain was reminding him that once the case got to court the accused was innocent until proven guilty. Until then a homicide detective didn't have the luxury of thinking about his suspect that way.

"Let's go back to Dorie Wineski," Bern said. "During the time she worked for you, did she ever bring a friend to your house?"

"I don't think so. Not when Natalie and I were around."

"Anybody pick her up after work?"

"She had her own car. Tell me something, are you guys doing anything at all to find the man who kidnapped my son? Besides harassing me, that is."

From Glen's perspective, Bern figured it was a legitimate question. He said, "We picked up somebody. A boyfriend of Ms. Wineski's. As soon as Dr. Menlo okays it, I'd like Danny to take a look at him. Meanwhile, I have a tape of the man's voice for you to listen to."

He formally ended the interview recording, then played

the tape of Tony reading what Glen had said was the gist of his conversation with the kidnapper.

"Can I hear it again?" Glen concentrated, frowning, then shook his head. "I just don't know. The guy's voice was muffled, but—no, I don't think so."

"You're sure? Listen."

Glen shook his head slowly while the tape repeated. "I'm sorry, I can't say for sure."

"All right," Bern said. "I'll probably have another one for you tomorrow."

"You have another suspect?"

"We have managed to stumble across one, yes." Bern stood up. "Will you be at work?"

"Yes." Glen got up slowly. "Look, what I said before, I didn't mean to sound ungrateful. I know you're just doing your job."

He offered Bern his hand, and Bern took it. A firm grip, if a little moist.

"No problem," Bern said. "We'll have the interview tape typed up so you can sign it when you come in to-morrow."

"Meanwhile," Will said, "I'm going to walk Glen to his car and pick up that gas receipt. Okay with you, Glen?"

Anne had hoped to avoid Glen altogether, but he arrived just as she was backing down the driveway. He raised a hand, signaling *wait*, parked next to her, got out of the Lexus, and walked over.

She rolled down her window and said, "I just stopped by to see how Danny was doing," before he could speak, adding a nervous smile to answer his questioning look.

"How is he?"

"Good, all things considered. As I told you, therapy can't be hurried. How did it go at the police station? I know

Bern—Detective Pagett—had a tape he wanted you to hear.''

''I'm not sure. But I don't think it was the guy,'' Glen said.

''Oh—I was hoping—'' That Glen would recognize Tony's voice, that the case would be over, and that Danny would be safe. ''Well, you weren't certain, were you? And there may be another suspect.''

''Oh, yeah,'' he said derisively. ''A real great one. Listen, I better get inside. Pagett wants Natalie down there. See you tomorrow.''

He stepped back and let her go on down the driveway. Despite the heat, he stood watching as she drove away.

A few blocks away, her pager went off. Bern was trying to reach her. She could have called him on the cell phone, or turned the phone on so he could call her. She did neither because she didn't know what to tell him. There was just the feeling she'd had twice now that she was missing something important—once when Danny awoke from his nightmare and reacted so violently to the stuffed rabbit, and again today with the drawing.

She tried to visualize the sheet of construction paper, but she'd had only a quick look before Danny grabbed it away. All that remained of that fleeting glimpse was an impression of black vertical lines on red paper—unrecognizable and yet somehow tantalizingly familiar.

16

At home Anne went directly to the kitchen to find something cold to drink. Not much in the refrigerator. Orange juice. An opened bottle of white wine. Four cans of beer she kept on hand for Bern. She went out for the jar of sun tea brewing on the back deck, taking along two pot holders, and good thing because the glass was too hot to pick up with her bare hands.

The porch provided only a thin strip of late afternoon shade. The heat took her breath away as she stood for a second, looking up at the hills where nothing stirred. In these temperatures life only endured, hiding in tunnels beneath the ironwood and chain fruit cholla, or holed up in dens in the rocky outcroppings. North, over the mountains, clouds boiled, their undersides a bruised purple, but her practiced eye judged there would be no rain.

Back inside, she poured the tea over a full glass of ice and sipped it while she called the station from the wall phone in the kitchen and waited for Bern to come on the line.

"Anne?" he said. "You looked upset. Where did you go in such a hurry?"

"I went to the Lewises'. Sorry. I didn't mean to worry you."

This was true, but not the whole truth. She hadn't said anything to Bern about her memories of Nicki Craig or how she felt those memories were affecting her work with Danny.

And now all she said was, "I keep hoping he'll remember something."

"Did he?"

"Not exactly. I get the feeling his subconscious is sending out signals, only I'm just not picking up on them." The ice in her glass had melted. The phone cord was long enough so she could reach the fridge for more. "I saw Glen as I was leaving. He said he couldn't identify Tony's voice for sure. Does that rule Tony out?"

"Not completely. He might have disguised his voice somehow. We'll keep on him. Meanwhile, I've got somebody else to check out."

She listened with amazement as he told her about Glen's ex-business partner. "Good Lord, Bern, you actually think the *mafia* might be mixed up in Danny's kidnapping?"

"It's a stretch," Bern admitted. "Listen, after I talk to Natalie, I'm going to do some paperwork, then I want to go see Ferraro. How would you like to go with me? I'll pick you up, and we'll get dinner somewhere along the way."

"All right," she said, surprising herself. But suddenly she knew she didn't want to spend the evening alone, and to tell the truth she was intrigued by the thought of meeting somebody with mafia connections. "Is he expecting us?"

"No. One thing about being a cop, Annie, you don't have to make appointments, and when you get there, they have to let you in."

Bern had left the door open, hoping to air out the interrogation room, but it still smelled strongly of smoke. Natalie Lewis perched on the same chair Tony had been shackled to, looking tired and pale. Her thin stalk of a neck looked too fragile to bear the weight of the dark hair that was twisted into a knot on top of her head. A yellow T-shirt was tucked into a print skirt, one of those crumpled things Anne called a broomstick skirt. Above the scooped neckline of the top, her collarbones jutted sharply against the skin.

When Will took out his cigarettes, Bern shook his head, and Will put them away.

"You didn't let that man go? The one you thought might have taken Danny?" Natalie asked. "Glen said he couldn't tell for sure about the voice, but what do you think?"

"He's still a suspect," Bern said. "We're holding him on some other charges while we investigate."

There was none of Glen's resistance as they questioned her. Bern didn't attribute this solely to the fact that Natalie was being truthful, however. Some people were naturally secretive and didn't react well to scrutiny. And some people, he reminded himself, were good at appearing to be open and honest when they were, in fact, lying through their teeth.

Natalie told them about hiring Dorie Wineski. "I still can't believe I could be so wrong about her. She seemed to really love Danny."

Dorie had never spoken much about her personal life, never mentioned a boyfriend, never brought anybody around. She answered Natalie's newspaper ad, and as soon as Dorie began work, Natalie found a bookkeeping position in a small office. She had worked before Danny was born; as a matter of fact, she had helped Glen when he started the business. She wasn't crazy about leaving Danny, but she thought she should get back into the job market. Glen didn't like it; after taxes and paying Dorie, the money was little enough, and they certainly didn't need the income.

"And he was right," Natalie said miserably. "None of this would've happened if I'd listened to him."

Bern wondered if Glen had reminded her of that these past few days. He also wondered why a woman who wanted to stay home with her baby and could afford to do so felt driven to look for a job.

"I see a lot of tension between you and your husband," Bern said gently. "I'd expect some under the circumstances. But I'm wondering if the two of you had problems before the kidnapping."

Natalie hugged her arms across her thin chest. "We—yes, but we were trying to work things out, for Danny's sake."

"What kind of things?" Will asked.

Natalie turned to Bern. "Do we have to discuss this?"

"Not money," Will persisted. "Is it another woman?"

She hunched over, avoiding their eyes, and said softly, "Things are all right now. Please—I can't talk about this anymore."

So Glen Lewis was playing around. Bern made a mental note to find out who the playmate was.

"Okay," Bern said, and she gave him a grateful look. "Since you worked with Glen at Fitness Unlimited, you know Joe Ferraro."

"Not well. I'm not sure anybody did."

Busy with his other ventures, Ferraro pretty much left the business in Glen's hands, Natalie said. Things were fine until Joe started taking a more active role. He and Glen argued a lot, petty stuff. The real problems began after she became pregnant with Danny and quit working at Fitness Unlimited. Glen never explained in detail what those problems were.

Natalie registered shocked disbelief at the news of Ferraro's possible connection to organized crime. Obviously her husband kept a lot of things from her. Her reaction to the idea of Ferraro being involved in Danny's kidnapping reminded Bern of a nonswimmer thrown into deep water.

"Dorie—that was bad enough. But if it could be Joe—my God—it could be anybody." Her voice was choked with horror.

"That's right," Bern said, "so I want you to think about it, Natalie. Make us a list."

"Gardener, cleaning people, any workmen who've been around, especially anybody you deal with that Glen hasn't met," Will said.

"Why? I don't understand."

"You said you never spoke to the kidnapper," Bern said.

"No, I didn't."

"Tell me about that."

"That first time—I picked up the phone and said hello, but nobody answered. I knew somebody was there; I could tell. I—I said something like: Please, please, talk to me; tell me my baby's all right. Then Glen snatched the phone away."

"Did this happen more than once?"

"Yes. One other time. Glen told me to stop answering, that I was making the guy mad. I didn't want to do that. I was so afraid he'd do something to Danny." She hunched forward, giving Bern a startled look. "He was afraid I'd recognize his voice, wasn't he? That's why he wouldn't talk to me."

"It's possible. Let's talk about the night you and Glen paid the ransom."

She said Glen brought the money in a briefcase. They put it in a shopping bag with crumpled tissue paper on top. He left the house about seven-thirty. She left about eight.

"I'd been there ever since Danny was taken," Natalie said. "I couldn't stand it anymore."

"Where did you go?"

"I don't know. Just—around."

"You stop someplace?" Will asked. "Visit a friend? Have coffee?"

"No, I just drove." A flush suffused her pale skin, a rosy stain blooming in her cheeks and down her face. "I wasn't gone that long. I had to get away, that's all."

They picked at it a little longer but got nowhere. She answered their questions in a tense monotone and bolted from the room when he ended the interview.

"Hiding something," Will observed. "Think she went to visit Dorie?"

"I wish to hell I knew," Bern said.

Bern arrived at Anne's around five o'clock, took a quick shower, and put on a suit, a white shirt, and a tie. Anne was never one to dither over what to wear, but she found herself at a loss: What is appropriate attire for visiting a member of the mob? A *suspected* member, she corrected herself quickly. Finding the whole train of thought a bit ridiculous, she dressed for dinner instead in light gray slacks and jacket made of crinkled rayon gauze and a white silk blouse.

Bern said he wanted to go by Ferraro's first. The fact that the dinner hour was fast approaching didn't bother Bern. "If he's eating in, it's a good time to catch him. If he's out, we'll go back later."

They went south through Cave Creek. The small downtown stuck close to the frontier look. A street sign pictured a serpentine squiggle and warned: SNAKE CROSSING. Another forbade shooting within one-quarter mile of any building. Past Carefree there were huge stretches of open land. The developers were steadily pushing north, however. It was only a matter of time before the roadside stands offering cattle skulls and strings of dried red chilies became just another memory of a picturesque past.

"These signals you think Danny's sending," Bern said. "Maybe we should talk about it. I'm not a psychologist, but I'm pretty good at solving puzzles."

"All right, but it's pretty vague. That first night at the Lewises'—remember when Danny woke up from the nightmare? He was saying 'bunny' or at least that's what I thought he was saying. I offered him his stuffed rabbit, and he got even more upset. I know that doesn't sound important. But at the time, I just got this feeling—" She broke off and shook her head.

"It's called a hunch," Bern said. "Cops get them, too. I trust your instincts. If you think it means something, it probably does. Anything else?"

She told him about the drawing. "I have no idea what it was, but I feel as if I *ought* to. I don't know. Maybe I just want Danny to tell us something so desperately, I'm reading things that aren't there."

She stared out the window. The first houses of a tract flashed by. A brand-new strip mall up ahead. Civilization.

"Anne, I know how something like this can drive you nuts," Bern said quietly, "but there's more going on here. I wish you'd tell me what it is."

And if she did tell him, what would he say? That Nicki's suicide all those years ago was not her fault. To let it go and stop beating up on herself. Well-intentioned advice that would be delivered with fierce protectiveness, but not what she needed to hear.

"I'm sorry. I can't talk about it right now."

"Is it that little girl back when you were in school? The one who—"

"Please, Bern. Let it alone."

He braked hard and turned into the last entrance to the strip mall, the sudden maneuver skidding the tires and giving Anne a little vertigo. As soon as he got the Jeep stopped, he undid his seat belt and reached for her, cursing at her shoulder belt and fumbling to undo the latch.

Then he pulled her into his arms and covered her mouth with his in a hard, demanding kiss. She didn't know if he was seeking affirmation or asserting some sort of relationship rights, but she did know that what she saw on his face had been closer to panic than anger.

Whatever the emotion was, she could feel it subsiding as his embrace loosened. He kissed her again, lightly, let her go, and moved back behind the wheel.

Anne didn't trust her voice until they were moving again. She said, "Not that I'm complaining, but what brought that on?"

"Nothing that I can talk about, babe. Nothing that makes sense."

"Well—okay. I can certainly understand that."

"Yeah, I'm sure you can. Oh, Annie." He gave her a wry grin. "Ain't we a pair?"

17

The Ferraros lived in Biltmore Estates, an area where huge old houses sat on half acres of lush lawns amid luxuriant trees and shrubs. Bern parked on the circular drive in the shade of mature oaks and royal palms. It was definitely cooler here. Anne thought about the amount of water required for that drop in temperature as she and Bern got out and went up five broad steps to the porticoed entry.

Mrs. Ferraro answered the door, summoning her husband immediately when Bern showed her his identification, more annoyed than flustered. Not a thick-necked bodyguard in sight, Anne noted.

Unless beaded gowns and tuxes were their standard dinner dress, the Ferraros were leaving for a big night out. The two conferred at the bottom of the sweeping staircase, Mrs. Ferraro doing most of the talking. Then she went upstairs, and Mr. Ferraro stalked over, tall and elegant in his Armani formal wear. His dark hair was streaked with gray and combed straight back. He had peculiar eyes, not quite brown, almost a feline yellow.

"I can't imagine what you want," Ferraro said, "but whatever it is can wait until tomorrow."

"No, sir, I'm afraid not," Bern said politely. "It concerns homicide and kidnapping. Bern Pagett,'' he added as introduction and nodded to Anne, ''Anne Menlo.''

Not Anne Menlo the psychologist, Anne noticed, which left her status open to interpretation. Ferraro gave her a speculative look, but if he had doubts about whether she met the height requirement for the police department, he kept them to himself.

''Someplace we can sit down and talk for a few minutes?'' Bern inquired, pleasantly enough.

''On second thought,'' Ferraro said, ''maybe I'd better have my attorney present.''

''Of course. Why don't we have him meet us downtown?''

''Oh, I suppose it's all right,'' Ferraro said with ill grace. ''In here.''

He led the way to a formal living room that looked as though nobody had ever sat in it. White carpeting and silky white-on-white-striped wallpaper formed the backdrop for furniture covered in pale green damask with carved fruitwood arms and legs. Anne was sure the shades of the peach and blue accent pillows had been chosen to match the colors in the floral paintings, two oils that were definitely originals. Cynthia would probably know the artist, but Anne didn't have a clue.

''I suppose this concerns Glen Lewis's boy,'' Ferraro said. ''Although I can't imagine why you'd want to question me about it.''

''Just routine,'' Bern assured him.

Ferraro waved them to two spindly chairs while he sat on a small sofa, careful of his jacket and the crease in his trousers. His didn't offer them anything to drink, flouting the unwritten code of Southwestern hospitality.

Anne could have used a glass of water, but mostly she wished she could exchange her thin gauze jacket for a sweater. The temperature in the room must have been below seventy degrees.

"The department hasn't released any information about the kidnapping victim," Bern said. "How did you know it was Danny Lewis?"

"I may be out of the company, but I still have sources."

"You and Glen Lewis were partners at one time," Bern said.

"That's right. I was the one with the money." Ferraro opened a silver box on an end table, took out a slender black cigarillo, and lit it with a silver lighter from his jacket pocket. The smoke drifted over, strong and acrid.

"How long were you in business together?"

"Two and a half years. Too long."

He blew more noxious smoke, and his gaze brushed over Anne. She had a sudden urge to do up another button on her blouse.

"I heard you had some problems," Bern said. "Tell us about that."

"He ran one of my fitness centers up in the Sunnyslope district. Good manager and a good salesman—well, he sold *me*. I put up some money to buy Fitness Unlimited. I was busy, so I let him run with it for a while. I didn't expect any profit right away, of course, but then I heard outside reports that the business was taking off, which sure as hell didn't match the reports I was getting from Glen. I decided to find out what was going on."

According to Ferraro, Glen Lewis had found ways to legally cook the books and then had managed to use clauses in their contract to force a buyout from Ferraro at about twenty-five cents on the dollar.

"You must have been furious," Anne said, the comment out before she remembered she was not really part of the official team here.

"I was damned pissed," Ferraro said. "I had reason to be."

"So I guess Glen's not one of your favorite people," Bern observed.

"He's a lying, double-crossing bastard," Ferraro said. "But I don't put people I despise under freeway footings, Detective, and I do not kidnap their children to recoup my losses."

"What did you do?" Anne asked.

"I fired my attorney and wrote it off." He looked pointedly at his watch.

Bern said, "And if I check around, I won't hear about any threats you made against Mr. Lewis."

Ferraro bristled. "Is he telling you that?"

"Nobody's told me much of anything yet, Mr. Ferraro. But once I start turning over rocks, who knows what I'll find. You know anybody else who might harbor a grudge against Glen Lewis?"

"There are probably lots of people, but I don't keep track of them. Is that all?" He looked at his watch again.

"One more thing: Where were you on Monday afternoon at three-thirty?"

"You want an *alibi*? Christ's sake, if I was going to try something so stupid, I certainly wouldn't snatch the kid myself."

"Probably not," Bern said. "I still want to know where you were on Monday afternoon."

"And I'm not going to answer any more of your damn questions without my lawyer." Ferraro ground out the cigar in a dainty silver ashtray and stood up, glowering. "So either charge me with something or get the hell out of my house."

Although there was no physical resemblance, Ferraro reminded Anne of Tony Sales. He gave off the same aura of violence, and if he was cornered, she thought he could be just as dangerous.

Bern got to his feet, his face hard and his eyes cold. "I guess we have enough for now. But I'll see you and your attorney downtown at ten in the morning. Keep in mind that I really don't like people to be late. Oh, and you and your wife have a nice evening."

In the Jeep driving away, Anne said, "I thought for sure you'd take him in."

"Not worth the aggravation. Anyway, I wanted us to have dinner someplace nice. If you still want to go, that is."

"What I'd like is to put all this stuff with Danny on hold for a while. Can we do that?"

"We can try."

They succeeded, keeping to small talk, until they were in the Latilla Room at the Boulders Resort, having a drink before they ordered, looking through a glass wall at the whole expanse of metropolitan Phoenix laid out below. By then they were reduced to debating about when the monsoons would arrive.

"Enough," Anne said. "Neither of us is very good at making chitchat."

Bern smiled. "Okay. Your impression of Joe Ferraro."

"I think he was a mean little boy who grew up to be a vicious man. If he kidnapped Danny, it certainly wasn't for the money."

"Yeah, I agree. It would have to be for revenge. Give me a gut response, Anne. Taking a child—that's nasty and very personal. Would the guy do something like that?"

"Oh, yes," Anne said. "I think that's exactly what he would do." She sipped her wine. "Ferraro is the easy choice, isn't he? The stereotypical bogeyman."

"You'd be surprised how often it's the easy solution to

a crime that's the right one. But if Ferraro's involved, it'll be hell to prove. Like the man said, he wouldn't dirty his own hands.''

Bern would work on Ferraro again tomorrow—or do as much as he could with a high-powered attorney in the room. He would also talk to Florence Mosk and take another shot at Tony Sales.

He drank the last of the double margarita and said, ''I think an investigation must be like doing a sculpture. You keep chipping away at a rock until a suspect appears.'' He gave her a slightly loopy grin and lifted his glass. ''Or these could be damned potent and I'm a little drunk.''

She offered to be designated driver, but he still turned down wine with his prime rib. At least he had avoided problems with alcohol, that policeman's curse.

As they drank coffee and watched the city lights blink on in the growing darkness, she reminded herself that so much about Bernard Pagett was good and kind and loving. And yet she'd turned away from him once and couldn't commit herself this time, either.

She had blamed their problems on Bern's outlook on life and could even remember the exact moment when she realized just how deep that dark vein in his personality went.

They had been eating a late Sunday breakfast and reading about a hit-and-run driver in the paper. A Mexican family had stopped beside Interstate 10 to change a tire. One of the children, a six-year-old girl, ran out in the road and was hit by a Thunderbird. A sunny April afternoon, and when the highway patrol finally stopped the car, they found a dent where the child's body had bounced off the hood. The man could not claim he didn't know he'd hit her, but he just kept driving.

Bern's summation was, ''I'm telling you, Anne, people are just no damn good.''

Anne realized he wasn't simply letting off steam; he meant it. She was no Pollyanna herself, even less so after Nicki's death, and while she could easily agree that this particular driver was indeed the lowest form of life, in her heart she truly felt that most people were decent, honest, and kind. Bern's statement jolted her because it crystallized the fundamental difference in the way they looked at life. And it marked the point when she began to hear every negative thing he said, to flag it, and to believe she couldn't deal with such cynicism on a daily basis for the rest of her life. Or at least that's what she'd told herself at the time. Now she had to wonder if it was really true, or if her turning away had been caused by some deeper problem.

"You've got that look on your face again," Bern said.

A frightened look, she assumed he meant, but was saved from having to give an explanation by her pager's muffled beep. The shoulder bag she had brought along held the beeper but was too small to carry her cellular phone. She excused herself to go use the pay phone outside the ladies' room.

The woman at the answering service said, "Dr. Menlo, I have this man who wouldn't give me a name or number, but he says it's an emergency. He's on the line, and I can patch you through. Do you want to talk to him?"

"Yes, of course."

"Hold, please."

A second of dead silence, then: "Anne? I didn't want to bother you, but—is it okay? I had a hell of a time talkin' that broad into hookin' me up with you."

"Yes, Tony," Anne said. "It's okay. What's wrong? Were you released?"

"Don't I wish. They got to let you use the phone here in jail. I didn't know who else to call, I mean nobody who would give a shit. I think I'm gettin' sick, Anne. Maybe something serious.''

"Then you need a medical doctor, Tony. I told you I'm not an M.D.''

"Yeah, but you know stuff, right? See, the way they are around here you say you got something major wrong, you better be throwin' up and pissin' blood or they just go yeah, yeah, and hand you a' aspirin. And this could be nothin', just gas, maybe, but it came on sudden a little while ago, kinda like bein' stabbed. The thing is, one night my mom had this attack. They rushed her to the hospital and operated, but she died. It was her gallbladder, infected they said. So I got this pain, and right away I start thinkin' about my mom, like is it inherited or something. I figure if it sounds serious, you'd make sure I got taken care of, wouldn't you?''

Was the man really sick or just angling for attention? She hadn't forgotten how he had tried to hit her up for some legal dope and wondered if that was his hidden agenda. In any case, her answer would be the same. She said, "Yes, Tony, I would. Tell me where it hurts.''

"Down low. Right in the middle of my stomach. And I'm feelin' kinda warm and feverish. I wouldn't worry about it so much except for what happened to my mom, you know?''

Her roommate in college had been a medical student whom Anne had helped study for exams. She tried to recall those cram sessions dealing with gallstones and ruptured appendixes.

"How long ago did you eat?'' she asked.

"About three hours.''

"I don't think it's gallbladder, Tony. An attack usually starts about an hour after eating fatty foods. The pain's under the ribcage but seems to go through to your back. It may not be bad at first, but gets steadily worse, particularly in a severe attack, until you can barely straighten up. Fever's not typical, but sometimes gallbladders can get infected like your mother's did, and that can be quite serious. What you have could be appendicitis. That's much more common.''

"No, I had my appendix out already."

"Well, then, I can't be sure, but more than likely you're just feeling indigestion or stress. Or even the flu."

"Yeah, you're probably right," he said, sounding relieved. "Probably nothin'."

"I still think you ought to see a doctor, just to be on the safe side. Okay?"

"Yeah, thanks, Anne. I feel better just talkin' to you."

"I'm glad it helped."

"Oh, it did," he said. "It really did."

Back at the table, Bern asked, "Was it about Danny?"

"No, it was Tony Sales."

"The son of a bitch is calling you up? What did he want?"

"Mostly reassurance, I think. It's not surprising, Bern. I doubt the man feels a connection to very many people."

"Well, I sure as hell don't want him connected to you. Jesus, Anne, what am I doing? You could've been killed yesterday, and now this. Not to mention dragging you along to meet the local chapter of the mob."

"We both know what you're doing," Anne said. "You're trying to get me interested in your work. Well, it's dangerous work, Bern. If I get involved, I'll be exposed to the danger, too. You can't have it both ways."

He brooded over that on the ride back to Cave Creek. When they were barely inside the door, he reached for her, kissing her with a hunger and intensity that mirrored the way he'd kissed her earlier in the Jeep. They went directly to the bedroom. Of course, the lovemaking didn't solve anything. It never did. It was a wonderful interlude, a way of putting off thinking about whatever problem they were facing.

Afterward, Bern held her, her body molded to his, stroking his fingers down the curve of her back.

"I should've listened to you," he said. "When I called from the Wineski house, you told me to get somebody else. I know you don't like working these cases. It was arrogant and selfish of me, putting you on the spot and forcing you into coming out there."

"It certainly was," Anne said.

"You don't have to be quite so eager to agree," he said dryly.

"Well, you said it."

"Yeah, and I meant it. I'm sorry, and it's over. I'm taking you off the department's list, and I'll call Karen Doheny, ask her to step in with Danny."

It would be so easy. Agree with Bern and be rid of all the doubt and second-guessing. Instead she pulled away from him and sat up. "No, Bern, I can't do that. I'm not going to desert that little boy."

"Dammit, Anne—" Bern broke off to give her a rueful look. "All right. I know enough not to argue with you when you set that stubborn jaw of yours. Go ahead and treat Danny, but no more interviews with suspects. And I don't want you talking to Tony Sales. I want you out of this. Okay?"

Anne nodded agreement and let him pull her back down into his arms. It was what she wanted, wasn't it? If she concentrated on her practice and stayed away from the police work, maybe the memories of Nicki would subside. Everything could go back to status quo, including her part-time relationship with Bern. On her terms. Always in control. Only why wasn't she happier at the prospect?

Neither of them slept soundly. Bern never did in her house. She dozed fitfully, too, starting awake at the sound of a pager beeping.

"Mine," Bern mumbled.

He got up to grope his way in the darkness out to the kitchen to call in. The bedroom window faced north. They hadn't pulled the shade. Nothing out there to spy on them except coyotes and bobcats. Forks of light arced in the night—heat lightning. Or maybe a storm really was brewing.

She heard Bern's voice, raised in anger, then he came hurrying back into the bedroom, turning on the lights, his face grim.

"What is it?" Anne asked. "What happened?"

"Tony Sales," Bern said. "The son of a bitch got away."

18

Anne sat up, wrapping the sheet around her bare breasts. Bern didn't have a stitch on either, a situation he immediately remedied, opening the bottom drawer of her dresser for shorts, a T-shirt, and socks, grabbing cotton slacks and a sports shirt from the closet.

Muzzy with sleep, Anne wrestled with what Bern had said. "What do you mean Tony got away? He escaped from jail?"

"From the hospital," Bern said. "Bastard faked some emergency. Good enough to convince the night-watch sergeant and the doctor that he needed immediate medical care."

"A gallbladder attack?" Anne asked, with a sinking feeling in her stomach.

Bern stopped in the act of buttoning his shirt to stare at her. "How did you know that?"

"Because that's what Tony and I talked about." Anne recounted her conversation with Tony, anger beginning to replace her instant reaction that she was at fault. "My God, Bern, wasn't there a guard? What were the hospital staff doing?"

"The way I got it, the nurse insisted the deputies undo one handcuff so she could insert an IV. So they cuffed

Tony to the bed. Then she ordered them out of the treatment area because Tony was so upset.''

"I'll bet," Anne said, remembering Bern's words: *He works me, he works you, he works the system.* "I still don't understand how he got away.''

"I'll tell you while you get dressed. And pack a bag. I'm taking you to my place.''

"You think he'll come looking for me? Why? He already got what he wanted.''

"Maybe so, but you can't predict what assholes like Tony will do.''

"Well, he won't come here," Anne said. "He has no way of knowing where I live. Danny's the one you should be worrying about.''

"I sent a patrol car out to the Lewises'. And don't change the subject. I'm not going to leave you here alone, and I'm not going to argue about it. If it comes down to it, I'm a hell of a lot bigger than you are. I'll cuff you and carry you out of here.''

Anne bristled at the threat, but she knew he meant it. She was ready to go in ten minutes, listening all that time to the rest of the story of Tony's escape.

"The ER was a madhouse," Bern said. "They were triaging because of an accident on the Squaw Peak Freeway. The nurse got called away, and Tony was in there long enough to rip out his IV needle and pick the handcuff lock, most likely with the needle.''

"You're kidding! How could it be that easy?''

"Babe, back when I was in a patrol car, I can't tell you how many people got out of their cuffs. If you were lucky, they'd just hand 'em to you. Couple of times I wasn't so lucky. Ask me, they ought to get rid of the damn things and go strictly to Flex-ties.''

Anne knew he was referring to the plastic strips used in place of handcuffs.

"Anyway," Bern went on, "Tony was in a curtained treatment area. I guess he waited until the deputies were distracted, and ducked out the back."

"How long before he was missed?"

"A good half an hour. Long enough."

Bern tailed her Camaro all the way into the city, making sure she didn't turn around and go home. He needn't have worried. Driving alone, she had time to think about the situation and concluded he was right. Tony was as sly as the creatures who prowled the mountains behind her house and a lot more unpredictable. It was stupid to take chances.

By the time she got to Bern's apartment, it was three in the morning, that nadir of insomniacs, the time most people die in hospitals. By then her anger was leaking away. She kept replaying her conversation with Tony. How could she let him sucker her that way? She was a *psychologist*, for God's sake.

She never did go back to sleep.

Tony was still at large when Jane Clawson arrived at work. By then Bern had been on the job for four hours, Will for almost as long. Not that they'd accomplished much. Once the APB went out, they had gone to sit in front of Tony's apartment house, taking along a Thermos of Mocha Cream and watching the bright sun begin its climb. The temperature must have been close to ninety degrees when another unmarked car came to relieve them at six A.M. They headed back to headquarters and feverishly attacked the paperwork until seven when a message came in that a stolen car report had been filed by a nurse, coming off the night shift at the hospital where Tony had been treated.

Well, they'd figured Tony probably had wheels. At least

now they had a description and plate number to add to the APB. As soon as Jane arrived, they followed her into her office. Jane's crisp beige suit worn over a black cotton knit top made Bern feel even grubbier, and he wished he'd stopped at home for a shower and a change of clothes. He and Will, both wired on too much caffeine and too little sleep, braced themselves for her reaction.

They didn't have long to wait. She closed the door behind them and said without preamble, "Can either of you guess what my wake-up call was like this morning? I'll give you a hint. The chief was on the horn telling me everything I missed over the weekend."

"Homicide didn't let Tony escape," Will said.

"We damn near did on Saturday. You think the TV and the newspapers are going to forget that? I imagine they've got their headlines and lead-ins all ready. Something that will lump us all together and make us look like horses' asses. Talk to me, guys. Tell me you're making some progress."

She took off her jacket, put it on a hanger, and went to sit behind her desk while they filled her in. Laying it out, Bern could see that aside from the fingerprints at the scene, they had little solid evidence linking Tony to the murder and kidnapping. Wayne Jensen and his friend Dale had failed to identify Tony in the lineup, Glen Lewis didn't recognize his voice, and a search of Tony's apartment the day before had turned up no sign of the ransom.

"So basically we have squat," Jane said. "Anything from Danny Lewis?"

"Not yet," Bern said, "but Anne thinks she's getting close. Meantime, we do have a couple of other suspects."

They gave her what they had on Florence Mosk and Joe Ferraro.

"Good luck tying anything to Ferraro. Christ." Her disgust summed up her feelings about the case. "We'd better hope we get lucky and pick up Sales."

Bern had never considered leaving Tony's call to Anne out of his report, but he did think twice about bringing it up now. There was always the chance Jane would read that detail when she was in a calmer mood. Picking up on Bern's hesitation, Will shot him a look that said: *Your call.*

Not like Bern really had an option, though. Not if he wanted protection for Anne.

Jane eyed him and asked, "Something else?"

He told her about the call.

"And Anne didn't tell you what they talked about?" Jane said, incredulous. "You didn't *ask*? *Jesus.* If the press gets hold of this, we're going to look worse than those idiots from the Sheriff's Department."

Bern had been kicking himself, remembering how he'd been too busy worrying about Anne's safety right after the call, too swept up in his passion for her later to think that the details of her talk with Tony might be important. But now he felt a hot surge of anger.

"Excuse me," he said, not really giving a shit if there was a caustic edge to his voice. "But we've got a couple of things here more important than press coverage. If Sales is our man, he could go after Danny. Or Anne. I don't like the way he's attached himself to her."

"If you're going to suggest twenty-four hours on them, forget it," Jane said. "I can ask, but it's not going to happen."

Bern stood up abruptly, enraged enough that the old saying about seeing red definitely applied. "So the department's cutting them loose." Will put a restraining hand on his arm, but Bern shook it off. "Sorry, don't call us until somebody else gets killed—is that the message?"

"Look," Jane said, "the guy's got some smarts. Chances are he's already long gone."

"Maybe you're willing to take that risk," Bern said. "I'm not."

"I didn't say I liked it." Jane's shoulders sagged, and she looked incredibly weary. "How about a tap on Anne's phone? He's called her before. Maybe he'll do it again."

"That's it?" Bern asked.

"That's all I can do." Jane spread her hands. "Take it or leave it."

Anne usually got together with Cynthia and Andrew for an informal half-hour meeting first thing on Monday mornings. Except for the times when Peggy was away and the temps turned everyday routines into crises, they mostly spent the time talking shop over a cup of coffee.

Today Anne asked Peggy to sit in, and the mood was grim as Anne gave them the highlights of what had happened over the weekend: the hostage situation at the police station on Saturday, her subsequent involvement in Tony's interrogation, the way she had unwittingly helped him escape, and Bern's fears that Tony would contact her.

"Jesus." Cynthia stared at her as though she couldn't quite believe her ears. Tall, blond, volatile Cynthia was always embroiled in high drama. But not Anne.

"You don't really think this Sales would show up here?" Andy asked anxiously. A gentle bear of a man, he didn't have an aggressive bone in his huge body.

"No, I doubt it. I think Bern is overreacting."

"It was his fault you got involved in this thing to start with," Peggy said darkly.

She was right, but of course it was more complicated than that. Most things were.

"Fixing blame isn't going to help the situation," Anne

said. "And this wasn't meant to scare you. I just wanted you to know what was going on."

"You'd think he'd at least send a police car over," Peggy said.

Anne had thought that was just what Bern would do and was surprised that a patrol car had not been stationed outside.

"Well, I'm just as glad," Cynthia said. "We still have patients to see."

And people who visited psychologists already had enough emotional roller coasters in their lives. With everybody on guard and practicing caution, they all dispersed to start the workday.

Alone in her office, Anne massaged her temples where spikes of pain seemed embedded in the bone. She was more than a little grateful for the busy day ahead that allowed no time to dwell on the frightening thought of Tony out there on the loose. She just hoped to God the Lewises were taking extra precautions to keep Danny safe.

Florence Mosk arrived at the police station at nine o'clock on the dot, but that was the end of her cooperation. She grunted her way through Bern's opening questions, sitting on the other side of the table from him and Will like one of those statues from Easter Island, airdropped into the interrogation room.

Joe Ferraro was due in forty-five minutes. Bern knew from experience how long it took to extract information from Florence. He decided to try another tack.

"Look," he said, injecting compassion and understanding into his voice, "I'm going to tell you up front we have a witness who says you not only knew Dorie Wineski, but also that the two of you were lovers." Well, they would have him, once he was caught. "Losing somebody you care about—that's truly terrible. I'm sure you're really hurting over this.''

To tell the truth he thought she had the emotional level of a turnip, but, curiously, something stirred behind the bland surface of her eyes.

"We know about Dorie's family," Bern went on. "They cut her out of their lives when she was alive, and now they don't even want to give her a decent burial. Isn't that the saddest thing?''

"Real sad," Will agreed because Florence wasn't saying a word.

"You're probably the only one who loved that poor woman, Florence, and you may be the only one who can help us figure out who took her life. You live right next door, and you talked on—what?—a daily basis? I'm sure she told you things—''

"We argued," Florence said.

With a little more prompting she said this happened the week before Dorie died. Yeah, Dorie was acting funny, but Florence blamed this on Tony coming around. She saw him at Dorie's on Friday. Florence had called and left a couple of messages, but Dorie never called her back.

When Bern suggested Florence was keeping an eye on Dorie, he got one of her massive shrugs in reply. She lapsed back into monosyllabic responses, and several questions were required to find out she claimed to be napping the evening Dorie was killed, getting ready for her graveyard shift at Good Sam. Asked about any other enemies Dorie might have had, Florence went back to shaking her head. Bern was set for more resistance when he requested that she record a reading of the kidnapper's words to Glen Lewis, but she took the written sample without comment and complied.

After that Bern made one last try. "Florence, I want you

to think about our conversation. If you remember anything that could help us find Dorie's killer, give me a call, day or night.''

She stared at him. ''Can I go now?''

''Yeah, sure,'' Bern said wearily.

After Will followed up with the don't-leave-town routine, she clomped over to the door, paused, and looked at them.

''Where'd they put Dorie?''

Will said, ''She's still at the morgue.''

''I'd like to do what's right for her,'' Florence said awkwardly, her face too stony to gauge the level of her grief. ''Would you tell 'em that?''

''Sure,'' Bern said. ''I'll tell them.''

Outside in the squad room, Joe Ferraro and his attorney were waiting and fuming. Bern had Will take them into the interrogation room to cool their heels while he made a couple of phone calls.

The first was to Glen at his office. Bern endured a minor tirade about the police department's bungling before informing Glen about the new voice sample and requesting that he drop by later that afternoon. Bern's second call was to Anne to ask her to stay put because he was coming over. He didn't explain the reason for his visit. Things like phone taps were better broached in person.

By then he was feeling mean and grungy and figured he looked worse, as if he were on undercover drug detail instead of homicide—but what the hell. He knew he'd get nothing out of Ferraro. Today was just an exercise of power. As Jane had said, tying Ferraro into the case would be a tall order. Nevertheless, unless they got a break soon, the investigation would have to be done.

So, after a little teeth baring and muscle flexing, he let Ferraro go. Then he set noon as the time he would meet the lab tech at Anne's office. He was heading out the door, bound for the gym for a quick shower, when Will yelled at him and waved him over to his desk.

Will was just hanging up the phone. "Two things. Robbery detail called a few minutes ago to tell me about a holdup—four A.M., all-night liquor store. Description of the robber matches Sales. And just now that was somebody in impound. That Honda Tony stole? It was towed at six forty-five this morning at Sky Harbor, sitting at the south curb at Terminal Four."

"*Shit,*" Bern said.

"The last place I would go," Will said. "You think he made it through security?"

"With our luck?"

The Sheriff's Department kept men at the airport in addition to Sky Harbor's own security force. With an APB out, they would all certainly be on the lookout for Tony. Still, Bern knew it was entirely possible Tony might slip through the net.

"At least if he left town he can't hurt Danny or Anne," Will offered. "Still a good idea to tap Anne's phone, though, don't you think?"

"Oh, yes," Bern said. "I just hope she agrees."

On the way to Anne's office, he could feel that sense of foreboding ballooning up like the clouds building to the north, huge, black, and threatening. He'd told Anne about cop's hunches. This was more than that.

He didn't believe in the power of crystals and pyramids, in telepathy or clairvoyance, none of that psychic crap. A short stint in bunco was enough to convince him that all those who claimed such ESP powers were either delusional or charlatans.

So exactly what was this overpowering sense of dread?

He didn't know, but he did give serious consideration to going back to headquarters, handing Jane his badge and his gun, then going to get Anne—by force, if necessary—and getting the hell out of town.

19

Anne stared at Bern, aghast at the suggestion of a stranger monitoring her every word.

When she finished with her last patient, Bern had been in the waiting room, pacing around, looking grim and haggard. A police tech arrived about that time, ready to install the equipment to bug her phone.

"I think we need to speak privately about this," she said and led the way back into her office without waiting for Bern's reply.

As soon as he closed the door behind him, he said, "Anne, please don't argue with me about this."

"No argument. I won't even discuss it. Something like this violates every principle of the therapist-patient relationship."

"For Christ's sake, your patients are children," Bern said. "How much consulting do you do with kids over the phone?"

"I speak with their parents. I speak to their teachers, their doctors. I told you, Bern. The answer is no."

Silent, he went to the window and stood, pushing the blinds apart to stare out into the parking lot.

"Anne, if I tell you something, will you believe I'm dead serious?"

"All right. What?"

"I've got a bad feeling, babe. About this case, about you. Us. Shit, I don't know." He turned from the window, the look on his face sending an icy crawl down her back. "I can't pin it down. It's just *there*. Jane won't authorize any protection. I'm thinking about calling a friend of mine, an ex-cop who's in security work, and hiring him—"

"Bern, no. Are you serious? Tony never threatened me. If anybody's in danger, it's Danny. And we don't even know that for sure. Do we?"

"No," he admitted. "Not for sure."

"Well, then, never mind the expense, I don't want a bodyguard. Darling, you're tired. Pressure and fatigue can do a number on your nerves, you know that." She certainly did. Taken in perspective, those two factors had to be contributing to her own level of stress these past few days. "I'm surrounded by people here, then I'll go to your place. And you'll be there. How safe can it get?"

"I guess so." He didn't sound convinced. "But I wish you'd reconsider letting us monitor the phone."

"I can't do that," she said firmly.

"God, you are stubborn."

"Yes, I am." She walked over, put her arms around him, and laid her head against his chest. "I'll be all right, Bern. Really."

He sighed and held her for a moment before he went out to confer with the technician. A few minutes later he was back with an alternate suggestion: the installation of a device that displayed the number of the calling party. She agreed. She was to buzz Peggy if Tony called, then try to keep him on the line while Peggy phoned the police and passed along the number that should pinpoint Tony's location.

After the lab tech finished his job, packed up, and left,

Anne tried to talk Bern into lunch, sure he hadn't had a decent meal since their dinner the evening before.

"Can't," Bern said. "Too much to do."

"All right," Anne said, "but promise me you'll make some time to come home for dinner."

"I'll try." He brushed a kiss across her forehead. "Call you later."

After he left, Anne debated about going out for a quick bite to eat, but the phone rang before she could make her exit. Two phone calls later, Peggy knocked and came in with a small paper bag and a mug of coffee.

"I saved you half my sandwich and some cookies," Peggy said.

"Oh, you didn't have to do that."

"Yes, I did. I knew you wouldn't eat otherwise. It's turkey and swiss from the deli and oatmeal cookies I baked last night."

Anne accepted gratefully, having managed to scrounge only juice and toast for breakfast at Bern's. By the time she finished lunch, her one o'clock patient had arrived. She spent a busy afternoon, thinking about Tony Sales only when somebody called and the number was displayed on the device attached to her phone. She decided that both she and Bern had given too much weight to the bond formed between Tony and her. The man had used her, that's all, and she hadn't been sharp enough to see what he was doing.

Natalie and Danny were due at four o'clock, but Natalie called a few minutes before that time to say she was running late.

"Danny's been just impossible," she said. "Terrible nightmares last night and temper tantrums twice today, kicking and screaming. He's rarely ever done that. There was a police car here earlier, but it left, and I'm so nervous, knowing that man escaped from jail. Have you heard anything?''

Anne wanted to tell her that Tony Sales was probably long gone, but she didn't want to offer false hope. ''I'm afraid he's still on the loose.''

''I'd feel better if Glen stayed home with us, but he insisted he had to go to work. We had a terrible fight about it. I tried not to let Danny hear all that. I know he needs to have things calm and low-key right now.''

''You can't expect not to react to the stress, Natalie. You're only human. And of course Danny's going to pick up on your feelings. He's a very sensitive little boy.''

''The worst is, a TV reporter showed up, Anne. That woman from Channel 12.''

Dear Lord, Anne thought, but she tried to sound unruffled and reassuring. ''I know it's upsetting, Natalie. Just hang in there, and don't worry about being late. Danny's my last patient. I'll wait for you.''

It was almost five o'clock when Natalie arrived with Danny, looking anxious and rattled. She wore no makeup, and strands of her dark hair had escaped from a fabric-covered elastic band to curl damply around her pale face. By contrast Danny seemed to almost crackle with undirected energy. Natalie stood in the doorway and kept one eye on him as he moved restlessly around the room.

''Glen promised he'd try to meet us here,'' Natalie said. ''But he called to say he has to work late, so he won't be coming. I know things have piled up on him; I know he can't let the business go down the tubes. But I really need him right now.''

''He probably feels very torn,'' Anne said. ''Just try to be understanding, and talk to him. Don't keep this bottled up inside.''

''I try. But it's not easy. There were—well—other problems. But never mind that. I want you to spend the time with Danny, not me.''

''Natalie, do something for me. Andrew Braemer has an office here, and he specializes in family counseling. Unfortunately he's left for the day, but have Peggy give you his card. I think you'll like him. He's a good man.''

Natalie agreed that she would get in touch with Andy and went to wait in the reception area. Anne sat on a floor pillow at the play table, hoping to encourage Danny to join her, but he could not—or perhaps would not—allow himself to settle down. Finally she got up to take a big throw rug from the closet and spread it on the floor. Then she returned and dragged out a pan filled with sand. The pan was a heavy-gauge plastic from a pet supply warehouse, intended for use as a litter box.

Immediately curious, Danny stopped bouncing around to watch. When she said the pan was heavy and she needed help, he came over to tug on the container and help her place it on the throw rug.

Once again the tray worked its magic. After she announced her rules pleasantly but firmly—only hands in the tray and no throwing sand—he sat down and began sifting the soft white grains through his fingers. The motion had its usual calming effect.

Danny began by heaping the sand in random piles, but gradually became more organized. He made a long swipe— a road—and went to get a car and a dump truck from the toy basket. Blocks became a bridge, then an overpass, a ramp from which cars crashed with appropriate sounds.

Ordinarily Anne would not interfere; she would sit quietly and allow him to proceed at his own pace. But with Tony Sales at large and so many questions unanswered, the circumstances were far from normal. So with trepidation and more than a few misgivings she smoothed a small area and made a finger drawing—a circle, two dots for eyes, a smiling mouth.

Danny stopped to watch. She dragged the edge of her palm across the sand for an eraser. Drew another circle, added rays for a sun. Danny took out the cars and blocks, put them on the rug, and leveled the surface. On it Anne made a long scalloped line.

"The ocean," she said, then waited.

He obliged with a big blob, nearly ovoid, and said, "Free Willy."

Anne's turn. She made little squiggles. "Fish."

Danny added a horizontal line bisected by a vertical line and pronounced it a boat. After several sharks and another boat, he showed signs of getting bored, so Anne started over with smooth sand and created a playground with Danny's help.

A sweep and another start. A round shape, droopy ears. "Doggie," Danny declared.

Obviously her artistic capabilities didn't extend to a front view of a rabbit. She added a lolling tongue to fulfill Danny's observation and began again, this time a side view: a round body with a powder-puff tail, the long ears, whiskers.

Beside her Danny grew very still. He stared silently at the sand sketch with a kind of frightened fascination.

"What's that?" Anne prompted.

"Bunny," he whispered.

"Can you tell me about him?"

He gave his head a quick, hard shake.

"That's all right. You don't have to. Maybe later."

As she spoke she began making straight lines next to the rabbit, three before she heard Danny suck in a breath. She was merely repeating her impression from his drawing and had no idea what the lines were supposed to represent. Clearly they meant something to Danny. His whole body tensed; he drew his head down into his shoulders; his breathing quickened, and his skin grew pale.

He made a quick line through the rabbit doodle, stabbing down so hard his finger sank to the bottom of the pan by the time he finished. He brought the finger up and then scrubbed furiously with his fist, the action sending sand flying out on the rug.

Time enough later to remind him of the rules. Now she pulled him on to her lap, wrapped her arms around his rigid body, and murmured soothing words. There was little left of her sketch. Danny had left marks obliterating most of it, savage and disturbing tracks in the sand.

What is it you see, Danny? Anne wondered. *What is it you see and I don't?*

Glen Lewis did not recognize the recorded voice of Florence Mosk...

When the words on the computer screen began to blur, Bern thought *enough*, saved the incomplete report, then sat, massaging the hard knot of muscle at the back of his neck. Summing up the progress of the case took only one word: zero. All he could do was hope that Danny would tell Anne something in their session today—which should be over by now.

He dialed her office, but Peggy said that Danny had arrived late and was still with Anne.

Bern gauged the paperwork he had yet to complete. Hours worth of the damned stuff. To hell with it. "Tell her I'll be home by eight, will you?"

"I'd be happy to."

Peggy's polite reply didn't quite conceal her hostility. Bern wasn't sure if she had problems with all men, or just him. Well, she was protective of Anne, and he couldn't fault her for that.

He supposed he'd made an idiot of himself in Anne's office today, but he didn't care because he could not shake his overwhelming feeling that something bad was on the way.

It didn't help at all that Tony had vanished. Maybe he had disguised himself, avoided security at Sky Harbor, and hopped on a plane. Maybe he was long gone. And maybe not.

Bern had asked the patrol officer in Anne's area to swing by her office as often as possible. It was all he could do for now, but if Tony wasn't picked up tonight, tomorrow morning he was going to arrange protection for Anne whether she liked it or not.

Peggy had waited for Anne even though it was past her normal quitting time. Both were on the alert, scanning the parking lot as they walked out, seeing nothing the least bit suspicious. In her car driving away, Anne kept checking the mass of vehicles surrounding her, feeling edgy but a little silly, too. In the movies they made it look easy to spot somebody following you, but Anne was sure it wouldn't be. Anyway, how much danger was there? Why would Tony abandon his car at the airport unless he planned to leave town?

Her stomach growled, shifting her thoughts to food. Peggy had relayed the message that Bern would be at the apartment by eight. But Anne realized that getting Bern home was one thing; feeding him quite another. His pantry—not to mention his refrigerator—had looked glaringly bare. There was nothing for it; she would have to stop at the supermarket although she was exhausted and hated the lines this time of day.

Gasoline first, she told herself, eyeing the gauge.

She pulled into a Circle K. Lines there, too. She went

inside to leave her credit card, noting the groceries in the mart and wondering if she could come up with something to make for dinner and save herself that trip to the super-market.

Outside, the air stank of fuel as she pumped the gas. Three cars were lined up behind her, so after she filled the tank, she decided to move the Camaro out of the way since she wanted time to check out the minimart's shelves. Leaving her car by the side of the building, she went in to retrieve her credit card and credit slip, then assembled enough supplies for a ham and cheese omelet, sourdough toast, and canned pears for dessert.

Not exactly a feast, but good enough.

Back at her car, she dug out her keys, intending to put the groceries on the floor rather than in the hatchback trunk where things had a tendency to slide out of a slippery plastic bag and roll around.

The Camaro was nose-in to the building. An old Toyota pickup had parked nose-out next to her, leaving just enough space to walk between the two vehicles. The pickup's engine was running, pumping out superheated air, but she didn't see the driver.

She was just about to insert the key into the lock when the door to the pickup flew open behind her, banging into her car with a thunk of metal against metal.

"Hey, watch it," she said, turning, the protest dying in her throat as she saw who was snaking out of the truck cab: Tony Sales, a gun in his hand, his body and the truck door trapping her in the space between the Camaro and the pickup.

20

"**Hey, Dr. Anne.**" Tony bared his teeth in a feral smile. He'd chopped off his hair, the uneven cut looking worse than his scraggly ponytail. An olive-green army cami shirt tucked into worn jeans hid the jailhouse tattoos.

The plastic shopping bag slipped from Anne's nerveless hand onto the asphalt. He must have waited somewhere outside her office complex, then trailed her here, and she'd never seen him. Bern had been right to worry. *Oh, Bern . . .*

"Are you okay?" Tony asked solicitously. "Didn't mean to scare you. Sorry about this—" He gestured with the gun. "Just hafta make sure you don't do nothin' stupid."

"What do you want, Tony?"

"Just to talk. We'll take a little drive and talk."

Anne's heart hammered her ribs, and she had difficulty getting her breath. "First put the gun away."

"Can't do that, Anne. Wish I could. I wish I could trust you that much, but—you understand, don't you?"

She understood, all right. He'd shoot her where she stood and tell his next shrink and his next lawyer that he had to do it; that she left him no choice.

She took a desperate look around the busy station. All

those people coming and going. None of them paying any attention to what was happening here. To be fair the pickup blocked the view on one side, the open door shielded another. Still, you'd think one person would look her way . . .

As though he'd picked up on her thoughts, Tony said, "Okay, let's do it," with a rough edge to his voice. When she didn't move fast enough, he grabbed her arm and pulled her with him up into the truck cab, keeping the gun jammed in her ribs as he slid over to the passenger side and left her behind the wheel. She realized she still had her purse over her shoulder, but she had dropped her car keys along with the grocery bag.

He leaned across her to slam the door, his body hard against her breasts, then lingered in that position, pinning her against the seat, his face inches from hers. Sweat oiled his skin, and his black eyes gleamed. She saw his pupils were dilated. Some of that money he took in the liquor store robbery must have been spent on drugs.

She forced herself not to look away. Control—that's what men like Tony wanted, what she dared not let him have.

He gave her a knowing smirk, slid a thumb under the shoulder strap of her purse, and took it with him as he shifted away. "Let's go, Anne. Take it nice and easy."

Amazing how instinctive driving had become. She maneuvered out of the station and into the busy flow of traffic. The steering wheel felt slick with skin oil. A weak flow of cool air from the vents did little to mitigate the stifling heat. She could smell Tony's perspiration mixed with the cigarette odor that permeated the truck.

Stay calm, she told herself. *Keep it together.*

Surely somebody would notice. But why should they? Tony had shifted the gun into his left hand. She could feel the hard round barrel just above her hipbone. But he was turned a little, angled toward her, close, like an attentive lover, his body hiding the weapon.

What if she slammed on the brakes? Rammed another car? He hadn't put his seat belt on. But then, neither had she. Assuming she didn't hurt herself and that she bought a few seconds to escape, he might still shoot her—or somebody else. In the car next to them, a toddler was strapped into a car seat beside his mother. On the other side, a white-haired couple waited patiently for the traffic light to change.

No, she couldn't take the chance. Talk to him, that's what she had to do. It was her job, for God's sake. And she'd done it before, in Bern's office, when Tony flipped out.

"Where are we going?" she asked, trying to keep her voice steady.

"Someplace cool. This fuckin' truck—well, I grabbed the first thing I could find. Didn't stop to check the air-conditionin'." He opened her purse. Took out her wallet and flipped it open. "Hey, this sounds good." He read off her address from her driver's license. "Oh, yeah, that's where I wanna go. And you know the way, don't you, Anne?"

"Dammit, Anne," Bern muttered as he listened to his own voice on the answering machine at his apartment. Unable to concentrate, he had called to make sure she had arrived home safely.

He glanced at his watch while he left a message asking Anne to call as soon as possible. Ten minutes until seven. Maybe she'd decided to stop at the grocery store, planning to cook instead of going out. Maybe she was in the shower. It was too soon to panic.

He stared down at the reports covering the top of the desk and rubbed his temples where a headache, compounded of fatigue, worry, and continuing overdoses of caffeine, radiated into the bone.

If he didn't finish the frigging reports Jane would really be on the warpath. What he could do was call it quits now and come in early in the morning to finish them. But knowing how poorly he functioned first thing in the A.M., he knew he'd better just do it and get it over with.

He worked for five minutes, then reached for the phone.

Anne braked the pickup to a stop in the driveway of her house in Cave Creek. Tony surveyed the place and said, "You gotta be rakin' it in, Anne. Figured you'd live someplace with a little more class."

Anne said nothing. She sat with her hands on the wheel, utterly drained, knowing the last thing in the world she wanted to do was to let this man into her home.

The drive had taken about thirty minutes, but it felt like hours. They'd talked; oh, God, yes. The man was a nonstop conversationalist. He could use more words and say less than anybody she'd ever met. She realized now he'd just kept her busy so she wouldn't attempt to escape. About the only thing she'd learned was that he took the Toyota pickup from long-term parking at Sky Harbor after he left the stolen car there. No wonder the airport police hadn't caught him. He'd never gone inside the terminal.

"Well, come on," Tony said. "Let's don't sit out here and gawk at the view."

He opened his door, grabbed her arm, and pulled her out of the truck behind him. He reached back in for her purse and handed it to her.

"Keys," he said.

She fumbled them out, and he marched her up to the

front door. All this lovely isolation. Nobody to see her; nobody to hear her scream. Inside was worse. When the door closed behind her, she felt totally cut off and alone.

Tony snatched the purse away and tossed it on a hall table, then stuck the gun in the waistband of his jeans, right at the small of his back, and gave her what might have passed for a disarming grin if she hadn't seen that same smirk come and go ever since he took her from the gas station.

"Jesus, I'm thirsty," Tony said. "How about something to drink?"

Knowing this was an order, not a request, she led the way into the kitchen, trying to marshal her thoughts. It was more than an hour before Bern was due to arrive at his apartment. She remembered his face when he said, "I've got a bad feeling." He'd know something was wrong when she wasn't there, and he'd look for her. But how long before he found her?

Tony went right to the refrigerator and opened the door. "Hey, Bud, great." He grabbed two cans, popped the tops, then held one out to her as if he were the host.

"No, that's okay," she said. "You go ahead."

"What—you don't want to drink with me? Come on."

Anne didn't like beer much. She took the can anyway, not wanting to provoke an argument. At least it was cold. She took a long swallow, grateful just to quench her thirst.

Tony said, "Bottoms up," and guzzled his straight down. He tossed the empty in the sink, took another one from the fridge, and opened it. He leaned against the counter and squinted out the window at the mountains, shadowed a dark indigo by brooding storm clouds that had risen to towering heights.

"Gonna rain," Tony said, then turned and went to sit at the table.

A heavy china cache pot sat on the counter close by, holding a spider plant. If she moved quickly, picked it up, and smashed it down on the back of his head . . .

"Well, come on," Tony said. "Sit."

There was also a knife block on the counter. Forget it. Even if she could get to the pot or pull out one of the knives, she wasn't sure she could use it. And if she faltered she'd have to deal with his reaction. Suddenly she remembered the two women Tony had beaten up, one badly enough to put her in the hospital.

Outside, lightning flickered up high in the clouds, and by the time she took the chair opposite him, thunder played a distant drumroll.

Tony sat sideways, his legs stretched out, making himself at home. She'd bet he got the clothes in a thrift shop, but he'd splurged on the needle-toed boots. An intricate design of bucking broncos was carved into the soft glossy leather. Was there enough money from the holdup for the outfit? Or had he recovered the ransom money?

"Tony, you keep telling me you didn't kill Dorie, that you didn't kidnap Danny—"

"I didn't."

"But don't you see? Escaping the way you did—it's like admitting you're guilty. If the police catch you, they'll shoot first."

He gave her a sly grin. "Oh, I don't think so, not with you around. Hey, stop worryin'. I ain't hangin' around much longer. There's this guy owes me some money. Soon's I get it, I'm gonna take off."

Without her? She wished she could believe that he'd leave her behind, but she had an awful feeling he wasn't going to abandon a useful hostage. She tried again. "Don't do this, Tony. You'll be living the rest of your life as a fugitive. Think about what that means."

"I did. I thought about it good'n hard. You know, I could lay something in the cops' lap, something that ought to get me a real sweet deal—if I could trust 'em. But they're out to screw me over, Anne. People been doin' that all my life. So you know what? I'm gonna get my money and take my chances. Yeah, that's what I'm gonna do."

He tipped the can, drank the rest of the beer, and flipped the can into the sink where it clattered against the other empty. Questions whirled in her head. What money was he going to get? This debt he talked about? If he'd kidnapped Danny, why didn't he just go collect the ransom from its hiding place and get the hell out of Dodge?

The phone rang, impossibly loud. *Bern.* Anne jumped up, quickly covered the few steps to the counter, and reached for it. Tony was quicker. Just as she was about to lift the receiver, he disconnected the cord where it was plugged in at the bottom, leaving the curly wire dangling free from the wall unit. The phone rang twice more before the answering machine in her bedroom picked up the call.

Tony took the receiver from her hand, put it on the counter, and flashed his smirky half smile. "Sorry. Can't take a chance, Anne. In case you slip, let the cat outta the bag—you understand."

"Yes," she said dully. "Oh, yes, I understand."

Faintly, off in the bedroom, she could hear a man's voice leaving a message—Bern. She recognized the timbre and pitch, but, *Please God, don't let Tony know it's him.* Because if he was calling here, then maybe Bern was home a few minutes early and was already looking for her. He'd come here, of course he would. Bern was smart and thorough. If she could only distract Tony, keep him here, keep *them* here, until Bern could arrive . . .

She forced a normal tone in her voice. "Tony, I don't

know about you, but I'm hungry. Why don't I make us something to eat?''

"Nah," Tony said. "I had a burger a while ago. But I'll have another Bud. You just sit."

She sank into the chair while he popped the tab on the beer, sipped, and opened a drawer in the cabinet next to the refrigerator.

"You know, Anne, I can see you're nervous, but you don't hafta be scared of me. I ain't hurt you, have I?"

"No, you haven't hurt me." Not yet. "But you took me against my will, Tony. You forced me to go with you at gunpoint."

"Yeah, well, I had to."

He closed that drawer and moved on to the next one. Something about the deliberate way he moved made her heart feel as though it had expanded and was pushing up into her throat. He drank another big swig of beer and put the can on the counter.

My God, she thought, *he must have a bladder like a horse.*

"I didn't *like* doing it this way. But you wouldn't have come with me otherwise." He opened a drawer that contained an assortment of plastic bags, everything from sandwich-sized Ziplocs to large ones for trash. "Look at this. Everything all neat and organized. Comes from bein' a doctor, I guess."

He poked through the collection and took out some plastic fasteners—big, sturdy ones, the kind that had teeth cut into the sides at one end and a slot in the other. Idly he stuck the toothed end of one fastener into the slotted end of another, cinched it closed to link the two. All the while he rambled on about how his mother had been a neat housekeeper, too—well, a damn fanatic, if you want to know the truth—unless she was drinking, and then she didn't give a shit about the house or him or anything.

Anne stared in horrified fascination as he added a third fastener, making a chain—no, that wasn't it. She thought, *I know what he's doing* just as he took a step toward her and reached down for her right hand.

He looped the fastener chain around her wrist—Flex-ties, that's what the police called the plastic substitute for hand-cuffs. He'd made a set, crude but effective.

She tried to keep her other hand away, but he grabbed it, saying, "Just relax, Anne, I ain't gonna hurt you, but I gotta do this," as he wound the plastic strip around that wrist.

Then he threaded the toothed end into the free slot and pulled the makeshift Flex-tie tight.

The worst thing that can happen ...

His father's voice croaked in his head as Bern punched in the Lewises' number. He had an unreasonable hope that Anne was there, but of course she wasn't. Natalie said she had arrived late for Danny's appointment. It was almost six when the session ended, and she was sure Anne was going home right after they left.

Feeling as though he had fallen into deep water with cement weights tied to his feet, Bern called the Beidermans. Norman told him they had not spoken to Anne today.

"What's wrong? You sound worried." Norman probably recognized worry more readily than other men.

"I am, but I don't have time to explain," Bern said. "If you happen to hear from her, for God's sake call me."

The next step was an APB on Anne and her car, then he was out of here to look for her himself. Before he could make the call, the phone rang.

It was the patrol officer in Anne's area, already alerted to keep an eye on her office. "Detective Pagett? I'm at the Circle K on—" He gave the address. "I think you'd better get over here. I just found Dr. Menlo's car—abandoned."

21

The shocking swiftness of Tony's actions kept Anne immobilized for several seconds. Such a feeling of unreality, but the hard edges of the plastic strips tight against her wrist bones were all too real.

He had moved behind her, standing there with his hands on her shoulders, pressing her down in the chair. Outside, the storm closed in, bringing a swift blackness cut with bright knives of lightning.

"This way you don't hafta have a gun in your ribs." Tony moved his thumbs in a circular caress that made her skin crawl. "This'll be a lot better."

"No, it won't be *better*." Anger—reckless, maybe, but righteous—cut through her fear, and she twisted away from his grasp. "This is kidnapping. You might not be charged for taking Danny, but you will be for this."

"Yeah? Well, they gotta catch me first, don't they?" He clamped his hands around her upper arms and jerked her up from the chair, reminding her of the strength in that wiry body. "Come on. I gotta see a man about a dog."

He kept hold of her left arm and hustled her along, into the living room, down the hall leading to the bedroom, turning on wall switches with his other hand clenched into a fist and banging upward. He stopped at the bathroom. Her heart gave a sickening lurch as he fumbled with his jeans zipper.

"Damn beer," he said, yanking her in with him. "You can watch if you want to. I don't care."

He kept one hand firmly on her arm. Laughed softly as she turned away. A steady stream splashed in the toilet, and the strong smell of urine filled the room.

Her mind seemed split in two. One side still worked furiously, trying to come up with options—shampoo, hair spray in his eyes—but the other side was filling rapidly with a howling panic that threatened to drown out rational thought.

This was how Nicki must have felt, totally helpless, at the mercy of her father's strength and perverted appetites. But Anne wasn't a child; she couldn't think like that. *Do something.* Before she could overcome her terror, Tony finished, zipped up his pants, then hauled her along through the house to the front door.

Useless to beg him to reconsider. A show of weakness might encourage a greater display of power. He was reaching for the front doorknob when he stopped, went back to the hall table, and picked up her purse from where he had tossed it when they came in.

"Never know," he said. "I didn't see much cash in there. But you got an ATM card. Not to mention a gold VISA."

He put the strap over her head so it hung just below her breasts and behind her hands bound in front with the plastic fasteners, then gave her a rough yank that made her stumble into the table. A pot filled with blooming pink violets toppled off, spilled dirt and mangled blossoms on the tile floor. He opened the door and shoved her outside.

The air was not only oppressively hot, but also humidity was creeping in. Anne could smell water falling on hot earth, rain somewhere in the mountains. She hugged the purse against her as they hurried to the truck, a faint hope revived by the weight of the bag—heavy because of the cellular phone down in the bottom.

"This is the way the manager found the car," the patrolman told Bern. "Except the keys were on the ground. He picked them up. Afraid somebody might take off with it before we got here."

A grocery bag on the asphalt beside Anne's Camaro spilled bread, ham, a carton leaking broken eggs. Nothing else unusual except Bern was sure there was a fresh dent in the left rear panel, a small vertical nick deep enough to mar the paint.

He followed her here.

That's how it had to be. Tony could find Anne's office easily enough in the phone book. He had gone there, lurked around until she left, and found the opportunity to take her when she stopped for gas and food supplies.

And where the hell was Bern the cop? Writing fucking reports, covering his ass with Jane, instead of listening to the alarm bells clanging in his head.

The patrol officer stared at Bern uneasily. "I went by her building several times, like you asked me. Never noticed anything wrong."

Bern nodded curtly. "The manager?"

"Inside."

Tom Laine, the manager, was a pudgy man with permanent worry lines around his eyes, thinning blond hair, and a caterpillar mustache.

"We were real busy," he said. "Don't even know why I noticed the lady, except she moved her car over before she came in to pick up some stuff. Real thoughtful, you know, so's not to make other people wait."

He remembered ringing up Anne's groceries but didn't see her go out to the car. "And then, a little later, I noticed it's still out there. Soon's I got a minute, I went to take a look, and then I saw the stuff on the ground and the keys and got worried. What do you think happened to her?"

"I think she may have been kidnapped."

Bern described Tony Sales. The other cashier had come over to listen. Both he and Laine shook their heads. They hadn't seen anybody that fit Tony's description or noticed a vehicle that seemed out of place.

From his cell phone Bern called in the APB on Anne, setting the full strength of the police force in search of the woman he loved, realizing even as he did it how pitiful the army he marshaled was against the legions of evil possibilities that waited in the coming darkness.

Anne expected to be driven out in the country, to have Tony's meeting take place on some deserted road. Instead he had taken a slow, circuitous route down into Phoenix. She had known where they were when the storm hit—Indian School and Twenty-fourth Avenue. After that she had a hard time tracking their course.

The wipers left oily streaks on the outside of the windshield. Inside, the ventilation system in the old Toyota was no match for the humidity, so fog quickly condensed on the glass. Tony took out a dirty handkerchief and cleared a round circle right in front of him. For Anne, the world was reduced to a surrealistic display of neon and traffic lights that seemed to dissolve in the rain and run down the windows.

Her head ached, and her hands were beginning to swell. She should ask him to loosen the ties. She could at least do that. But the words stuck in her throat because she didn't want him to touch her. She understood something else, too.

She knew now how victims die so meekly, frightened lambs led away to the abattoir.

Stop it, she told herself. The worst thing she could do was give in to the terror that invaded her mind like a narcotic, keeping her numb and living on a second-to-second basis. She hugged the purse against her. Help was a call away if she could only figure out a way to get to the phone.

Country music blasted from the radio, perfect for line dancing. The cab smelled of male sweat and of the fast-food wrappers that littered the floor under Anne's feet. Soon after they left Cave Creek, Tony had dry-swallowed a pill and turned on the radio. Anne didn't see what he'd taken but suspected amphetamine because he'd been wired ever since, unable to sit still, telling her his life story non-stop until she wished he'd shut up—a few sad, telling glimpses mixed in with the swaggering hyperbole. He'd come down a little after that and lapsed into beating out a rhythm on the steering wheel in time to the music.

She pictured Tony as a child. An alcoholic mother, deserted by his father; a thin little boy bullied at school. She could see that poor little boy and understand what had molded him into the man who sat beside her. All that empathy and knowledge, all her training and experience, and she had failed once again to see what was coming, failed to do something to prevent it from happening.

Bern went to his apartment, back to Anne's office, and then headed toward Cave Creek. He had no real hope of finding Anne but he had to check all these places anyway. He sure as hell couldn't just sit in his office, waiting.

There was one light on in Anne's house—a lamp in the living room that he knew was on a timer. No vehicles on the driveway. Despair settled over Bern like a blanket soaked in ice water. All this time—more than two hours since she was at the gas station. Tony could have taken her anywhere. They could be almost to the Mexican border by now.

The first drops of rain hissed down as he approached the house, frying on hot pavement, sucked instantly into the rocky earth. By the time he braked to a stop, rain drummed loudly on the top of the Cherokee. Lightning sizzled, bright enough to illuminate the whole area with an eerie greenish glow.

Thunder crashed as he got out and ran up to the front door. Rain soaked his shirt and dripped off his hair as he slid under the overhang of the front entry and inserted his key. He felt a cold stillness in his chest. The dead bolt had not been turned, just the spring lock. And he distinctly remembered turning the bolt when they left the night before.

He slid the Glock from his hip holster, pushed the door open slowly, and went in fast, flattening himself against the hallway wall. Light spilled in from the living room, enough to see the potted plant broken on the floor.

She was here.

Maybe when he called. Surely while he began his search, never thinking to come here first. It made sense though. Tony probably wanted a place to hole up until dark. And then he'd left—taking Anne along?

Bern searched the house, the entry into each room bringing a new wave of dread. But at least Sales hadn't left Anne violated and bleeding, choked by a gag. Say it: *Dead.*

And Bern had no doubt about what had happened, didn't need a fingerprint match with the ones they would find on the beer cans to know it. He was tracking on a more primal level, and the odor of strong male urine in the unflushed toilet made the hair rise all over his body.

He called it in, asked for backup, and then went himself to the other houses in the area, splashing up muddy drive-

ways and pounding on doors. But out here in this godfor-
saken place without even the protection of close neighbors,
nobody had seen Anne arrive and nobody had seen her go.
She had simply vanished into the stormy darkness.

Outside the pickup this street was much darker. Anne
had no idea where they were as Tony turned into a parking
lot and stopped. He rolled the side window up and down
to wipe it. Anne caught a glimpse of a small abandoned
building with a sign that read OH BOY BURGERS and a
round-bellied statue, an obvious ripoff of the old Bob's Big
Boy logo, standing forlornly in the rain.

Tony pulled around in back and parked, front out, tail-
gate against a high, cement-block wall. Another larger
building loomed behind the wall. Atop this building was a
huge sign that said ROADRUNNER TRUCKING in red and yellow neon while a brightly lit cartoon bird ran endlessly.

Tony switched off the engine, killing the radio. The silence seemed louder than the music as he checked the gun
stuck in his waistband, pulled his shirt out of the jeans, and
let the shirt fall back to hide the revolver. Headlights sliced
the darkness—a vehicle approaching on the street.

"Slide down on the seat," he said.

"But what—"

"Just fuckin' do it." His voice was full of ugly tension.

She did what he said, helpless as she slid down to rest
on her spine, her head level with the armrest. Somebody
turned into the parking lot. The side window had fogged
back over. All she could see was a strobe of light on the
windshield.

*As soon as he leaves, I'm getting out of here. I'll open
the door and run like hell.*

She might have done it, too, and never mind the gun,
but Tony grabbed her arm and hauled her over against him

so she was angled on the seat with her feet still on the floor on the passenger side. He undid the plastic ties, put her hands by the steering wheel, and reconnected the strips, leaving her attached to the wheel.

"Take my word," he said. "You don't want this guy to see you or know you're within a mile of here. So you lay down on the seat and don't do nothin' else 'til I get back."

He got out and slammed the door, letting in a puff of cool, rain-drenched air, leaving Anne to such a bleak wave of despair he was gone at least a minute before she realized that the pressure on her hands had been eased and that her purse lay on the seat almost under her chin.

She slid up a little higher against the door, still keeping her head below the edge of the window. Moving carefully, heart trip-hammering, she used the surfaces of her body to push the purse up until the top was close enough to grab the zipper in her teeth and pull it open.

Then, with even more care, she let the bag drop down and maneuvered it to tilt the opened top forward. The rough serrated edges of the plastic ties dug into her skin as she swung her right hand enough so she could reach into the bag.

The rain had stopped. She could hear male voices—Tony's raised in anger. *Hurry.* Collecting this debt was probably a pipe dream. Men like Tony convinced themselves of lots of things that never happened. He'd give up and come storming back while she was still fishing through the useless junk in her stupid, goddamn purse.

A sob caught in her throat as her fingers found the leather case with the hard flat phone inside. Three steps: get the phone out of the case, turn it on, dial the one number programmed in to quickly connect the caller to 911. *Concentrate,* she ordered herself, trying to ignore the argument that had grown so loud she could almost make out the words.

Her hands were slippery with sweat as she inched the phone out of the case.

Outside in the parking lot, a gun went off, the sound so sudden and loud, she cried out, tugged too hard on the phone, and it flew from her hands.

No more arguing. Tony had shot the man. He'd take his money now and come running. She found she cared nothing at all for the poor man who lay dead or dying out on the wet, oily asphalt, that she was only concerned with the prospect of Tony jumping in the pickup and finding the cellular phone on the floor under his feet.

She yanked wildly against her restraints, ignoring the pain as the edges bit deep into her flesh, tears running down her face. An engine roared to life; lights blazed on. Tires screamed as the other vehicle peeled out of the parking lot. She lay very still, almost afraid to hope. Tony had taken the man's car and gone away, leaving her there. All she had to do was wait. Somebody would come by. If not today, tomorrow morning.

Even as hope flared brightly, a man's shadow loomed up above her, filling the side window between her and the neon roadrunner. He fell forward against the glass. Even through the fogged window, she knew it was Tony.

His nose was flattened, his hands out, palms red on either side of the distorted face. Then, very slowly, he slid down, his hands leaving wide scarlet smears behind. She heard the thump as he hit pavement beside the door.

Terror clamped a band around her chest. She lay there, exerting all her effort simply trying to breathe as fresh gusts of wind rocked the truck, and she watched the rain pour down, washing Tony's blood off the window.

22

Anne had no idea how much time passed before an overpowering sense of urgency got her moving. Frantically she ratcheted her wrists around the lower part of the steering wheel, squirmed up against the door, and used her head to push down the lock.

This wouldn't stop Tony. He could still break the glass. All she could hope to do was slow him down—if he was alive. She wanted him dead so badly, she was afraid to admit the possibility. She knew he planned to keep her as a hostage until he was away from Phoenix, out of Arizona, and then . . . She wouldn't think about what that would mean, wouldn't allow it to happen.

The thunderstorm must have dropped the outside temperature dramatically. She was shivering in her thin cotton slacks and blouse. Bern had to be looking for her by now. But she couldn't just sit here and wait. Tony might only be unconscious. Could she reach the phone with her foot, use her toes like fingers and get the receiver back up on the seat? She thought she might, with time. What she had to do was to get free of the plastic ties. She studied them in the dim, underwater glow of the Roadrunner Trucking sign. Human teeth had once crunched bones. She could probably chew through the strips. But there was something else she might try first.

The toothed end of the strip fed sideways into a slot, then turned to lock. Unlocking it could also be accomplished by reversing the action. She grasped the serrated plastic between her teeth and tried to turn it. This was more difficult than it looked. The hard, slick surface had to be rotated at just the right angle, then she had to adjust the pressure and try to jerk the strips apart.

Over and over she manipulated the plastic, only to have it snap back into place. She tasted blood as the rough edges cut into her mouth. Just when she was ready to give up and begin chewing, the strips came apart, and she was free.

She grabbed up the phone and dialed 911.

Bern was back in his office when the call from Anne came in. He had left a county patrol car to stake out the house in Cave Creek, although he couldn't imagine Tony bringing Anne back there, and returned to the station only so he could hear any reports as soon as they came in. While he waited, he tried not to think how bad the news would be and attempted to fill the time with paperwork, but ended up staring blindly at the computer screen.

Frank Trusey arrived about eight-thirty. "Figured I'd find you here. Anything?"

"Not yet."

"Well, I have some. Bartender at Aces says Tony Sales was in there on Wednesday. Not sure when he came in, left about eight-thirty. Showed up at The Irish Hound at nine, was there until eleven being loud and unruly, and believe me, you gotta go some to get attention in a place like that."

Last Wednesday. The day Dorie Wineski died.

"So he has an alibi?"

"Seems that way. Say, how about I brew us a fresh pot of Kona? You look like you need some."

"Sure, why not," Bern said.

He was drinking what must have been his fifteenth cup of coffee for the day when the desk sergeant called to pass on the word from emergency response, and to say a patrol car was waiting at the door.

As the patrol officer expertly maneuvered the car on wet pavement at full throttle with siren wailing, dispatch patched them through to the unit patrolling the area around Roadrunner Trucking. That officer was already on the scene, reported Anne was in his car, and handed the mike to her. The sweetest thing Bern had ever heard was the sound of Anne's voice. But this was nothing compared to the feeling of having her in his arms ten minutes later.

The officer had the heat on in his unit, and Anne was wrapped in a blanket. She was soaking wet because she'd jumped out of the old Toyota pickup as soon as she freed herself and called the police, running down the block in the rain to meet the patrol car. Now she was shaking, both from shock and from cold. Bern had seen an outdoor sign on the way over that read sixty-nine, a good forty-five degrees less than it had been at noon, downright chilly to those used to soaring temperatures.

Anne had refused the patrolman's offer to call the paramedics. Bern knew how hard it was to overrule one of Anne's decisions, but in this case he wished the officer had done just that.

"Is Tony really dead?" Anne asked.

"Oh, yes," Bern said.

Tony Sales was sprawled next to the pickup with the two patrol officers standing beside his body. He'd been shot in the chest at close range. A Smith & Wesson .38 revolver lay on the asphalt about twenty feet away. If they were lucky, there would be prints on the gun, although the rain had more than likely washed away most other physical evidence.

Will arrived just then. He parked beside them, got out, stopped to lean down beside the window, and when Bern cracked it, Will asked, "You all right, Anne?"

"I'm fine now," Anne assured him.

"Good. I'll get started out here, then."

After Bern rolled the window back up, Anne said, "Shouldn't you be out there?"

"No," Bern said. "I'm right where I ought to be. Tell me what happened, babe. Just take your time."

As she related how Tony had followed her to the gas station, Bern cursed department budgets and unheeding superior officers, but mostly he cursed himself again for not following his instincts.

Bern listened with special interest to Anne's story of the meeting Tony had here in the parking lot. "You didn't see the man or the car?"

"No, I told you. Tony forced me down on the seat and ordered me to stay there. And it was all fogged up inside the truck."

"Then how do you know the man was driving a car?" Bern asked.

"It was just an impression. I may be wrong. Oh, Bern, I was so scared. I would never have believed I could feel so helpless, so totally powerless. I'm a *psychologist*, for God's sake. I'm trained to talk to people. I did my job that day in your office, but this time . . ." She shuddered and huddled against him. "He even gave me an opening. He said he had information that he could use to bargain with the police. I should have tried to convince him to talk to you."

"Annie, love, stop beating up on yourself. The kind of

work you do—it's a long way from dealing with guys like Tony Sales.''

''I know, but it doesn't make me feel any better.''

''Any hint of what this bargaining chip was?''

''No—'' She hesitated. ''This is not based on anything he said. It's just a feeling. But somehow I think it had to do with Dorie's murder.''

''Why do you think that?''

''I don't know, it's just—'' She slipped away, pulled the blanket tight around her shoulders, and sat, staring out the window. ''Remember when you questioned Tony? The way he kept fooling around with the paper cup?''

''I thought that was nerves.''

''So did I, but now I think he was using that repetitive motion as a mnemonic device, that he was trying to jog his memory.''

''And maybe he succeeded,'' Bern said.

''If I'm right.'' She turned back to look at him, her face pale in the glow of the Roadrunner Trucking neon. ''Do you know what that would mean? He didn't kill Dorie.''

Bern sighed and told her about Frank's report. As he spoke, he watched Will searching the wet pavement around Tony's body, and he began adding things up, not happy at all with the answer.

Anne followed his gaze and was not far behind him. ''Oh, Lord,'' she whispered. ''That man Tony met—here, tonight. Do you think it's possible he was the one who killed Dorie?''

''I think it's damn likely,'' Bern said grimly.

She kept staring blindly out the window. ''I had it all planned. As soon as Tony got out of the truck, I was going to jump out and run. In his own strange way, Tony probably saved my life.'' She crept back into Bern's arms, shivering again. ''If only I'd gotten a look at that man.''

"Thank God you didn't because he might have been looking back at you." And if he had, there was no way the man who had kidnapped Danny and killed two people would have let Anne live.

They sat silently, holding each other, knowing they were together only by a whim of fate. Bern ought to have been cheered to think that his father's old prediction had been wrong. He had not lost Anne.

This time.

The pessimistic thought popped up, right on cue. He told himself he was just tired. It would take very little, here in the warm car with Anne safe in his arms, to succumb to the fatigue weighing down his shoulders and dulling his brain and drift off.

"Listen, babe," he said, "I have to give Will a hand. I'll have you driven over to my apartment, okay? You need a hot shower and some sleep."

She protested, saying he was dead on his feet; Will was more blunt when Anne called him over.

"Pal, you look like shit," he said. "And I don't need you messing things up. You did your part. You questioned the only witness. Now take your woman home and don't come back."

Driving away in the patrol car, they met a TV news van rolling in. Tony Sales was really dead now, Bern thought. The vultures had come to pick the bones.

They detoured by the station for Bern's Jeep. He insisted that Anne stay in the patrol car until he warmed up the Cherokee's engine, so she wouldn't have to ride without heat. While she waited, Anne made a call to Peggy at her home from her cellular phone, cutting short Peggy's worried questions by saying she was all right, just too tired to explain. She asked that Peggy reschedule her appointments for tomorrow.

"Danny Lewis, too?" Peggy asked.

Anne had forgotten that Danny's next appointment was for three. She told Peggy she would call the Lewises herself and then decide. It was even more urgent now that Danny remember what had happened to him. She would see him if she possibly could.

At Bern's apartment after the prescribed hot shower, they ate canned chicken noodle soup and went to bed. Cradled against Bern, Anne finally felt warm. Or at least her flesh did. But there was a place back in some primitive center of her mind where the memory of her brush with death lingered and the coldness remained.

Sleep came instantly, dark and seamless, and she did not dream. Or if she did, the dreams were too terrifying to remember.

23

Bern slept a solid eight hours and awoke a few minutes before the alarm went off. He took a shower, got dressed without waking Anne, then stood for a moment beside the bed, looking down at her.

Asleep, she looked as small and vulnerable as one of the children she treated. She lay with one hand cupped under her face. The bruises and freshly scabbed cuts on her wrists reminded him of how close he had come to losing her. But she had survived. She was safe. So why didn't he feel more reassured?

Anne would say he was obsessing. He supposed she was right. At any rate, even if absolute safety were possible, there was no way to guarantee it short of staying by her side twenty-four hours a day. The best thing he could do for her was stick to his job and close the case as quickly as possible.

He brushed his lips against her forehead, wrote a note asking her to call the station when she woke up, and left the apartment quietly, making sure to lock the dead bolt behind him.

Approaching the Police and Public Safety Building, he saw the Channel 12 news van parked along Sixth but paid little attention. The press often stormed the department ramparts. It was the job of the media rep to keep them from breaching the outer walls.

He left the Cherokee in the lot on the other side of Washington and headed for the station. It was only seven-fifteen, but the sun was already beating down with unrelenting brightness. Whatever coolness the storm had brought was fast dissipating. He saw two people leave the news van just as he crossed the street, a woman and a man, the man with a video camera on his shoulder.

They had timed it perfectly, nailing him before he reached the building entrance. Bern recognized the woman who moved with lean, predatory ease, although he couldn't remember her name. She was the reporter who regularly ambushed grief-stricken survivors right after tragedy struck and then followed up with muckraking inside stories.

The cameraman charged around Bern, then walked backward, video rolling, as the woman stuck a microphone in Bern's face.

"Detective Pagett? Grace Safely, News at Ten. Do you know who shot Anthony Sales last night? Did Tony really kidnap Danny Lewis?"

He muttered, "No comment," following standing department orders, which also included the command to resist all temptation to shove the microphone down the reporter's throat. This was a real exercise in self-control as she went on with her questions.

"Is it true Tony Sales was going to sue for false arrest? Are the real criminals still on the loose?"

Bern shouldered past her and pushed open the front door. The two followed him through the small reception area and into the station where a couple of alert uniformed officers hustled over to bar the way. Grace Safely kept shouting her questions the whole time.

"Who let Tony escape, Bern? Why was your girlfriend in the truck with him? Did she see who shot Tony?"

Upstairs at his desk, Bern called the chief's office and told them to get somebody to deal with Safely—about like asking them to handle a rabid dog.

Will was already in the squad room with the morning paper. Bern barely had time to scan it, grab a cup of coffee, and make a phone call before Jane summoned them into her office. At least the shooting had not been splashed on the front page. An article on page two mentioned that Anne was with Tony and speculated this may have been against her will. Tomorrow's reports were bound to be a different matter after Grace Safely did her number on TV tonight.

One look at Jane's face told him she'd already heard about his encounter with the reporter.

"I have an appointment with the chief in one hour," Jane said. "I hope to God you've got something good for me to tell him."

"You can say that Anne's alive," Bern said coldly. "Terrorized, but breathing."

"I understand that you're upset," Jane said. "The night detectives fielded a call early this morning from a woman who had finally dragged herself to a phone after lying at her front door bleeding for hours. She was stabbed by a guy who's been stalking her for months now. She needed protection, too, Bern. But the bottom line is, we can't protect everybody."

"Yeah, I know," he conceded. There was really no point in harping on it with Jane, especially since he was really mad at himself. He asked, "The stabbing victim—did she make it?"

"Survived the surgery, but she's critical. Now, tell me about Sales."

Will went over the physical evidence from the night before. Tony Sales had been killed by a bullet from the gun left in the parking lot, identified by Anne to the first officer on the scene as belonging to Tony. The serial number had been filed off so there was no way to trace it.

Powder burns confirmed that Tony had been shot at close range; there was gunpowder residue on Tony's hands, indicating that he had been holding the gun when it was fired, and they'd found no prints on the revolver except his.

Bern reported what Anne had told him: Tony's reference to the person he was meeting as male, Tony's expectation of coming into money, and Anne's feeling that this person was connected to Danny's kidnapping.

"I figure Tony remembered something that led him to the kidnapper, then hit him up for money," Bern said.

"Makes sense," Will said. "The guy was just the type to try a little blackmail."

"Wait a second," Jane said. "When did you eliminate Sales as a suspect for the kidnapping and murder?"

"Last night, when we found out he really did have an alibi for the time Dorie Wineski was killed."

Jane's face got grimmer. "And all this speculation—no hard evidence to confirm any of it. So what I get to tell the chief is that not only are we making no progress, we've added another body."

"Well," Will said, "it could be just what Tony said: He was meeting a guy who owed him money. A drug deal gone sour, or—who knows?"

Jane looked at Bern. "But you don't think so?"

"No," Bern said.

Jane listened gloomily as he finished his report. According to his wife, Glen Lewis had been working late. They hadn't checked on Joe Ferraro yet, but expected an ironclad alibi when they did. They also needed to check out Florence Mosk. Although Glen Lewis had failed to identify Florence's voice, Bern wasn't ready to write her off as a suspect. Tony Sales might have led Anne to believe he was meeting a man, but Tony had lied as naturally as he breathed.

"I'd like to get a warrant for her house," Bern said. He could cite bloodstained clothing as the reason for the search as well as the ransom money.

"You really think she'd be stupid enough to keep the cash there?" Jane asked. "No, scratch that. We've both seen people do dumber things. Okay. Go ahead. Now, what about Danny? I thought Anne was making progress."

"She is. She's spent a lot of time with him, but it's not an instant process."

"Well, she'd better have a breakthrough soon. That boy's our best chance to clear up this mess."

Bern couldn't argue the point. He thought she was right.

The phone rang. Jane picked it up and exchanged a few words with the caller, then hung up, took out a bottle of Mylanta from her desk, shook out a couple of gel tabs, and washed them down with coffee.

"The bloodsuckers are really going to have a field day," she said bitterly. "That stabbing victim just died."

"At least we'll be able to clear that one," Will said.

"Somehow I don't think that's going to help the chief's mood very much," Jane said. "For Christ's sake, please, catch me some bad guys."

About the only good thing about the stabbing was that since the night detectives caught the call, they'd handle the case. Still, Bern could hear the clock ticking away. Only a matter of time before somebody else was killed, and the folder was put ahead of the Wineski murder.

Back at his desk, Bern phoned the Lewises. Natalie answered.

"Glen heard on the radio that Tony Sales was shot," she said. "Is it true? He's dead?"

"It's true," Bern said. "While I have you on the phone—did you complete that list yet?"

"List? Oh—you mean the people working around here? I hoped—you think somebody else took Danny? That it wasn't Tony Sales?"

"We think so," Bern said. "I need to speak to your husband. Is he there?"

"Yes. I'll get him."

She put down the phone. Bern waited several seconds until Glen picked it up.

"Detective Pagett? According to what Natalie says, you're back to square one." There was scorn in his voice and just a hint of something else. Disgust? Or gloating?

"Not exactly," Bern said. "I understand you didn't get home last night until ten-thirty."

"That's right. I was at work. Why?" Glen asked sharply.

"Anybody stay there with you at work? Secretary? Assistant?"

"No. I was mostly going over reports, and I didn't see any point in keeping people late. Why are you asking me these questions? Oh, I see. You think I need an alibi. I'm getting pretty damn sick of this, Pagett. And I'll tell you something else. I was right in the first place. If I'd called you people, the way you screw up, Danny would probably be dead."

Bern grimaced at the sound of the phone being slammed down. Then he hung up and began preparing an affidavit to obtain a warrant to search Florence Mosk's house.

Anne's ordeal had left her with sore muscles, assorted bruises, and cuts on her wrists. Another hot shower helped a little. Afterward she tended to the cuts with antibiotic ointment and bandages, had tea and toast, took some Advil, and called Bern while she waited for the ibuprofen to kick in. His line was busy, so she was put through to Frank Trusey.

After asking how she was, Frank said, "Did you see the papers this morning?"

"No. Should I?"

"The department tried to keep a lid on things, but some of those reporters got their ears glued to their scanners. They know that Tony had you with him last night when he was shot. And this morning some TV reporter was laying for Bern."

"Great," Anne said.

She left word for Bern to call, that she really needed to pick up her car, then she checked in with Peggy at the office.

"And you told me not to worry last night," Peggy said. "I thought Bern was supposed to be watching out for you."

"It wasn't his fault, Peggy. Has the press been trying to find me?"

"Oh, yes," Peggy said. "The phone's been ringing off the hook, and that Grace Safely from Channel 12 was waiting when I got here. Don't worry. I told them you left town."

"I hope they believed you. Tell Cynthia and Andy I'm sorry for the disruption."

"Never mind that. Are you sure you're okay?"

"I will be. Were you able to reschedule everybody?"

"Everybody except the Lewises. You remember you were going to call them?"

"Yes, I'll do it now."

Natalie answered the phone sounding upset, and Danny was whimpering. "Anne, there was a reporter here. She said you were there when Tony Sales was killed, that you probably saw the man who shot him. And Detective Pagett was asking me if Glen was home last night. You didn't tell them—I mean, that Glen—'' She broke off, as though the rest of the question was too awful to voice.

"No, of course not. That reporter doesn't know what she's talking about. I couldn't identify the man who shot Tony."

"You mean you didn't know him?"

"I didn't *see* him, Natalie."

"I don't understand. Why were you there?"

"Tony Sales kidnapped me," Anne said.

"Oh, *Anne*. Oh, God. Did he hurt you?"

"No, I'm all right."

Anne could hear Danny's whining change to shrieks for attention, and Natalie saying, "Just a minute, baby."

"I called about Danny's therapy session." Anne offered to come to the Lewis house for the session since the last thing she needed was for Natalie to encounter TV reporters who might still be lurking at the office.

"Are you sure you're really up to it?"

"I'm sure." She had to be because she was convinced that Danny was the key to finding Dorie's and Tony's killer. "I'll see you at three."

After that Anne checked her answering machine at home. Grace Safely was among the enterprising reporters who had found Anne's unlisted number—no surprise. There was also an alarmed message from Rosemary.

Before she could disconnect to dial Rosemary, call waiting beeped—Bern, harried and rushed, making sure she was okay, then adding, "I have to serve a search warrant. So I can either run you home first, or you'll have to wait until I'm finished."

Somehow, during the confusion the night before, a helpful patrol officer had driven Anne's car from the gas station to her house in Cave Creek.

"I guess I could take a cab," Anne said, "but it would be expensive."

"No, I don't want you going up there alone. Why don't we do it now?"

"All right," Anne said gratefully.

Would her parents have heard about what happened? Probably not, she decided. At least not yet. It struck Anne that, other than Rosemary, there were few people she felt needed an immediate call. Work took most of her time, and her relationship with Bern didn't promote much of a social life.

Anne played down the account to Rosemary, emphasizing that she was fine now. She could hear the falseness as she spoke, so it didn't surprise her when Rosemary heard it, too.

"Anne, you are not okay," Rosemary said. "Nobody would be after an ordeal like that. Why don't you come over here so we can talk about it?"

"I can't." Anne explained about the logistics with her car. "Let me see how it goes. There are things I have to do. Maybe later?"

"Come anytime," Rosemary said.

Having somebody force his way into your home and make you a prisoner was a lot like rape. Anne understood that; she could catalog the anticipated emotions. But preparation was one thing, reality quite another.

Tony had left his mark in her house like an animal leaving spoor, and her reaction was immediate and visceral. She had expected anger, but nothing like the rage that ballooned swiftly in her chest and left her trembling with its intensity.

"You okay?" Bern asked.

"No, but I will be."

She banged open a cupboard under the sink and took out Ajax, a sponge, rubber gloves, and a scrub brush. She opened a drawer for a trash bag, the yellow plastic tie strips the first thing to go in for disposal. Not saying a word, Bern took the trash bag from her, dumped in the beer cans, and took the bag out to the garbage while she began scrubbing the sink, the counter, the table, anything Tony had touched.

They worked fast and furiously for a while, Bern cleaning the bathroom while Anne mopped the kitchen floor and the front hall. The house smelled of lemon additives and bleach when they finished. Anne was sweaty and tired, but she had stopped shaking.

"All right?" Bern asked.

She nodded and went into his arms there in the sunny kitchen, hugging him tightly. She had probably never loved him more than she had at that moment, so much she couldn't possibly put it into words.

"Go ahead and take a quick shower if you want to," Bern said. "I'll call Will."

"You don't have to stay," Anne said. "I know you're running late. I'm okay here now."

"You're sure?"

"I'm sure."

When the door closed behind him, she had a few panicked moments, but they passed. She had begun to relax when somebody starting banging on her front door. A look out the front window confirmed that this invasion was the press. The van had the Channel 12 logo, and the woman identifying herself loudly was Grace Safely.

24

Anne had said she was all right and she seemed to be, but Bern hated to leave her alone in that house. Add over-protective to obsessive. He lead-footed it down Cave Creek Road back into Phoenix. Traffic was light, and he made good time, but Will was already waiting a block from Florence Mosk's house, with a patrol car parked behind him.

Will and the patrol officer left their vehicles, got into Bern's Jeep, and Bern drove on down to Florence's. He had checked with the hospital. Florence's shift didn't start until three, and, sure enough, the old white Monte Carlo was on the driveway.

They got out to heat so intense you'd never guess there had been a downpour the night before. The only blessing was that the rain had been sucked right into the bone-dry earth. Contrary to outsider perceptions, the Arizona desert got most of its rain during the summer, much of it coming in violent thunderstorms. When that humidity was added to the high temperature, you felt as if you had been suddenly beamed to Jakarta. No wonder the locals referred to the rainy season as the monsoons.

Will eyed the Mosk house warily. "Thought you said there was a dog."

"Under the porch."

"Hate fucking dogs," the patrolman muttered, drawing his gun.

The dog, Duke, was there. Bern could see his eyes, a yellow gleam in the cave of shadow, and hear his harsh panting. Duke rumbled a low growl as they went through the gate in the chain-link fence and walked up to the porch steps but stayed where he was. Too much effort in the heat to get up and come out, Bern supposed.

At least there was no barking to alert Florence. Bern motioned the patrolman to stand to one side out of peephole range and knocked. He could hear heavy footsteps on the other side of the door, then sensed she was just standing there.

"Florence, can we talk to you?" he called. "It's about Dorie."

He deliberately kept his tone nonthreatening. If she believed they had come about the disposition of Dorie's body, well, her mistake. It was always better to get inside before mentioning search warrants even if subterfuge was required.

After a moment the door opened. Bern went right in, Will close behind. Florence's eyes widened as the uniformed officer quickly brought up the rear, and there was a sudden ugly set to her face.

"We were hoping you'd call and talk to us, Florence," Bern said, "but you didn't, so I'm afraid we're going to have to search your place."

Will produced the warrant and made it official. There was a tense moment when Bern wondered if he'd misjudged the situation, if he should've brought a half-dozen uniforms, but then she turned, stomped into the living room, and sat in one of the oversize chairs, not saying a word as they began the work.

The patrolman was the slash-and-burn type, but neither

Bern nor Will believed in trashing the place and told him so. Still, the job by its nature leaves a mess, and this one was no exception. They found no cash, but down in the bottom of the bathroom hamper, Will discovered an over-size blue T-shirt with a reddish-brown stain on the right sleeve.

Florence wouldn't answer any questions about the garment. She just sat, huge and unmovable, and stared at Bern with her stolid gaze.

Bern said, "Florence, you have anything to say to us, now's the time."

But Florence, true to form, said nothing.

Midday traffic was so light, Anne arrived at the Lewises' a few minutes early. There was an unfamiliar tan Audi in the driveway, and before Anne could touch the bell, the front door opened to reveal a man taking his leave, saying, "I worry about you, Natalie. Please, you have to—" He broke off as he saw Anne standing there.

He was about Natalie's height, slender in a gray suit, white shirt, and conservative striped tie. His dark hair was threaded with a little silver. He regarded Anne through glasses with metal frames, surprised and a little flustered.

"Sorry," Anne said. "I guess I'm early."

Without makeup Natalie's face had a scrubbed, vulnerable look, and her blush was an unattractive red stain on her pale skin. Her coral-colored tank dress hung loosely; cheekbones and clavicles appeared even more pronounced as though stress was rendering the fat from her body.

"Oh, Anne—Elliot just stopped because of the newspaper reports. I worked for him—the job I had a few months ago. Elliot Wray. This is Dr. Menlo."

"Dr. Menlo. I know you're treating Danny, but I wish you'd get Natalie to take better care of herself."

"I'm all right, Elliot, really," Natalie said quickly. "We need to get out of the heat, and I know you have to go back to work. Thanks for coming by."

He looked as though he would have liked to say more, but nodded instead. "All right. Call me. Dr. Menlo."

Natalie quickly shut the door as soon as Anne was across the threshold.

"He seems nice," Anne offered.

"He's a kind man. We can talk. We're just *friends*."

Anne had no intention of prying, but she wasn't blind, and it was obvious that there was something more to the relationship between Natalie and her ex-boss. For one thing he'd come here when Glen wasn't at home. Out in the kitchen, a teakettle began a shrill whistle.

"I was going to make tea," Natalie said, distracted. "Danny's sleeping. Unless you want something cold?"

"No, tea's fine."

"I'll be right back. Please—go sit down."

She gestured to the living room and rushed off toward the kitchen. Anne went in and sat on the blue-striped couch to wait. The room had been restored to order since Anne was here last, the mattress returned upstairs. Natalie was back in minutes with a tray containing a flowered teapot, matching cups, pink paper napkins, and a plate of short-bread cookies.

"I know I should've woke Danny and had him ready, but—do you mind if we talk first?" Natalie put the tray on the coffee table and sank down on the couch beside Anne.

"If it's about your friend Elliot, you don't owe me any explanations."

"No, it's not about Elliot. It's just the reporters and everything—" She poured tea, then glanced down, suddenly panicked. "I forgot sugar and lemon."

"That's all right. I don't need them."

"You're sure? I can just—" She stared at the teapot and looked ready to cry.

Anne gently took away the pot and held Natalie's hands between both of hers. Natalie was trembling, like a tuning fork lightly struck.

"Take a couple of deep breaths," Anne advised, and when Natalie complied, she asked, "Did you eat any lunch?"

"A little soup. I can't—it's like I have a big knot in my stomach. I can barely force anything down."

"Stress can do that to you." She gave Natalie the poured tea. "Here, drink some. And eat a cookie."

Natalie nibbled a few bites, sipped, then put down the cup. "I know people—parents—do horrible things. I watch TV. I read the papers. And we're strangers to the police. I understand they have to assume the worst. But the awful thing is what their suspicions are doing to me." She began breaking the cookie into smaller and smaller pieces, hunched over the coffee table, letting the crumbs fall into the tray. "At first the questions Detective Pagett was asking us—asking Glen—well, I just felt sick. But then I started thinking about how I never talked to the kidnapper. I mean, it is odd. And I didn't see Glen that evening when Dorie was killed until later, maybe nine-thirty, and he wasn't home last night—God, this is making me crazy."

Or she was making sure Anne saw that she was upset about her doubts, meanwhile focusing attention on her husband. But wait—Natalie was home last night, and Tony's killer was a man. So that would eliminate Natalie as a suspect, wouldn't it?

"I didn't even tell Glen you were coming here today," Natalie confessed. "I let him think the session was off, because I wanted to see you alone. You've talked to him,

Anne. You understand people. Please tell me—could he have done something like this?''

''You know him better than I do, Natalie. What do you think?''

''He's lied to me before,'' she said bleakly. ''He had an affair. A woman who worked in the advertising department at Fitness Unlimited. Kristobel—with a K. Kristobel Jones. He hired her while I was still working there. I knew he was attracted to her. All the men were.''

''He's not still seeing her?''

''He swears it's over. I know she left the company. I insisted on that. But all that time he was sleeping with her, I never suspected. I guess that's what scares me—I remember how he came home and acted as though nothing was going on. But this—an affair is one thing. This kind of— of *evil*—no, it can't be true. I don't believe it.''

Upstairs, Danny called for his mother, sounding sleepy and querulous. Natalie jumped up as though responding to a fire alarm.

''I'll come with you,'' Anne said.

''No, drink your tea. I'll get him dressed.''

Anne stared after her as she rushed upstairs, remembering something—the announcement for the new art gallery in Scottsdale, the one Cynthia wanted Anne to attend with her. Kristobel's. And the owner was Kristobel Jones. The same woman? Probably. It was an unusual name.

Did Bern know about Glen's affair? Surely he would have told her if he did. Distasteful as it was, Anne would have to pass along the information and tell him about Natalie's concerned friend Elliot.

Anne sighed, slipped off her shoes, tucked her feet under her, and leaned back on the couch. She had dressed in beige cotton slacks and a gauzy, white, long-sleeved blouse with wide cuffs that drooped well below her wrist bones and covered her bandages and bruises, but she felt chilled. She sipped the tea, grateful for the warmth, and told herself Natalie was right. An affair was one thing; kidnapping and murder quite another.

She wondered if Bern's search of Florence Mosk's house was finished and how it had gone. He had assured her he was taking backup; still, she worried. Reclaiming her own house had calmed her nerves a little, but being stalked by the reporter had generated a much deeper undercurrent of unease.

As if to prove how jumpy she still was, she started at the sound of the front door opening and closing, sat up, and felt for her shoes with her toes as Glen walked down the hall. Seeing her there, he stopped and looked at her with surprise.

"Anne? I didn't know you would be here."

No sense making things worse between the Lewises. She covered for Natalie by saying, "I hated to miss Danny's session, so I took a chance and came over. He was sleeping, but he just woke up. Natalie went up to get him."

"Are you okay? I couldn't believe it when Natalie said that Sales kidnapped you, that you were there when he got shot."

"It was bad," Anne admitted.

"It could've been much worse, though. Lucky for you the man who killed Sales didn't see you."

She listened for a false note but heard only honest concern in his voice.

He sat down in one of the navy-blue chairs. "Did you hear? The cops are still wasting their time, treating me like a suspect."

"Natalie told me." Anne stayed carefully neutral.

"Be nice if they stuck to looking for the real criminals. I know I shouldn't let it get to me. It's just so damned hard on top of trying to keep up with the business and worrying about Danny. I'm sorry, Anne, but I can't see that he's getting any better. Maybe if I understood what happens in these therapy sessions with you. Why is it you don't want us to sit in?''

''I build a certain rapport with the children,'' Anne explained. ''If the parents are there, the dynamics change. To be honest, Glen, quite often the parents are part of the problem.''

''But not in our case,'' he said.

''To a degree,'' Anne said. ''I sense that things were not right between you and Natalie and that Danny was experiencing a lot of anxiety before the kidnapping.'' Of course, she was not going to tell Glen that Natalie had just confirmed her suspicions.

''Danny told you that?''

''Not in so many words.''

''There were problems,'' Glen admitted. ''But we're handling them. I can see your point about working alone with Danny. But what exactly do you do?''

He was entitled to know what the therapy process entailed. She hated the reservations she had about explaining fully. Still, the reality of the situation dictated caution, so she opted for generalities.

''Play is serious business for children. It's a sort of psycho-drama where they can act out troubling things and come to terms with them.''

''So then you can see what's wrong. In Danny's case you can tell what happened to him.''

''Not necessarily. Quite often the therapist can't translate the play.'' True, although for Danny's safety she was going to try. She didn't give this information to Glen, however. Instead she said carefully, ''The most important thing is for the child to deal with his fears in a secure environment.''

To Anne's relief, Natalie and Danny came downstairs then.

"Hey, Dan, my man," Glen said. "How about a hug?"

Danny held up his arms, and Glen scooped him up, but Danny's eyes fixed on Anne, a sober blue gaze shadowed with dread.

"I thought we could play with your toys today, Danny," Anne said.

"Won't that be fun?" Natalie said brightly. "Why don't you take Dr. Anne up to your room?"

Danny shook his head. "No. Don't wanna."

"But, Danny, Dr. Anne came all the way out here."

"No. No *play*."

"If you don't want to, you don't have to," Glen said to his son, adding with a challenging tone, "Isn't that right, Anne?"

She had worried all along that she was pushing Danny too hard. If she insisted on another session and he wasn't ready, she could be doing more harm than good. Was her sense of urgency driving her or her concern for the child?

"Of course," Anne said, not at all sure how good a job she was doing at hiding her uncertainty. "We'll do what's best for Danny." Knowing Glen's distrust of the therapy process, she didn't want to give him the opportunity to put off the next session too long, so she added to Danny, "Maybe you'd like to come and play at my office tomorrow. Okay?"

But Danny turned away and buried his face in his father's neck. Glen's look contained triumph, quickly veiled as he carried the boy off in the direction of the kitchen, promising a snack, crackers and juice, maybe even a chocolate chip cookie.

Watching them go, Anne said, "Natalie, I know it's difficult for Glen after what happened to his sister, but it's vital that I work with Danny as quickly as possible. Please—you have to make sure Glen sees that.''

"His sister?''

"Natalie?'' Glen called from the kitchen. "Give me a hand, will you?''

"I'd better see what he wants,'' Natalie said. "But don't worry. I'll have Danny at your office tomorrow.''

Anne believed her because for an instant she glimpsed a core of strength—resilient and resolute—beneath the fragile, anxious exterior.

25

Until they heard from the lab about the stains on Florence's shirt, all Bern could do was mark time and do paperwork. To be honest, case reports did serve one good purpose. The writing forced him to summarize the things he'd done, to look at them objectively, and once in a while to pick up on anything he had overlooked.

"Follow the money," was the standard police maxim. But where the hell was the ransom? The FBI reported no large deposits made in any Arizona banks. Search warrants had turned up nothing. Could Glen Lewis slip the cash back into his business? Joe Ferraro seemed to think his ex-partner was a pro at manipulating the books. Of course, talk about the pot describing the kettle. And, speaking of Joe, if he'd gotten his hands on the money it would be off to the Cayman Islands faster than you could say private jet.

They had wasted a lot of time on Sales, but the case was not dead—not by a long shot. There was the list coming from Natalie to be checked out, in-depth backgrounds on both the Lewises to be completed—and Bern had not forgotten that Glen might have a girlfriend on the side. Another go-round with Dorie's neighbors might not be a bad idea. See if anybody else had noticed the mysterious man on the street that Wayne Jensen and his pal Dale had reported. And, of course, there was always Danny . . .

Finally, too tired to think straight, Bern left to spend a fast, furious hour on the handball court down in the gym. After a shower, he went back to his desk physically tired but with some of the mental cobwebs cleared away. Now if only he could find a form of exercise that would get rid of that grim old specter of dread that had settled in once again like an unwanted guest in the back of his mind.

His messages included one from Anne. He called her house and got the machine.

"Thought I'd knock off early," he said after the beep. "Maybe I'll bring you a pizza. On second thought, guess I'd better have you paged."

Before he could redial her answering service, Will hurried over.

"Drive-by in the area near Christown Mall," Will said grimly. "We're up."

Bern called Anne's house again and amended his message. "Sorry, babe, no pizza delivery tonight. I caught another case. I'll call when I can."

Anne considered going to see Rosemary after she left the Lewises but found herself heading toward Cave Creek instead. She knew she should not put off talking about what had happened with Tony Sales. But the open wound of her experience last night was not the only thing to be explored. She would also have to open up the old pain of Nicki's death. Confronting her fears, old and new, was going to drain her physically and mentally. She had to find the strength for it, but not now, not tonight.

She knew Bern wouldn't want her to be alone. And she certainly wouldn't argue with him about that. Even a meal in one of the noisy little western-styled cafés in town sounded good to her.

A message from Bern was waiting to scuttle those plans and start a drumbeat of panic in her head. Just as Bern had feared, the Wineski case would go on hold. For the moment any progress would rest entirely on her work with Danny.

So what had she done? Missed an opportunity to work with him just now, given up too soon . . . *Don't do this*, she told herself. She had used her best judgment in deciding to wait and not push the child. Second-guessing was a useless exercise.

Too edgy to rest, she changed the bed and started a load of laundry. There was still an aura of Tony Sales's violent intrusion in her house, like an odor of smoke after a grease fire that only time would dissipate. One thing for sure, she didn't want to be by herself this evening, and if she could do something that might have some bearing on the case, so much the better.

She called her office. Peggy said that Grace Safely had camped out in the parking lot for a while, but had finally given up. Anne suspected the reporter had simply moved on, perhaps to Bern's new case.

"You going to be all right out there tonight?" Peggy asked.

"I'm sure I'll be fine," Anne said. "What does my schedule look like tomorrow? Do I have a slot?"

"It's pretty full. Nothing open until four."

Anne told Peggy to reserve the time for Danny, then asked, "Is Cynthia still there?"

She was, and her last patient had just left.

After assuring Cynthia that she was suffering no ill effects from her trauma, Anne said, "Bern's working, and I'd just as soon not stay home. Are you busy tonight?"

"Lots of things I should be doing," Cynthia said, "but nothing that can't wait. You want to get some dinner?"

"That would be great. Cyn, remember that gallery opening? Would you like to check it out?"

"I'd love to if you're up to going. And it'll take your mind off what happened last night, so that's good."

Cynthia couldn't know it, but distraction was not the issue here. Not that Anne really knew what she was doing. She'd acted on impulse. Dumb impulse—because what could she possibly accomplish by going to take a look at Glen Lewis's ex-lover?

Anne arranged to meet Cynthia at a small café in Scottsdale at seven. This gave Anne time to sit on the couch with her feet up for a short rest before she exchanged her slacks for a long denim skirt and added a silver and turquoise necklace and earrings. Southwestern chic, perfect for the café that was decorated in soft green and peach with sleekly modern white and chrome fixtures.

Cynthia had opted for a white knit halter dress that showed off shoulders and arms toned and tanned by tennis. Good thing Anne had a healthy self-image. Many women suffered a massive attack of insecurity in the presence of slim, blond Cynthia Lynde.

By the time they finished a prickly pear margarita, Anne was starving. The food was overpriced but surprisingly good, leaning heavily on blue corn tortillas, black beans, and fire-roasted chilies. Since both women were skilled in the art of directing conversation, they chatted casually, a surface skimming of art and movies with a smattering of family news.

Over in the far corner a young couple was having dinner with their little daughter who entertained herself by blowing on a red-and-gold pinwheel. Something about the spinning wheel riveted Anne's attention.

"Anne?" Cynthia said.

The elusive memory vanished. "I'm sorry. What?"

"Are you okay?" Cynthia asked, studying her. "I mean, really."

"What's the line?" Anne gave her a wry smile. "As well as can be expected."

The waitress brought their check. Anne glanced at the child with her pinwheel again as they left the café, but whatever memory the sight had stirred stayed frustratingly unclear.

Outside the nice little stucco and frame house just off Bethany Home Road, Will was wrapping up the physical investigation of the blood-soaked Voyager on the driveway. The street was crowded with police vehicles, news vans, and a horde of people curious enough to gather even in one hundred-plus heat. Inside, Bern sat on the couch in the pleasantly furnished living room with the woman whose husband had been shot to death right in front of her horrified eyes a few hours ago.

Mike and Cathy Matoosian and their six-year-old son, Mike Jr., had returned home from Smitty's supermarket at approximately four P.M. From Cathy's hysterical call to 911 and the report of a neighbor, Bern learned that two white males in a blue Chevy pickup had followed the Matoosians into the driveway, pulled up right beside their Voyager on the driver's side, and opened fire. Considering the number of spent .45 shells Will had recovered, it was a miracle that only Mike had been killed. Cathy and Mike Jr. escaped with minor cuts from auto glass turned into beaded shrapnel by the gunfire.

Bern had canvassed the neighborhood while paramedics attended the two survivors. A sedative was finally required to calm the little boy. His mother stayed with him until he fell asleep.

She had been in the bloodstained outfit she had worn on her trip to the store until a few minutes ago when the policewoman who was up sitting with Mike Jr. had tactfully suggested Cathy change her clothes.

Now she sat next to Bern in a mismatched print T-shirt and plaid shorts. She hunched forward, wrapping her arms around herself as though she were holding her body together.

She said, "Are you from this area, Lieutenant?"

She had watched too many TV shows that always gave detectives a rank, but this was not the time to correct her misconception.

"Yes, ma'am," Bern said. "My folks moved here when I was two years old, so I'm practically a native."

"Then explain this to me. We lived in L.A. There was so much crime. Every night on the news all these horrible things happening. I was afraid all the time."

Her voice had a remote, brittle quality, a product of tranquilizers and shock.

"I told Mike we had to get out. I wouldn't stay there and have something happen to Mikey. So we came here. We heard Phoenix was such a nice place. Different. Safe. We've only been here two months—*two months*—and now—" She drew a ragged breath and looked at him with big, tortured eyes. "How could this happen, Lieutenant? Could you please tell me that? I don't understand. *How could this happen?*"

"Phoenix really is a good city," Bern said, "but it's not perfect. Mrs. Matoosian, we need to talk about the shooting now."

She shook her head back and forth and hugged herself tighter.

"I know it's hard," Bern said gently, "but you have to tell me what you remember so we can catch these men and make sure they don't kill somebody else."

Eventually he got the story from her, or as much as she could remember. The men were in their early thirties. She didn't know either of them. She was sure they hadn't been at the supermarket. The truck had started tailgating about a block from home. If it had been following them, she wasn't aware of it and didn't think her husband had been either. What happened on the driveway was a blur. The two men were yelling, but the window was rolled up in the Matoosians' car, and she couldn't make out what they were saying.

She hadn't seen the gun. Mike had shouted to get down, turning in the seat to reach her with one hand and Mike Jr. in back with the other. Then there were several explosions, glass shattering, Mike Jr. screaming. Mike had slumped down on top of her, and she heard tires screeching as the truck roared away.

"They were so angry," Cathy said. "Oh, God, what could we have done to make them so angry?"

"I don't know, Mrs. Matoosian, but I'll do my best to find out."

He had reason to hope he'd be talking to the two slime-bags soon because a neighbor had provided a partial plate number. Meanwhile, he thought about the little boy upstairs. Anne was the person he wanted to recommend, but he honored his promise to keep her out of police work and gave Mrs. Matoosian Karen Doheny's number instead.

Perhaps because Anne suspected that Kristobel Jones had come from a job in advertising at Fitness Unlimited, she was expecting a small place with modest stock, a first rung on a long, difficult ladder to success. Instead, Kristobel's offered works by several well-known local artists and sculptors along with some talented unknowns and was well lit and spacious with just enough odd corners to make it interesting.

Suddenly Anne wished she were here just to enjoy the art. Coming to spy on the owner was alien to her nature. Still, it was what she'd intended to do. Might as well get on with it.

The gallery had attracted a goodly number of people for a summer opening. The food and drink and live music helped. A table offered an array of hors d'oeuvres, a waiter circulated with a tray of glasses filled with champagne, and a string trio played something soft and baroque.

"Oh, Lord," Cynthia said, accepting a glass of champagne and looking around. "Promise me if I reach for my charge card you'll take it away."

"Remember you told me to do it." Anne took a glass for herself. "Come on, it doesn't cost to look."

"She said with the conviction of a shopper without a compulsive bone in her body."

They began a slow circuit, went about ten feet, then Cynthia stopped in her tracks to stare at a bronze sculpture that looked to Anne like a mass of bronze spaghetti noodles.

"Oh, I don't believe it," Cynthia said. "That piece is exactly what I've been looking for. You know the table in my front entry—"

"Forget it," Anne said. "Keep walking."

"No, Anne, I mean it. Scratch all that stuff I said before. This is not just compulsive buying. This is serious."

"You're impossible," Anne said with a laugh.

"I know I am. Listen, let me stand here and drool for a while. You go ahead and wander."

Anne didn't have to wander far before she spotted the owner of the gallery. Cynthia was beautiful; this woman was breathtaking. A froth of Nordic, white-blond hair framed a perfect oval face. Ice-blue silk displayed a body that managed to look lush without carrying an extra ounce of fat. Anne knew for certain the woman was Kristobel Jones, not because of her stunning beauty, but because Glen Lewis was standing next to her.

They were not touching, but something about the way they stood, ignoring the bounds of personal space, suggested intimacy. Or maybe it was the way Kristobel smiled at what Glen was saying, her face tipped up toward him. Anne had only seconds to observe before Glen looked up and saw her.

Glen froze, his expression going blank and then rearranging itself into a smile as she walked toward them.

"Anne," he said. "I'm surprised to see you out. I guess you really do recover fast. Come and meet Kristobel."

He made formal introductions, adding that Anne was the psychologist who was taking care of Danny.

"Poor little boy," Kristobel said. "Such a terrible thing."

Her eyes were a dark shade of blue, almost purple, wide and earnest; the musical voice was full of serious concern.

"Good thing we have Anne to get him through it," Glen said. "So you're an art lover, Anne. Do you go to all the gallery openings?"

"Most of them," Anne said. "I have a friend who's on a list somewhere, probably because of the money she spends. She gets invited, and I tag along."

"Well, I'm so glad you came to my opening," Kristobel said. "Oops, somebody's waving to me. Would you excuse me for a minute?"

"I'm afraid I have to go," Glen said. "I just wanted to say good luck."

They both looked ill at ease, not knowing how to bridge the awkward moment.

Glen said, "I mean it, Krissy. I hope the place is a smash."

She murmured her thanks and hurried off, leaving Anne and Glen with some awkwardness of their own.

"You know, don't you?" Glen asked. "About Kristobel and me. I suppose Natalie told you."

Anne didn't enjoy lying and wasn't good at it, but a little guile was called for here or else she'd find herself having to explain the huge coincidence of being in the gallery.

"She confided in me, yes. When my friend brought me along tonight and I saw Kristobel listed as the owner on the brochure, I wondered. It's an unusual name. And then when I saw the two of you together—" Anne shrugged.

The explanation seemed to satisfy any suspicions he might have.

"I hope you won't tell Natalie about seeing me here," he said. A couple moved in to look at a painting on the wall behind Glen. He touched Anne's elbow and guided her over to where their conversation could be private.

"Natalie would be upset," Glen said, "and there's no reason for her to be."

"I don't plan to say anything," Anne assured him. She might have pointed out that if he'd stayed away from his ex-lover, he would have nothing to worry about. Assuming he really had broken off the relationship, that is.

"I was on my way back to the office," Glen said. "I'm having to go back every night just to keep on top of things. I decided to stop by and wish a friend well. I meant what I told Natalie. I'm not going to see Kristobel anymore. But I still care about her, and these few days are very important to her." He gave Anne a shamed-face grimace of a smile. "I guess this wasn't the smartest thing I've ever done. Now

I'm wondering if anybody else is going to tell Natalie about my being here. Of course, it's my fault things are such a mess, and now I may make it worse. I just wish we could get over this bad spot, you know?''

"I recommended a family counselor to Natalie. Did she tell you?''

He nodded. "I said I'd think about it. This damned hang-up of mine—well, I told you. I seem to always be confiding in you, Anne. And look at me—I'm doing it again.''

"That's what I'm here for,'' Anne said. "I don't mind. But the man I suggested to Natalie is much better at family relationships than I am. I urge you to consider going to him.''

Glen promised he would, then looked at his watch, and said he really had to go on to the office. He would see her tomorrow with Danny. On his way out, he detoured to say a few words to Kristobel.

Anne speculated on what they were saying as Cynthia came to join her. Congratulations and best wishes again? Or a warning that Anne knew about them?

"I didn't want to interrupt,'' Cynthia said. "Couldn't be competition for Bern, could it?''

"Not likely.'' Anne wasn't ready to answer questions Cynthia was sure to ask if she knew the man was Glen Lewis, so she said only, "He's the father of one of my patients. What did you decide on the sculpture?''

"I talked myself out of buying it. Now would be a good time to leave while I'm still solvent.''

"Can you hold out for a few more minutes? I'd like a few words with the owner.''

"Well, if I have to. Just don't leave me alone for too long.''

Anne promised to make it quick and idled her way over to Kristobel, arriving as the couple she had been talking to was leaving and Kristobel was putting a sold sign on the painting the two had been looking at.

"My friend and I have to go," Anne said. "I wanted to tell you your gallery is wonderful. A place like this must be a dream come true for you."

"You could say that." The open gaze had grown cool and watchful. "Thank you for coming."

She nodded and glided away toward a more promising customer, leaving no doubt in Anne's mind what Glen's final words to Kristobel had been: a warning that Anne knew about them.

26

With a high-profile case like the Matoosian shooting, there were department media people on hand to keep the reporters at bay. Bern glimpsed Grace Safely trying to make an end run, but a burly uniformed officer stopped her before she could duck under the crime-scene tape. Bern was aware of her presence, however, as he helped Will complete the processing of the scene. When they finished, a couple of uniforms ran interference as the two detectives made a dash for Will's car.

Since they had missed dinner, they went through the drive-up window at Taco Bell and ate on the way back to the station.

In the squad room Bern sat behind his desk, and Will dragged over a chair and sank down wearily into it. Besides the ton of paperwork, there was little to be done on the Matoosian shooting until the lab finished its job or there was a hit on the plate. Bern let his mind skip a track back over to the Wineski murder.

''We're pretty rapidly running out of leads,'' he said without preface.

They had worked together enough so that Will followed the change of subject. ''Except for Ferraro, and that's going to take a hell of a lot of digging.''

He got up and trudged over to the coffee machine and came back with two filled mugs. He asked, "You ever partner with Lou Halley before he retired?"

"No," Bern said. "I met him, though, and I've heard plenty about him."

Halley had been a slender, balding man, famous for his photographic memory and for his phenomenal clearance rate.

"I worked with him for about a year," Will said. "We had this case—dozens of leads, every one leading nowhere. I was beating my head against the wall, rechecking everything. Not Lou. He took a day off and went to the zoo. He used to do that. Came back and told me who did it and damned if he wasn't right. Told me that's how he cleared so many cases. Said he just settled back and waited and pretty soon his gut told him who was guilty."

Most cops knew what Lou Halley meant. You do all the investigation, but in the end sometimes instinct, honed by years of experience, is the best tool a detective has.

There was nothing Bern would like better than a gut feeling about who had killed Dorie Wineski and Tony Sales and had kidnapped Danny. What he was lacking in crime-solving instinct he was making up for in foreboding because that sense of impending doom lurked, perched in a corner of his mind like a buzzard in a tree.

He reached for the phone and called Anne, but they seemed destined to play phone tag. She had left him a message saying she was having dinner with Cynthia. Now he left one asking her to please call so he'd know she got home all right.

She did, but by then Bern had left with Will to investigate a pickup, abandoned a few blocks from the Matoosians' house, with a license plate matching the partial number the witness had given them.

• • •

Anne kept checking her rearview mirror on the drive home to Cave Creek. Nobody there. Still, when she left her car, she found herself daunted by the prospect of entering the dark house, and when she opened the front door, such a powerful wave of dread swept over her she almost ran to the Camaro and headed back to Phoenix to Bern's apartment.

This is ridiculous, she told herself as she reached for the hallway light switch.

But she stood there, like an animal scenting the wind, until she was satisfied that the only apparent odor was lemon cleaner and the only sound the quiet hum of appliances—refrigerator, air conditioner, clock.

Without realizing it, she had been holding her breath. She let it out and walked slowly into the living room to turn on a lamp. The fear didn't retreat until every light in the house was blazing.

She wished now that she'd gone to talk to Rosemary instead of taking that trip to the art gallery. All she had done tonight was to indulge in a kind of voyeuristic look at Glen and Kristobel. So Glen might still have feelings for the woman—so what? Emotions are not easily turned off. Anne certainly knew that from her own on-again, off-again relationship with Bern. What mattered was whether Glen was making a sincere effort to keep his affair in the past and salvage his marriage. Anne could give him the benefit of the doubt and assume he was. Of course, Bern might come up with a different interpretation since Bern saw everything in the worst possible light.

She wondered what his take would be on Elliot Wray, but she couldn't reach Bern, so she'd have to wait to hear his reaction.

One thing she decided she had to do was to call her

parents. Chances were good that Tony's death and her connection to the incident would remain local news, but she didn't want to count on it.

Her mother answered the phone, and they chatted for about a minute before her mother said, "What is it, Anne? What's wrong?"

Her father heard and picked up the extension. After assuring them that she was fine, Anne gave a fairly accurate report of what had happened to her, although she downplayed the danger she had faced and the terror she felt and emphasized that she was safe now.

"Seems to me it might not be over yet," her dad said. "What if this guy thinks you saw him, but that the police are keeping it quiet?"

"Oh, I don't think that's likely, Dad," Anne said even as a chill crept along her spine.

"Anyway, Bern's going to stay there, isn't he, Anne?" her mother asked. "You're not going to be alone."

Even though she was thirty-four years old, a grown woman living five hundred miles away, she still found it impossible to lie to her mother.

"Bern's on another case, so I'm not sure he'll make it here tonight," Anne said. "But he's keeping close tabs on me."

"I think we ought to come over," her dad said. "I don't know if we can still get a flight, but we can jump in the car and be there by three or four in the morning."

Yes, Anne wanted to cry, *come right away.*

Instead she said, "Dad, you told me you had a busy couple of weeks coming up. You can't just leave like that."

"Honey, I'm the boss. I can do what I want."

Sam Menlo was past the age when he could install tile and shingles, but he did everything else for his small roofing company—estimating, scheduling, ordering, and managing the crews.

"You know if you need us," her mother said, "we'll be there."

Anne remembered that night years before when she got the phone call about Nicki Craig's death. Unable to reach Rosemary, she'd called home. Hearing the shock in Anne's voice, her mother had declared, "We're coming right over there."

Now Anne said, "Well, I love you for offering, but really, Mom, it's not necessary."

Eventually she convinced them they didn't have to drop everything and rush over. She asked them to say hi to Kevin, Tammy, and her four nieces and nephews and promised to come for a visit soon.

After she hung up, Anne prowled the house restlessly, watching distant lightning from the kitchen window. The night she heard about Nicki she had sat in her dark bedroom, staring at the glowing numbers on a digital clock that counted down the hours until her folks would arrive. Just knowing they were on their way kept her from falling apart.

Their love had helped, no doubt about it, but some things can't be fixed with hugs and reassurance. Anyway, her parents were in their early sixties now, old enough so they didn't need the stress of charging off in the night to rush to her side.

At ten o'clock, Anne decided she'd better watch the news to see exactly what was being said about Tony's death. The lead story was the drive-by shooting. Bern's case. She saw him in the footage, a cold, remote stranger doing his job and ignoring the cameras. Grace Safely gave a report, black eyes burning with anger and voice snapping with exasperation because the cops wouldn't allow her to talk to Mrs. Matoosian.

Anne began to think that the reporter had been side-tracked by the newer tragedy and that nothing would be said about Tony Sales's murder. The broadcast was almost over before Anne learned it was a mistake to underestimate the tenacity of a determined reporter.

The anchor announced a live report, and there was Grace Safely in the patchy, oil-stained parking lot behind the abandoned Oh Boy Burgers stand with the Roadrunner Trucking sign strobing her face with red and yellow neon.

With her sleek black hair and slightly beaky nose, in the surreal light Grace looked like a bird of prey. Anne would be willing to bet the woman was still fuming at being denied access to Mrs. Matoosian and had decided to get some of her own back against the police department. As she spoke, Anne could see that anger and exasperation had changed to vindictiveness.

"The tragic death of Michael Matoosian was the second shooting in Phoenix in less than twenty-four hours. Police are working all out on this murder, and that's as it should be. A good man is dead. His wife and child are lucky to be left alive.

"But another man died here in this parking lot last night. Tony Sales was a convicted felon, an escapee from jail, but he was gunned down just as viciously as Mr. Matoosian. What are the police doing to find his killer? Nobody's talking. Including the detective assigned to the case . . ."

Here the screen showed footage shot outside the police station, Bern giving Grace the cold shoulder and a terse, "No comment," and then a segue to Grace knocking on Anne's door.

". . . and Dr. Anne Menlo, the woman who claims to have been Tony Sales's hostage, isn't talking either.

"Tony Sales was the chief suspect in the kidnapping of three-year-old Danny Lewis . . ." Inserts of telephoto views of the Lewis house, of Natalie and Danny getting into their car. "But Tony was never charged, and he denied the crime. Strangely enough, Dr. Menlo is Danny Lewis's therapist, and inside sources confirm that although little Danny Lewis was traumatized and hasn't talked about his ordeal yet, he may be an eyewitness to the murder of his ex-nanny, Dorie Wineski—who was also Tony Sales's girlfriend."

Grace shook her head in puzzlement. "As I said, stranger and stranger. Tony Sales died right here on this very spot. Let's just hope the police remember that Dorie Wineski and Tony Sales may not have been perfect people, but solving their murders requires the same diligence as finding the men who killed Michael Matoosian."

As the anchors thanked Grace and got in a few knowing nods, Anne seethed with outraged anger. All this time the police had kept a lid on the news that Danny might have witnessed a murder. Now, for any mathematically challenged killer who hadn't put two and two together, Grace Safely had provided that information and then identified Anne as Danny's therapist. In addition to the danger for Danny, it shouldn't be too great a leap to figure out that if Danny saw anything and talked, Anne would likely be the one he would talk to.

As late as it was, Anne called the Lewises. Their machine answered, but as soon as she identified herself, Glen picked up the phone.

"Did you see the Channel 12 news?" Anne asked.

"No, I've been avoiding newscasts. Natalie gets too upset. Why?"

Anne explained what the reporter had said.

Glen swore bitterly, then said he would alert the security patrol and ask them to make extra swings past his house.

"I have an opening at four tomorrow," Anne said. "We need to find out what Danny knows, Glen. Especially since his identity and mine have been on TV and are bound to be all over the papers.''

"Is he really remembering anything?'' Glen asked. "Don't you think he's put the whole thing out of his mind? And how do you know that forgetting wouldn't be the best thing for him?''

"You can't bury trauma forever. It needs to be brought out in the open and dealt with. I think Danny's getting ready to do that.''

He was silent for a moment. "Well, okay. But I really don't want Natalie to bring Danny to your office. I think he ought to stay right here where he'll be safe.''

"All right,'' Anne agreed. "Tell Natalie I'll be there about four-fifteen.''

After she hung up, Anne knew she wouldn't be able to sleep. She made herself a cup of tea and went to sit in the living room. No television. She needed to think.

As she had told Glen, burying a traumatic event was like covering up an infection. Although the ugly sore was out of sight, it did not stop festering. And sometimes, even when you thought the wound had healed, you found out you were wrong. She had had her own reminder of this lately.

For the sake of Danny's mental health, as well as keeping him physically safe, she hoped he would have a breakthrough soon. Even though she had let Glen believe this might be about to happen, she really wasn't so sure. There was always the possibility that Danny had repressed so much of the trauma he might never recall everything. And so far the things that he had revealed made very little sense.

To you, she reminded herself.

A child's perceptions are very different from an adult's. On some level he knew he had seen a dead body, but so far he was not ready to claim the experience with all its ramifications. As for the rest of it—rabbits and those impressionistic straight lights that seemed familiar somehow . . . Well, what did the rabbit suggest?

A toy, maybe. Something brought along to calm him when he was taken from his father's car, much the way Anne herself offered teddy bears to distraught children? But there was no reaction when she told Bern about Danny's nightmare and his reaction to the stuffed bunny. Surely he would have remembered if they found such a toy at Dorie's house.

As for the drawing . . .

She sat very still as an image leapt to her mind: a pinwheel held by the little girl in the restaurant, red and gold blades spinning. And she knew what the pinwheel reminded her of: a house in Dorie's neighborhood with a yard full of windmills twirling in the hot breeze.

It was a good forty-five-minute drive to the area where Dorie lived, even with the light traffic at this time of night. Anne didn't care, because she was sure she'd never get to sleep unless she verified what she suspected.

The house with the windmills was on a corner on an intersecting street, which made it about a block and a half from Dorie's. Anne parked out front. A lot of people were still up, but not those who lived here. The windows were dark.

Most of the clouds were to the north except for one big thunderstorm cell to the south toward Tucson. The sky was clear to the east where a pumpkin-seed moon rose. A gibbous moon, she recalled from an astronomy course, a few days past full. It supplemented the weak illumination from a lone streetlamp, providing enough light to observe the yard.

If anything, the light level was better than daytime because the moonlit scene was rendered in impressionistic shadow. Support towers were reduced to strong straight lines, the vanes to X's. Some, at least in the darkness, appeared undecorated. Others, however, had cutouts of animal shapes: a pig, a cow, a rooster.

And there atop the closest windmill was the silhouette of a rabbit.

27

Anne sat gripping the steering wheel, her heart racing. Danny had been here, possibly in this very spot. She stared at the dark, silent house with fear drying her mouth. What had she been thinking of coming here alone?

She hadn't been using her head, that was the problem. She had been too caught up in trying to find out what Danny's memories meant. A quick check of the street showed nothing moving. Her doors were locked and the engine running. She decided she was safe enough to sit for a few more minutes, reached into her purse for her cell phone, and called Bern's pager. She punched in her mobile number plus 911, their code for emergencies.

Strictly speaking, this wasn't an emergency, but it would guarantee his calling back immediately. Less than a minute later, the phone rang.

She picked it up and said, "Bern? I'm all right."

"Jesus," he said, his voice rough with a mixture of anger and relief. "You scared the hell out of me. Where are you?"

"I'm sitting in front of a house about a block from Dorie's."

"You're *what*?" He yelled so loud she had to hold the phone away from her ear. "What the *fuck* are you doing?"

"You can lecture me later." She could hear a police scanner in the background and other male voices. "Can you talk for a minute?"

"Yes, but—"

"Just listen. Do you remember the house with all the windmills in the yard?"

She told him the correlation she had made to the windmills with Danny's nightmare, his reaction to the toy bunny, and the drawing.

"Did you interview the person who lives here?" she asked.

"Persons—yeah. An elderly couple. He's blind, and she uses a walker."

Anne sighed with disappointment. "I really hoped—did the woman maybe see anything unusual?"

"No, she said not. I'm glad you made some sense out of Danny's dream, babe, but I'm afraid it doesn't help."

"It may not point out the murderer," Anne said, "but it does tell me something for sure."

"What?"

"I knew Danny remembered Dorie's fall and seeing her body, but I was beginning to be afraid he'd repressed the rest of it to such an extent he might never recall the details. Now I know that everything is there, Bern. The memories are surfacing in bits and pieces, but they are coming back."

"When will you see Danny again?"

"Late tomorrow afternoon."

"Okay, listen up. If he remembers anything else, you call me immediately. No running off to check it out, you hear?"

She bit back a tart reply. After the incident with Tony Sales, Bern had a right to worry. "I promise not to do anything stupid."

"That's not the same thing, and you know it." He

paused—counting to ten maybe—then said wearily, "Anne, go home. Please. Leave the cop stuff to me."

There was not a chance she was going to tell him about her trip to Kristobel Jones's art gallery. Not now. He was angry enough already.

"And call when you get to Cave Creek," he added.

She promised she would leave a message to let him know she was safely home.

Next morning, after a brief meeting with Andy and Cynthia, Anne plunged into a full day of work. Rescheduled patients made sure of that. Even though she had gotten to bed late, she felt charged with energy from a bike ride and more confident than she had for a long time. Despite her doubts, her work with Danny had produced results.

Jason Sills was coming in at one. Anne used her spare minutes to call some other psychologists. What they told her left her shaken to the core. Two other children from Jason's class were in therapy. Something was terribly wrong, and she had not picked up on the severity of the situation. While she'd delayed checking with other therapists, Jason had spent extra time in a classroom with a woman who was obviously unfit to teach.

She had asked Peggy to bring her a sandwich from the deli, but she could barely eat anything because of the knot in her stomach.

When Deena arrived with Jason, the boy's actions confirmed her worst fears. Jason walked in quietly with his mother, sat down beside her on the couch, and responded politely when Anne spoke to him.

"Why don't you go over and set up our toys, Jason," Anne said. "Your mom and I need to talk for a minute."

He got up obediently and went to the play table.

"Whatever you're doing seems to be working," Deena

said. "I haven't had a complaint from his teacher all week. He seems tired, though. I hope he's not getting a bug."

Across the room, Jason sat listlessly beside the table, staring at the basket of toys Anne had put out. The borderline hyperactive, mischievous hell-raiser was gone; in his place was a passive, well-behaved little boy with the saddest eyes Anne had ever seen.

Anne leaned forward and pitched her voice low so that Jason wouldn't hear. "Deena, Jason's behavior hasn't improved because of my therapy, and I don't think he's tired because of a virus. Your son's exhibiting signs of depression."

"He's depressed?" Deena said incredulously. "But he's only five years old."

"Believe me, children can suffer from depression as well as adults."

Anne had to make sure Deena understood the seriousness while calming Deena's growing alarm. With that accomplished, Anne had to move on to the next part, which was not going to be easy for Deena Sills. Like many young women these days, she was torn between needing to work and finding safe, dependable care for her child. The private school Jason attended had seemed a godsend, offering an extended program after the kindergarten class.

But despite any personal hardship the decision would cause, Deena agreed to remove Jason from the school at once, adding, "I've got to do something about that teacher, Anne. Surely she won't be allowed to go on working there?"

"Not if I can help it," Anne said.

Together she and Deena called Jason's doctor who agreed to give the boy a physical evaluation as soon as Deena could bring him in.

Seeing them out, Anne gave Jason a quick hug and said, "He'll be all right, Deena. We'll make sure of it."

Deena looked ready to cry. "I just knew something was wrong. I had this feeling. And I could see how Jason was acting. But I kept telling myself it couldn't be true. I should've trusted my instincts. I should've done something."

"You did," Anne said. "You came to me."

I'm the one who failed him.

All she could do now was to make sure that Jason would recover and that the rest of those children would be all right.

She spent her odd moments of free time that afternoon talking to other therapists and to the principal of Jason's school who reacted with such hostility that Anne realized it would not be easy to get the teacher out of the kindergarten classroom; it might even be impossible. Private schools were not subject to the same safeguards as public education. But Anne would not give up. She would have to regroup and plan some strategy.

After her last patient, Anne quickly packed up a plastic crate with toys. Then, balancing the doll house on top of the crate, she left her office to drive to the Lewises'. Last night she'd felt so sure Danny's therapy was going well that she had instinctively done the right things. Now, after the bombshell with Jason, she wondered how many other mistakes she'd made, how many warnings she'd played down or overlooked.

At least no news van was lurking outside the Lewis house when she arrived. Maybe Grace Safely had done her hatchet job and moved on. Anne hoped so.

There was a delay while Natalie disengaged the security system and turned the dead bolt. As soon as Anne was inside, Natalie locked the door and reset the alarm.

"I hate this," Natalie said. "It's like we're hiding out. That can't be good for Danny.'' She looked anxiously at her son who had come to stand in the entry to the living room, regarding Anne and his mother soberly. So small, so dependent. "I made sure he was up early from his nap today, and I gave him a snack. Danny, come and say hi to Dr. Anne.''

He came over shyly, intrigued by the toys she carried. Anne dropped down on her heels to say hello, resisting the urge to gather him into her arms. It was essential that she keep her chaotic emotions in check. Children were little walking sensors, picking up on everything.

"Anne? You said something yesterday that's been puzzling me. What did you mean it's difficult for Glen after what happened to his sister?''

Anne picked up the toy crate and stood, holding the doll house in place with her chin. "Just that he's leery about therapy since it didn't help her.'' At Anne's puzzled look, Anne said, "You didn't know his sister was in therapy before she died?''

Natalie shook her head. "He never told me. Which shouldn't surprise me, I guess. He won't talk about things, just like his folks.''

Anne would bet Glen had not told his wife about visiting Kristobel's gallery the night before, either. Well, Anne wouldn't be the one to hurt her. Anyway, she had her hands full trying to help Danny.

"Maybe Danny and I could play in his room,'' Anne suggested. "Do you want to help me carry the toys, Danny?''

She offered a truck from the crate. He took it and went with her, looking resigned. Anne closed the door, and they settled down on the floor in his room. He sat, his sturdy body touching hers, watching her set up the doll house, his eyes wide and serious. His straw-blond hair had grown shaggy and feathered against his ears. He smelled of baby shampoo and vanilla wafers.

Oh, God, she thought, *let me do this right.*

The crate contained several toy figures, an assortment of cars, and a pickup truck. She began the play by putting two figures in the house.

"This little boy and his mom are at home," she said. "The boy's been playing, and he's getting tired. What do you think he's doing now?"

Danny hesitated, then said reluctantly, "Watching cartoons."

Anne let him manipulate the toys for a minute, the mother cleaning the kitchen, the boy in the family area nearby jumping on the sofa. Then Anne put a male figure in a car and brought the car to the house.

"Dad's home now," she said. "He's going to run some errands and take the boy along."

The toy child didn't want to go. Danny had him whine and cry and cling to his mother. All the while tension built in Danny's face. Anne wasn't sure whether this scene was a re-creation of what had happened the day of the kidnapping or an indication of Danny's reluctance to reenact the real events.

When it looked as though the boy was going to convince his mother to let him stay home, Anne said, "Mom's getting a really bad headache. She has to lie down for a while, so the boy has to go with his dad."

Danny gave her an imploring look. "Even if he promises to be really quiet and not do anything bad?"

She was pushing him—too much? The safest thing was to back off for now. No, the safest thing was to have let him dictate the pace to begin with, and she was far beyond that now.

"Yes, Danny," she said. "He still has to go."

He sat holding the boy figure, staring at the scene. Anne

picked up the toy father and made him walk out the door. "The dad's going to get his car, Danny. He says: 'Come on, son. We're going to run some errands.' "

"No." Danny shook his head. "It's not the right one. No, he can't."

"Yes, Danny. The boy has to go."

"*No.*"

He threw the boy figure down, his behavior rapidly turning frenetic as he went to rummage frantically in the crate, then in his toy chest.

Anne went to him, put her arms around him, and said, "It's all right, Danny. We can stop now. It's okay."

He was sweaty and trembling as he finally calmed enough to sit on her lap. Did she dare go on? All she wanted was this little boy safe and whole, but he never would be until the person who kidnapped him and killed Dorie was caught.

Feeling torn and fearful, she said, "Tell you what, Danny, how about we tell a story instead? Okay? Is that all right?"

A hesitant nod.

Anne took a steadying breath. "Once upon a time . . ."

She spun out the tale of a boy who lived with his father and mother who loved him very much, arriving eventually at the day when the father takes the boy along to the bank and the drycleaners.

"So the little boy and the dad drove away in the dad's car—"

"No," Danny said. "No, they didn't."

"Yes, Danny. That's what they did."

"No," he insisted, growing tense and agitated again. "It was the Big Foot. The Big Foot," he declared.

"Okay," Anne said. Anything to keep him calm. "Then what happened?"

"The boy was crabby. He wouldn't put the seat belt on. Daddy said you have to. And I—and the boy kicked his feet. But the daddy made him. Then he went to sleep. And then he waked up."

"At the dry cleaners?"

Danny shook his head.

"Where did the boy wake up?"

"The bunny place." He was very pale. His blue eyes were fixed on some terrible middle distance. "I wanta go home. But I have to go with Dorie. Dorie was sad 'cause I didn't like it there, and I cried, and then she falled down. I was bad, and she falled down."

"No, Danny. You did not make her fall down," Anne said. "It wasn't your fault. Who else was there, Danny? Who else was with Dorie?"

"She went to sleep and she *died*," he said, so caught up in the horror of the memory that she wasn't sure he had heard her. "I said I'd be good. I promised. But she wouldn't w-wake up." Tears rolled down his cheeks. "There was b-b-blood, and b-b-b-bugs—" The word ended on a wail.

"What's going on in here?"

She looked up to see Glen standing in the doorway, his face grim. Absorbed in Danny's anguish, she hadn't heard the door open.

"Please give us a minute," Anne said. "I'm not quite finished—"

"Oh, yes, you are."

He closed the distance in two long strides and took Danny from her. "It's okay, son. Daddy's got you."

Jarred from the remembered scene, the boy looked like a frightened and bewildered sleepwalker. Anne got to her feet, feeling suddenly uneasy with Glen towering over her, and tried to keep her voice calm to keep from scaring Danny further.

"Glen, he's starting to remember what happened to him. That's a painful thing, but it's necessary."

"Maybe so, but I'm not so sure." He turned stony and resolute. "I know one thing—no more today. Come on, son."

He carried Danny from the room, brushing past Natalie at the door on the way out.

"Anne?" Natalie said. "What's going on?"

"Glen walked in just as Danny began to talk about what happened to him. Nobody wants to see Danny upset, Natalie, but it's inevitable. He's remembering a horrible thing."

"It's just so hard to see him like that, Anne."

"I know it is. But for his sake, to help him get over the trauma and to keep him safe, it's essential that he go through the process. Whatever Glen's hang-ups about his sister, he has to let me finish what I started here today."

"Yes, okay," Natalie agreed, looking tense and distracted. "I'll talk to him."

On the drive home, Anne hit rush-hour traffic, so she had plenty of time to think about the aborted session with Danny. Had Glen been right to rush in and rescue his son? Had he recognized some breaking point she hadn't seen?

No, what she told Natalie was true. Recalling the trauma was painful but necessary. The thing that worried her the most was that Danny had been left with all those frightening images, all that horror raw in his mind. Even an adult would have difficulty coping, and Danny was just a scared baby.

She was very much afraid he would deal with the memories the way he had in the beginning. He would cram them into a room in the deepest corner of his mind and slam the door. And she might not be able to get him to open up to her again.

28

The first truck Bern and Will checked out proved to be a false lead. It had been almost noon today when patrol spotted another Chevy pickup that looked to be a match; two hours later, Bern and Will found the men suspected of killing Mike Matoosian. After that Bern was too busy to worry about Anne and the stunt she'd pulled the night before, going off on her own to check out the house in Dorie's neighborhood.

The truck was registered to one Calvin Rupp. His wife was just leaving for work from their tiny cinder-block rental house; they caught her on the driveway, getting into a car with a friend. She said she hadn't seen Cal since about noon, but she kept shooting such fearful glances back at the house that Will asked her to step out of the car. The friend, sensing trouble, promptly left. Protesting, Mrs. Rupp led them across a weedy lawn and let them into the house.

There they found two children, ages four and seven, who were being left without a baby-sitter. The first time she'd ever done such a thing, according to Mrs. Rupp, and all her husband's fault. *Somebody* had to work. He certainly wouldn't, the no-good son of a bitch. Wouldn't you think he'd at least come home to watch the kids?

She thought he was where he always was: Off with that

bastard Pete Norbert, a bigger loser than Cal, they were probably at Pete's apartment. Mrs. Rupp gave Will the address, showing no desire to know why the cops were looking for her husband. Bern guessed police interest in Calvin Rupp was old hat; the guy had a record of repeated arrests for drunk driving and bar fights. Neither Bern nor Will was going to tell her just how much trouble he was in this time. They didn't want Rupp alerted.

What Bern told Mrs. Rupp was that he expected her to stay home until she got somebody to watch her children, and that Child Protective Services was going to be around to make sure of it in the future.

Then he and Will drove over to Norbert's apartment where they found Pete and Calvin drinking tequila and Dos Equis, smoking marijuana, and debating whether to head for Nogales or to go out for pizza.

Too drunk and too stoned to put up much resistance, the two were taken down to headquarters where they began to sober up fast when they realized the charges they were facing.

After taking a look in her refrigerator, Anne had to go out again if she wanted something more than scrambled eggs or yogurt for dinner. She found herself oddly reassured by the bright lights and abundance in the supermarket. Surrounded by the earthy smells and bright colors in the produce department, the disappointments and worries of her grinding day seemed distant and unreal.

But the illusion faded fast as she drove home. She wanted to see Danny again as soon as possible, both to reassure herself that he was handling what had happened today and to make sure he didn't bury the trauma again. Before she even unloaded the grocery bags in the kitchen, she called the Lewises. She expected to get the answering machine first. With the publicity, they were screening their calls. But nobody picked up the phone.

Maybe the Lewises were avoiding her. Considering her own self-doubts, how could she blame them?

She picked at a lamb chop and a salad, cleaned up the kitchen, then went out to turn on the outside tap for the line that ran to the watering basin up in the rocks. All the while she kept going over what Danny had told her.

In Danny's version, he had fallen asleep in his dad's car just as Glen said, but he didn't wake up until he was on the street near Dorie's, the "bunny place." If that were true, it meant Dorie or her accomplice had picked the boy up and transferred him to another vehicle without awakening him.

Or that his father had taken him to Dorie's.

Anne felt cold even though the western sky glowed with a bright, fierce twilight, and she could feel heat on her face radiating from the rocky earth and the building.

Don't jump to conclusions, she cautioned herself.

Back inside, Anne took a legal pad and wrote down everything that had happened during the session. The Big Foot, Danny had said. What exactly did that mean? Did the name describe the accomplice—a big man or a big woman?

Children Danny's age did not always have the necessary vocabulary to express themselves. Quite often they used tags taken from TV or else the names they used were corrupted or misunderstood terms. Sometimes the connections were easy to see. For instance, Danny had named his stuffed bunny Easter Eggs; he called the whale in his picture Free Willy.

Occasionally it was almost impossible to figure out the reference. Anne remembered that her nephew Benjamin told his grandmother one morning that he wanted Chicken Cereal for breakfast. The more baffled the adults looked, the more he insisted, working himself toward a full-blown tantrum. Finally Anne had opened the pantry, asking him to point out what he wanted.

"Chicken Cereal!" he had cried, tearfully triumphant as he pointed to a Kellogg's Corn Flakes box with its big red, green, and yellow rooster.

To Benjamin who couldn't read, the name had made perfect sense. Danny's Big Foot reference would, too—to Danny.

She decided to call Bern and tell him about the session. Maybe he'd see something she missed. She put down the pad and went into the kitchen. Before she could pick up the phone, it rang.

"Anne?" Glen said. "About what happened earlier— I'm sorry I flew off the handle like that. I'm sure you know what you're doing and you have Danny's best interests at heart."

"I'm glad you think so," Anne said. "And I'm happy you called. I tried to reach you earlier, but nobody picked up the phone."

"Oh, boy, I was hoping Natalie just didn't want to talk to me. I'm worried about her, Anne. She was really depressed after you saw Danny today. I should never have left her, but there's just so much to do. I haven't let on to Natalie; I didn't want to worry her. But paying the ransom, all that money gone—well, I'm fighting tooth and nail just to keep the business going."

"You're at the office?"

"Yes, but I decided work could wait and planned to go home, but the car won't start. Damned auto club—I've called twice now."

"Well, I think you're overreacting," Anne said. "Natalie seemed all right to me. Maybe she went to bed early. She's missed a lot of sleep, and she's really drained."

"Yeah, I know. I'm sure you're right. It's just—I keep thinking about the way she looked—almost, well, despondent, and the things she was saying—"

"Like what?" Anne asked sharply.

"That maybe Danny was never going to get any better. She blamed herself, as though the kidnapping was somehow her fault. I told her not to be silly. I mean, I'm the one who's had the problems with Danny's therapy. She's been hopeful, until now. I hate to ask you, Anne. We always seem to be asking you favors. But if you could talk to her—" He broke off, leaving the request unspoken.

"But if she's not answering the phone—you want me to go over there?"

"I know it's an imposition. I just have this feeling she *needs* somebody, and God knows how long I'll be stuck out here."

Anne thought it likely that Glen was feeling guilty for leaving his wife alone, maybe even for stopping by to see Kristobel last night. Bone-weary herself, Anne had no desire to drive all the way to the Lewises' only to awaken Natalie from well-deserved sleep. Her instinct was to offer reassurances and say no, but suddenly she remembered Deena Sills, eyes brimming with tears, saying, "I had this *feeling*. I should've done something." And Anne remembered how she had waited to make those phone calls to other psychologists; her delay may have triggered little Jason's slide into depression.

Wasn't it entirely possible she had misjudged Natalie's frame of mind? Could she afford to take the chance?

"All right," Anne said. "I'll go over to check on Natalie."

Finding Calvin Rupp and Pete Norbert turned out to have been the hard part. Once Bern and Will put a little pressure on the two, Rupp couldn't wait to give Norbert up as the shooter. Informed of this, Norbert immediately told them that Calvin had urged him to open fire, that Cal was the one who was royally pissed when Matoosian cut him off in the Smitty's lot so that they would have to park way the hell down at the end and walk in the heat to go buy some liver sausage and Swiss cheese for sandwiches.

They never had gone into Smitty's; they went through a nearby Burger King drive-up window instead. Then, still fuming, about halfway to Norbert's apartment Cal had wheeled around and headed back to the supermarket, arriving just as the Voyager was leaving. They followed the Matoosians home—definitely Cal's idea. To teach them a thing or two, Norbert said.

It wasn't his fault, naturally, even though he'd pulled the trigger. He was drunk, and Cal had told him to do it, practically forced him, if you want to know the truth.

Bern, already exhausted by the long hours, was sickened by the prospect of having to tell Cathy Matoosian why her husband had been killed. He surely wasn't up to the task tonight. Neither was Will who said he was going home.

Bern desperately needed a shower, a decent meal, and—eventually—sleep. But what he wanted most of all was to see Anne, to be reassured that there was still decency, tenderness, and love in the world and to quiet the worry that still gnawed at him by having her safe in his arms.

If he had left the office at that moment he would've headed north like a homing pigeon toward Cave Creek. But he sat there five seconds too long. The phone rang. It was the lab with a report on Florence Mosk's shirt. The stain was blood, all right.

Canine blood.

Bern had investigated twenty-five homicides in the past year, including four stabbings, thirteen shootings, two poisonings, two hit-and-runs, three bludgeonings, and one strangulation. He had taken all that tearing and bruising of flesh, all that spilling of blood and brain matter in stride as part of the job. Yet now, the thought of Florence's dog—injured, lying out there in the dirt, heat, and flies—provided the final gram of outrage, tipping the scale.

The sensible thing to do was call animal control. He was beyond being sensible. Operating on narrowly focused, blind fury, he charged out of the office, got into the Jeep, and headed toward South Mountain.

Instead of taking her usual route, Anne thought it would be faster to go south through Carefree, jogging over to miss downtown Scottsdale. Times like this made her think how nice it would be to have a freeway in this part of town.

She caught the news on the radio that the police had announced arrests in the drive-by shooting case. Bern might be tied up all night with the suspects, but at least if the charges stuck, he should be free to give his attention to finding the person who kidnapped Danny and killed Dorie and Tony. This would be especially important if Danny retreated again, if he refused to process his memories.

No, don't think like that, she told herself.

Her experience and training would help her find a way to help Danny. Meanwhile, she had to do what she could for Natalie. Anne might have discounted Glen's worries except for Natalie's behavior the day before. Although she seemed okay earlier, Natalie could be heading for a breakdown if her fears for Danny weren't relieved soon—along with her suspicions of her husband.

Anne had been careful not to fuel those suspicions, but Natalie had a right to be alarmed. As Bern once explained, "Remember that old song: 'You Always Hurt the One You Love'? Well, that's the first tenet of police work."

As for Anne, she simply didn't know what to think. What did she really know about Glen Lewis? He was competitive and hard-driving. He cheated his business partner—if you could believe Joseph Ferraro. He cheated on his wife for sure, yet Anne really felt he loved Danny, and he had promised Natalie to work out their problems before the kidnapping. A flawed man, but then there were lots of men like that in the world.

But Anne couldn't forget what Danny had told her, that he woke up in the "bunny place," a house located a block and a half from Dorie's.

She called the station from her cell phone. Somebody else picked up at Bern's desk and said he'd left. At his apartment she got the machine and left a message telling him where she'd gone and that she needed to talk to him right away.

Night had come swiftly while she drove. The Lewises' street was lit well enough, but trees shaded the front of the house, and the bright, outdoor security lights, installed with motion detectors, did not switch on as she turned into the Lewises' driveway. Another vehicle was already parked there, a Pathfinder, huge, gray, with oversize tires and darkly tinted windows.

She sat there for a second, considering. If Natalie already had company, she wouldn't need Anne. Maybe this explained why Natalie was ignoring the phone.

Still, Anne had driven all the way over here. She ought to go and say hello. It might be good for Natalie to know that her husband was worried enough to send Anne to check on her.

She shut off the engine, left her car, and walked up to the front door. The only illumination was from the window in the living room where a lamp burned, visible behind the closed blinds. Maybe it was the darkness, but she was filled with uneasiness. Something was blooming in the neighborhood, exuding a heavy tropical scent, alien in the desert air. The night seemed almost preternaturally silent.

She reached out to ring the bell, paused, and looked back at the Pathfinder looming over her car.

"It was the Big Foot," Danny had said.

And suddenly Anne remembered the toy ads on TV during the last Christmas season, a remote-controlled vehicle with outsized tires lumbering over a sandbox terrain: Big Foot.

If that vehicle was here, the one that transported Danny to Dorie Wineski's house, then the person who took Danny and killed two people was here, too.

29

Anne's mind sent out a barrage of commands. *Run. Get to the car. Call Bern.*

Before she could act on that first most important one, the door opened. Although she had no idea whom she expected to see, she was not surprised that it was Glen who stood there.

"I guess you made it home after all," she said. Her mouth was dry, and her heart began to hammer so loudly she was afraid he would hear.

"I gave up on the auto club," Glen said. "The Path's my company car."

"Well, now that you're here, you don't need me."

She started to back away. He reached out and put his hand on her arm, lightly, with just a hint of the strength she knew he could wield with those pumped-up biceps.

"I do need you, Anne. Natalie's in the living room. I think she took something."

"Do you know what it was?"

"Sleeping pills. I found the bottle."

Anne's concern for Natalie overcame her fear for her own safety. She went into the house.

Glen released her, and she hurried down the hall, putting her alarm on hold because she saw Natalie slumped on the sofa. She looked as though she'd been sitting there and had just keeled over to one side. Her head was propped on the arm of the couch. Enough fine dark hair had worked loose from a fabric-covered elastic band to veil her face. In the dim light, the flesh on her thin arms looked pale as marble.

Anne picked up the limp wrist and searched for a pulse. "Natalie," she said sharply. "Natalie, can you hear me?"

The heart rate was slow, much too slow. The bony chest barely moved with her shallow breathing. Anne brushed the hair back and found that Natalie's eyes were open, the pupils huge. Saliva trickled from her mouth, staining a needlepoint pillow wedged in the angle of the sofa.

Glen had come to stand behind Anne on the other side of the coffee table. Had he gone to work in cotton slacks and a loose shirt? Surely he wouldn't have taken the time to change.

"How soon will the paramedics arrive?" Anne asked urgently.

"What do you mean?"

"Did they give you an ETA?"

She glanced up. His face was curiously flat, without expression, and he was taking a pair of white latex gloves from his pocket and pulling them on. The action was so peculiar that a moment passed before all the alarms began to clamor in her mind.

She stood up and edged around the coffee table that sat between them. He said, "You know, don't you?"

She ran out into the entry, skidding on the tile, regaining her footing, and heading for the front door. As she reached for the dead bolt, Glen said, "Stop right there."

She could see him lifting the loose shirt and taking a gun from the back waistband of his trousers. She turned, her back against the heavy wood of the door, to face him.

There was enough light to glint off the steel barrel as he

pointed the gun at her and said, "Come on. Let's get this over with."

Bern's rage had been enough to propel him blindly to Florence Mosk's house. He was pulling up along the curb when rationality began to kick in; common sense returned as he got out of the Jeep and slammed the door behind him.

This is totally dumb, he told himself.

Maybe so, but he was here now and he'd be damned if he'd leave without doing what he came for. The old Monte Carlo was under the carport; Florence must be home. The house was dark, but light flickered behind the blinds, strobing blue to green—the TV.

The street was dark, too. He remembered Wayne Jensen talking about how poorly lit the area was. You could see the stars out here, diamond points against a sky that was blacker away from the city, South Mountain a broad silhouette against the spangled brightness.

Bern went warily up the driveway to the gate, stopped, and drew his gun before he went inside the chain-link fence. The irony did not escape him. He'd come to save the dog, but if Duke charged him, he'd have to shoot the poor beast.

A low growl rumbled from under the porch.

"Easy, boy," Bern said softly. "Easy."

The growl grew deeper but seemed to come from the same place. The dog stayed put the day before, too, when he and Will had served the warrant. Now Bern wondered if this was because Duke hurt too much to move. It was going to be a hell of thing to get him out from under the porch, something Bern was not about to tackle on his own. He would call animal control as soon as he dealt with Florence.

He went up on the porch and banged on the door. He

could hear voices over the labored noise of the window air conditioner. A television drama. Funny how you could tell just by listening that the conversation was not between real people.

He felt the vibration of Florence's heavy footsteps, transmitted through the floor to the planked surface of the porch, knew she stood on the other side of the wooden panel.

He knocked again and said loudly, "Florence? It's Detective Pagett. Open up. I know you're in there."

A short wait, then the door swung inward. Her huge body blocked the view of the TV. Glow from the tube seemed to radiate around the massive head and shoulders like some kind of weird aura. He got a whiff of her winy breath and saw she was carrying a bottle, about a one-and-a-half-liter jug, judging from the size and shape.

"I want to talk to you," Bern said.

As usual, Florence said nothing.

He remembered then that he still had the gun in his hand and was in the act of holstering it when she started to move, coming outside, so he automatically backed up a step or two. Beneath the porch, Duke began to rev up his fierce rumble.

Under the overhang of the porch cover there was little ambient light from either stars or street lamps, and damn little from the TV with Florence in the way, so he sensed rather than saw her arm swing up. And then he heard the sudden chuff of air compressed out in front of the bottom of the wine bottle as it rocketed toward his head.

For the second time within a week Anne was staring down the barrel of a gun. This one was bigger than Tony's, the sheer size an ominous warning of the kind of wound it could inflict.

"Back in the living room," Glen said.

She stared at him, an awful realization dawning. "You drugged Natalie. But why? Danny's the one who—my God, Danny. Is he—what have you done to him?"

"He's all right. He's sleeping."

"Like Natalie?"

"Don't worry. I just gave him some of that stuff his doctor prescribed. Now move."

He grabbed her arm and shoved her ahead of him, the hard finger of the gun prodding her back. She banged her leg against the coffee table as he hustled her around it and thrust her down on the couch beside his wife. Then he sank into one of the dark blue chairs with a weary sigh and leveled the revolver at her.

She could feel the panic rising. Remembering how terror had threatened to paralyze her when Tony held her captive, she fought to stay calm and rational. And she did have one small hope: Bern would be home anytime now; he would get her message and find her. On the sofa beside her, Natalie moaned.

"She's going to die if you don't get her to a hospital," Anne said.

"I don't think so. I didn't give her a big enough dose for that."

"Why are you doing this? She found out, didn't she? That you were still seeing Kristobel. That you arranged the kidnapping. Did she find the ransom money?"

"*Natalie?*" He smiled thinly. "Not likely. You're the real problem, Anne. You digging around and stirring her up."

"How long were you standing there today when I was with Danny? How much did you hear?"

"Enough to know Danny was going to tell you everything if I didn't do something."

"He told me enough," Anne said. "I just didn't understand what he was saying. The day Danny was supposed to be kidnapped you took him in the Pathfinder. You lied about going in your car. What I don't understand is why Natalie lied, too."

"She didn't." He gave Anne a smug look. "I left the Path at the Mobile station for an oil change the night before. The station's right next to the bank, so after we went through the drive-up, I switched cars; came back later and switched back. I thought the Lexus would stick out like a sore thumb in the area where Dorie lived."

"And you didn't worry that somebody would see you in front of Dorie's house no matter what you were driving?"

"Give me a break," Glen said. "Dorie met me a few blocks away."

In front of the bunny place, the house with the windmills. No wonder the memory upset Danny so much.

"Then what happened to make you go to Dorie's house two days later? Were you so angry you forgot about how risky it was?"

"What are you talking about?"

"Danny saw you," Anne said. "He saw you hit Dorie. No wonder he repressed the memory."

"I wouldn't do something like that in front of Danny," Glen said indignantly. "Anyway, I'm not that stupid. I never went near that house while Danny was there. He did it—Sales. Then he tried to blackmail me. Called me from jail, can you believe that? I thought he was just fishing around, that he really didn't know anything, but I couldn't take a chance on it."

"So you shot him."

"Naturally. It was self-defense. The asshole pulled a gun first. Too bad I didn't know you were in the truck. I could've taken care of you right then."

"Tony didn't kill Dorie," Anne said. "The police accounted for his time all evening."

That stopped Glen for a moment. He said, "Yeah, well," shrugging it off, but Anne could tell the idea bothered him, that it was something he hadn't planned for. If Tony had been able to link Glen to the kidnapping, maybe the person who killed Dorie could, too.

Natalie's eyelids fluttered, and her lips moved, but she didn't make a sound. Anne was afraid Natalie was sinking into a drug-induced coma from which she might never awaken.

Do something, she told herself.

Should she tell him she had called Bern? Or would this mean he would simply shoot her right away before Bern could arrive? Glen was a talker. Better to keep him talking and wait for Bern.

The wine bottle smashed into Bern just above his left ear. A conflagration of stars burst in his head, brilliant colors that outdid the stellar display over South Mountain— no contest. He dropped like a felled tree.

Beneath the porch, Duke barked in short, harsh yelps that sounded as though the effort hurt. The dog was the one creature in the world that knew exactly how Bern felt the next moment when the freight train slammed into his chest. At least that's what it felt like. Some rational corner of his mind that had not been short-circuited by the overload of pain insisted the blow was dealt by Florence's shoe, driven into his ribs hard enough to skid his 175-pound body across the planks.

In the time it took for her to draw back and aim another kick, he remembered dimly he'd been holding his gun when she hit him, but his brain was too busy processing the massive amount of distress that afflicted his head and torso, so all the sensory messages from his extremities were on hold. He had no idea if he still held the gun.

Since he was incapable of defending himself, he simply lay there like a football ready for the field goal, and sure enough Florence scored. There was a brief sensation of flying off into space, an almost pleasant feeling of weightlessness, over too soon. And the pain he'd experienced before was nothing compared to the agony when he landed with a jarring thump on the unyielding, sunbaked earth.

It was no wonder that after a few seconds of this, his brain simply shut down.

"Glen, you really ought to think this through," Anne said earnestly, hoping the words sounded sincere and not just like shrink-speak.

"You think I haven't? Christ! It was going to be so simple."

"How could it be?" Anne asked, amazed. "Even if the police hadn't become involved, Danny would've told Natalie where he had been held and that you gave him to Dorie. And Dorie never would have taken the blame alone."

At the sound of her name, Natalie stirred, her fingers twitching against Anne's hip. Anne squeezed her hand and sent a silent message: *Fight, Natalie. Stay awake.*

"As soon as Dorie got her money, she was leaving town," Glen said. "That was the agreement. I was going to make sure she stuck to it."

The implacable note in his voice told Anne he hadn't intended for Dorie to go far, that she was probably headed for a lonely grave out in the desert.

"And Danny," Glen said, "he's only three. Little kids get confused. I figured I'd be all right if they couldn't tie the ransom to me."

"So you took it but you weren't going to spend it? I wish you'd explain that to me. I could understand if you were trying to keep the money out of a divorce settlement, but you told Natalie you wanted to make your marriage work." Anne shook her head, showing confusion. A put-up job, because she knew exactly what the bastard had planned. She just wanted to hear him say it, and she thought it would appeal to his ego to show her how smart he was.

"Of course I was making sure the money stayed out of a settlement. I killed myself building up that business. I wasn't going to hand half of it to Natalie. And I wasn't going to give up Kristobel. Well, you saw her."

Oh, yes, Anne thought. And she was sure that Glen, used to docile, manageable Natalie, had no idea what marriage to Kristobel would be like.

"I had to make it look as though Natalie and I were patching things up, so that later when we broke up, everybody would think how hard I had tried. The money would just vanish. I'd tuck it away somewhere. I had it all worked out. But now you've forced me to change everything."

Anne caught it then—a tentative note in his voice. He wasn't so sure of the brilliance of his plan as it first appeared. Anne was the expert here on emotion and human reaction. He was using her for a sounding board, figuring out where his logic was faulty or if he'd covered everything.

That was okay with Anne. Glen could talk to her all night, giving Bern time to get to his apartment, check his machine, and hear her message. Bern would call, and when she wasn't at home, surely he would try to reach her here. He'd suspect the worst—he always did.

All she had to do was stay in control and keep Glen talking.

Bern, for God's sake, where are you?

30

Given a choice, Bern might have opted for the anesthetic of unconsciousness. But shock recedes, the heart pumps, and like it or not conscious thought swims back across a sea of pain.

He lay flat on his face on the ground. The earth retained the heat like a brick baked in an oven, and for a moment he found the warmth soothing. Then all his injuries began checking in, and nothing helped. He drew a ragged breath and stifled a groan. He thought the moon was rising in the east out over the Superstitions. Although he could see neither moon nor mountains, the light was bright enough so he could see the shadow cast by his body, and he could definitely see Florence sitting on the edge of the porch.

Light winked off glass as she lifted a wine bottle and drank from it. Jesus, the same bottle she'd slugged him with? He didn't see how it could be, not the way his head hurt, but as far as he remembered, there was no broken glass on the porch. Sure that she'd be delighted to try breaking the bottle again, he lay very still while he assessed his injuries.

There was the head wound, of course. Without being able to touch it, he couldn't be sure, but he thought his scalp was a pulpy, bloody mess above his ear. Concussion? Oh, yeah, very likely because to tell the truth he was seeing a second hulking image on the porch, and beneath the porch two sets of eyes glowed in the blackness.

He tried not to think about Dorie Wineski dying of a subdural hemorrhage or of his own blood seeping into his brain. His more immediate concern was the grating feeling in his ribs when he breathed.

He remembered that he was just holstering his gun when Florence hit him. Had he completed the action? His right arm was close enough to his body, so he thought if he moved it very slowly, Florence might not notice.

He inched the arm in, wondering how he could have found the hot ground a comfort. Small stones dug into his face, and sweat trickled down his temples and dampened his clothes. He touched the holster.

No gun.

And no help likely to arrive. He'd charged off on his errand of mercy without telling anybody. Even Anne wasn't going to suspect anything was wrong. They'd been playing phone tag all day.

Anne . . . Could it be that nasty old vulture of foreboding that had flown back to perch on his shoulder hadn't been for Anne after all? Maybe the real thing, bald-headed and sharp-beaked, was out there, sitting in an ironwood tree, waiting for Florence to finish him off.

Anne remembered her sessions in the clinic while she was still at ASU, and particularly one woman who could talk for her allotted hour nonstop. That patient more than any other had taught Anne how to *appear* to be giving her full attention even though her eyes were glazing over with boredom.

Boredom was not the problem here. Still, the situation was similar: She must appear to be hanging on to Glen's every word while engaged in a kind of three-dimensional mental chess, always assessing the level of the immediate danger, keeping track of Natalie's physical status, and trying to outguess the man who was intent on murdering her and Natalie to cover his tracks.

She leaned forward slightly, as though completely absorbed, trying not to let her glance stray to the unblinking eye of the ugly gun he held.

He said, spinning out his scenario, "Natalie was just so jealous. She never believed I'd broken it off with Kristobel, and she was determined to pay me back somehow. So she kidnapped Danny. Her plan was to drain off the ransom money. Then when she filed for divorce she'd get half of what was left."

He stopped and waited for her reaction.

"But what if Natalie found somebody else?"

"Who? Oh, *Elliot*." He chuckled quietly, blowing little puffs of air out his nostrils. "Even better. She leaves me for another man—if you can believe she'd go for that wimp. And—hey—how's this for an idea: Those ransom calls were from a *man*, right? Maybe ole Elliot made them."

The calls hadn't been from a man at all; Anne was sure that *Dorie* had made them. Now the fact that the caller wouldn't speak to Natalie made perfect sense: Natalie would recognize her voice.

"The thing you may have some trouble explaining is why Natalie allowed me to treat Danny," Anne said. "She wanted help for him. Wouldn't she have tried to keep him away?"

Like you did.

Bern didn't know the reason Glen had given Anne for resisting treatment for his son, but he certainly knew it was Glen who had stalled, so Bern would suspect . . .

Her stomach gave a sick lurch as she realized the path her thoughts were taking: Bern would only be sorting through these suspicions if she and Natalie weren't around to tell him otherwise.

While these thoughts went through Anne's mind, Glen was considering the question. He dismissed it with a shrug. "Natalie had to make it *seem* as though she wanted help for Danny. She was afraid it would look suspicious if she didn't. But she had you coming out here to the house to treat Danny so she could keep an eye on you. And when it looked like you were going to find out what happened, she knew everything she'd done was going to come out. She couldn't face that.

"She gave Danny his medication to make sure he'd sleep until I came home, so that he wouldn't come down and find her. Well, we all know she loves him. Your being here— I'll blame myself for that."

"The police will be skeptical," Anne warned. "Natalie might be depressed, but why would she shoot me? And if she took sleeping pills before I arrived—" Anne shook her head. "It doesn't make sense."

He considered, annoyed that she was finding holes in his reasoning, then said slyly, "Who's to say she wasn't going to shoot herself? At first, I mean. You came. Tried to talk her out of it. Maybe you tried to get the gun away. It goes off. She sees what it's like, all the blood and gore. Can't do that to herself, so she takes the pills. I'll have to give her a few more. Make sure she has enough to do the trick."

Anne had to admit his analysis followed a kind of sick logic. Worse, she could feel hopelessness creeping into her mind. She might be buying time, but in the end, maybe all she was doing was helping Glen hone his story. Still, what choice did she have?

Anne had been told by everybody—friends, family,

Rosemary—that Nicki Craig's death was not her fault, that she could not have foreseen what would happen. Well, this time she knew. Danny might not experience the same kind of abuse that Nicki Craig had been subjected to, but he'd live with a monster all the same.

She had to find a way to keep that from happening, and the only thing she could think of was to get him to continue with this macabre game.

"You can sit here and rationalize things," she said, "but the police won't necessarily follow your chain of reasoning. Maybe they won't add it up that way at all."

"Oh, I think they will. They'll know Natalie kidnapped Danny because they'll find a locker key in her purse, and when they check, they'll find the ransom sitting in a locker at the bus station. They'll probably assume Natalie killed Dorie, too. Maybe Dorie demanded more money. They argued. It got violent. The cops're dying to pin the murder on somebody, and here's Natalie on a silver platter."

"Bern would never believe it."

But even as Anne said it, she knew he might. Trained by experience to imagine the worst, blinded by grief and holding himself accountable, maybe the explanation would be just awful enough so that Bern would buy it. And for an instant Anne could see with terrible clarity how Bern's life would be altered by what might happen here, how the corrosive effects of despair and guilt could so easily ruin his life.

"Bern," Glen said, speculation edged by that hateful slyness. "You two got a thing going, haven't you?"

She couldn't answer without screaming out her loathing and fear.

He grinned. "Hit the mark, didn't I? Tells me how I'll play it for ole Bernard. Who knows? Maybe we'll become buddies—both of us losing the woman we love."

More than anything Anne wanted to tear the smirk off his face. Beside her, Natalie gripped Anne's hand tightly, reminding her of all that was at stake.

Forcing herself to remain calm, Anne said, "But you're still forgetting one thing. Natalie didn't kill Dorie, and neither did Tony. Maybe Dorie talked, and there's somebody else out there who knows what you did."

"So what? I dealt with Tony Sales. I'll deal with anyone else, too, when the time comes. How hard could it be?"

So he had a minor concussion—pray God it was minor—a bitch of a headache, and a couple of broken ribs. Lying in the moonlit yard, Bern told himself that at least he was alive. Of course, he knew what his father would say: *Just wait; things are bound to get worse.*

Between his eyes adjusting and the increasing illumination as the moon rose, it was damn near bright as day. Without moving his head, he could still take in the few feet of dirt between him and the porch, part of the planked structure, and more of Florence than he wanted to see.

She sat, knees apart, a female Neanderthal lined in silver and black, motionless except for hefting the jug now and then. When she threw back her head to drink, her eyes gleamed briefly, a flash of white in the dark sockets of bone. He didn't want to think about the view of Florence in a skirt. Thank God she always wore pants.

The visibility worked both ways: If he could see her, she could see him, too. He lay still, playing possum. Fortunately his face was in shadow. He hoped she couldn't tell that his eyes were open.

Yelling for help was not an option. This was not a neighborhood where people responded to such cries. Besides, one peep, and Florence would be on him like a duck on a grasshopper.

The situation wasn't exactly like old Lou Halley's trip to the zoo, but it was great for tapping into those gut feelings Halley touted. One thing Bern's gut told him: Florence had killed Dorie Wineski.

He and Will had scared her by taking the shirt, so it was either the one she had been wearing when she killed Dorie or one she *thought* she may have worn. Oh, there was none of Dorie's blood visible on the garment; Florence worked in a commercial laundry, and she understood all about removing stains. As soon as she did the wash again, the dog's blood would also have been history. Thanks to all those cop shows on TV, however, she had heard plenty about the magic of forensic science. So Florence must have believed the lab found something, that Bern had come to arrest her, and that he was stupid enough to come alone.

Well, she was right about that last part.

She hefted the bottle and took another slug of wine. How long before she killed the jug? Maybe she'd drink enough to simply pass out there on the porch, but he was his father's son and he knew he couldn't count on it. He needed an alternate plan.

Problem was he couldn't think of anything that didn't require him to move. Even breathing hurt.

Beneath the porch, Duke had stopped growling. The area was inky black, but suddenly Bern thought he saw movement, a shifting of shadow on shadow. He supposed the topper to all this would be when the dog he came to save rushed out and sunk his teeth in Bern's leg.

Before he could get too worried about Duke, Florence got up and stood there swaying for a minute, and Bern knew that things were bound to get a lot worse just like his father always predicted because now he could see what had happened to his Glock semiautomatic revolver. Florence had it. The wine jug was in her left hand, the gun in her right as she clomped up the steps, walked unsteadily across the porch, went into the house, and closed the door.

Losing his weapon had narrowed his options considerably. Nothing left to do but get the hell out of here. He tried to get up. This should have been a simple operation: push with the hands, bring up the knees. Pain sledgehammered his head, just as intense as when Florence hit him. There was a tearing in his chest, and sickness rose from his stomach.

He had no sensation of collapsing, but found himself back on the ground. Above him, the stars seemed to be rushing together into one brilliant pinpoint of light that rapidly dimmed, then winked out into blackness.

31

"**Good thing I** didn't have to use this on Sales," Glen said, raising the gun so Anne had no doubt what *this* referred to. "I had it with me. Couldn't get to it. The idiot drew first. Now—well—about time I had some luck." He stood and said, "Okay, up." His eyes shone with a dark, brutish gleam.

On the couch beside Anne, Natalie moaned. Her eyes were open, huge and imploring. Terrified.

Anne tried to signal reassurance, but the truth was she could feel a black tide of despair rising. She had to keep her head; had to come up with something else to buy them time.

Dammit, Bern, I need you.

"Come on," Glen said sharply.

"Glen, please, think of Danny. You love that boy. I know you do."

"Of course I love him."

"Then don't do this to him. He's already traumatized by Dorie's death—"

"That's not my fault. I didn't plan for him to be there when she died."

"But he *was* there," Anne said. "Let me tell you something about children. You can't fool them very easily.

Danny knows you put him in that situation. Even if he's not down here watching you, he'll know on some level that you killed his mother.''

"That's bullshit," Glen said. "Don't play head games with me. I'm not buying it."

"No games. I've seen what happens to kids like Danny. He may bury the memories. You'll help him do that. But they won't go away. They'll fester and turn ugly. He'll have behavior problems. He'll probably do drugs. One day you may find him gone, out on the streets. He might even die in an institution like your sister."

"The only institution my sister was in was jail. She died after she sampled some angel dust and tried to fly out a hotel window on the tenth floor." Glen came around the coffee table and put the gun to Natalie's head. "Now, do what I tell you, or I'll shoot her right now and figure out the details later."

Anne rose slowly, unsure whether her legs would support her. Natalie made feeble, clawing motions. Her face contorted as she tried to speak.

Until that moment Anne had a small reserve of hope. Bern would come. She'd be able to reason with Glen. She'd seize some opportunity to get away. Now she knew she'd only been fooling herself, buying time with the coin of desperation.

Never taking his eyes off Anne, Glen eased Natalie up enough so he could slide in beside her. Then he snaked his left arm around her, clamped it just under her breasts, and stood up, lifting her limp body. Instinctively wanting to put distance between them, Anne took a step backward. Natalie struggled feebly and cried out, the sound a muted wail.

Glen gave her a shake, prodded her ribs with the gun, and said harshly, "Cut it out."

Anne backed up another step.

He said, "Stay right there."

But Anne's brain was crying *danger*, and her feet seemed to move of their own volition, toward the hallway, toward the door.

"Hey, what're you trying to pull?" He was both annoyed and incredulous that Anne wasn't doing what she was told.

Glen was also having a hard time with Natalie. Although he was a big, strong man and she was slender, his wife was also dead weight as he hefted her and came after Anne.

"I mean it," he said. "You stop, or I'll fucking kill her."

Anne pictured him as a child, determined to gain control over his life, learning that charm and persistence usually did the trick. If that didn't work, he would resort to tantrums and other destructive behavior to get what he wanted. The child begets the man; the adult has much more power and cunning, and more determination than ever to have things the way he wanted.

"You'll kill her anyway." Anne felt the tiles of the hallway under her feet.

From experience and training, Anne knew you never reward a child's bad behavior. A little late to do anything about Glen's formative years, but damned if she'd let him run the show. Still, it was an awful decision. She knew she couldn't save Natalie. Probably couldn't save herself either, but she had to try.

Crabbing sideways on the slick tiles, she saw what he intended to do. He wrapped both arms around Natalie, took Natalie's hands one at a time, and placed them on the gun, his own hands holding them in position, pointing the gun at Anne. He was going to make sure Natalie's fingerprints were on the weapon, and that his weren't. That's why he was wearing the gloves.

There might be gunpowder residue on his wrists, his clothes, but who would check?

A great plan, but Natalie was fighting him and fighting the drug in her system. His face was slicked with sweat. He cursed in a monotone and squeezed Natalie savagely in a futile effort to make her stay still. He might be able to fire at Anne; hitting her was another matter. No lights on in the hall. That would help.

Now, she told herself. *Run.*

Not the front door. The back door in the kitchen. Probably locked. He would drop Natalie and come after her, but there might be a few precious seconds . . .

She bolted down the hall.

He fired.

Sound thundered in the entry, echoing off the hard surfaces, and pain sliced along the top of Anne's shoulder as the bullet plowed a bloody furrow through fabric and skin. She staggered and missed the framed opening that led to the kitchen area. Her momentum sent her crashing into the wall.

Trying to regain her footing and run again, she turned enough to see Glen with Natalie thrashing wildly in his arms, and something else, movement glimpsed from the edge of her vision: Danny, coming into the shadowy landing above the stairs.

"Daddy? Mommy?"

The sight of Danny and the sound of his dazed, frightened voice froze Anne in place.

Busy subduing Natalie and trying for another shot at Anne, Glen hadn't noticed his son until Danny spoke. Natalie stopped struggling, and they both looked up.

Anne could have taken advantage of the distraction then, could easily have gotten away into the kitchen, but fear for Danny kept her there.

In the dim spill of light from the living room, she could see he was wearing short pajamas, his straw-blond hair tousled and sticking out. And he was walking slowly, staggering toward the stairs.

"Dan-nee." Natalie's cry was hoarse and distorted.

"Danny, go back to your room," Glen said sharply.

"Daddy?" Danny sounded bewildered and lost.

"Danny, get back," Glen called. "Stay there. Stop!"

Anne didn't waste time yelling at the disoriented little boy. She ran back into the hall, her fear for his safety blocking out her own pain and shock. She moved as fast as she could, but time seemed to stretch like taffy to that hideous slowed motion where the mind observes so much faster than the body can ever react. What she saw, what she knew, was that she'd never make it up the stairs before Danny got to the edge of the landing.

She was only at the bottom of the stairway when he stepped off the top.

Regaining consciousness the second time around was far worse for Bern than the first. Whatever natural painkillers the body produced—endorphins, whatever the hell they were—just plain weren't cutting it.

He had no idea how much time had passed, but he could see the moon now, risen high enough so it was in his field of vision. Florence? He remembered she'd gone inside. Maybe she'd passed out. Maybe—no. No such luck.

She was sitting on the porch with her back up against the wall, concealed in shadow. Concentrating, he could see movement, thought she was hefting a wine bottle. The observation was confirmed by the sound of her swallowing.

Plan—he had a plan, didn't he?

Oh, yeah. Stand up. That was a good one. That really

worked. Looked like he was stuck with Plan B. Which was: Do nothing and hope she would drink herself into a stupor.

Meanwhile, pain ate at his body like flame. He longed for the sweet blackness of unconsciousness, but this time it didn't come.

Danny gave a startled cry as his bare foot skidded off the top step, then there was only a terrible thumping noise as his little body tumbled down the stairs. The sound mixed with a ululating wail from Natalie and a despairing shout from Glen.

Anne kept moving, rushing up—two, three steps as Danny hurtled down. All she could think of was his head hitting the hard surface of the tiles at the bottom of the stairs. His solid little body collided into hers with more force than she had expected. She grabbed him tightly and fell backward with him in her arms, doing nothing to break her fall, using her body to protect him.

She hit the tile with stunning force, the breath knocked out of her lungs by the impact. Danny was a boneless little bundle clasped to her heart.

Dazed and helpless, she could only watch the scene that was being played in front of her. At first she thought Glen was trying to restrain Natalie, to keep her from Anne and Danny. Then Anne realized that Natalie had latched on to the gun, the gun Glen had placed in her hands, and that she was clinging to it stubbornly as her husband tried to take it away.

Glen was no longer holding her from the back, propping her up and using her like a living puppet. He'd let her go to give his full attention to regaining possession of the gun. Maybe fear for her son had accelerated the recovery process. Natalie swayed and staggered, but she stayed upright and fought him.

Unable to pry her fingers loose, Glen grabbed the barrel of the revolver and yanked, pulling Natalie around in a ghastly pirouette.

Anne was looking at Glen's face over Natalie's shoulder when the gun went off. There wasn't much light in the hall, but enough to see his surprise before he slumped to the floor. *All my plans!* that look seemed to say. *How could it go so wrong?*

Anne whooped in a breath as Natalie sank down beside her, sobbing "OhGodOhGod." Natalie still held the gun. Anne's first words were a sharp warning. Natalie stared at the revolver as though it were a snake, quickly put it down, and shoved it away.

"Danny, oh, Jesus, Danny—is he—"

Slowly, cautiously, Anne slid the child off her body and onto the floor, checking first for respiration and pulse. "He's breathing."

That's when she noticed the blood on Natalie's blouse, a bright red blossom, more streaks down her arms.

"Natalie, you're hurt."

Natalie looked down, puzzled, shook her head. "Not mine. His. Glen's. I sh-sh-shot—" She began trembling violently.

"Never mind. Forget it," Anne ordered as she swiftly moved her hands over Danny's body.

No obvious breaks. That didn't rule out concussion or— even more serious—injuries to the spine or internal organs.

"Is he—? He's not—" Natalie touched her son's hair, her voice full of blind panic.

"He seems okay." No point in alarming her. "But we need the paramedics. Can you get to the phone?"

Natalie shook her head, rocking back and forth.

"Okay, I'll be right back."

Concentrating on Danny, Anne had forgotten her own

jolting fall and the wound in the top of her shoulder. Pain came in a rush as she stood up. She took a couple of steadying breaths and started toward the kitchen.

And stopped when she saw Glen.

He was still breathing, but there was a massive wound in his chest, and blood pooled around him, staining the grout in the tiles. His eyes were open, and he was staring up at her. When she hesitated, he spoke. One word, the last thing Glen Lewis ever said to her.

He said, "Danny," with such urgency that she knew whatever heinous acts the man had committed, he did love his son and wanted her to put Danny first.

She stepped around him and hurried out to call 911.

32

Anne insisted that Glen be taken in a separate ambulance, and that she should ride with Natalie and Danny. She knew she must look like a crazy woman, wild-eyed, smeared with the blood that had oozed from her own shoulder. She kept telling the patrolman who had responded along with the paramedics that she worked for the department and ordering him to find Detective Bernard Pagett in Homicide.

On the ride to the hospital, Danny's eyes fluttered open. For a second there was no recognition, then he said, "Dr. Anne? I falled down."

"I know you did, baby, but you're all right."

She kept repeating her reassurances all the way to the emergency room.

And he was all right, according to the doctor there. The sedative had relaxed his body, so that he appeared to have suffered nothing more than bumps and bruises. As a precaution, he would be kept for observation. Natalie was in worse shape. It was too early to tell if the overdose had done any long-term damage. With luck, she would recover.

As for Glen, about half an hour after they all arrived at the hospital, a doctor came to tell Anne that Glen had died while being prepped for surgery.

There was no time to sort out the welter of emotions this news brought. Anne was too busy making sure that Danny and his mother were going to survive, so preoccupied that it was a while before another nagging worry began to surface.

She had asked both the police and the hospital to contact Bern. She knew wherever he was he would drop what he was doing and rush here. But he didn't come and he didn't call.

After her shoulder was dressed, she went up with Danny to get him settled into the children's ward. As she left to go back to Natalie in ER, a nurse at the front station said, "Dr. Menlo, somebody's here for you," and motioned.

Relief quickly turned to anxiety as she saw that it was Will who waited for her, not Bern.

"Will? Where is he? What's wrong?"

"I don't know where he is, Anne." Schooled as he was to cover his emotions, Will couldn't hide the worry in his eyes. "Come on. Let's sit down. You look dead on your feet."

"I don't want to sit. You must know something. Tell me."

"He's not answering his car phone or his pager. I sent somebody to his apartment building. He's not there. Neither is the Jeep."

"Maybe he went to my place."

"I thought of that. I called the sheriff's office and had them send a deputy. No sign of Bern."

Anne's anxiety was rapidly turning to fear. She swayed slightly, her strength running out like sand. Will took her arm and steered her over to a small waiting area. This time she didn't protest, but sank down, grateful for the solid feel of a chair beneath her.

"How about some coffee?" Will asked. "Or maybe tea."

She shook her head. "Could Bern have been in an accident? Did you check—"

"I checked."

"Was he still working on the shooting?"

"No, we wrapped it up. And there was nothing new on this case until I got the news about your 911 call."

"Nothing? You're sure? Bern told me you were waiting on some lab tests—clothing you picked up at Florence Mosk's house."

"Yeah, but they were negative for human blood. And now, well, guess we were hassling Florence for nothing."

"Then who did kill Dorie?"

Will stared at her. "What do you mean? Glen Lewis—"

"He told me he didn't kill her. I think he was telling the truth."

"Jesus. Maybe I'd better hear exactly what he said."

Anne recapped the story she heard from Glen, how he had used Dorie as an accomplice to kidnap Danny, how Tony had tried to blackmail him, how he shot Tony in a struggle for the gun that night in the parking lot. While she talked, something Will had mentioned earlier popped into her mind.

"Will, what you said before—about the lab's findings—do you mean they found no blood at all on Florence's clothes?"

"No, they found blood all right, but it wasn't human. It was canine."

Anne thought of the big black dog she saw that day in the house next door to Dorie's—Florence's house. She thought about Bern who could maintain a glacial wall between himself and the most gruesome of crime scenes, but for all that had the softest of hearts when it came to the weak and helpless.

"I know where he is," Anne said.

•   •   •

Anne and Will were flying across town in Will's unmarked sedan with a patrol car ahead clearing the way, emergency flashers and siren going, when the report came in. Will had ordered patrol to do a casual drive-by. No spotlights. Observation only. According to the officer in the car, the Cherokee was parked on the street in front of Florence's house. He saw nothing else suspicious.

Bern had left the station just before Anne called him from her car on the way to the Lewises'. Three hours ago. Anne pictured wounds that could be inflicted by animals mad with pain. She remembered Bern's account of why Florence had been sent to jail, how she'd attacked a man with only the slightest provocation.

She imagined losing Bern, but quickly pushed the thought away because the idea was unthinkable.

Several blocks from Florence's address, their escort cut the siren and flashing beacons. Neither the patrol officer nor Will reduced their speed, however. Anne held her breath as they approached a traffic light changing to red, slowing only a little to adroitly thread their way through the sparse traffic at the intersection.

Will got on the radio to tell the two patrol cars to wait for him around the block. He would do a drive-by himself in his Plymouth.

As they cruised slowly down the poorly lit street, Anne could feel her heart beating all the way up in the top of her throat. The house was on her side of the car. She rolled down her window so that even the glass would not obstruct her view. There was only one dim light in the house and a lone streetlamp at the corner. Still, the moon was very bright. She had no problem seeing the figure that came out of the shadowy porch and down some steps into the yard. And even though Anne had never seen Florence Mosk, she recognized the huge woman from Bern's description.

Florence stood there for a brief second, staring out at them as they passed, and then her arm came up. Moonlight glinted on the gun in her hand.

"Fuck!" Will said, stomping on the accelerator. As the car leapt forward, the back window exploded in a shower of glass.

Anne was aware of what went on during the next few minutes: the patrol cars roaring up, lights blazing on in the houses nearby, Will pulling her from the car and making sure she was all right. But her mind's eye was focused back there on Florence's yard, on her fleeting glimpse of what lay, barely visible, behind that chain-link fence.

Will was swearing a blue streak and calling for more backup on the radio. "Officer involved," he said. "No, I don't know how—"

Anne grabbed his arm and said urgently, "Bern's there. He's lying on the ground."

Will handed the mike to one of the patrolmen, "Fill 'em in on the rest." To Anne he said, "You're sure?"

"*Yes*. I don't think—I couldn't tell if he was moving."

Will unlocked the trunk of his car, selected a pair of night-vision glasses from the gear inside, and trained them on the yard. "I see him," he said grimly.

He put the glasses down and turned to one of the officers who was attaching a night scope to a rifle. "You any good with that thing?"

"Yeah, I'm good." The answer didn't sound boastful, just honest. The man lifted the rifle, squinted into the sight, then lowered it. "But I don't know if I ought to try it. You'd better have another look."

Will's second scan seemed to take forever.

"What is it?" Anne demanded. "What's going on?"

"She's sitting on the ground next to Bern. She's got the gun to his head."

"Call it," the patrolman said.

"Are you crazy?" Anne cried. She turned on Will. "Don't you dare let him fire that rifle."

Will considered for an agonizing second before he said, "Okay. We'll wait. We have an ETA for the SWAT team?" he asked the patrolman who had been on the radio.

"Thirty minutes."

"You're going to just sit here?" Anne asked, appalled.

"I don't like it either," Will said. "But it's all we can do. And even when SWAT gets here, it's going to take a while. They'll want to evacuate the area, bring in a hostage negotiator—"

"He must be hurt, Will. Even if she doesn't shoot him, he could die while all this is going on."

"You think I don't know that?" Will's voice was rough with emotion. "Shit, Anne, we either take our chances and shoot the fucking bitch or we wait. That's the choices."

"No," Anne said. "I can go and talk to her."

"You got to be kidding. Uh-uh, Anne, no way. The woman probably murdered Dorie Wineski. At the very least, she's gone nuts."

"Will, please. You must've heard how I worked with Tony Sales that day at headquarters. Will, I can do this. It's his best chance, and you know it."

"Christ," Will said. He paced back and forth beside the car. "Headquarters will never okay it."

"Then don't ask. I'm going anyway."

He stopped pacing to regard her gloomily. "Ah, Anne, there are three of us. We can put you in cuffs."

"Then you better do it."

"If we all survive, Bern's gonna kill me for letting you do something this risky." He sighed. "Yeah, okay, but we take a few precautions."

They made her wear a Kevlar vest. It was way too big

and would never fit under her clothes, so she wore it over her blouse, gritting her teeth against the fresh pain in her shoulder where the vest was a cruel weight against the wound. Will took off his own shirt so she could slip it over the armor. She was sure she looked ludicrous in the huge garment, but nobody was laughing.

Will clipped a two-way radio to her belt. "I'll make sure we keep the channel clear. I want to hear everything that goes on in there."

She'd never been so frightened as when she began that block-long walk. Maybe she had badly misjudged the situation. Maybe any movement would set Florence off. What if she opened fire on Anne—or worse, shot Bern? But every step brought Anne a little more confidence. She could do this. She had to.

Her mouth was dry, and sweat coated her skin beneath the heavy vest as she reached the driveway and stopped behind the big white car parked there. A chain-link fence enclosed the yard where moonlight reduced everything to stark black and white with no shades of gray. Florence's mountainous silhouette loomed over Bern's prone body. Anne could not see her face.

"Florence?" Anne raised her voice enough so the woman could hear her. "I don't have a weapon, and I'm not with the police. My name is Anne Menlo. Is it okay if I come a little closer?"

"Whaddaya want?" The reply was harsh and slurred.

Anne thought she heard a moan then. She knew she saw Bern's legs move. Her joy was unreasonable given the situation. She couldn't help it. At least he was alive.

"I just want to talk to you, Florence. This is all kind of a mess right now, but maybe if we talk we can figure a way to clear things up. It can't hurt to try, can it?"

Nothing.

Anne could hear her own heartbeat ticking in her ears.

"All right," she said, "I guess you don't mind, then. I'm going to come over and open the gate. Okay?"

Still nothing.

I'll take that for a yes, Anne thought.

She managed to flip on the two-way radio as she fumbled with the gate latch. A low growl rumbled from beneath the porch. The dog was alive. Did it attack on command? She knew there were at least two rifles with night scopes trained on the yard. Surely the patrolmen would kill the dog if it came out and lunged at her. Filled with misgivings, she slipped through the gate.

"Okay, Florence, this is a lot better, isn't it? We don't have to shout now." She held her arms wide so the woman could see she didn't have a weapon. "I'll just come a few steps closer—"

"Anne, no—" Bern's voice was so hoarse, almost unrecognizable, his words quickly changing to a gasp of pain as Florence grabbed his hair with her free hand and thumped his head against the ground.

"Shut up," Florence growled.

Anne had to choke off the cry rising in her own throat. Under the porch, the dog barked, loud and vicious.

"Shut up, Duke!" Florence ordered, and the barking subsided to a low menacing buzz.

Anne said, "Florence, please, I'm here so nobody gets hurt. Not you, or me, or Detective Pagett."

"Bullshit," the woman said. "All's you care about is *him*."

"No, that's not true. Naturally I'm concerned about Bern—that's his name, Florence. Bern Pagett. He's hurt. I'd like to help him. I'm a doctor, did I tell you that?"

This wasn't exactly a lie. It didn't matter. She remembered one of her teacher's maxims about handling crisis situations: *Whatever works*.

She took another step.

"Stop," Florence said. "Don't come any closer."

Anne was about eight feet away. "All right. I'll tell you what. I'm going to sit down now. We can talk better that way."

She sank down on the bare dirt which was still hot from the scalding sun. A strong, almost medicinal odor exuded from rank weeds that grew along the fence, was overlaid by the stench of dog urine and feces and a smell of perspiration and cheap wine.

From this perspective Anne could see the woman only marginally better. Her face was cast in skeletal shadow, the eye sockets dark beneath the orbital bone. What was horrifyingly clear was that Bern's head was propped on one of her massive knees. Florence held him there with her left hand tangled in his hair; the right pressed an automatic pistol to his temple.

Anne strained to see if he was conscious and almost wished he wasn't. Then Florence grunted and shifted her weight so that moonlight illuminated his face. He was awake, all right, his eyes open and staring at Anne, his jaw set against the pain.

Say something, Anne ordered herself.

"It's still awfully hot, isn't it?" Weak, but a start. "Are you all right, Florence? Would you like something to drink?"

"Wine."

"I'm sorry. I don't think they'll bring you that. How about something cold—a soft drink, maybe?"

"No," she said sullenly. "I just want the cops to leave me alone."

Anne decided to play it as though she had no suspicions

of what the woman had done. She said, "I think they will, Florence, if you let Bern go."

Florence snorted her disbelief.

"They might," Anne insisted. "What if Bern agreed not to press charges against you? I think you've been drinking, Florence. People will understand if you have a problem with alcohol. Maybe if you promise to get treatment—"

"Do you think I'm stupid? He came here to arrest me."

"Oh, no, Florence, you're wrong. Bern was worried about your dog." Anne searched her memory for the damned animal's name. "Duke. He came about Duke. He'll tell you. Bern?"

"Yeah," Bern said thickly. "That's why I came, all right."

"He came about Dorie," Florence said. "Maybe I could stand going to jail. I been there before. But they'll say I helped Dorie kidnap that little kid. They send you to the federal pen for that. I ain't going to no federal pen."

Oh, God, Anne thought, *she really did kill Dorie.*

Had Bern figured it out? Maybe now, but not before he arrived, otherwise he was too smart a cop to come alone.

"Florence, you're wrong," Anne said, trying to keep the realization from her tone. "I know for a fact that you had no part in kidnapping Danny Lewis. Danny's father was in it with Dorie." The revelation drew a startled sound from Bern. "We just found out tonight."

"His dad?"

"Yes. It was a scheme to hide money before he divorced his wife."

"That's sick," Florence said.

"Yes, it is. But you see? You won't be charged for kidnapping."

"They'll still get me for killing Dorie," Florence said heavily.

"Maybe not—murder—" Bern said, each word sounding as though it hurt. "Maybe—manslaughter."

"Bern's right," Anne said. "Why don't we talk about it? There might have been extenuating circumstances. The charges could be reduced."

Florence sat still as stone.

"I know you cared about her," Anne said gently. "Tell me what happened, Florence."

Florence hunched her shoulders, rocked back and forth. "She was—she was putting me off, making excuses that she was busy. I went over there." Once started, the words came in a rush. "She didn't want me to come in, but I did anyway. Knew she had somebody in there with her. That Tony or somebody else in the back room. We argued, and I—I hit her. She fell and banged her head on the table. Then I heard it—this little kid crying. I guess we woke him up. I think maybe she had the door locked 'cause he kept crying for her to open it."

So Anne had been wrong. Danny had not seen the murder. Dorie must have let him out of his room after Florence left. He saw Dorie fall in her bedroom, that second fall from which she never recovered.

"I told her I was sorry," Florence went on. "Dorie said it was okay, that we'd talk about it later. So I left. She didn't seem hurt bad. Not bad enough to die. I didn't—didn't"—the shoulders heaved, and Anne realized she was crying—"didn't mean to—" She let go of Bern's hair, let him slide away.

A tumult of emotions filled Anne's mind: sympathy for the woman, elation, hope that she could talk Florence into giving up the gun. All of it instantly swept away by the overpowering onrush of fear that the patrolmen would misinterpret what was going on, suddenly knowing what was going to happen next, knowing it even as she saw a red dot appear on Florence's forehead—a laser marking its target.

Anne cried out, but the rifle went off, and almost simultaneously Florence's head jerked back. Blood and bone fragments sprayed out as the bullet exited the skull. Even in the moonlight Anne could see the redness of the droplets falling on the bare earth.

The dog gave a startled, frightened howl, but it stayed under the porch. Anne scrambled on hands and knees to Bern, afraid to do more than crouch down beside him and touch him with trembling hands.

" 'S okay, babe," he croaked. "You did good."

There was no time to say more before the yard was swarming with police. Will dropped down beside them. His flashlight shone on Bern's face, powerful enough to see that Bern's hair was matted with blood and his skin was gray from shock and pain.

"Jesus Christ, Bern," Will said, a mixture of anger and relief in his voice.

"Screwed up—" Bern mumbled.

"Yeah, you did. Big time," Will said, still hovering as the paramedics moved in.

Bern grabbed on to Anne's hand and held it while the medics checked him over. The strength of his grip went a long way to assure Anne of the power of his life force even as the medics spoke of concussion, broken ribs, a punctured lung.

"Danny?" he asked as the paramedics prepared to transfer him to a stretcher.

"Danny's okay. I'll explain it all to you later."

"Annie—"

"Shh, be quiet now. Don't talk."

"Tell Will—the dog—"

"I'll take care of the goddamned mutt," Will promised, then slapped a hand against the ambulance. "Now go. Get him to the hospital."

33

The dun-colored hills shimmered in the late morning heat beyond Rosemary's cool patio retreat, miragelike in the water vapor sprayed by the roof misters. Anne sat next to her friend, sipping tea and talking quietly.

She had come here four times in the past three weeks. She would have come more frequently if Rosemary's health had permitted and if she could have fitted the visits into her schedule. There were never enough hours in the day to keep up with her patients and to spend as much time as possible with Bern during his painful recovery.

Facing death three times within a week had been a kind of shock therapy for Anne, exhuming her guilt over Nicki Craig's death and forcing her to consider how that guilt had influenced her life. So at least those four visits—approximately four hours—had not been wasted in denial.

Anne knew that people chart their lives to avoid pain, so it was not surprising that she had limited her practice to keep out the neediest children, the ones who, as Rosemary said, "attach themselves to your heart." What amazed her was how blind she'd been to what she was doing.

There was also her relationship with Bern to consider. The more she thought about it, the more complicated she knew it to be. Figuring that one out was going to take some doing. As she told her patients, therapy was slow. And—what she usually hesitated to add—it was painful.

Today she'd announced to Rosemary that she was here for a social visit. It was Sunday. They both needed a rest.

"I went to see Danny before I came," Anne said. Natalie's parents had come right away to care for the boy, while Natalie was in the hospital. They had gone back to Buffalo last week after helping their daughter to settle into a rental condo.

"Poor child," Rosemary said soberly. "Life has dealt him a terrible hand."

But Anne would help him handle it, and Natalie would, too. Anne had once told Glen not to underestimate his wife's strength; Natalie was proving her right. And somebody else was there offering support.

Elliot Wray had come every day to the hospital, and when Natalie said she couldn't bear the thought of going back to a house that was filled with so many horrible memories, Elliot had found the condo, rented furniture, and had it ready for Natalie and Danny to move in as soon as Natalie was released.

"How's Bern doing?" Rosemary asked.

"He went up to his mother's for a few days. He said it would make her happy to fuss over him. He'll have desk duty for a while, after he goes back to work."

Norman had come to the patio door and stood looking out, silently reminding Anne not to overtire his wife. Anne put her cup on the round glass table.

"I suppose Norman's giving you the high sign," Rosemary said.

"Yes, and he's right. You need a rest, and I have lots of things to do at home."

"I know we agreed no therapy, but tell me how you are, Anne, before you leave. Honestly."

"I'm sleeping better. I think maybe just surviving those ordeals at the Lewises' house and with Florence restored some of my self-confidence. But I don't know—sometimes I think no matter how long I work at it, I won't ever stop feeling guilty about Nicki. I'm beginning to think the real question is whether I can forgive myself."

"Oh, my dear Anne," Rosemary said. "Didn't you know? That's always been the question."

Anne was home making lunch when the doorbell rang. A glance out the window revealed Bern's Cherokee parked on the driveway. She opened the door, saying, "Did you forget your key—?"

She broke off to stare in astonishment. He was standing there with a duffel bag in one hand and a leash in the other. Attached to the leash was a scroungy, all too familiar, black dog.

"Bern, is that—?"

"Yeah." He grinned sheepishly. "He's looking pretty good, don't you think?"

Duke's dull, matted fur had been shaved in three places; the largest swath coming from the belly still had the black threads of stitches used to close a ragged wound. One ear drooped, and his tail had a pronounced kink where it had been broken. He pulled his lip back over ugly yellow teeth and growled, the sound a low rumble in his throat.

"Be nice," Bern said, giving the leash a tug.

The animal glared at him but stopped growling.

"I had about all the fussing over from my mother I could stand." Bern didn't look a lot better than the dog. He'd lost weight. He needed a haircut, and there were a few silver strands in the dark hair that just touched his ears. "Anyway, the vet called and said he couldn't keep Duke any longer, and he couldn't find anybody who would take him."

"Why does that surprise you? Bern, he's a vicious animal."

Bern glanced down at the dog. "Maybe he just expects the worst of the world, and so far the world has obliged." He looked back at her and added, "He needs a place to recuperate. I do, too."

What had she told herself earlier about complications? Her head advised going slowly. Maybe to draw back and get some perspective. To be really sure this time.

"I have serious doubts that this will work out, Bern."

"I know you do, babe. We can at least try, can't we?"

Listening to her heart, she stepped back, holding open the door, so he and the dog could come inside.

JUDITH KELMAN

__While Angels Sleep 0-425-11093-1/$5.99

"Swift, suspenseful, and highly entertaining."—Dean Koontz
Strange, terrible things happened at Thornwood, years ago,
when Emily was a child. Now Emily has returned, a grown
woman with children, ready to start anew. But somehow
the shadows of the past seem to linger in this lonely place...

__Where Shadows Fall 0-425-10181-9/$5.99

"Gripping...it swept me along to the shocking climax."

—Mary Higgins Clark

Sarah Spooner's son is the eleventh suicide at Cromwell
University. With neither the police nor the school officials
investigating, Sarah has no choice but to go to Cromwell
herself to see what madness lies behind the deaths of so
many innocent young men and women.

__Hush Little Darlings 0-425-11739-1/$5.99

The four young girls remember little of their abduction—just
a strange dream of black velvet walls. But her investigation
will lead D.A. investigator Sarah Spooner to dangers far
more terrifying and personal than she ever imagined...
because Sarah has a daughter of her own.